# Praise for

"A fun, escapist read witl ........................ ...orical
morsels."
—*Kirkus Reviews*

"Camalliere's work spans several genres: historical fiction, paranormal suspense, and women's lit.... The prologue grabs the reader's attention [and] the book delivers an action-packed finale."
—Windy City Reviews

"Takes a mystery and runs with it through generations of family entanglements, the lasting impact of life choices, and the consequences of love.... Highly recommended for both mystery and historical fiction readers searching for something different."   —Midwest Book Review

"Stands out from its genre!... Thrilling, captivating, and addictive from beginning to end... Should not be missed!" —Red Headed Book Lover

## Other Writers

"A complex and satisfying tale of crime, friendship, and one woman's relentless search for truth."
—Patricia Skalka, author, *Dave Cubiak Door County Mystery series*

"Captured me with her first sentences and kept me engaged throughout the story."   —Dan Burns, author, *Grace: Stories and a Novella*

"Camalliere's pedigree as a top-notch historian of the fascinating world of southwest Chicago shines through every page...she perfectly captures the magic of these storied places. Native American heritage, paranormal intrigue...you [will be] completely enmeshed."
—Ursula Bielski, author, *Haunts of the White City*

"A joy... Filled with everything you want in a mystery—smart narrative, great research... It rings with authenticity. Read this!"
—David W. Berner, author, *Things Behind the Sun*

"A Chicago area writer with a deep grasp of the history in our area…a delightful read and highly recommended…It combines elements of historical fiction, women's fiction, and paranormal in a wonderfully crafted tale…I couldn't put it down."

—Brigid Johnson, author, *True Course: Lessons from a Life Aloft*

## What Readers are Saying

"With a mystery story that spans generations, pristine character development, and in-depth detective work this book never slows down."

"Love her books! Always look forward to the next one. So much history about the area crafted into the story."

"Her pedigree as a top-notch historian of the fascinating world of southwest Chicago shines through every page, ancient ravines and waterways, haunted roads… Perfectly captures the magic of these storied places."

"I especially enjoyed learning about the locations and the history and mysteries buried there."

"Five-star rating based on wonderfully well-drawn characters, their relationships and development…There is depth and authenticity to these people that had me rooting for them."

"Wonderfully conceived and beautifully written… A cadre of exceptionally well-drawn characters… Splendid and satisfying mystery with the many parts tied up nicely. A dab of paranormal seamlessly adds an additional dreamy dimension."

"To all my reader friends, run don't walk to pick up or order my new favorite novel, *The Mystery at Sag Bridge* by Pat Camalliere. As God is my judge, this is the best fiction book I have read in years…Murders and mysteries, my fav! Book club anyone?"

# The Miracle at Assisi Hill

# The
# Miracle
# at Assisi
# Hill

*Pat Camalliere*

~~~

Books by Pat Camalliere

*The Miracle at Assisi Hill*
*The Mystery at Mount Forest Island*
*The Mystery at Black Partridge Woods*
*The Mystery at Sag Bridge*

~~~

Paperback First Edition   ISBN 13: 979-8-8971624-0-8

CAMPAT Publications   Lemont, Illinois 60439

Edited by Diane Piron-Gelman. Cover photography by Pat Camalliere. Designed and typeset by Sarah Koz. Body in Janson Text, designed by Miklós Tótfalusi Kis in the 1690s, revived for Mergenthaler Linotype by Chauncey H. Griffith in 1937, digitized by Adrian Frutiger in 1985; also in Franklin Gothic, designed by Morris Fuller Benton in 1903–1912, digitized by Linotype in 1995. Titles in Dwiggins Uncial, designed by William Addison Dwiggins in 1935, digitized by Richard Kegler in 2001. Thanks to Nathan Matteson.

~~~

Dedicated with love to my husband and best friend, Chris.

Cora's inclination was to either draw back and watch unseen or leave, but again curiosity drove her on. As she approached, she noticed that Maryam was barefoot today despite the chill and the rough, rocky, muddy ground. She wasn't wearing a jacket either. And she wasn't doing anything except staring at a spot above the station, where a small tree, no more than a shrub, grew. Was she praying? Did this station have some significance for her?

A thick branch of the tree seemed to be encased in pale fog that appeared slightly brighter than the surrounding area. Why would fog appear on such a sunny afternoon? Also, the branch was bent down, as if a heavy weight were on it, yet nothing was there. A low buzzing, in a cadence resembling speech but without words, seemed to originate from that spot.

Maryam gave no sign of having noticed Cora, despite the fact that she was now only ten feet away. The nun's hands were pressed together in prayerful pose, fingertips touching the base of her chin, a smile of total delight on her face, her eyes bright, her attention on the tree and foggy patch absolute. She nodded her head seriously and murmured, "Of course. I will always do anything you ask."

# Prologue

**1886**

Careening down a rough dirt road, an open-bed buggy races through the misted woods of slender trees and brush, thick drops falling sporadically from the branches above. Under other circumstances in such gloom, the young woman driving would be watching for some creature, a vampire or stolemy, to leap from the trees, but today she has more menacing fears.

The woman steals a glance behind her. Dim light penetrates the forest, enough to confirm her suspicion that the dark-skinned man on the buckskin is gaining. He will overtake her soon.

*Dear Lord! If it is Your will, please help me!*

Fearfully, she checks the bed of the buggy. The blankets appear dark, wet, but the bundle remains tied securely, despite being tossed about.

Ahead, a gap in the trees. She flaps the reins recklessly, urging the horse, desperate to flee the forbidding forest. The horse bolts wildly, beyond her intent. A terrible mistake, due to her youth and inexperience at driving a horse-drawn vehicle.

The trees drop behind. The buggy enters a vast, empty plain, dampened by a light, steady rainfall. The road is smoother here, the bouncing less, but her relief is momentary. The plain presents new challenges. Her pursuer could catch her more easily in the open.

Although still too far from safety, she might encounter others who could help her. She must keep going.

She glances back again. Man and horse are less than a hundred yards away.

And then she remembers the bridge.

A short way ahead, a narrow wooden bridge with no rails crosses a deep wash. She has to slow the horse's pace. But the horse runs wildly, out of control, ignoring her frantic tugs on the reins.

The horse plunges onto the bridge, misses its footing on the slippery wood, falters, and goes down. Momentum carries the buggy into the horse. The vehicle upends, throwing the woman into the air. The buggy slides into the wash, pulling the screaming horse with it.

# Chapter 1

**May 2015**

Clear, mournful music pierced the solitude and Cora's troubled thoughts. The notes floated like feathers on the breeze, dipped, soared, and wailed through the deserted ravine, the musician unseen, the instrument unidentifiable at first. Before the music began, the solemn silence in the isolated valley had been broken only by rustling leaves, the occasional distant chirp of some spring bird, or the drumming of a woodpecker.

The hymn did not disturb, but seemed instead to enhance the peace of the secluded garden. Cora Tozzi recognized the melody, remembered the words:

*Immaculate Mary, your praises we sing. You reign now in Heaven with Jesus our King. Ave, Ave, Ave Maria…*

Cora reached into the pocket of her denim jacket, found her rosary and gathered it into the palm of her hand without withdrawing it. Before she left home to visit this place she was inspired to search in a box of old religious articles for her childhood rosary and tuck it in her pocket. Its image filled her mind when she touched it: a chain of pale-blue crystal beads attached to a silver cross. The cross was tarnished a dull gray now—so many years, some sixty-five of them, since her mother had given her the rosary when Cora made her First Holy Communion as a child.

If only life was as simple now as it was then, when she trusted God to lead her to heaven.

An hour earlier, she had left Main Street and turned up the drive to St. Marija's, stopping for a moment in front of the Slovenian Catholic

Center to overlook the Des Plaines River Valley. Quarries, now filled with water, glistened in the valley floor and Argonne National Laboratory sat on the far ridge. After driving uphill, she passed the immense red brick Franciscan monastery and the retreat house, where she parked in an empty lot hidden from the road and surveyed the surrounding woods and fields.

Then she had exited her car, shivered, tugged her broad-brimmed hat tightly over her white hair, and fastened the upper button of her jeans jacket against the chilly breeze. Although the sun was bright and the sky cloudless, the temperature was in the low sixties even this late in May. The car door made a soft, dull thunk in the hushed surroundings when she gently pushed it closed; the following chirp of the lock seemed jarring in the silence.

As archivist for the Lemont Historical Society, Cora had a rudimentary knowledge of the large number of religious institutions that had been established in and near Lemont in the 1920s. This included a Catholic Franciscan monastery, St. Marija's, and an adjacent convent of sisters, Assisi Hill. Both sat on a bluff overlooking the Des Plaines River Valley about two miles east of downtown Lemont. A third order, the Franciscan Sisters of Our Lady, had purchased land a half mile west of St. Marija's.

Although Cora had passed these institutions many times, she had never explored them. She had come to St. Marija's today seeking comfort, to walk in a place of reverence and prepare for the dreaded journey she would soon begin. She wanted to be alone to face her fear, although she acted brave in front of Cisco, her family, and friends.

What lay ahead would be difficult. Perhaps here she could figure out how to survive the ordeal.

She had walked up the only path in sight, north from where she left her car. She was looking for a grotto and Stations of the Cross she'd heard were here.

When she came to the stone grotto, it was more impressive than she had imagined. A large structure composed of ancient-looking rock enclosed an altar, with smaller enclosures on either side and steps leading to another level. Ivy, leafless in early spring, grew above the altar, and in a niche capping the entire shrine was a statue of the Virgin Mary, her light blue gown and white veil shining between the branches of adjacent trees. It reminded Cora of photos she had seen of the shrine at Lourdes, where the Virgin Mary had appeared to Bernadette. The grotto faced a large pond with a small island in its center. Stations of the Cross circled the pond and were reflected in the clear blue water.

Cora had expected only a peaceful place to think, not such an elaborate display. Amazed, she forgot her personal problems for the moment, following a path that traveled through the Stations of the Cross. At each stop was a sculpture with a memorial plaque embedded in a tall column of multicolored rock that resembled rough gravel. She had never seen stone like this before: it seemed to be composed of intricately convoluted materials in brown, reddish, and tan tones with crystal encrustations. It struck her as gaudy and not very attractive, but certainly eye-catching and memorable.

Midway around the pond, a sign pointed downhill to the monastery's cemetery. After a moment's hesitation, remembering why she had come here, she decided to visit. She had always feared death, but if death lay at the end of the journey she was about to embark upon, it was time she faced that possibility.

Did she have the courage to power through what was ahead? Was it the treatment itself she feared, or the possibility she would not survive it?

The cemetery was a small square plot, about half an acre, filled with gravestones and a monument that faced the gate at its far end. Like everything she had seen so far, the spot was peaceful but desolate. Despite the chill air, Cora felt warm and safe as she wandered in dappled shade, pausing to read grave markers and a stone tablet inscribed with a history of the monastery.

Cora was not a strongly religious person, but cancer was bound to affect one's outlook. Catholic guilt had tortured her: what had she done to cause this disease? Then she turned to the saints: Mary, of course; St. Jude, patron of impossible causes; St. Peregrine, the patron saint of cancer; St. Blaise, patron of diseases of the throat. There was a saint out there for just about anything. Despite turning to the saints, she had doubts. She wished she could fully believe the saints could help her.

After a time, she left the cemetery and went back up the hill, intending to return to her car, composed and resigned to reality by the peaceful atmosphere but still sad. She would soon be on an express train headed to an unfamiliar destination, but she would do what it took to beat this thing. She had no other choice.

As she approached the parking lot again, legs burning and out of breath, she came to a side path she hadn't noticed before. She followed it, descended a few stone steps and came to a thin, meandering stream at the base of a ravine. A path circled both sides of the stream. At the entrance to a statuary garden, rocks on the ground spelled out: *Franciscan Rosary of the Seven Joys of Mary.* Next to them was a brown stone crucifix, a larger-than-life-size Christ in carved white stone affixed to the Cross.

After passing the crucifix and entering a narrow valley, Cora stopped at the first structure, made of stone similar to the Stations of the Cross she had just seen. Here a round bas-relief plaque of white stone was embedded in the rough rocks of the column, depicting The Annunciation, when the Angel Gabriel told Mary she was to bear the Son of God.

Ahead was a group of statues depicting the Miracle at Fatima: the Virgin Mary, three kneeling children, and two sheep, all carved from similar white stone. Mary stood on a column of the same unusual reddish rock, the stone embedded with numerous bubbles, cavities and crevices in which visitors had placed coins. A rosary of large jade-like beads identified this place as one devoted to prayer and reflection.

Like its name, this valley was all about Mary, the mother of God. Despite being surrounded by images of Mary, Cora couldn't capture a feeling of knowing the woman. Mary was at the heart of her religion, and being unable to feel a connection made Cora sad.

That was the moment Cora first heard the music. How appropriate the song seemed for this time and place, she thought. She clutched the rosary in her pocket again, awed, then filled with curiosity. A harmonica, she realized. The melody changed to Schubert's "Ave, Maria," a favorite of Cora's. The musician was quite accomplished, the notes on pitch, the expression haunting and masterful, filled with embellishments, trills, vibrato and warbles that only harmonica virtuosos can produce.

Where was the music coming from? When she got here, her car had been the only one in the parking lot. Was the instrument being played by another visitor, or by someone who lived here, perhaps a Franciscan Father? How extensive were these grounds? She was on private property.

If she explored beyond the gardens, would that be trespassing? She didn't know, but decided to take the opportunity. If stopped, she would plead ignorance.

She walked to the far end of the valley and ascended steps dug into its side, exiting onto a vast lawn studded with ancient oaks. The music seemed to be coming from her left, away from the lawn and behind an area of thick brush and scrub trees. Skirting the brush, she came to a break—a short tunnel through dense undergrowth. After about fifty feet, Cora stepped onto a large sunny field. In the center of the field, apparently unmindful of the crushed dry grass that she sat on, was a nun, dressed in a black skirt, white blouse, and black jacket. On her head was a white headband attached to a short black veil. The sister's hands were clamped around her mouth. It was clear she was the musician Cora heard.

Cora had expected a male harmonica player, not a woman, and certainly not a nun!

She stood for a time, unsure if she should approach and introduce herself. As she wrestled with her thoughts, the musician started a new hymn that Cora also knew, "Be Not Afraid." Cora froze. It was as if the nun had read Cora's mind, knew she was here to confront her fears, to gain the courage needed to face her future. Her eyes filled with silent tears, her legs shook. She took a few steps toward the nun, but felt too weak to go any farther and sank to the ground.

The nun looked in Cora's direction and finished playing the hymn. *Be not afraid. I go before you always. Come. Follow me. And I will give you rest.* She stood up, tucked the harmonica somewhere in her clothing, and walked toward Cora, hesitating a couple of times along the way. "Are you okay?" she asked as she drew near, her voice soft and warm.

"I'll be fine. I just need a moment…" Cora murmured, brushing tears away with a shaking hand.

The nun was young, probably not older than twenty, short, a little pudgy, and barefoot. Walking in such a rough field with the temperature barely out of the fifties must be painful, and Cora wondered why the nun didn't wear shoes.

"Should I…sit here with you…until you feel better?" the sister asked.

"I'll be fine," Cora repeated. Her gaze met the young woman's eyes inquiringly. The eyes were hazel, reflected warm gold in the light, and filled with concern. "But is it okay for me to be here? Please *do* sit. Is this field part of the monastery?"

The nun smoothed the back of her skirt and seated herself on the grass beside Cora. "No, it's Assisi Hill grounds. The monastery property ends somewhere around those trees." She pointed to the wooded area Cora had just come through. "Technically, you're trespassing, but we don't mind as long as people aren't here to cause damage." Her gaze was downcast, avoiding Cora's eyes. "It's a beautiful spot isn't it? God meant for people to see His beauty."

Cora glanced around, a bit more at ease now that the shock of the hymn was over. "That's a good attitude to take. This place reminds me of the opening scene of *The Sound of Music*—you know, 'the hills are alive', and all that?"

The nun looked at the tall grass surrounding them. "I see what you mean. Nothing but hills here, and me, a nun, playing music in the field." She turned to Cora and grinned. "I feel like standing up with my arms in the air, twirling in circles."

Cora managed a smile. "That would make it perfect, wouldn't it?" She felt stronger by the minute. "So, are you in the convent here?"

"Yes. I'm preparing to take final vows. I've chosen the name Sister Maryam." She pronounced the name Mary-am.

"I haven't heard that name before."

"It's the Aramaic pronunciation of Mary—the language Jesus and Mary spoke. I'm a Mary devotee, you see." She giggled shyly, and reached for a tall blade of grass, broke it off, and ran her fingers up and down the stalk before stopping to caress the fuzzy seed head.

"It's a lovely name. As is your playing. Where did you learn to do that?"

"Did you ever hear Howard Levy play? He's incredible. The first time I heard him play 'Amazing Grace' I became fascinated with the harmonica." The nun beamed. "Harmonica music is for anyone, you know. A harmonica is cheap, and you can just noodle with it until it does what you want. And it fits in your pocket so you always have it with you—when you want to make music."

"Well, your noodling really paid off. I can't imagine that Levy is any better than you are."

"Oh, he is! I just play for myself—and for Mary." She dropped her gaze again.

Cora studied the shy young woman. Her skin was pale with freckles and acne, her face oval, with a small turned-up nose. Wisps of red hair escaped from her headband. She looked to Cora like a typical Irish girl. Her eyes sparkled with good humor, making Cora think that, despite her shyness, the girl had a vivid imagination and had probably been a prankster as a child.

Much like the half-Irish girl Cora had been at that age, except that Cora had nondescript light brown hair and tended toward plumpness even then. How she wished that today she had the energy of youth, the carefree hours, and could shed thirty pounds.

Although they had just met, she felt an immediate fondness for this nun, a feeling that they were destined to become friends.

"I've been to Assisi Hill before, down by the convent and school, for events," Cora said. "Actually, Sister Lorita called me a couple of weeks ago to see if I was interested in helping her write a history of your order. I'm a bit of a historian. I'm going to have to put it off, though." She swallowed somewhat painfully, then went on. "Something's come up that's going to take a while."

"Oh, no," said Sister Maryam, putting her hand on Cora's forearm. "It's serious, isn't it? An illness? That's why you're here today. Our Lady told me to play for someone who needed comfort. Someone who's afraid. She said you must trust in God now, and to assure you that you are in His hands."

# Chapter 2

**March 2020**

Cora Tozzi stared out the passenger-side window at the traffic merging onto northbound I-294 and then glanced quickly at Cisco, waiting for him to complain about her silence. She wanted to chatter excitedly about the upcoming weeks, but she was too fixated on their imminent separation to fake it convincingly. In the fifty-plus years they'd been married, they'd been separated only for hospital stays or tragedies. With separations linked so clearly to unpleasant memories, it was no wonder she was worried. But then, Cora was an incorrigible worrier.

All morning she'd tried to reassure herself. Cisco was going on this golfing vacation to Arizona without her, but with her blessing—in fact, it had been her idea. She hoped he would relax and have fun with her cousin Barney, Cisco's old golf buddy who had moved to Phoenix to golf year-round. She would spend the time at a nearby convent, having agreed to help write and publish the order's history. Living in, she would be free to devote every minute to the book without feeling guilty about sacrificing together-time, and Cisco would be free to engage in the activity he loved best without worrying about leaving her alone. A win-win.

Or so it seemed when they planned it. It was another story now that he was actually leaving. Would he eat properly? Cisco didn't remember to eat when he was busy. Recent weight loss was noticeable on his too-thin, five-foot eight-inch frame, and in his gaunt face, accentuating his generous Roman nose and baldness. Would he find his way around without her? She did the planning and navigating, things he preferred not to do. Surely Barney would show him around and arrange meals. And it was only for two weeks.

She'd miss him. She was missing him already. Her eyes burned from unshed tears she didn't want Cisco to see, and she stared out the window again. She'd never have let him go alone if she didn't believe it would be good for him. Something had to bring him out of the mood he'd been in for over six months now. Everything she'd tried hadn't worked.

He had been at her side five years ago during every moment of her cancer treatment and recovery, but recently the stress of the experience seemed to have taken a toll on him. He spent many hours in front of the television now, sometimes slept in his chair in the afternoon, and took little interest in household chores, or anything else for that matter, even activities he had always enjoyed. Everything seemed to irritate him, and his language—which had always been "colorful"—had gotten annoying.

This behavior was unlike Cisco, who, although outspoken, had always been energetic and accepting. Cora knew that sometimes an experience with cancer traumatized the spouse even more than the patient, but Cisco had never given any indication of that. Perhaps he had suppressed his feelings and they were coming out now. She shied away from using the word *depression*, but she thought he needed something to do—a distraction. He loved golf, but it was too cold to golf in Illinois in March, which is why she came up with this idea and arranged the trip.

She'd just have to swallow her worries for his benefit. This had to work.

"We're getting close to O'Hare. You're awfully quiet," Cisco said—as she'd predicted—steering the car aggressively into the left lane to pass a truck.

Cora winced as he made the move, but instead of complaining she said, "I'm going to miss you."

"I'll miss you too. But it's only two weeks. This is supposed to be a vacation for both of us."

"It's *all of* two weeks," she said.

"We've got our phones, and you'll get wrapped up in your project. We'll be home before you know it, and I bet you'll be wishing you had more time to yourself. Didn't you say the sisters were fun to be around?"

"Daytime will probably be okay. I'll miss you at night."

"Don't forget to turn down the heat, check the stove and coffeepot, and be sure everything is locked. Maybe you should unplug the television and computers, in case there's a power failure," Cisco said.

As if she needed to be told. "We did most of that already, but I'll double-check. I'll have the laptop with me. You didn't forget your range-finder, did you?"

"Nope—got it. And before you ask, yes, I have my wallet and my phone."

"Remember, I can always run home if something comes up."

"I remember."

They were approaching the terminals. Cora watched the signs carefully. "There," she said. "Departures, Terminal 3, American, stay on the left."

Cisco followed her directions. They passed the first two terminals, then moved to an inner lane, searching for a place to pull over. As always, cars and buses moved in and out of the lanes. Driving slowly, Cisco spotted a gap as a car pulled away and darted into it. A security guard walked by, reminding drivers no parking was allowed.

Cisco and Cora both got out of the car and he retrieved his suitcase and golf bag from the rear of their SUV, setting them on the ground. He drew her into a hug and kissed her.

"Have a good trip," Cora said. She grinned. "Safety ride." It was a family phrase first used by her Polish grandmother.

"I will. Love ya, hon," Cisco said.

"I love you. Call me as soon as the plane lands, okay?"

Cisco eyed the security guard, who looked as if he was heading their way. "I will. And you take care of yourself, too. We'll be fine, both of us. If anything goes wrong, we'll just come home."

"Okay." She blinked rapidly.

He hugged her again and rubbed his cheek against hers. "Bye."

"Bye." She tightened her arms for a moment, then let go and backed away. He picked up his luggage and turned to her, eyeing the security guard again.

"Get in the car—go!" Cisco said, pointing.

"Bye," she said again. She got into the driver's seat, but sat watching him walk away until he entered the terminal and was lost to sight. She hated goodbyes. They always felt permanent to her.

As she drove off, she felt empty and so, so alone. She'd never been able to explain why this man meant so much to her. She recalled little things now, like how they bumped into each other accidentally when they walked, how they caught each other's eye when they both had the same thought, how they pitched in to make things easier for each other, the feeling of his hand on her back. Nothing anyone would think important, but uniquely theirs.

Like when she was pregnant with Patrick, their first son. She'd stepped out of the shower and noticed a piece of paper on the floor. It said, *Just sitting here thinking how glad I am that you are in my life.* Cisco often left little messages like that, finding it difficult to speak the words.

Enough self-pity. Sister Lorita was expecting her, and she had to swing by the house to pick up her own possessions and check the house one more time. She remembered a cartoon on her desk backboard. It showed a headstone above a recent grave, with a word bubble that said, *Did I leave the iron on?*

# Chapter 3

The door clicked shut behind Sister Lorita, leaving Cora alone in one of the convent's guest rooms. She sighed and set her suitcase, purse, and duffel bag on the puffy comforter that covered the queen-sized bed and surveyed the small room that would be her home for the next two weeks.

A comfortable-looking, navy-blue easy chair sat next to two large windows with a stunning view of the Des Plaines River Valley. Good—a nightstand next to the bed had a lamp. She'd be able to read at night, and the oak desk with matching captain's chair would be a suitable work space. There was no television, but she had books, her phone and her laptop, and she would be busy. Two doors on her right led to a closet and a bathroom. She had expected something more spartan than these almost-spacious guest quarters—provided she stayed. If it didn't work out, she lived only two miles away.

Abruptly, Cora felt uneasy. It had been years since the house was unoccupied for more than a few days. Perhaps she was uneasy because she didn't know if her decision to stay at the convent had been a wise one.

Before she knew she had cancer, Cora had agreed to Sister Lorita's request to help write a history of the order, the Sisters of St. Francis of Christ the Teacher. A mouthful, but apparently there were a plethora of Franciscan orders. Then, before the project began, Cora had been diagnosed and the long treatment and slow recovery intervened. The history was put back on the table this past January, but after the long delay the work was going slowly and both women were feeling frustrated.

It was now early March. Sister Lorita had suggested laughingly that

Cora should just move into the convent so they could concentrate their efforts. Cora immediately saw that she could write the better story she envisioned if she involved herself directly in convent life. That is, if she could convince Sister Lorita of her concept for the book.

Sister Lorita didn't know that Cora had other reasons for wanting to live in the convent. Not only did Cora think Cisco needed a vacation, but she had problems of her own. Specifically, getting her life back on track after her cancer. She was in remission, her doctors said, but they were cautious about using the word "cure." She had given up over a year of her life to cancer treatment and another year trying to bring her old life back. Then more years working her way through a new normal and an accumulation of two years of postponed projects. In her seventies, that time was precious. Cora had so much more she wanted to do, but had trouble prioritizing, and she had had a bad scare.

Cora opened the drapes, slumped in the easy chair, and gave in to memories of how it all began.

It was April of 2015 when she'd noticed a small lump, about the size of a pea, just below her jaw. She and Cisco were in their family room, watching an old season of *Vera*. She rested her jaw on the palm of her hand, as she often did, and there it was.

She didn't think much of it, not then. It was probably a dental infection, and an antibiotic would take care of it. But she procrastinated until her son Joe, his wife Rosie, and one-year-old Maria came from Indiana for a weekend. During their visit she was alarmed to find that the lump was no longer pea-sized, but larger, like a grape.

She had wandered into the guest bedroom where Joe was checking emails. "There's something in my neck," she said, tilting her head to the side and pointing. "What do you think?"

Joe, a gastroenterologist, felt her neck. "How long has this been here?"

"Only a few days…well, less than a week."

"Does it hurt?" he asked, gently probing the area.

"No. Just a little sore when you press on it. I think it's an infection. The teeth right above have been giving me trouble."

He lowered his hands and nodded. "That makes sense. You're probably right. This isn't my field, but an antibiotic until you see your dentist can't hurt."

By the time Joe and his family left for home, the lump was even larger. She saw her dentist a few days later.

"It's likely you have a periodontal infection," he said. "I'm going to give you a stronger antibiotic. Come see me if it's not better in a couple of days."

Two days later it wasn't better.

Still not really alarmed, Cora complained to Cisco. "I've been on antibiotics for a week. Maybe I should see Dr. Papanastos."

"At our age, it's best to be cautious," Cisco agreed.

"I don't like how this feels," Sophia Papanastos, her internist, said. "Your ENT is Dr. Thomas, right? I'm going to see if I can reach him on the phone right now. Stay here." She left the room.

Cora was glad Dr. Papanastos was thorough, but surely she was overreacting. Dr. Thomas would probably be unavailable, or would think it was of no concern. But when Dr. Papanastos returned to the room a few minutes later, she looked concerned.

"Dr. Thomas agrees that this is suspicious. We'd like you to get a CT scan. Then he wants to see you in his office. Can you do that?"

Cora's gaze met Cisco's, sitting in a visitor's chair across the exam room. He nodded, his tense jaw and drawn eyebrows reflecting his worry.

"We can, but I feel fine. Do I really need all this fuss?"

Dr. Papanastos lowered her chin and raised her eyebrows. Cora got the point.

"Okay, we'll go."

Fortunately, there was an available CT appointment in an hour. Afterward, they stopped to pick up Mexican food and by early afternoon were munching at their kitchen table.

"The technicians never say anything, only that the doctor will call. But it's going to turn out negative, I just know," Cora said, although doubt was beginning to enter her mind. "After having the kids here last weekend, I should be exhausted, but I'm not. Wouldn't I feel bad if there was something really wrong? And I think it's getting smaller now that I've been on the antibiotic for a while." She looked at Cisco for confirmation.

"You'd think so," Cisco said, over a mouthful of chicken burrito. His eyes avoided hers.

They were watching television when the phone rang at eight that evening. When Cora saw the caller ID she answered, then jumped up and moved to the kitchen, away from the sound of the TV.

"We have the results of the CT scan," Dr. Thomas said.

"Already?" Cora had expected to wait a few days. She heard road noise in the background. He must be calling from his car.

"Yes. I'm afraid the scan *is* suspicious. It shows enlarged lymph nodes on both sides of your neck. The swelling you feel is invading your neck muscles. I'd like to examine you in the office tomorrow and take a biopsy."

Cora's mouth went dry and her heart pounded. "Wait," she said. "Let me put you on speaker so my husband can hear."

She beckoned to Cisco, who got up and moved to her side at the kitchen island. He touched her arm but stared at the floor. Dr. Thomas repeated what he had told Cora.

Cora understood medical terminology, having worked with doctors all her adult life. But a little knowledge could be more alarming than reassuring, and being on the receiving end of bad news was another matter.

"You're saying I have…cancer?" Cora asked. Her mind felt numb. She thought, *I should be scared to death but this seems unreal.*

"We don't know for sure," the doctor replied. "But if it is, we have ways to fix this." At her regular appointments, Dr. Thomas was always cheerful. Today he seemed professionally positive, but Cora had trouble believing what he was telling her.

"Tell me about what you're going to do tomorrow," she asked, her voice weak and a little shaky.

"I'll do an endoscopic exam, just insert a thin, flexible tube through your nose so I can look at the back of your throat. You've had that done before."

"Yes," she said. It had been only mildly uncomfortable.

"We need to know where this may have started. The CT showed a suspicious area at the base of your tongue, and I want to look at it with the scope. Then we want to see what that swelling in your neck is. So, I'll numb it, put in a tiny needle, drain it, and send the fluid to pathology."

"My *tongue?*" Cora said, surprised. "I don't feel anything wrong with my tongue. I feel fine."

"Let's hope it turns out that way," Dr. Thomas said. "I'll have my secretary call you first thing in the morning to give you a time for tomorrow."

Cora managed to murmur an *okay* and end the call. She set the phone down and looked at Cisco. When she got up that morning she had expected to check off a minor health detail. Instead she had been seen, scanned, and her world turned upside down in a single day.

"This has to be a mistake," she said, her cheeks burning and her head buzzing.

Cisco drew her close, rubbing his head against hers and stroking her back. "You're probably right."

Fear of the unknown surged inside her. If it wasn't a mistake, would she live? What would happen to Cisco if she didn't? Maria, her only granddaughter, was just a year old!

Bringing herself back to the present, Cora got up, moved to the window, and gazed out on the sweeping grounds of the convent. She'd come to realize that the fear of cancer was even worse for those who had been through it, because now they knew firsthand what they had to dread. Also, who said she wouldn't have other health issues in the future, unrelated to the cancer? And she had been told that "late effects" of cancer treatment might occur even years in the future. Could she go through the exhausting ordeal all over again? Were there things she should do while she still could?

During her treatment, she had pushed off unpleasant thoughts about death as soon as they entered her mind. She wasn't sure she believed in heaven and hell anymore, even though she had had experiences with ghosts that should bear witness to an afterlife of some kind. She had been born and raised Catholic, had raised her children Catholic. She did not consider herself a *lapsed* Catholic now, as she still belonged to and supported her parish and was friends with the pastor and other priests. Yet she rarely made time to attend Mass or the sacraments. She prayed daily, but her prayers seemed more like meditation. Was that what prayer really was? Or was it an appeal for urgent favors to some entity that might or might not be out there? Covering the bases, to put it bluntly.

When she was younger she went to Mass frequently and sought out quiet chapels for peace in times of need. The rituals, ceremonies, churches, and chapels gave her comfort. But that closeness to God now seemed lost. Could she get it back? Or was it gone forever?

Cisco would not understand. He had seen poor examples of religious life in his childhood, and evils committed by religious zealots and extremists who claimed their actions were in the name of God, and scandals within the church. He appreciated Cora's need to feel a part of her faith, and wanted that for her. He would go to Mass with her but would not—no, *could* not—understand her discomfort about her faith. Despite his differing ideas about religion, he was sensitive to her needs, but she couldn't discuss her feelings with him. He would listen, and he would care, but he wouldn't be able to help her figure out what was missing.

She *could* talk to her friend Frannie, of course. But even though Frannie was Catholic and they were close, preparing for life after death was not something Cora felt comfortable discussing with Frannie. She was a great friend, always there with a helping hand and a sympathetic ear, but they never talked about deep personal matters.

Cora was also good friends with a local priest who would have been the ideal confidant, except he was on a six-month sabbatical.

But if she lived in the convent, among believers who dedicated their lives to God, and who followed the comfortable traditions she remembered so fondly—among kindly strangers with compassionate ears—perhaps she could put her thoughts and priorities in order and decide what God's place would be in her life going forward. She could try.

She had revealed none of these personal issues to Sister Lorita. Friendly as the woman was, she seemed more businesslike than intimate. In fact, Cora found her a little scary.

She turned from the window, approached the bed, and unzipped her suitcase and duffel bag. She hung clothes in the closet, doubling up on an insufficient number of hangers, and stacked more items on shelves and in drawers. She had brought too much, of course—she had never learned how to travel light.

Many of the items she had brought, she had never worn. She recalled how, after losing thirty pounds to cancer, she had asked Marty, her son Patrick's wife, to help her weed out her wardrobe.

"Do women my age wear skinny pants and leggings?" she had asked. "My shoes still fit but I don't have any dress boots."

Marty pulled out a gray linen suit that Cora had loved and kept so long it was back in style. "I can alter this a little," she said. "Put it on so I can mark it."

In the suit, standing in front of a mirror, tears had come to Cora's eyes. She looked good! When was the last time she saw herself in a mirror and thought that?

A few days later Joe's wife, Rosie, took her clothes shopping. "You're not a 16 anymore, you're size 10," Rosie said, pulling items off the rack for Cora to try on. At the register, Rosie pulled out her charge card. "It's on me. You've worked hard and deserve a reward," she said. "Let's check out some bras and panties."

Now, her suitcase empty, Cora noted a chill in the room. She hoped the radiator under the windows would provide enough heat and not keep her awake banging and wheezing all night. The building was old, built around 1940, a stately three stories of orangey-colored brick that proudly represented religious institutional architecture of the time. Like other structures of that era, it was likely poorly insulated.

She draped a warm cardigan over the back of a chair and threw her fluffy robe across the foot of the bed.

Her duffel held her computer, references, and notes. She placed her laptop on the desk, plugged it in, and connected to Wi-Fi using the password Sister Lorita had provided, FunNuns104—the numbers for October 4, the feast day of the convent's patron, St. Francis of Assisi. Her reference books went on the desktop, reading books on the nightstand, notes, notepads, and writing implements in the center desk drawer.

The bathroom was nothing fancy, but functional. She checked herself in the mirror over the sink, picked up her purse, searched in it for a moment, and retrieved her pale-blue crystal rosary. She held it until it felt warm in her hand and then slipped it in the top drawer of the nightstand, where she could reach it easily. She hadn't used it for a while, but found its presence reassuring.

Lunch was promptly at noon, a communal meal. Cora was invited to attend as a temporary part of the community. It was time to get to know the good sisters and test her ideas for the book. Sister Lorita's plan had been a simple, straightforward chronological presentation of important people and events, but Cora had a different structure in mind. Her concept would entail a lot more work than Sister's, and the project had already been severely delayed.

Under most circumstances, Cora found embarking on new projects, being in new places, and meeting new people fun, but was she doing the right thing? She looked in the mirror again. She had chosen a high-necked, long-sleeved knit top in a narrow blue-and-white stripe, over slim-legged navy-blue knit pants, and comfortable black Sketchers. She tried a closed-mouth smile, the same smile she had seen so often on her own mother's face, and drew back her shoulders. She would set her personal problems aside for the moment and immerse herself in the project she had committed to.

*The coming weeks may not be all wine and roses, but I can do it—I've done it before!*

# Chapter 4

**W**ooden tables for four were scattered around the spacious dining room, the tabletops covered with pale pink tablecloths, a vase of cheerful deep pink lilies in the center, each table surrounded by armchairs with deep green padded seats. The room could accommodate about forty diners, but was less than half occupied with sisters in black veils, black skirts, white blouses, and an assortment of black vests or jackets.

Amidst a low murmur of voices, Cora glanced around, wondering where she should sit. An elderly sister at one of the tables beckoned to her, and she gratefully joined that table.

The sisters introduced themselves, then immediately the office prayers began, followed by grace. The prayer period seemed interminable to Cora. She tried to concentrate reverently, but her mind drifted, wondering what the sisters thought of this woman who had suddenly arrived at their table. Did they know why she was here? Did they approve, or think of her as a nuisance? Would she have anything in common with them? Usually Cora was at her best when first meeting people, but....

After about twenty minutes the sisters made the sign of the Cross, went to the serving table to fill their plates, and began to chat.

"I'm Sister Fatima. It's about time we got to meet you," said the sister who'd invited Cora to join them. "I'm surprised she's given you a room in the convent. Visitors usually stay at Assisi Manor."

Cora wondered what prompted Sister Fatima's comment. The slight woman looked sweet and innocent, with her fringe of graying light brown hair and rimless glasses, but her voice verged on a whine and she sounded annoyed.

THE MIRACLE AT ASSISI HILL

Anxious to make a good impression, Cora felt blindsided. She forced a smile in Sister Fatima's direction. "I guess you've heard why I'm here and what Sister Lorita and I are working on? She thought I would have a better understanding of convent life if I observed it directly."

Cora picked up her tuna salad sandwich and took a bite. It was surprisingly good. Sister Fatima, she noticed, was the only one at the table with toasted cheese, explaining that she was allergic to fish.

"I really don't know why she needs anyone to help document our history, especially someone who doesn't know our order at all. There are plenty of us here that would be happy to contribute," Fatima said.

*Got her! She's played right into my hands!*

"I'm so glad to hear you say that," Cora said, beaming. "That's what I've been suggesting to Sister Lorita. I suspect you don't really want another dry recital of facts. Wouldn't it be better if the sisters use their own words, stories from their lives, or stories passed down from sisters who aren't with us anymore?" She looked each woman in the eyes. "What do you think?"

Sister Agnes was the oldest woman at the table, probably in her eighties. She set down her sandwich, swallowed, and rubbed at her nose, knocking her round, metal-framed glasses off-kilter. She was rather stout with white hair, her lively eyes and energy belying her age. "Oh, I love that idea, and many of the sisters would too. Especially those of us who've been here so long and have time on our hands." She poked at her glasses to straighten them. "But I don't know. Sister Lorita has been planning this history for a long time and has pretty firm ideas. From what I understand, she favors a more academic approach."

"Well, you're right there," Cora said. "And she only asked for my input, not for me to take over. In either case, the material we're gathering will be useful to structure the book, as well as to pinpoint the best sisters to interview." She took another bite of her sandwich and swallowed. "Sister's approach is of value even if it's not compelling reading."

"Our written history should be a resource for anyone who wants to know about our good works," Sister Fatima insisted. "A reference—a gathering of important facts and dates. People ask, you know. Our history is already on our website and in promotional material, but having a single updated resource will be helpful when developing new materials. We can always write stories later. There's no need to delay things by doing it now."

*Oh, great. Everyone wants to drive in different directions.* Did some of the sisters, like Sister Fatima, view this as a committee project? Sensing that she was unpopular with Sister Fatima already, Cora wondered if that opinion extended to anyone else.

She turned to Sister Bernadette, a timid, slender, fortyish woman with warm, medium-brown skin and gentle, dark brown eyes behind square, tortoise-framed eyeglasses. The nun had identified herself as supervisor of the convent's infirmary, which housed elderly sisters as well as those that needed assistance with daily living.

"What do you think, Sister?" Cora asked.

The nun placed her fingers against her cheeks, then dropped her hands and her gaze to the table, and finally looked modestly at Cora.

"I agree that an outline of all the important facts should come first," she said, her words precise in a soft, eastern Indian accent. "But I also think we should use this opportunity to make it the best history it can be. Why not make it something *all* readers will enjoy, not only our community? If it is popular reading, it can spread our mission to a wider world and benefit us in many ways. Stories told by our sisters will be entertaining, and that will bring us income, not only from book sales, but will generate bigger donations if more people think our mission worthwhile."

Cora peeked at Sister Fatima out of the corner of her eye and bit her cheeks to stifle a smile. *Three to one, Sister.*

Sister Fatima slowly applauded with a wry grin. "Admirable sentiment but wasted effort in my opinion. It sounds to me like you're more interested in controlling the project than in helping with it, Cora. But it won't be our decision anyway—it's up to Sister Lorita. So there's not much point in discussing it further."

Sister Fatima's accusation stung. Cora felt as if she had been put in her place, a place she didn't deserve. Or did she? It wouldn't be the first time she was accused of being controlling, when her intent was only to convince others to consider a good idea.

Her cell phone rang. She glanced at the caller ID. It was Cisco.

"Excuse me just a minute—I have to take this," she said, and hurried into the hallway.

Cisco sounded rushed. "I'm waiting for my luggage They better not have damaged my clubs—cost enough to get the damn bag on the plane."

"I'm sure they'll be fine. Have you heard from Barney yet?" Cisco would likely be golfing every day while staying with Barney and his wife, Connie, in a suburb of Phoenix.

"Not yet. I'll text him as soon as I hang up with you."

"How was the trip?"

"Uneventful, except the blabbermouth in the seat next to me pissing me off, filled with doom and gloom about some virus in China. Says it's going to be a big problem. I didn't need to hear that."

"Joe said that too, hon. Let's just hope it doesn't come here."

"If the asshole was right it's already too late—apparently there were some cases on some ship offshore of California. They'll contain it, I'm sure. Oops! Here comes the luggage—got to run."

"Okay. Have fun. Talk to you tomorrow?"

"Yeah. Love ya!"

"Too!"

Cora stood in the empty hallway a moment after the call ended, fighting off a sudden feeling of foreboding. She'd get used to it in a day or two, and then it would come back.

She leaned against a nearby wall and closed her eyes, feeling a little lonely and sorry for herself. She didn't want to go back to the past, yet memories of her battle against cancer kept popping up, triggered today by her loneliness, perhaps. As much as everyone told her she was not alone, cancer was ultimately a solitary battle.

Oh, her family and friends had tried to be helpful. Cisco, of course, was at her side every step. Frannie called to cheer her up. Family, and old and new friends, showered her with cards and gifts. It had meant a lot.

Many offered suggestions. She found herself trying to avoid visitors. She didn't want people, although well-meaning, to tell her what they thought she should do, or to bring over dinner and wine that she couldn't eat or drink to remind her of what she was missing. She was frustrated by their lack of understanding, even as she knew they intended to be kind and only wanted to help. Then she got angry with herself for not appreciating their efforts.

Friends said she had a lot of courage, but she didn't think that way. She thought she was cooperating fully because she wanted to live.

But now, she had been away from the dining room too long. Despite the fact that she had come here intending to deal with her lingering problems once and for all, this was not the right time to dwell on the past. She took a deep breath, put on her business persona, and headed back to her table.

"I wanted your opinion on another matter," she said as soon as she rejoined the sisters. "History does not stop with the past and with the older members of the community, you know. Today's events are tomorrow's history. What do you think about including stories from the younger women in the community—novices and postulants? Are there many here?"

The timid Sister Bernadette answered. "We don't have any novices or postulants right now, but we do have one woman in temporary commitment. Few young women are called to a life of devotion these days, sad to say."

"What's temporary commitment?" Cora asked.

"Postulants usually come right out of high school, sometimes college, although some years ago we had a woman who joined our order when she was thirty-two and had worked in the secular world for almost ten years," the elderly Sister Agnes said. "After one year as a postulant, if a woman decides to stay, she enters the novitiate, where she stays for a number of years before taking temporary vows. These are years of prayer, and she lives in the convent, assisting us in any way we ask. After she proves herself in the novitiate, she takes final vows and is assigned a regular job."

"I also took a non-traditional path to God," said Sister Bernadette. "I entered a mission convent in India when I was twenty-three years old, and after my first vows I discovered the Sisters of St. Francis of Christ the Teacher and sought to be admitted here, where I took my final vows. So, there are many paths to God, you see."

"How long does temporary commitment last?" Cora asked.

"It all depends on the sister. As little as three years, or as long as six."

Cora added the years together in her head. "That's quite a commitment!"

"Yes, well, turning one's back on the secular world and devoting oneself to God does not come easy. One has to be sure. That takes time," the timid sister said.

"Yes, I can see that. Living in a supportive community and relief from some day-to-day decision-making must be attractive. But you give up so much—family, independence, just…things! I don't think I could do that."

"Yes," Sister Fatima cut in, "and you never had a desire to be a sister, did you? Why would you think you would understand?" She pushed her plate away. She hadn't touched her French fries and half of her sandwich was uneaten. Cora supposed that explained why the nun was so exceedingly thin, with a gaunt, bony face, like someone with chronic digestive problems.

But she'd had enough of Sister Fatima. "I never had a desire to be a cancer patient either, but was forced to ultimately understand cancer."

Her comment was greeted with silence. Sister Fatima glared but the other sisters stared at their plates.

Cora blushed and shook her head, thinking about her moments of introspection after Cisco's phone call and regretting her words. "I'm sorry. My remark may be irrelevant, but one doesn't have to *personally* have a desire to understand another person's attraction to it."

"Well, when you get around to trying to understand non-professed sisters, I suggest you don't waste time talking to Sister Maryam," Sister Fatima said. "She loves God, I admit, but I doubt she'll ever take permanent vows. She has no clue how to get on in the community."

Sister Maryam. The harmonica-playing nun who had consoled Cora before her cancer treatment, who she hadn't seen since. Cora had looked for her since her first visit to Assisi Hill but was disappointed, thinking maybe she had left the convent. Apparently, she was here after all.

Sister Agnes looked a little embarrassed. "Isn't that a little harsh, Fatima? She means well. She's just not as disciplined as the rest of us." She turned to Cora. "Sister Maryam is a sweet person, but she's had a hard time fitting in. Some of the sisters think she's undependable and she can be flippant or even scatter-brained at times. She does behave somewhat unusually, but the residents at Assisi Manor love her."

So that was it. The reason she hadn't seen Sister Maryam was that she was assigned to the senior residences at Assisi Manor, not to the convent. Perhaps they would get a chance to rekindle a friendship after all. She remembered the peace she had experienced after she spoke with Sister Maryam years ago. She might need a sympathetic ear, with Sister Fatima snapping at her heels.

Cora's thoughts drifted to the day she met Sister Maryam in the field. She raised her eyes and gazed randomly around the room, and there was Sister Maryam, seated at a table alone in a back corner. Catching Cora's eye, the young nun smiled in recognition and lifted a hand in greeting.

"Excuse me," Cora said, setting down her fork. She stood and hooked her purse over her shoulder. "I see an old friend." She moved off, hoping she hadn't revealed the triumph she felt at the irritated expression that appeared on Sister Fatima's face.

# Chapter 5

At nine o'clock the next morning, finding the dining room deserted, Cora went to the convent's kitchen. The cook wasn't there, so she poured herself a cup of coffee, added Italian sweet creamer she had brought from home, and put two slices of whole wheat bread into the toaster.

She rubbed her eyes. Without Cisco beside her, she hadn't slept well.

She missed him even at home, when she went to bed and he stayed downstairs watching television—she couldn't really sleep until he joined her. She missed him whenever she didn't hear him moving around the house, missed the footsteps, doors closing, water running, dishes clinking. And that was when she knew he would return shortly.

Although he didn't say so, she knew he felt the same way.

They were an improbable pair who bickered relentlessly—good-natured, most of the time. Others probably wondered why they were together, with so little in common. Cora was a take-charge person, involved in community activities, committing herself to projects, post-graduate-educated, a serious reader and writer, with over thirty years of administrative experience before retiring some ten years ago. Cisco had a high school education and rarely read books, relying on insight and common sense. More of a homebody than a joiner, a hard worker with a devil-may-care attitude, and instantly likeable. He was addicted to news on any level, local to worldwide, whereas Cora cared less about what was going on outside her home and community.

Cora had been known to say that opposites attract because they fill in the gaps to make a better whole, and that explained why those relationships became so intense. She believed it. Cisco went along with her. As he did on most things. He disapproved of the level at which she sometimes involved herself, but he was the first person with an astute suggestion or a helping hand when she got out of her depth—more frequently than she liked to admit.

While she waited for her toast, she called Cisco's cell phone. It would be seven in Arizona. She could catch him before he left for the golf course.

"Hey hon," she said when he answered. "Are you having fun?"

"Shot 83 yesterday afternoon," he said. He was less anxious; she could hear it in his voice. "I could have shot a few strokes less if it wasn't for my putting…" He rambled on about the previous day's game. No matter how well he played, he always said he could have played better. It wasn't that he was disappointed, Cora understood. It was his unique way of bragging. While he went on, her mind drifted.

The toast popped up. Still alone in the kitchen, she hit the speaker button and set the phone on the counter while she grabbed a jar of peanut butter, her favorite quick-start breakfast.

"I'm meeting with Sister Lorita soon," she said, as she spread peanut butter on the toast.

"Did you work out your differences yet?"

"Not yet. I'm a little worried about that. I hope we settle some things this morning so I can start actually putting words on paper. It's been too long as it is."

"It has been a long time. Well, it's her project. You should let her lead."

"I would, but there's really no point in my being involved at all if she doesn't let me do my thing. I mean, she asked me because she liked the book I wrote about Wawetseka and my knowledge of local history. If all I do is put facts together like she wants, then she could have done that herself and just gotten an editor. She said she liked my imagination, but the way she envisions the book doesn't let me use it."

"Well, you're good with people. I'm sure you'll work it out. Anything important going on there?" Cora knew Cisco was referring to local news. She guessed he felt out of things without constant newspaper and television broadcasts.

"Not much."

"Any talk about that virus? People here don't seem to think it's important. At least the golfers I've been around don't. But I did see something on my phone about possibly restricting travel. Some people seem to be worried."

"Sorry, but I've been busy learning about this place. I feel like I'm in a little pocket of isolation. Haven't been near a television or newspaper."

"Okay. How are you getting on with the good sisters?"

Cora took a bite of toast, a sip of coffee, and swallowed. Swallowing took concentration after her cancer. She joked that she could no longer walk and chew gum at the same time. Hearing the now-familiar sounds, Cisco waited patiently.

Cora moved to the kitchen door to be sure no one was in the dining room to overhear. "I didn't get to tell you when you called from the airport, but I met some nuns yesterday. Sister Agnes and Sister Bernadette are delightful, but Sister Fatima may be a challenge. She's rather opinionated and outspoken, and she doesn't get along with Sister Maryam, the young nun I met before I started cancer treatment. Do you remember?"

"The one that plays the harmonica?"

"Yeah, that one. I saw her in the dining room when I was leaving. We went for a walk and I'm meeting her later. She's still the sweetest thing. That's why I couldn't imagine what Sister Fatima had against her."

"Knowing you, you'll get to the bottom of it."

Cora giggled. "I already did. When I hinted about it to Maryam, she told me. It seems Fatima is terrified of cats, and assumes everyone knows it. So, one day Fatima was out walking and there was a cat standing in front of the convent door blocking her entry, so she froze. Maryam, who had only been at the convent a short time, happened to be walking nearby. She didn't know about Fatima's fear and, in fact, didn't even see the cat. But she did see Fatima, so she smiled and waved at her. When Fatima just stood there Maryam was confused as to why she didn't smile and wave back, but she just waved again and went on her way, thinking nothing of it."

"But Fatima didn't think nothing of it, I suspect."

"Exactly. Fatima thought Maryam was laughing at her. She dramatized the episode over time, going so far as to claim Maryam set the whole thing up as a practical joke."

"But it's been years, hasn't it?"

"It's hard to forget when you think someone is making fun of you, especially for Fatima. Maryam didn't understand what happened until one of the other sisters told her. She tried to explain, but Fatima wouldn't believe her."

"Yeah, some people are like that. Thin-skinned."

"You got it. But that was only the trigger. From then on Fatima has looked at everything Maryam does with a jaundiced eye. From what I gather, Maryam marches to her own drummer, and that doesn't help. Fatima complains to the other sisters relentlessly. Some of them believe her, some just don't want to take sides. The background of the convent is Slovenian, like the monastery next door. Maryam is young and second generation Irish and doesn't have much in common with them. From what I gather, she's pretty much a loner, which is a shame because she has such a kind heart and doesn't deserve the cold shoulder."

Cora heard a voice in the background and assumed Barney had entered the room. The voice was muted; Cisco rarely put his phone on speaker.

"Barney said to say hello." He cleared his throat. "He also said I'd better get a move on if we're going to make our tee time."

"Well, have fun today, hon. I'm really so happy to hear you're having a good time. Makes me feel better too."

"Take care, hon. Love ya."

"Too."

After ending the call, Cora finished her toast and swallowed her coffee slowly and carefully. Liquids were trickier than solids. She remembered the first time she saw her speech therapist, two weeks after beginning radiation, before she started having serious trouble eating. He tested her ability to swallow a variety of foods: water, applesauce, graham cracker. She passed the test but he gave her exercises to strengthen and train the muscles, which were likely to be affected by radiation soon.

"You try this," she had told Cisco while doing one of the exercises. "See if you can do it. Stick out your tongue and hold it between your teeth, then swallow."

Cisco, who didn't like to look foolish, just said, "I believe you."

Despite doing the exercises three times a day, swallowing did get more difficult, not just from pain but from lack of saliva. She could chew her food into a ball, but it was too thick to swallow. She'd add water to thin it out, but the water would drizzle down her throat and make her cough. "Swallowing different consistencies is hard," the therapist had explained. "After you add water, drop your chin and let the food and water come forward. There's more room there for it to mix." The trick did help, but even today she still had trouble with liquids sneaking down the back of her throat or food sticking.

Her breakfast done, she put her plate, knife, and cup in the dishwasher and headed to Sister Lorita's office.

Sister Mary Lorita, the Provincial Superior of Assisi Hill, was flipping through a stack of manila folders on her large, old-fashioned mahogany desk. Apparently finding what she was looking for, she pulled a file out and opened it, then looked up at Cora. "Here it is—the timeline. Let's go over this together and pick out what we want to highlight. All of it needs to be included, of course, but as you pointed out, some parts deserve more attention than others." She grinned. "See, I considered your thoughts on structure."

Remembering Cisco's advice about letting Sister Lorita lead, Cora said nothing, only pulled out a pencil and notepad and moved her chair over so both of them could look at the file.

The nun's enthusiasm was boundless. Of average height and about forty pounds overweight, she moved with an energy that made her always a little out of breath. She was clearly excited about what she was doing, speaking so rapidly that saliva gathered around the corners of her mouth. Cora found this passionate and animated woman magnetic, if just a little scary.

"This folder has copies of the displays in our Heritage Hall. As we've already discussed, Mother Margareta Pucher founded the Sisters of St. Francis of Christ the Teacher in 1869 in Maribor, Slovenia," Sister Lorita said.

"I've been to Heritage Hall and studied the information. Yes, Mother Margareta has to be one of our main focuses. But what do we know about her? For instance, how old was she at the time, what was she like, what was important to her?" Cora asked.

Sister Lorita riffled through the folder. "There's some information here."

But there wasn't, or at least not much. A photo of a painting of Margareta showed an austere-looking stocky woman in traditional nun's habit, seated with two young girls, one of whom held an embroidery hoop. Aside from that, there were a few dates and locations, but little else.

"Are there any interviews with people who knew her, any stories or anecdotes?" Cora asked.

"There must be—somewhere. She never came to the States. I suppose one of our sisters could do further research." Sister Lorita punctuated her words with lively gestures.

Cora sighed. "That's what I mean. Readers care little about what people do unless they understand why they do it. And that comes through personal details. What made them do what they did? How did they feel about it? How did it turn out and why was it important to them?"

Sister Lorita rested her chin in her hand but said nothing.

Cora pointed to the folder. "We can organize and enlarge on the information in this folder and the others there." She nodded toward the stack on the desk. "It will be like an expanded version of what's in Heritage Hall. It will be good, and the sisters will treasure it. But if you want the *world* to know about your order and your good work, you need more than dates and facts. You need to entertain readers. You need to touch their emotions, move them."

"I didn't have a wider audience in mind until you brought it up," Sister Lorita said, her gaze unfocused. "Now, I don't know…maybe you have a point."

"Yesterday at lunch, the sisters mentioned that vocations have been declining. Isn't that a good reason to tell young women inspiring stories they can identify with, so when they have an interest in joining a convent they aren't discouraged by the decline? If we wait too long, there won't be any sisters left to tell their stories."

"Of course, we would like to attract young women…."

Cora pushed her chair back from the desk and held Sister Lorita's gaze. "Why did you ask me to help, Sister? Why me, particularly? Why did you put the project on hold until I could help write this book?"

Sister Lorita looked down at her hands. She fidgeted with her nails for a moment and then looked back into Cora's eyes. "I read *Wawetseka's Tale*. I loved it. I thought, here is a woman who made the history of early Lemont come to life. I wanted that for the history of our order. I'm good at organizing facts, but I wanted you to put the facts into words for us."

"Then you know the history came to life because it told of one woman's journey. Deep down that's what you wanted for your book—the history of your order to come alive."

Sister Lorita was nodding slowly, her expression thoughtful.

"Look, Sister, I'm not suggesting we write about only one person, Mother Margareta, for instance. She never came to the United States, and there are many more stories: the order's arrival in America in 1909, the expansion to the Midwest, the move to Lemont, the founding of Assisi Hill Academy for girls and then Assisi Manor for seniors. They're all important stories."

The nun's eyes indicated she appreciated Cora's passion.

"Why don't we decide which events are the most important," Cora said, "identify a person involved in each event, and tell that person's story in detail? That will make readers care and appreciate the significance of the event itself."

Sister Lorita rubbed her forehead and then folded her hands in front of her on her desk. "Okay, let's try it. Let's pick a few milestones, and decide who might be the best person to tell that story. I'll get one of the sisters to look for details. We'll get the facts and you rough out a draft." She held up a forefinger and tapped her nose. "But this is a trial. It's not decided until we see what it looks like. Agreed?"

Cora grinned. "That's great. I even have an idea where to start. A recent event, so it's easier to get first-hand information. Begin with Assisi Manor being built in 1970. Surely there are people right here who remember. We won't think about other stories until I give you a first draft about Assisi Manor and see how you like it."

Sister Lorita returned the grin. "I like the way you think. Maybe this will work out after all. I have to confess I was starting to have doubts."

Feeling like she had made her point at last, Cora laughed. "Waited for me almost five years and then I turn out to be on another page entirely? All that wasted time? How disappointing!"

"Well, maybe you're right. Let's see. But didn't you also say you were interested in other religious communities in Lemont? What are your plans in that regard?"

Cora leaned back in her chair. "I suspect there's a reason so many religious communities, especially Catholic communities, settled in Lemont. Something drew them, something common to all of them. I want to find that reason and compare it to what's unique to each community. Ultimately, I'd like to write a history that includes all the Lemont communities—including Assisi Hill, of course."

"Rather ambitious, but if there's a common theme I'm convinced you're the person who can find it."

"Take the Poor Clares, for instance. They date back to 1212, came to America in the 1870s. I have vivid memories of visiting their garden in Chicago with my grandmother when I was a little girl. There was a grotto with a trickle of water Grandma said was holy, and I should say a prayer and drink some, using a metal cup hanging there. I told Grandma we'd get sick drinking from the same cup as everyone else, and she said God wouldn't let that happen."

They shared a laugh.

"Anyway, I was surprised to find the Poor Clares moved here. There has always been a mystique about what would attract a young woman to a contemplative order, but why did they move to Lemont? You see what I mean?"

"Not to mention that a small town like Lemont has four Catholic parishes, and St. Marija's Monastery next door." Sister Lorita held up a hand and started counting off on her fingers. "St. Joseph Convent and St. Joseph Village, St. Vincent De Paul Seminary, and De Andreis School of Theology have closed, but the Lithuanian World Center and Mission is there now, and nearby are Holy Family Villas, St. Francis of Assisi Residence, and Bishop Lyne Residence for retired priests...it is quite a list, isn't it?"

"And the Carmelites and the St. Theresa Shrine. For a small, semi-isolated town, yes. There's even a local saint in the making, I hear."

"Mother Mary Josepha, yes. I can see why you'd be interested." Sister Lorita stood up abruptly. "Well, I don't intend to work on other communities—that's up to you. But you might as well start your research now while I gather the facts you'll need for Assisi Manor. Father Bozic at St. Marija's Monastery is a good friend of ours here at Assisi Hill. I'll give him a call and see if he can show you around. Is that okay with you?"

Cora felt like hugging the woman. She loved it when a plan came together!

# Chapter 6

Assisi Manor was a senior housing facility run by the Sisters of St. Francis of Christ the Teacher on their Assisi Hill property. The buildings sat atop a bluff and provided an excellent view north across the Des Plaines River Valley. In addition to Assisi Hill Convent and Assisi Manor, the sisters had operated Assisi Hill Academy, a high school for girls, for sixty years. The Academy closed in 2014 and was now a daycare and retreat center. Extensive grounds included tennis courts, baseball fields, and vast open areas where a variety of events took place.

"I was so glad to see you yesterday," Sister Maryam said when Cora met her at Assisi Manor that afternoon. "How did your meeting with Sister Lorita go this morning?" Sister Maryam's hazel eyes shone warm gold in the lights of the lobby.

Cora said, "Promising, I think. You know, earlier this year I looked for you, but never saw you. I was about to ask her if you had left."

"Oh, I'd never leave," Sister Maryam said. Her broad grin revealed perfect white teeth, but her eyes were serious. "Our Lady wants me to stay, and I'd want to, even if she hadn't said so."

Cora wondered what that meant, but it seemed rude to ask. Today was only the third time the two women had met. Sister Maryam looked much the same as at their first meeting, though, still youthful and delightful, although she had lost some of her pudginess and her acne had cleared up nicely.

"I asked Sister Lorita if you could show me around," Cora said.

Sister Maryam took Cora's arm. "Let's get started, then. I forgot to mention when you called, but I have something to do at three."

"It's two now. Are you sure you have time?"

"No problem." She smiled. "I'm really glad you're here. I think you'll like what you see."

Sister Maryam led the way out of the homey lobby and down a brightly lit corridor into a generous space, filled with dining tables and chairs. Tall windows set in a brick wall provided an unobstructed view of the Des Plaines River Valley.

"What a pretty room!" Cora said.

"Yes, it is, isn't it? Especially on sunny days like today. It's so bright and cheerful. We hold parties and events here, like our annual spaghetti dinner in June. You should come."

As Cora followed Sister Maryam from the gathering room down a series of corridors, she realized that the building was much larger than it appeared from the outside. A number of wings extended into areas that led to gardens, patios, lawns, and a lovely modern chapel with floor-to-ceiling stained glass. A back road connected the center to the convent just uphill.

The young nun described the manor as they went. "Some residents have private rooms, some suites. Some are furnished, or residents can bring their own things if they prefer. Many seniors here are independent, but some need help with medications, bathing, or other things. We serve three meals a day, tailored to individual diets. Our mission is to provide an active, pleasant place for independent seniors without the burdens of living alone."

In a large open lobby adjacent to the chapel, a tall, smiling, gray-haired man who appeared to be in his early seventies stopped Sister Maryam. "Hope it warms up soon," he said. "We're anxious to get started on this year's garden."

After the man left, Sister Maryam said, "Our garden has raised beds to make it easier. Some residents miss gardening they did in their own homes. We can't get enough homegrown tomatoes here, but a fair amount of the zucchini goes begging." She laughed. "We offer a lot of activities and most of the residents participate. Games, music, exercise programs, outings for shopping, local events, entertainment. Of course, we have Wi-Fi."

They passed a number of residents in the halls. One used a walker and another was in a wheelchair pushed by an attendant. All appeared alert, happy, and smiling.

"Hold up a minute," Sister Maryam said as an extremely thin woman in short heels and a tailored pants suit approached them. The woman's face was badly disfigured, the left side caved in where the jaw should be, the mouth unable to close fully, the skin shiny, red, and badly wrinkled. Her nose was pushed upward, two large dark nostrils apparent. The face reminded Cora of Edvard Munch's painting, *The Scream*. She had to force herself to smile and not look away.

"This is Cora Tozzi," Sister Maryam told the woman. "She writes about Lemont history and is going to help write a book about us." Maryam turned to Cora. "Winnie Garth runs our book discussion group. I'm sure they'd like to meet you."

Winnie said a few unintelligible words. Some saliva escaped the corner of her mouth, which she carefully wiped with a handkerchief.

Sister Maryam smiled fondly at Winnie, gave her a hug, patted the collapsed cheek, then leaned forward, and whispered something in Winnie's ear. It struck Cora that touching was probably meaningful to this woman whose looks would repel most people.

When Winnie was out of earshot, Cora commented, "She seems careful of her appearance, dresses well, hair and makeup carefully done. I couldn't...one wouldn't expect...."

"Yes, she's proud. I'm sure you're curious. She was in a bad auto accident when she was only in her twenties. The left side of her face was crushed by the steering wheel and then the car burst into flame. Bystanders saved her, but much of her jaw couldn't be reconstructed, also part of her tongue and nose. The scarring is from the burns. Today they could minimize all of that, but back then they didn't have the skills."

Cora felt a chill in her stomach. She couldn't help but wonder if she would have looked like Winnie if she'd had surgery for her cancer instead of radiation and chemotherapy. At the thought, her own jaw began to ache and she wagged it to loosen it up. The encounter shocked her back to the terror she'd experienced when she feared her cancer would cause disfigurement.

In his office, Dr. Thomas had done a laryngoscopy.

"There's a small lesion at the base of your tongue. About the size of the tip of my little finger," he said, holding up his hand and pinching the tip of his pinky with his thumbnail. "Now let's check that lump in your neck."

"It was bigger," Cora had said nervously. "It's gone down a bit."

Dr. Thomas nodded. After he numbed the area, Cora felt only the sting of the anesthetic and then nothing more as he inserted the needle and drew fluid into the syringe. She glanced at Cisco, sitting across the room. It was comforting to have him there but, as she expected, he was looking at the floor, not watching the procedure. He was squeamish about such things, but he'd stay at her side.

"Interesting," Dr. Thomas said, busy at the right side of Cora's neck. "This looks like pus."

"Yay! Pus!" Cora said. Then she giggled. How ludicrous to feel relieved by the presence of pus. "That might mean infection, not cancer." Her words were meant as a question, not a statement.

Dr. Thomas only said, "Let's let the pathologist tell us."

*God*, she prayed, *please let it be infection.*

Afterward, she called her son Joe to give him what she thought was an encouraging update.

"I hope it's not cancer too, but that would be hard to believe in view of the CT report," Joe said. "It's fortunate Rosie is an oncologist and can help you if need be. She'd like to believe it's an infection, but we're both concerned."

Another week had passed before Dr. Thomas called with results of the culture and pathology. The report showed infection. "Unfortunately, that's not all," he said. "Cancer cells were also present." It would take more studies to be sure the cancer hadn't spread to other areas of her neck or elsewhere.

Dr. Thomas told her the prognosis for treatment and cure was good. It looked as if the diagnosis had been made early, and there was a good chance they could avoid the seven-hour radical neck surgery that often went with tongue cancer. Cora could be part of a study offering an alternative treatment that would be easier for her body to tolerate than standard treatments.

"What will happen if I don't treat it?" she asked.

"It will spread. There's no ignoring this, Cora." So she went ahead with the radiation and chemo, secretly terrified it wouldn't work. If she had to have surgery after all, how disfiguring would it be? Would they remove part of her jaw? Would she still be able to eat? To talk? Would people look away when they saw her, or treat her like a dummy? What if surgery didn't stop the cancer either?

*If* she actually had cancer, she thought, sure they'd find an error before she started treatment. But she wasn't going to risk her life based on her doubt. She would follow the advice of her doctors and family.

*If* what they said was true, there was every reason to believe the cancer would have been well along by the time it was noticed, had she not gotten the infection and investigated the neck swelling. The infection may well have saved her life. Indeed, God worked in mysterious ways.

Sister Maryam's voice brought her back. The nun was looking at her with concern. "Are you okay?"

She tore herself away from her private thoughts. "Oh, yes. I was just remembering something that isn't too pleasant." She hesitated, then asked, "How does Winnie communicate to run book discussions?"

"Oh, she's a stubborn little thing. Had to be, to get through life with her handicaps. She uses whiteboards and hand gestures, and her friends have learned to recognize some of her speech."

A wave of sadness struck Cora, not just for Winnie. When shopping for a place for her own mother for short stays, a lingering memory was a home where the residents were lined up, slumped and dozing in wheel chairs, waiting an hour for the dining hall to open. The incident fed her mother's fear of living in a nursing home.

What a difference. None of those places had seemed as vibrant and comfortable as this one, where every resident appeared happy.

Sister Maryam had a personal comment or joke for each resident they met. The affection between the sister and the residents was obvious, but her attitude toward Cora was a little puzzling. One moment she was open and friendly, but other times she avoided eye contact. Out of shyness, or reluctance? Or was it only Cora's imagination?

But then, Cora was a bit of a fraud herself. She hadn't admitted her religious doubts to Sister Maryam. Maryam probably thought Cora's faith was as strong as her own.

"There's even a dog," Cora commented, laughing, as they re-entered the lobby and a big, friendly golden retriever ran to her side.

Maryam grinned. "Meet Butch, our family dog. He lives in our common rooms and is everyone's pet. He's amazingly sweet, aren't you, boy?" She stooped to rub the dog's shoulder, but Butch seemed more interested in Cora, nudging her knee with his muzzle, tail wagging, hindquarters swaying side to side with every swipe. Cora fondled one of the dog's ears. She liked dogs and this one seemed charming.

"Let's sit here. I have a little time left." Sister Maryam pointed to a comfortable-looking, yellow-and-brown-fabric sofa near a fireplace in which a few large logs burned gently. Butch followed and curled up at Cora's feet.

"Obviously your cancer treatment was successful. You're looking much better than that day we met—it must be close to five years ago. Really good, as a matter of fact," Sister Maryam said.

"People say that, probably because of my weight loss. I needed to lose about forty pounds before I got sick, and the treatment took care of most of that. But yes, it went well, and now I have to watch my weight again." Cora turned her eyes to the fire and thought for a while.

"It wasn't ever awful, but it was hard. I think the worst part is how much of your life it takes up. You just don't feel good for a long, long time. You think once treatment is over, that's the end, but all that's over is the treatment itself. You feel even worse in the three to six months *after* ending the treatment, when the cumulative effects of radiation and chemo kick in and then your body tries to heal itself. It goes on and on before you start to feel better, and then what they call "late effects" are always out there potentially, even *years* later."

"Is that why it took you so long to find time for our book?"

Cora nodded. "It was almost a year after treatment before I started to feel even a little bit like myself again. Then there was so much I'd put off while I was sick, it took time to catch up. And there were projects that I'd stopped in the middle of to complete. I never forgot my promise, but there was always something more urgent. It's a good thing Sister Lorita was patient."

"She had no choice, from what I understand. She's not a writer by any stretch, and although this book is a dream of hers, she needed someone to do the actual writing, to put all the details she's gathered into words. She really counted on you for that, and was willing to wait unless you pulled out completely."

"Yes, well...I want her to realize her dream, of course. But we have... um...some details to work out." Cora sighed. "Just between us, Sister Lorita and I aren't really in agreement about the purpose and structure of the book, but I think we've ironed that out. At least for now."

"Can I help in any way?"

"I doubt it. I'm a storyteller, Sister Maryam. I think the book would be richer if we let the sisters tell their stories. For instance, how many people know there's a woman who may be a saint affiliated with Lemont? Sister Lorita is letting me try it my way, but I'm not sure she's sold yet."

"Well, it's her book, isn't it?"

"My husband said that too. But she asked for my opinion."

"Sounds like you gave it to her." They laughed. "I get the sense you're pretty determined."

"Like I said, we're working it out. But enough about the book and about my cancer. What do you do here, Sister? Aside from giving tours and reading to residents."

"Just call me Maryam, okay? My title is Activity Director. I plan indoor and outdoor activities, coordinate transportation, lead programs, things like that. Keep everyone busy and entertained." She broke into a grin. "Hey, how would you like to give a lecture about local history, or any topic really? Our residents love to meet new people and question them—maybe I should say grill them!" She chuckled.

"Sure—anytime. If I can't fit it in while I'm here, I live nearby."

Sister Maryam sighed. "When I first came here, I just sat with the residents who had few or no visitors. Just talked with them and read to them if they liked. I loved doing that. Some I've known for years, so I still try to make time for them."

"And do you still play the harmonica? Do you play for the residents?"

The nun laughed. "I still play, yes. But if I played every time someone asked, other residents would complain. Music travels, you know. So, I play outside, alone, occasionally on the patio when the weather's good. Or I'll entertain a group in one of the common rooms now and then. They sing along when they know the words."

Cora glanced down. "You're wearing shoes, I see. You weren't when I first met you."

Maryam laughed again. "I am. And not because I want to, but there were complaints." She shrugged. "It didn't seem productive to argue. Better to pick my battles."

It seemed Sister Maryam was aware of her unpopularity with some of the other sisters. Maybe that explained the unease Cora sensed in her earlier. But after spending time with her in her own setting, Cora couldn't imagine how anyone saw anything in Maryam to dislike. Surely everyone should recognize her cheerfulness, high energy, positive attitude, and real compassion, something Cora envied. Couldn't the sisters see these things? How unhappy was Maryam because of their cold shoulder?

Maryam glanced at her watch. "I have to get going," she said, and stood up.

Cora looked at her inquiringly, hoping she would explain, but Maryam didn't. "I really want to see more of you while I'm here," Cora said.

"I'd like that. I live here in the Manor, but I'm not working all the time. Can you come back tomorrow after dinner? Just show up, the receptionist will ring me."

With a parting smile, Maryam walked away. Cora watched as she stepped into a glass-walled office behind the reception desk and slipped her arms into a black jacket before hurrying out of the building through the front door. She looked like a little girl going to her first birthday party, Cora thought, delirious with excitement but a little scared at the same time. Of course, it would have been impolite to ask. Maryam had dodged Cora's implied question about why she went barefoot, too.

Cora frowned slightly. Something seemed a little "off." Could Sister Fatima be right? No, surely not.

# Chapter 7

Father Anthony Bozic's intelligent, pale blue eyes sparkled through round, wire-framed glasses. "Now that you've had the tour, what do you think of St. Marija's?" he asked with a quiet smile. A serious demeanor, but gentle, if Cora had to use a single word to describe him. He spoke with an obvious eastern European accent, but she had been relieved to discover that his English was excellent, even colloquial, and she liked him immediately.

Fond thoughts of another friend came to her. A very different priest with a wry sense of humor, who had been her confidant and counselor through her fight against cancer. He had joked about how they could be such good friends despite her poor attendance at Mass, and that was before she admitted to herself the extent of her religious doubts. But he was away.

Now Cora sat across from Father Bozic in the library at St. Marija's Monastery after completing a tour of the property. A notepad was in front of her on the long wooden table that filled the center of the room. Three walls were lined with built-in shelves filled with neatly arranged books, and light flowed through a wall of large windows that overlooked the expansive grounds surrounding the building.

She took in the priest's tall, slender build, in his dark brown robe belted with a long, white, rope-like cord. His full head of brown hair was cropped short.

Cora smiled but raised an eyebrow. "It's amazing to me that you can live here alone in this huge building with so little help. How do you do it?"

He chuckled and shook his head. "I don't need much. There are always people about, and they are good to me. The women try to impress me with their cooking, and I have only to point out something that needs doing and a volunteer arrives to do it." He paused for a moment, and then explained, "There are only three Slovenian Franciscan priests in the United States now: me, one in New York, and one in Pennsylvania. The parishioners, I think, fear that I will be called back to Slovenia, so they are very grateful and support the mission."

Cora flipped through her notes. "Slovenia is a small country, about two million people, is that right?"

Father Bozic nodded.

"How large is the mission's membership?"

"About three hundred families."

Cora thought the average Catholic parish these days had about a thousand families. She made a note to check online. Three hundred families was still a larger number than she would have guessed.

Father continued. "Many of our members are skilled craftsmen: masons, carpenters, electricians, plumbers, and the like. As you've seen, we don't use much space in our buildings presently, but we keep the place from deteriorating."

Since the priest was the only resident, Cora had been surprised at how much of the property actually *was* used, with two Masses each Sunday, one said in English and one in Slovenian. The chapel in the monastery was impressive, similar in size to other churches in the area. She estimated it would seat over two hundred, and the stained glass and altars were lovely, traditionally designed. The most prominent features were the windows, the vaulted ceilings, and a large, ornate, gold-framed painting of the Madonna and Child behind the altar. Father had told her that the crowns on the mother and child were real crowns incorporated into the painting, which depicted Our Lady Help of Christians, the patron of Slovenia, known in their language as Marija Pomagaj. "Can you spell that," she had asked.

"We have a hundred and thirty acres." Father Bozic spoke as if he had rehearsed the history. "We bought the farmland in 1923 and built a temporary wooden building. Construction of this brick building started in 1939 and was completed in 1940. At one time, in addition to our friars and Franciscan brothers, we had a seminary, and a farm on the property provided much of our food until 1961."

Cora jotted a note. *What is the difference between a priest, a friar, and a brother? Between a parish and a mission?* She wouldn't take Father's time with that now—she could find out online. A lifelong Catholic, she was embarrassed at how much of the jargon she didn't know.

"There was even a slaughterhouse located in the basement of our garage," the priest was saying, "and a print shop in the basement of the monastery. We printed a newspaper, magazine, books, and other publications for all Slovenian Catholics throughout the United States. The newspaper alone had a circulation of thirty thousand. The farmers and print shop workers also lived here. The seminarians lived in the separate red brick building at the end of our parking lot."

She found the detail interesting. None of these operations was going on now, although the archives had been meticulously preserved, stacked in string-tied bundles she had seen on shelves in the print shop library in the basement. The extent of what had once been a busy monastery was impressive, but the present situation seemed sad.

"But tell me something, Cora. Sister Lorita said you're helping to document the history of their order but she didn't say why you're interested in St. Marija's."

Cora waved her arm as if taking in the entire location. "Since I moved to Lemont, I've developed a passion for local history. There are so many Catholic communities here, impressive places, but except to their members, they are little known. It's a shame. We have photos and articles at the historical society, but I'd like to find some commonality or theme that explains why these institutions settled here."

She wished she had brought a bottle of water. After her radiation, she had regained most of her sense of taste, but her mouth remained dry, triggering an uncontrolled cough if she didn't pause often to moisten it when talking. She swept her tongue around the inside of her mouth and swallowed hard, then went on, hoping he didn't notice.

"Not just facts, but stories that happened at these places. I'd love to find those stories and put them together so everyone can know about the hidden gems right where they live. Assisi Hill is only one of the places, so my own interests are wider than Sister Lorita's—St. Marija's, St.

Joseph's…" She stopped and snickered. "Sorry, I've gotten a little carried away."

Father Bozic chuckled. "No, I admire your enthusiasm. I sense that you like to do things your way, but I like your way. I think Sister Lorita picked a winner." He folded his hands on the table in front of him, leaned back and closed his eyes in thought. After a time, his eyes still closed, he said, "Would your vision include telling the story of why our priests were sent here from Slovenia, why Slovenians immigrated, what their lives were like, secular as well as religious?"

"The short answer is yes. I like to describe particular events as told through the eyes of particular people. Stories, like I said." Not for the first time, Cora cursed the Irish complexion that sent blood rushing to her cheeks. She wondered if Father would interpret the telltale flush as excitement or apprehension. It was likely both. He clearly had a strong academic background. He might think stories were inferior to an academic manuscript.

He opened his eyes and his gaze met hers. His eyes seemed to twinkle and she sensed that he liked her. "Have you seen our Stations of the Cross, the Lourdes Grotto and the Rosary Valley?"

Cora nodded, remembering that first day walking in the Rosary Valley, when she discovered Sister Maryam with her harmonica. She'd been fascinated by the unusual stone used to make the monuments, and wondered again now why the builder made that choice.

"Yes, they're wonderful. I went to the cemetery too. Those are some of the hidden gems I mentioned, and that stone they're all made of—I've never seen anything like it. Does it have any religious or ethnic significance?"

"Not that I know of. Well, if you've seen them already, let me have someone take you through our retreat house, too. St. Marija's is a mission but it's also a shrine. Slovenians come here on pilgrimage, not only from the United States but from around the world. They needed somewhere to stay, so we built a place. Children used to stay for weeks in the summers. Our families will love to talk to you about those days. Are those the sort of stories you're looking for?"

Cora grinned. "Absolutely."

Father Bozic grew serious. "So now I must make a confession. I agreed

THE MIRACLE AT ASSISI HILL

to talk to you because Sister Lorita said you're a historian and a writer. So I was interested in meeting you. For a while now, I've shared Sister Lorita's wish, as I've wanted to create a book too. Not, like Sister Lorita, exclusively about our order, but about the Slovenian Catholic people we serve through our mission. I understand you have some interest in Mother Josepha who is awaiting sainthood. We also have our Bishop Baraga's cause for sainthood here."

Mother Josepha's name kept coming up wherever she went. Now Father had brought up another saint-in-the-making. Cora's mind raced.

"I'd like to pick your brain about these things," he went on. "Now that I've met you, I see it as a project that would best be put into your hands. Are you interested?"

Everyone wanted a book! Sister Lorita's book, and the book she wanted to write herself, and a factual presentation of the material, and now Father Bozic wanted still another slant on things…. It was overwhelming. They couldn't be a single book because the themes, structure, and audiences were different. Although they came from the same research, each would take at least a year to write. But why not, if the material was all gathered and the projects were all of value?

*Four years at a minimum, that's why not,* she thought.

Cisco would have a fit. He'd been complaining for years that she was filling her plate with an impossible array of projects. Her struggle with cancer had taught her nothing if she was considering doing just that again. Did she still have enough energy to complete the tasks she was agreeing to? Would she live long enough to do them justice?

Not knowing what to say, she fidgeted nervously, slipping a hand into her pocket. Her fingers bumped against her crystal rosary, reminding her why she was really here.

Cora Tozzi, *History of the Religious Institutions of Lemont*
(Chicago, Madonna Press, 2024), 3–10

*Author's Note: I didn't know, years ago when I took on the task of writing a book about the outstanding religious institutions in Lemont, that as a result I would become a participant in the canonization of a saint. After beginning my research, I realized that the story of Mother Josepha of Chicago would not only be a major part of the book I would eventually write, but that she would change my own life in many ways.*

*It has long been my belief that stories are best told by the people that experienced them. For this reason, I have chosen to write the story of Josie Mrozek, now Venerable Mother Josepha of Chicago, as if she was telling her own story in a personal journal. In reality, there is no such journal, although* The Chronicles of Venerable Mother Josepha of Chicago, *which deals with a portion of her life and from which selected quotes appear as epigraphs, is a real book.*

*It was only after years of research that I knew enough about Mother Josepha to have the courage to write her story from her viewpoint. Portions of this fictional journal are excerpted here. The author hopes that readers will believe the excerpts reflect the real life of this remarkable woman.*

*—Cora Tozzi*

*"I felt the misery and suffering of others, and it seemed
to me that I could not love Jesus, or even expect Heaven,
if I were concerned only about myself..."*
—*The Chronicles of Venerable Mother Josepha of Chicago*

## Josie's Journal
### Translated by Jadwiga Kierkowski

### January 15, 1880, Plocicz, Poland

I have not written in a journal since I was a child, but recent events have threatened the future of our family, and I do not want to lose to poor memory the facts that led to these changes. And so, I sit down this evening after all are asleep to make a record of this eventful day.

It all started when we lost our barn.

Despite the heat pouring off our burning barn, I found myself shivering in front of our porch in the darkness before dawn. I clutched my woolen shawl tightly around my neck and shoulders. The smoke struck in waves, its odor acrid, its taste filling my mouth, its roaring, sizzling, and popping sounds in my ears. Although it was barely light enough to see, my vision was distorted by glare from the flames and the tears in my eyes.

Katy clutched my hand fiercely as we stood silently watching. All hope was gone and there was nothing to say.

There had been rumors of Prussian informants lurking and keeping tabs on Catholics. Had they found out Masses were being held in our barn, and burned it down? I glanced nervously at the woods at the edge of our farm. What might the Prussians do next?

Katy, so sensitive for a child of twelve, noticed my distress. "What is wrong?" she asked me. "Are you hurt?"

I smiled at her. "No, dear. Only a little sore from rushing to save what we could, and cold. And sad, of course."

We had done everything possible: led the animals to safety, dragged out tools and equipment. Everything of value had been removed, but the barn itself was a complete loss. The cries of Konrad Wojda, who had been sleeping in the barn, had woken us from our beds in early-morning darkness. Everyone in the household, all except Hennie Danek's bed-ridden mother and two-year-old son, had raced outside to rescue the plow and harnesses, the horses, cows, pigs and sheep, and so nothing of importance was sacrificed to the fire.

Except the barn.

We stacked the farm equipment near the house and covered it with tarps. Later the rescued animals went to neighboring farms to be board-ed until we figured out what to do. A hard decision, not only because the loss changed our family's financial situation, but because it seemed the last straw. Our town is being persecuted from all sides and has been for years.

Katy tugged my arm, and I stooped to give her a firm hug. "Thank God we are all safe," I said against her golden hair.

Katy is more like a daughter than a sister to me. She is a sweet, laugh-ing child, a pure delight, and the prettiest of us. I was eight years old the day she was born. Mama had little time for an infant then, the last of her six children. My other sisters were at school and needed to work on the farm, and so the raising of Katy fell to me. Not that I minded at all—I wanted to be with her anyway.

"Mr. Wojda does not look well," Katy said, glancing toward the cov-ered farm equipment where our "tenant" leaned against the salvaged items. "Do you think he was hurt in the fire? Thanks be to God he sounded the alarm so we could get everything out, especially the poor animals."

I looked at the man, who was sulking, staring at the ground and shuf-fling his feet. He acted as if it was he who was being inconvenienced, when it was more likely that he, rather than the Prussians, had been to blame for the fire.

"Mr. Wojda can take care of himself, I think," I said. I did not share my thoughts with Katy.

Since Mr. Wojda came to us after falling on hard times, Papa had repeatedly warned him against using a fire in the barn to warm himself. Tonight was especially cold. While we were scrambling to empty the barn, I noticed the angry looks Papa gave our boarder. From the beginning Papa had not been happy about allowing him to sleep in the barn, but Father Felix had asked our help, since the poor man had nowhere to go. It was not that Papa was unwilling, but we had already taken in a widow, Hennie, along with her five children and bedridden mother, after she lost her home to a greedy German immigrant. Theo had to give up his bed for the old woman and he now slept on the floor beside the kitchen stove with Hennie and her children. Our small farmhouse barely served for our own family; there was no space for still another person, and certainly no place for a man to sleep with five children and their widowed mother.

Not that Mr. Wojda had not suggested that very thing.

But Hennie had seen the homeless man's sly looks at her fourteen-year-old daughter Gizela, and spoke to Mama, reminding Mama that her own daughters could be threatened by such a man under their roof. Mama had put her foot down and relegated Mr. Wojda to the barn.

I think Mr. Wojda is about thirty. He is a stocky man near 5'10" who wears rough-textured brown clothes, with chestnut-colored hair that is already thinning, and discolored teeth. The look on his face often seems shifty and self-seeking.

But does not God want us to treat all His creatures without judgment? Surely Mr. Wojda is not a cruel or evil man, just an unfortunate man who is not very smart and rather crude. If he did have anything to do with the fire, it is likely he feels guilty, but even more so, desperate. He will not be welcome to sleep in our house, and where will he go now that our barn is gone? I was struck with pity and made the sign of the Cross, trusting him to God's hands.

Later in the morning, after breakfast, Hennie took her family into her mother's room so they could bathe the old woman and she and the children could clean themselves at the washstand and spend time with their grandma. They deserved a break before helping to put the hastily piled farm implements in order. Hopefully we could salvage enough wood and stone to build a temporary shelter for the equipment and supplies. Farm work is always there to be done.

But Papa had other ideas. He took advantage of Hennie's absence to have a private talk. The whole family sat around our large oak kitchen table, and he began by saying, "I think it is time to accept my brother's offer to bring us to America."

I was dismayed. Uncle John lived in America, in Chicago with his family. He had asked many times for us to join them there, and my older sisters Rosalie and Marianne had gone. Sadly, Marianne died from complications after giving birth to her daughter, but Rosalie and Uncle John were very happy and wished the rest of us would come to Chicago, to unite our family again. But I loved our home, our farm, and my life in Poland, and did not want to leave.

"But Papa," I said, "surely we can rebuild the barn! Warm weather will be here soon, and this sad time is only temporary. We are not poor people. Why should we leave behind our beloved home and everything we have, for some place we do not know?"

Papa sighed and put his hand over mine on the table. "Josie, I know you do not want to give up your dressmaking and needlework. You are respected and have steady customers, but these skills are just as valuable in Chicago and soon you will be busy again."

I pulled my hand away. "But what will happen to my garden, and the church, Papa! What will Father Felix do without us?"

"Father Felix will have to find some other place in any event, now that we have no barn where we can assemble for Mass. He will ask other Catholics."

"But I want to help him! He looks to me to find places for the needy, to teach religion to the children, and so many other things. And...not only will he miss me, but I will miss him."

Papa shook his head, but he looked at me kindly. "You are not indispensable, Josie. John tells me his Catholic parish in Chicago is one of the biggest in the world, and the need for devoted people there is just as great."

"But Papa...." I was at a loss for how else to convince him. I looked around the table, at my mother, at my only brother Theo, nineteen years of age now, at my seventeen-year-old sister Frances, and twelve-year-old Katy. My sweet baby sister was no longer a baby. I saw sadness and fear in their eyes, but no one spoke up to argue with Papa. It was up to me, since I was twenty and the oldest still at home.

I took a deep breath and squared my shoulders. "Papa, I think you have decided already. Please explain to me."

He smiled gently. "So you can argue against my reasons?"

I smiled back. "If I can do so. But surely that is my right."

"Yes, yes, I suppose it is, if I expect you to follow me willingly." He sighed again. "You know the sad state of things here. We have grumbled about it many times, and you cannot be unaware of the hardships that have stricken Poland since we were occupied by the Prussians."

"Sadly, Catholics have suffered," I admitted.

How well I knew that Bismarck is no friend to Catholics. He thinks we are a threat to his plan for a unified Germany. Bismarck persecutes Catholics because our Pope is not in favor of what the Prussians are doing and our priests have spoken out about it. He has abolished our schools and dictated what our priests can do or say. They cannot even perform marriages anymore. Any priest who fails to comply with his orders is exiled. We are forbidden even to speak our Polish language and have to constantly look around to see who is listening so no one reports us. The sanctions are so bad that our Blessed Virgin Mary appeared at Gietrzwald to inspire Catholic people in hopes of reviving our Polish spirit. These conditions are why our priests must hide, and Father Felix says Mass in our barn in secret.

Only now we had no barn.

I could not escape these facts, but the thought of leaving my beloved country and the only life I knew brought tears to my eyes. I reached into my pocket for a handkerchief and blotted my face.

I said, "Do you not remember that only last year I walked ninety kilometers on pilgrimage to visit the shrine at Gietrzwald, to pray for liberation of the church and to drink from the holy spring? If Our Lady must come from Heaven to give us heart, how can I not know how bad our troubles are?"

Papa reached for my chin and tilted it up to look into my eyes.

"You are making my point exactly, Josie. In America we can worship freely in great churches, and speak our language among ourselves as we will. Do you not want that?"

"Yes, Papa, of course I do. But surely this situation will get better one day and our freedoms will return."

"We do not have to live in America forever, Josie. We can come back to Poland when life here improves. I have never thought of living in America permanently. But now is not a good time for us in Poland. Our religion is not the only reason. The Prussians do not want us here and, if we stay, it is only to serve their needs. They are making it difficult for us in every way. Do you not love your brother?"

"Theo? Of course."

"If we stay, Theo will be forced to fight in their wars against countries we Poles have no quarrel with. He is of age, and I am surprised he has not been called already. Prussian wars are not our wars. Do we feel any loyalty to Prussia? To Bismarck?"

I glanced at Theo. I saw anger on his face.

"The abuses go on and on, Josie," Papa said. "Their government gives Germans incentives to settle in our cities, towns, and farms. They push Polish people out of their established businesses so that German merchants can take them over. Only Germans are given government contracts and Poles always lose."

"But we are still surviving, are we not?"

"We are, but how much longer? And how much more abuse can we take? Do you not see the writing on the wall? Do you not want to see your sister again? Her letters home always beg us to join them in Chicago."

I wagged my forefinger in the air and then pointed it at him. "Do you not see the fallacy in your own words, Papa? You just said she is sending letters home. Poland is our home, not America."

He shook his head sadly. "America will soon seem like home, with half of our family already happy there. They would not urge us to come if America was not what they say."

This was a good point. I trusted Uncle John and my sister; they were happy and prosperous. Rosalie had married Adam, a successful young man who owned many properties. She worked as housekeeper at her parish rectory, and in her most recent letter had said, "We will send prepaid tickets for all of you. Come, stay a few years, and then, when things are better, return to Europe."

I had run out of arguments.

"If you are right, Papa, will we be allowed to leave?"

He laughed bitterly. "They will escort us out the door. This is what they want, for us to leave, so they can control everything. They are treating us poorly to make us leave. There will be buyers for our farm—not as much as it is worth, of course. But the money will go far in America. If we go now, we go on our terms, to a place where we have family established, a house and jobs waiting for us."

"And Theo," I said.

"Yes, and Theo will be with us, not on some battlefield."

"And you promise we can come back when life here is better?"

"Poland is our country, Josie. We will always be Poles."

Papa had not made a promise, but I thought he was sincere. Papa is a good man and wants the best for us.

I looked at Mama, at Theo, at Frances. They were not smiling. They looked worried, but each in turn nodded. The last face I looked at was Katy's. Her eyes were shining with excitement.

"It will be such an adventure, Josie," she said. "How soon can we leave, Papa?"

# Chapter 8

That night Cora did not sleep well again, tossing and turning with memories that kept surfacing despite efforts to distract herself. Well, she had come here with the intent of wrestling with her demons. Let the memory demons triumph!

Tonight, the demons took her back to another day when she lay in bed, the sun promising a glorious morning. But she lay motionless then with her eyes shut tight, pretending to sleep, her stomach queasy. Cisco wasn't fooled. He curled around her, spooning, his cheek against her hair. "Are you ready for today?" he had asked, his voice almost a whisper. She knew he intended to sound encouraging, but she heard anxiety in his voice. Sometimes cancer was even harder on the loved one, but it would be like him to hide his fear from her.

"How can I be ready, when I can't believe it's happening?" she said. His warm breath gently ruffled her hair.

Despite all the preparation, despite hearing the sounds of Joe and Rosie getting dressed in the next room, she still felt her diagnosis was a mistake. She thought that's what the doctors would say when they saw her later this morning in the hospital oncology department—*there's been a mistake.*

"I'm resigned to whatever I have to do, I guess," she went on after a moment. "My biggest fear is chemotherapy. You know I get sick to my stomach for every little thing. I hate that feeling! I'm even a little sick now, probably from nerves. I could be vomiting for months. That's going to be hard…" Her voice broke. "Really hard."

The treatment frightened her more than the disease itself. The pained, defeated expression on the face of a cancer patient she once knew stuck in her mind. The woman had such severe and constant bouts of vomiting, she had to stop therapy before it was completed.

Would she be able to eat? Would she need a feeding tube? This, she had read, sometimes occurred. Was she healthy enough to withstand the fight her body was about to wage? What if the radiation swelling was so bad her airway was cut off and she couldn't breathe? What if she was forced to stop treatment and surrender to cancer?

She refused to talk about whether she would survive. Or even consider it.

At 10:30 A.M. they were escorted to an examining room in the oncology department at Rush University Medical Center, with a wall of windows overlooking another building, an exam table, a desk with a computer and stool, and a side chair. Two more side chairs were brought in for Joe and Rosie. They had been making small talk during the ninety-minute ride from Lemont on Chicago's Stevenson Expressway, but now sat speechless, nervously avoiding each other's eyes.

After ten minutes, a short, slender, dark-skinned man wearing black pants, a white shirt, and maroon tie came into the room and introduced himself as Dr. Kenan Muni, her radiation oncologist, specializing in head and neck radiation. Cora thought he looked young, almost like a medical student.

"We talked about your case at tumor board," he said, sitting on the computer stool. "Dr. Thomas already discussed the surgical option with you. Radical neck dissection is a seven-hour surgery to remove the tumor as well as the lymph nodes in your neck. However, we feel your cancer will respond to more conservative treatment, a clinical trial using radiation and chemotherapy alone. You would need radiation and chemotherapy even if you had the surgery, but we feel we'll get a good result without the surgery."

Dr. Muni paused for her reaction. When she said nothing, he continued, his manner calm, his explanations thorough and easy to understand.

"Standard treatment is for radiation of a large area of your head, neck, and upper chest to destroy the tumor in your tongue and any existing cancer in your head and neck. Chemotherapy is done at the same time, in case your cancer has spread undetected to other areas of your body." He was interrupted by an "L" train rumbling loudly on the tracks between the two buildings.

"But you said a trial. This isn't what you're recommending for me," Cora said, her voice faint.

"Yes, you're correct. There's good evidence that less radiation and an alternate drug is effective for your particular cancer. There are many vital structures in the head and neck—major nerves, muscles, blood vessels, airway and voice box, mouth and esophagus. Tailoring radiation to avoid injury to these vital structures while destroying the cancer is not easy, but we can do it using computer mapping and details from your PET scan. We can direct your radiation dose at the lowest exposure and area possible, targeting only areas we know are cancerous and the most likely areas for spread. This does not mean that you will have no side effects, but they will be reduced."

"You feel this is enough? What happens if you don't get it all?"

"Then you have the surgery."

"Not more radiation and chemo?"

"No. We do this one time."

"And there is a risk?"

"Medicine is not an exact science. There's always a risk. But again, we feel this is the best option for you, that it's safe, and that you'll have a good result."

"But it's my decision? I can opt for the surgery or for the standard treatment?"

"Yes. You decide." His words were direct, but she saw compassion in his eyes.

"If I was your mother, what would you advise?" she said.

"I'd advise the trial," he said without hesitation.

She clasped her hands in her lap to keep them from shaking and swallowed hard. She looked at Cisco, Joe, and Rosie. Rosie, the oncologist, said nothing but was nodding her head.

"What do you all think?" Cora asked. She could hardly hear her own voice over her heartbeat pounding in her ears.

Rosie said, "I'm familiar with this trial. I think it's the right thing to do. For squamous cell tongue cancer, the results are very good. We can cure this kind of cancer now."

Cisco and Joe nodded.

"You're in good hands here. Let the experts do what they do," Joe said.

Cora and Cisco exchanged a long look. He nodded. This was real. Tears stung her eyes but did not fall. She nodded slowly.

"Good," Dr. Muni said. "Let me examine you."

As he looked in her mouth and felt her neck carefully, he explained more about her treatment, but she wasn't taking it all in; she trusted Joe and Rosie to do that. But she was glad he kept talking, because his voice was calming.

"We'll give you a binder to take home that explains everything. You'll come in five times a week for eight weeks. The treatment will affect your taste buds and your salivary glands, and that will happen pretty soon. Your mouth will be dry and you won't want to eat all the foods you normally eat. Expect your appetite to be poor and to lose weight, so we'll have a dietitian follow you. Toward the end of radiation, the skin on your neck will burn, but aside from that you shouldn't have much pain. The symptoms will start slow, increase over the course of treatment, and continue for a time after treatment."

"Will I be nauseous? I'm really afraid of that."

"We don't expect that from radiation, but you should ask your medical oncologist. If you have more questions, here's where you can reach me." He handed her a card. "My email and cell phone number. Contact me any time you have questions, problems, or just want to talk. We'll start in about three weeks."

Cisco got up and put his arm around her after the doctor left.

"You made the right decision, Mom," Joe said. Rosie nodded.

Cisco was still standing at her side when the medical oncologist came into the room. Dr. Deanna Coppin was short, thirty-something, with curly light brown hair, kind light blue eyes, a pleasant smile, and a quiet professional demeanor. She was plump, almost looking pregnant. Maybe she *was* pregnant, Cora thought. She was one of the leading experts in her field, but appeared to Cora like any other young mother, maybe a neighbor.

Her manner was warm and reassuring as she gave Cora another thorough examination and answered her nervous questions about the chemo and its side effects. "Because your cancer has spread, radiation alone won't stop it, so you'll need chemotherapy at the same time as radiation. The drug we're suggesting for you is Cetuximab, a monoclonal antibody. It has less side effects than standard treatment, but if you do have nausea, we'll give you medication to help with that. Unlike standard chemotherapy, which can't distinguish between cancer cells and healthy cells, Cetuximab recognizes and attaches to cancer cells and works with the body's immune system to attack only abnormal cells."

"Standard chemotherapy wouldn't increase my chances for cure?"

"You might term it overkill," Joe said. He was probably trying to lighten things up. Cora shot him a dirty look she didn't really mean.

"Chemotherapy is once a week. The first dose is what we call a loading dose. It's stronger, to give you a boost at the beginning. There will be eight doses, or eight weeks. Someone will need to drive you home." She glanced at Cisco.

"Sure. I'll be with her for all her appointments."

Dr. Coppin put a hand on Cora's arm and squeezed gently. "Good," she said, looking into Cora's eyes. "We're going to take good care of you."

Had she made the right choice? Cora wasn't confident. Why was she going to make herself sick when she didn't feel sick to begin with? Why do all this at all if she didn't feel sick? Especially when the treatment was going to make her miserable for months. Two months of chemotherapy and radiation, and who knows how long before she got back to normal. There seemed to be no good reason to opt for a more difficult treatment. If it worked….

*Well, in for a penny…* She would do the best she could, tough it out and try to think positively. Any other attitude would only make the journey worse.

Lying here in bed now, five years later, she reflected on her cancer battle. It had been tough, but she had made it through. As a consequence, her life would never be the same, and she was left troubled by unresolved questions about her religious beliefs. She had come to Assisi Hill in an effort to stop procrastinating and face the issue, to revive the faith she had once depended upon, which she now saw as too small a part of her life.

What she wanted was the comfort she remembered from her childhood years, the security of God's protection. But she could no longer *feel*

His presence, not as a constant companion, nor even when she reached out for Him.

What would happen if she decided there was no God and no afterlife, and lived the rest of her days based on that conclusion? Then, if she discovered there was a God and an afterlife, it would be too late. She had only one life to prepare, and she didn't want to blow it by making the wrong decision. Wouldn't it be wiser to prepare for either eventuality?

Cora had taken her degree at a Catholic women's college, where four years of theology had been required. She was well-versed in the Catholic religion, but after marriage and children she had allowed herself to get too involved in daily activities and had drifted away. Was she using the excuse of busyness to avoid facing her doubts about God? Cisco had been telling her for years that she took on too many obligations. Did that come from a feeling that only she could do things best?

Cora glanced at the clock on the nightstand. It was two in the morning and she was wide awake. She'd be a zombie the next day if she didn't get some rest. Maybe one of the anxiety pills left over from her cancer treatment would relax her enough to sleep.

She got up, turned on the light, and rummaged through the top drawer of the nightstand until she found the container of Lorazepam and a pill-cutter. The tiny white tablet was only about an eighth of an inch in diameter and had to be cut in half for the correct dose. She carefully positioned the tablet in the pill-cutter. The result was one half-sized piece and crumbs. She wet her finger, picked up and swallowed the crumbs, put the half-piece back into the pill container, and got back in bed.

In the morning, she would have to write down her thoughts. Writing thoughts down committed her to them. That was the first step. Then would come analysis, decision, and action. That was the routine she was comfortable with.

# Chapter 9

The minute dose of Lorazepam did the trick. Cora slept deeply until she woke up at seven o'clock the next morning, feeling rested. She pulled the covers around her neck and snuggled down for a last few minutes, not to sleep but just to feel cozy and warm. It wasn't the same when Cisco wasn't beside her, though. She felt an unexpected surge of apprehension, like she used to get when her sons were young. Whenever they were out of her sight she had a constant sense of foreboding, as if they would only be safe if she was with them. It began when she became a mother, this illogical fear when separated from loved ones. Did all mothers feel like that? It was only her third day since Cisco had left. She sighed and forced herself to get up, ignoring the nagging uneasiness. It was silly then, and it was silly now.

Nonetheless, she was relieved when she dialed Cisco's number a short time later and he answered immediately.

"We're doing something a little different today," he said. "We're going to some place called South Mountain Park. There's supposed to be a great overlook there." He paused and dropped his voice, probably to be sure he wasn't overheard. "I'd love to explore, but Barney isn't much of a hiker. We'll be touring by car. I'm the guest here so I can't complain."

"No golf today?"

"Oh, yeah. We'll play nine this afternoon." Not surprisingly, Cora detected disdain in Cisco's voice. To him, anything less than eighteen holes was a waste of time.

"What's on your agenda today?" he asked.

"I'm heading back to Assisi Manor after breakfast. I want to pick Sister Maryam's brains about aspects of the book."

"You don't sound too enthused."

"I need more background before my creative juices start flowing. Enthusiasm will come but it's a bit soon."

"Well, don't take up too much of her time. I'm sure she's busy."

Cora sighed. He didn't have to tell her these things. She knew how to treat people. But whatever.

"Are you worried about getting home at all?" she asked.

"Because of that virus, you mean?"

"Yeah. Aren't they saying air travel might not be a good idea? Do you think they'll stop flights?"

"Oh, I'm sure they'll never do that—all airlines think about is making money. Even if it *was* to get that bad there'd be some warning and I can head home."

"I thought Barney doesn't watch the news. And you forget everything else when you're golfing."

"Don't worry. I'll be fine. Look, Barney's standing at the door. I gotta go."

~~~

When she arrived at Assisi Manor, Maryam suggested they talk in the large open room next to the chapel. They settled into comfortable overstuffed chairs in the deserted space, morning sun streaming through the tall wall of windows.

"What made you decide to become a nun, Maryam?" Cora hadn't planned to ask the question, but the words slipped out.

Maryam turned to the windows, as if considering how to answer. After a time, she said, "I was a tomboy as a kid, but I had this great love for the Virgin Mary. Typical Irish thing, I guess. My father, who immigrated here about ten years before I was born, couldn't afford to send me to Assisi Hill Academy, but he used to bring me out here to get me away from hanging with boys all the time—to spend some time around girls. I'm not sure that plan worked, but I was fascinated with the place and spent a lot of time wandering the property and playing my harmonica. It got to feel like the right place to be."

She stopped and shifted her eyes away from Cora again. Cora got the feeling there was something she didn't want to say, but couldn't imagine what that was. Then Maryam gave a short laugh. "I felt Mary's presence here in a special way, I suppose you could say. I wanted to be here all the time, and becoming a nun just seemed like the right thing to do. The sisters weren't so sure at first. It had been a while since they had a postulant, and they were out of practice. It's been a bit rough, but I'm very close to taking permanent vows now."

"Are you happy here?"

"Happy?" She beamed. "I couldn't be happier, Cora. It's more than I ever could have dreamed. God, and Mary, have been…I can't explain." Maryam turned away, again giving the impression she was hiding something.

"But you came here to talk about the book," she said. "I know how important it is to Sister Lorita, so I want to help in any way I can."

Cora pulled out a notepad and fished a pen out of her purse. "I wonder if you know anyone who was here when Assisi Manor was built? I hoped to find someone who may remember and can give me firsthand information—tell me her story, you know?"

Maryam laughed, more open and relaxed now. "That's a tall order. We opened this building in 1971—that's fifty years ago, but it's not impossible to find someone, I suppose. By the way, I understand you've talked to Father Bozic?"

"Yes. What a lovely man. I'm gathering some history about St. Marija's, too."

Maryam thought that over. "What's on your agenda today?"

"I'd like to drive around to some other communities this afternoon, introduce myself, get some sense of what they're all about. The Poor Clares, maybe, or the other Franciscan convent off Walker Road."

"If you're seeing the Franciscan Sisters at St. Joseph's, ask for Sister Elizabeth. Not only can she show you around, she's in charge of the canonization process for Mother Josepha. You know about her?"

"Only that there's a woman from that order who's a candidate for sainthood."

"She's been declared venerable at this point, and is awaiting canonization. The process is a long one."

"What makes her worthy of being a saint?"

"She founded the order, the Franciscan Sisters of Our Lady. Like most saints, what she did wasn't easy and her life was full of challenges. Sister Elizabeth is a much better person than I am to tell you about it. Should I call her and set it up?"

"Could you? That would be wonderful."

Soon, Cora had an appointment to meet Sister Elizabeth after lunch. On her own it probably would have taken days just to get a callback. Things were falling into place so easily. Cora felt the beginnings of the spark that was missing when she talked to Cisco earlier.

As they walked toward the manor entrance, she saw Winnie, the disfigured woman she had met yesterday, seated with two other elderly women.

"She's remarkable, isn't she?" Cora said.

"Oh, yes," Maryam said. "Quite an inspiration. People who meet her end up believing they can deal with their own problems when they realize what she's managed to accomplish."

Their own problems. Cora was grateful once again that she'd escaped the possibility of disfigurement like Winnie's.

With the exception of Sister Fatima, the more she got to know these religious women, the more Cora felt at home. They were warm, welcoming, and inspiring—exactly what she hoped for when she decided to stay at the convent.

At the door, Maryam said, "By the way, when you're going back and forth to St. Marija's, you don't have to drive. There's a path between our convent and the monastery. Just walk toward the back of our property and you'll come to a bridge that leads to a field. Cut through the trees and you'll come to St. Marija's pond. It's about a quarter mile and a pleasant walk."

Abruptly, Maryam looked away, as if she had said something she shouldn't. Once again, Cora had the feeling there was something she wasn't meant to know. Something that involved Maryam in a very personal way.

# Chapter 10

St. Joseph Village was about a half mile west of St. Marija's and Assisi Hill, off the same road. Cora was discovering that religious communities did not consist of a single building that housed nuns, but multiple buildings that carried out the orders' missions. St. Marija's, in addition to the monastery, had a retreat house, the Catholic Slovenian Center and School, and at one time a seminary. Assisi Hill on 77 acres had not only their provincial center, but also senior residences (Assisi Manor), the recently closed high school (Assisi Hill Academy), and presently day care and retreat facilities. St. Joseph Village was the largest complex of the three, stretching out over 155 acres south of Main Street.

Although Assisi Hill and St. Joseph were both run by Franciscan Sisters and St. Marija's by Franciscan Fathers, they were completely independent communities with different histories and structures. All three places had their administrative center, monastery, or mother house in Lemont.

Cora drove through St. Joseph Village, viewing fields, maintenance buildings, a monument, a small cemetery, and a pond. She passed a development of duplex-style ranch homes before coming to a large tan stucco and red brick three-story building. Cora had been here years ago looking for short-term care for her mother, and knew the duplexes housed senior residents and the large building contained independent and assisted living suites. A wing of the building was the Mother Josepha Home, a skilled nursing facility.

Cora parked near the Mother Josepha Home, then got out and walked through an area that resembled the Stations of the Cross at St. Marija's. The stations here, however, were composed of stone that was brown and rough but without the unique bubbles and crystals that had intrigued her in the rock at St. Marija's. This location was not isolated, but placed where it would attract visitors. Like St. Marija's, there was a grotto here: a statue of the Virgin Mary in the center, sculptures of saints on either side, and white stone figures of young girls kneeling in prayer.

At the far end of the Stations of the Cross was a white stone statue on a pedestal with a plaque that read *Mother Mary Josepha, Founder of the Franciscan Sisters of Our Lady.* In the nun's arms was a boy of perhaps ten years. Both of the boy's legs were missing, starting from above the knees. *What's the story here?* Cora wondered.

She went back to her car, got in, and drove a short distance to St. Joseph Convent, the mother house of the Franciscan Sisters of Our Lady. Cora's prior research revealed that the sisters had about a dozen ministries across five states, the majority in Illinois. She assumed retired sisters would live here, and perhaps there was a novitiate for sisters-in-training. The two-story building was of modern, light-orange brick construction.

Cora parked near the front entrance. From a vestibule, she was buzzed in and walked up to a large semi-circular reception desk. A middle-aged receptionist told her that Sister Elizabeth was expecting her and would be down shortly. Would she care to visit the gift shop while she waited?

The gift shop was typical, with figurines, holy cards, wall decorations, rosaries and other spiritual memorabilia, racks of books about God and the saints, and more. Cora found a book about Mother Mary Josepha of Chicago and was flipping through it when Sister Elizabeth called her name.

Having been told that Sister Elizabeth was near her own age, Cora was surprised to discover a woman who looked at least ten years younger, with a welcoming smile and an abundance of energy that reminded her of Sister Lorita. It dawned on Cora that all the nuns she had been meeting seemed younger than their years and remarkably energetic. Was there something about religious life that upped the odds in that direction?

*This order must have lenient rules about dress,* she thought. Sister Elizabeth wore a bright floral-print jacket over a black, mid-calf skirt and a black top, with no veil over her curly red hair. This was far different from the black habits, starched white wimples, and black veils worn by the nuns who had taught Cora many years ago.

"Let's go to Heritage Hall," the sister said, after firmly shaking Cora's hand. "If you want to learn our history, that's the best place to start."

Cora followed Sister Elizabeth down a hallway and past white columns into a large, comfortable exhibit hall. "This is amazing!" she said, looking at the displays behind glass. "It's a regular museum."

Sister Elizabeth grinned. "We're proud of it."

Cora reached into her carry-all and pulled out her notepad and pen, ready to take notes and ask the questions she had prepared. She circled the exhibits, stopping to jot things down and take photos with her phone. This place was a historian's treasure, too comprehensive to take in at a single visit. She hoped she could get free access here.

She could have stayed for hours, as all the order's history seemed to be on display. The museum focused on the foundress who had been declared venerable, on the road to sainthood. It began with the birth in Poland of Josephine Mrozek—later Mother Mary Josepha—in 1860, and continued with her arrival in Chicago with her family, her founding of the Franciscan Sisters of Our Lady in 1894, the building of the St. Joseph Home for the Aged and Crippled, the move to Lemont, and the expansion of the Lemont properties and other locations.

Cora's mother had never made a big deal of her heritage, but Cora had dearly loved her Polish grandmother and the time she had spent with relatives during her childhood. Her background inclined her to think fondly of Mother Josepha.

"She is here in our chapel now," Sister Elizabeth said. "We'll go there next."

They left the museum and Sister Elizabeth locked the door behind them. "How much do you know about Mother Josepha?" she asked as they started down the hall.

"Very little until now. Just that she founded the order, is a candidate for sainthood, and her remains are here. I'd like to know more."

Sister Elizabeth smiled. "You will if you spend any time with me. I'm quite passionate about her candidacy, you know."

Cora laughed. "I'm getting that impression."

They reached their destination, and the nun pushed open the door to a chapel of modern, clean, simple lines. Instead of pews, tan armchairs with padded seats were set in rows. Behind the altar was a lovely twelve-foot high painting of Jesus depicted as the Sacred Heart. Tall stained-glass windows flanked the altar and sides of the chapel in brilliant shades of blue, red, gold and green. In the center of the ceiling was a spectacular dome in gold leaf.

Another sister was dusting near the altar. She was elderly, dressed in a brown jacket and mid-calf-length skirt, with a white headband and black veil. It seemed some nuns preferred more traditional habits.

Sister Elizabeth brought Cora into a side chapel. At the back of the recess was a large red granite sarcophagus that almost filled the niche from wall to wall. On it was engraved in gold lettering, *Servant of God, Mother Mary Josepha Mrozek, 1860–1918*. A spray of flowers lay on top.

Cora did the math in her head. "She was only fifty-eight when she died. What does 'Servant of God' mean?"

"The term 'Servant of God' is not a description, but a title," Sister Elizabeth said. "It designates that the Vatican has said there is enough evidence for the person to be considered for canonization—to become known as a saint."

Cora made a sign of the Cross and then glanced at Sister Elizabeth, who nodded and did the same. Both women prayed silently in front of the sarcophagus for a few minutes, then signed again and turned to leave. The other sister had left the altar, and the chapel was deserted. They moved to the back of the room and sat in two of the armchairs.

"I'm the current liaison for the Cause of Sainthood for Mother Josepha," Sister Elizabeth said. "I publicize her cause and collect stories. In order to be finally declared a saint, there must be two miracles credited to her after her death, which must be authenticated by the Congregation of the Causes of Saints, to be sure the miracles cannot be explained by natural causes and were performed by *this* person, not some other."

"Why after her death?"

"To prove the candidate is in heaven and is capable of interceding with God on behalf of someone living on earth."

Cora experienced a moment of light-headedness. Evidence of a person in heaven acting on earth! A saint in the making, right here in Lemont.

Perhaps she could be part of the process! This was even more than she had signed on for. The idea awed her.

"The road to sainthood is a long process, obviously." Cora heard someone moving around behind them. Perhaps the elderly sister they'd seen at the altar earlier had returned.

"That's not unusual," Sister Elizabeth said. "St. Bernadette of Lourdes died in 1879 and wasn't made a saint until 1925. The three children at Fatima weren't granted sainthood until very recently, in 2017, and the Virgin Mary appeared to them in 1917, a hundred years before."

"I didn't realize it was that involved."

Sister Elizabeth went on, her words sounding rehearsed, like a tour guide. "The church is very careful in these matters. The Cause for Mother Josepha was started by Father Henryk Malak in 1963. The first step was to preserve her remains. After exhaustive research, detailed biographies and eyewitness accounts were gathered, and permission was given to exhume her body from St. Adalbert's Cemetery and bring her here. The exhumation process is very specific and detailed. It has to be done in the presence of a representative of the Vatican and each step carefully documented. It took fourteen hours. That was in 1972, over fifty years after her death and burial."

"What did they find?"

"It's helpful to the cause if there are findings that defy the laws of nature. In Mother Josepha's case, her bones were found to be much better preserved than was natural. She was wearing a crucifix with a wood inlay that had absolutely no decay, whereas the casket was almost completely rotted and the nails and hinges badly corroded. Also, a piece of her habit remained completely intact."

"I saw her referred to as 'Venerable' in Heritage Hall. Is that the same as Servant of God?"

"Venerable is the next step. Documentation is gathered and translated into Italian, and if it meets the criteria of the canonization committee, the candidate is declared Venerable. Mother Josepha is Venerable since 1994. Prior to that date she was called Servant of God."

"What comes next?"

"Beatification, or Blessed, is the next step. Then canonization—sainthood."

"What do you do to move her up to beatification?"

"We publicize her, pray to her, and document miracles. One for the beatification step, and a final one to declare her a saint."

"Are there any miracles?" Cora heard rustling sounds again, this time seeming to come from near the side chapel with the sarcophagus. Was it the same sister? She turned but couldn't see the area, yet she had a sense they were being watched. Were they interrupting something?

Sister Elizabeth didn't seem to notice. "Yes. The most recent was reviewed in 2003. A young man had been hit by a train, resulting in severe brain injury and unconsciousness. His doctors believed he would never recover. His mother prayed at the sarcophagus and took some petals from the flowers on top. She placed the petals on her son and said a novena asking Mother Josepha to intercede—to ask God to cure her son. On the last day of the novena her son opened his eyes and recognized her. His doctors testified at the investigation."

"And?"

"Unfortunately, this miracle was not deemed important enough, so the cause continues." Sister Elizabeth folded her arms across her chest and added, "When the documentation is presented to the committee, someone is appointed to argue against the cause. This person is called the Devil's Advocate—that's where the term comes from." She gave a crooked grin. "I think it helps the cause if the candidate is Italian, but you didn't hear me say that."

Cora smiled. "And this is what you do? Look for miracles to present?"

"Yes. I talk to people, at meetings, in person, on the radio, wherever I can. The more people who know of her and pray to her, the more possibility miracles will happen. I believe it."

"I'd like to believe it, too," Cora said.

"I'm glad. Before you leave, I'll give you a copy of her writings. That's the best way to get to know her."

They sat in silence for a moment and then Cora reached for her purse and slid it onto her lap. "The statue of Mother Josepha outside—what's the story about the little boy she's holding?"

"Ah, Tommy. He was an orphan who lost both his legs under the wheels of a locomotive. In the early days of the order, Mother Josepha took him in to live with the sisters in the convent. He knew nothing of catechism or how to pray, and she taught him and raised him. Many years later he helped the carpenters expand the order's orphanage. Oddly, he eventually got a job as a railway switchman."

"The boy in the miracle you told me about, that was a railroad accident too."

Sister Elizabeth raised her eyebrows. "I hadn't made that connection."

Cora was suddenly overwhelmed with emotion and an ache in her chest. She had come here looking for a story, and once again everything she heard promised more than she had expected. Her eyes grew moist, and she dropped her gaze and blinked rapidly. She had lost sight of her doubts about her faith in her excitement over discovering a saint in the making.

Distracted by emotion, Cora had almost forgotten about the other person in the chapel. As they got up and started to leave, she could see into the side niche and recognized a familiar figure. She turned to Sister Elizabeth in surprise.

"I know that woman. I met her at Assisi Manor."

"Oh yes, Winnie. She comes here about this time every day to say a rosary to Mother Josepha. Winnie is one of her biggest supporters, I guess you could say. Poor woman, but so brave. Too bad she and Mother Josepha didn't live at the same time. They would have been good friends."

Cora Tozzi, *History of the Religious Institutions of Lemont,*
(Chicago, Madonna Press, 2024), 16–23

*"It seemed to me that God was pleased even with the
little good that I could do for His glory."*
—*The Chronicles of Venerable Mother Josepha of Chicago*

### Josie's Journal
### June 21, 1886, Chicago

As often as I visit St. Stanislaus Kostka Church, it never fails to fill me
with awe. I love its vaulted ceiling, marble columns, intricately painted
arches and murals. Above its white, elaborately carved altar floats a dramatic dome with a wonderful depiction of Jesus surrounded by saints
and angels. On the wall behind the altar is painted our patron, St. Stanislaus, portraying his visitation by the Blessed Virgin.

Every day I stop here and kneel in the first pew in front of the portrait
of Our Lady of Perpetual Help. I pray with my eyes closed, the palms of
my hands pressed together and tips of my fingers against my lips, but
still I see the image of Mary as clearly as if my eyes were open. Her
painting hangs above its own carved white altar, adorned today with
pink and white lilies. A bank of tall, red votive candle holders, flames
flickering through the glass, stands in front. Mary holds the baby Jesus,
the Angel Gabriel on her right and St. Michael the Archangel on her left.
Her eyes look deep into mine, and always I feel Our Lady's presence.

This church is even more grand than the churches built in Poland from the 16th century, and will be grander still once it is finished. It may be some years yet, but the plans have been drawn, the money collected, and orders placed. One day there will be twin towers and stained-glass windows.

Some do not understand the passion Polish Catholics have for our faith. They say our plans are too opulent. But we want to show what each and every one of us is willing to sacrifice to make our devotion known. Would we not be criticized if we scrimped or gave the impression we did not value God enough to honor Him appropriately?

St. Stanislaus is the largest parish in the United States, with forty thousand parishioners. Even though it seats 1500 people, our priests say twelve Masses each Sunday, six in the upper church and six in the lower church, and still latecomers must stand in the back and along the aisles. I would say I was proud of my parish, but pride is an attitude God disdains, so I settle for happiness.

Yet this parish, and this country, wonderful as they are, are not immune to worldly troubles. Only Mary, I believe, by the will of God, can lead our world out of its abyss. This is why I pray each day.

Concentrating on my prayers, I jumped and my eyes flew open when I felt a hand on my shoulder. It was Father Barzynski. "I am sorry to startle you, Josie. Did I interrupt your prayers?"

My rapid heartbeat slowed but it was a while before my cheeks cooled. "I was thinking how lovely our church is," I told Father. I slid from the kneeler onto the seat and made room for him next to me.

"How fortunate to find you here. It saves me from walking to your home. I have a favor to ask."

Father Vincent Barzynski often visits us in our home and stays for dinner, like when we lived in Poland and Father Felix came to our farm. Our family is very involved at St. Stanislaus. Even with five priests, there are never enough hands for the work required, and so all of us help out. My sister Rosalie is housekeeper at the rectory, Uncle John and Rosalie's husband Adam serve on the parish board, and Papa supervises the maintenance staff. Theo helps Father Vincent in his office and is quickly becoming his right-hand man.

Only a few weeks after we arrived from Poland, Father Vincent learned of my dressmaking and needlecraft skills and asked me to take charge of the church linens. I was happy to do so, but lately Father was finding more and more use for me.

Now I smiled at him and said, "You have given the linens to me, I am superior of a tree of Rosary Sodality and president of the arch-confraternity of the Immaculate Heart—which now has over 300 members, I may remind you. Why do you think I need more to do?"

As with everything else at St. Stanislaus, the number of confraternities and societies is astounding. The Rosary Sodality alone has over four thousand members, with the young ladies' branch divided into trees of 330 women.

My words, though, had been meant in jest. Despite the extent of my commitments, I enjoyed all I did.

"Your devotion to Mary is legendary, Josie, and you are so good with these things!" he said, laughing. How well he knew I found it hard to turn him down.

I gave him a serious look. "I am sorry for making jokes, Father. There is no one who works harder than you. I do not know how you do it all."

"It is challenging, Josie, I must admit." He sighed. "Today I came across some amazing statistics. Did you know that last year we had over two thousand baptisms, almost four hundred weddings, and over a thousand funerals? Our school has five thousand students. The sisters teach the students, but the church oversees administration, maintenance, and religious education. We have over fifty societies and confraternities, and now that our orphanage serves all the Polish parishes in Chicago, we also have three hundred children to raise."

His eyes were kind, but he looked tired and almost desperate. I wanted to comfort him, but instead I took off my glasses and polished them on my skirt. I only said, "Of course I will do my part, Father. How can I help?"

The worried look on his face faded, not due to my words, I thought, but because he was good at facing his problems and finding solutions. In only moments his positive attitude returned.

"Lidia Kruzinski came to talk to me this morning," he said. "Her family has fallen into difficulty and they have decided to try their fortune in the West."

Some of our neighbors find it impossible to make a living in the city.

In fact, this is happening not only to Poles in Chicago but to everyone throughout the country. Now that railroads are laying more lines and Indian conflicts are dying down in western states, that part of the country is not only getting more populated but industrialization is growing. Many now think more opportunities are available in the West than here.

I put my glasses back on. "I will be sorry to see Lidia leave. I hope she will be happy."

"Yes, but now there is no one to preside over the Third Order of St. Francis," he said.

"I see." I belonged to this organization for young Catholic women, and I knew how hard Lidia worked. I suspect Father Vincent asked me because I am unwed. He has kidded me before about this very thing.

I had told him, "God, with your help, has trusted me with many obligations, so you must take some responsibility for my spinsterhood. How can I have time for men with all you have assigned to me, and the dressmaking, and Papa, Mama, and Theo to care for now that my sisters are gone?"

But Father was waiting for an answer, so I took a deep breath and said, "Of course, I will do it. I will find time somehow. I am, after all, still a young woman."

He smiled and patted my hand. "And one of the best."

After Father Vincent left, I brooded a little about my unmarried state. Or perhaps I should say, my disinterest in marriage. It was not that I had no suitors, but I had little time or energy to devote to them. Recently, my friend Sophie Wisneski brought the matter up. Sophie was ten years older than me and a mentor, but at times I thought of her more as a busybody. Nonetheless, we were both unwed, and both heavily involved with the church.

"You have so many suitors, Josie," Sophie had commented, "which is no wonder, with your happy blue eyes, fine figure, and fashionable dress. I am sure men find you not only lovely but cheerful and intelligent. Your dressmaking business is profitable, your good work here at St. Stanislaus is well known, and you still find time to cook and care for your family. Men want to marry a woman with such qualities, not to mention earning ability."

Sophie's words seemed kind, and yet I wondered if she was jealous, or hinting that there must be some flaw in me that drives men away. I hope she did not want me to stay a spinster like her. She was right: I do have many suitors, but with all my commitments, I am happy to just have a warm, soft bed to fall into at night—I have no time for courting. The truth is that my life is satisfactory without a man in it. God is more important to me than any man, and I am not willing to give up a single one of the minutes I cherish for Him.

Although, I must confess to warm thoughts about Stanley Mrozinski. Stanley stands behind me during choir practice, and last week he asked the director if he and I could prepare a duet for Communion. Stanley is a nice-enough-looking man who has recently come from Poland, though he has one leg shorter than the other and walks with a limp. He is even more shy than I am, and never speaks if he can avoid it. For him to make his request in front of the three hundred members of our choir took courage. He sometimes walks me home after rehearsals, but says little, only stares at me with what Mama calls "cow eyes." He told me I had the loveliest voice in the choir. I suppose he may be smitten with me, but I do not encourage him.

As I walked the three blocks from St. Stanislaus to my home, I could not help but notice the changes to the homes of our neighbors. The houses were built when the economy was strong, but now there are signs of declining wealth: chipping paint, uncovered windows, weeds. Many houses are now divided into multiple units, some with basement flats. I passed the apartment of the Kwiatek family, where I recently delivered a food package. The family takes in boarders to make ends meet—eighteen people crammed into three small bedrooms. No one in the family has been able to find a job, and they are dependent on church donations.

I continued south on Noble Street, thinking about how good God has been to my family. I no longer plan to go back to Poland, because our life here is so rich. Rosalie's husband owns many fine properties, and we live in an entire floor of one of Adam's buildings. We are well off, comfortable, and our work is satisfying and profitable, even my dressmaking business.

When I reached Holy Trinity Church and turned onto Haddon Avenue, I realized that I could not be content if I did not share my good fortune with those who have nothing. In fact, it seemed wrong to me that we had so much while so many around us had so little, as more and more of our community were living in poverty.

When I reached home, I sat awhile on the top step of the small porch at our entry door to finish my thoughts.

After this country's great Civil War, I learned, few men were left to re-build what was destroyed during the conflict. Then a great fire destroyed Chicago. Plans were made to rebuild on an even grander scale, but few men were left to do the work. So, people came from Europe, especially from Poland and Ireland. But then more and more heeded the call—too many. In the last twenty years the population doubled, and soon jobs that had once been plentiful were no longer available.

Unemployment and poverty were especially bad in Chicago. The law of the jungle, where only the strong and ruthless survived and the weak and infirm were crushed, became the way of life.

With so many men out of work, employers paid less and less, because they could—people took any job they could find, no matter how poor the wages. That led to labor demonstrations and then just weeks ago a mas-sacre at Haymarket Square. Labor organizers were only trying to sup-port workers striking for decent hours when the police came to break up the peaceful demonstration. Some unknown person in the crowd threw a bomb, and a fight broke out that resulted in death and injury. I found it sad that, in a country that gives men the right to speak free-ly, so many should be harmed in an effort to deprive them of that right.

I sighed and thought then of my own family—there is little I can do to put an end to poverty. Our religion is paramount in our lives, and to prove that we have given two of our family to the church. Three years ago, Frances joined the convent of the Sisters of Notre Dame who teach at St. Stanislaus School. She lives in their mother house in Milwaukee now, and is already rising in respect among her fellow sisters, but we see her only once or twice a year.

We were less happy, especially Mama, when Katy entered the Sis-ters of Charity only six months after Frances left. Katy was only fourteen years old. Sisters often start religious life at a young age, but Katy had just finished school. We begged and pleaded with her to wait until she was older and was sure she had a vocation.

Katy is more like my daughter than my sister. I consider her the most important person in my life, after God. The thought of her leaving home was devastating, but if Katy wanted a life devoted to God, and God had selected Katy as one of His own, how could I stand in her way? I wanted Katy to be happy...but could she not wait?

But no, Katy took every chance to run to the Sisters of Charity and do tasks for them. Selfishly, I hoped that over time her attraction to religious life would diminish, but her passion only grew stronger. Sister Superior at the convent suggested Katy spend time living there, to experience the difficulties of convent life and to better evaluate the seriousness of her interest. Instead of becoming discouraged, my baby sister only seemed to grow more radiant.

And then Katy told us she wanted to go to the novitiate, which was in San Antonio, Texas. San Antonio—1500 miles away! There was no good transportation, and it was possible we would never see Katy again. It seemed like she was going to the end of the world, living in a Wild West where she would encounter scorching weather, crude cowboys, and Indian attacks. Why must she go there?

Mama was horrified. "Is that not where Geronimo makes his raids? It cannot be safe there! No, Katy, please."

I put an arm around Mama. "Surely it is not that bad. There are missions, and the mother house has been there for fifteen years. The sisters built a hospital and the town is growing. I am sure Katy will be safe."

We were forced to decide when the Sisters of Charity chose to leave Chicago and return to San Antonio. Mama tried to make Katy feel guilty by telling her she was needed at home, but Katy burst into tears in fear of not following her dream.

Katy had turned to me with every need or problem since she was a small child. She turned to me then too, grasping both my hands and looking pleadingly into my eyes. I remembered the many times I had listened to her childish prattle, answered hundreds of questions, made her pretty dresses, played dolls, took her shopping. Was I never to see my baby again? Mama looked at me with tears in her eyes, hoping I would say something that would make Katy change her mind.

What I said was, "If Katy is certain that God is calling her, how can we stand in her way?"

Katy let out a squeal, delight all over her lovely face, and she threw her arms around me. As I hugged her, I murmured in her ear, "You will have your wish, you little imp."

And so, in 1884, Katy left. It has been two years since we have seen her. She writes every week, long letters full of happiness and enthusiasm. She has trained as a nurse, received the habit, and taken her first vows. She is now an angel of mercy to the sick.

And I am left to hold meetings, sew, do laundry, and take care of our little family.

Suddenly tired, I had to drag myself up to our apartment on the second floor. I felt overcome with responsibility. As fulfilling as my work is, something seems to be missing. Is this to be my life? Or does God have something else in mind for me?

# Chapter 11

"I want to order a truckload of mulch when I get home," Cisco said. "Alliums are out of control in the bed by the pines. I'll dig them out and transplant some hostas and daylilies. Simplify the yard. It's getting to be too much work."

"I'm all for that," Cora agreed, overjoyed to hear him making plans again. His energy and motivation must be coming back—the trip doing him good. She wished she had made as much progress about her relationship with God and her religion. She'd been at the convent for a week and seemed to have fallen into a familiar rut—sacrificing her personal goals for a project that demanded all her time.

"So, you and Sister Maryam are hitting it off? Spending a lot of time together, are you?" Cisco asked, not seeming to have noticed her distraction.

"What little time we find between her responsibilities and my writing. I've done a lot of research and I have ideas, but no words on paper yet."

Cisco laughed. "As usual. Do you miss your office at home?"

Cora laughed with him. "Not really. My room here is quiet. I can concentrate. I guess you might say it's inspirational." She chuckled again, wandering around the room as she talked, moving a pen on her desk and aimlessly straightening a pile of notes.

"How are the nuns? The ultra-religious getting to you?"

"No, they're...sort of...normal, you might say. And friendly. Except Fatima, of course. But..."

"But...?"

She sighed and thought for a moment. "Nothing, I guess. It's just...

mostly Sister Maryam and I just chat, you know, about what she's doing, Assisi's residents, brainstorming ideas to keep them involved. And ideas for the book."

Cora hadn't told Cisco about the evening she confessed her conflicted religious beliefs to Maryam, but now wasn't a good time to start a long philosophical discussion with him. Maryam had been sympathetic, but her beliefs were so ingrained that she was unable to offer any helpful advice. Then Cora asked Maryam to tell her what the Virgin Mary was like as a woman, hoping to see Mary in a more personal way herself. It might provide the inspiration she was missing. Surprisingly, Maryam seemed embarrassed and reluctant, mentioning only a few well-known facts about Mary instead of the passionate discourse Cora expected from the professed Mary devotee.

Cisco interrupted her thoughts. "I repeat, but?"

Cora plopped down on her bed, leaned against the headrest, and put her feet up.

"I don't know. There's something…I can't really describe it. Maryam drops these cryptic comments about 'Mary' and gets this weird, distracted look, like she's somewhere else, or I'm not even there. I don't know how to take her sometimes." She paused. Cisco had an intuitive common sense that at times supplied answers that escaped her. Maybe he could do that now.

"We'll be talking and with no warning she jumps up, says she has to go, and leaves the building. Sometimes she doesn't even take a jacket. Always about the same time, just before three in the afternoon. Where do you think she could be going?"

"How should I know? What does she say?"

"Just something like Mary or 'Our Lady' told her to do this or that. You probably won't agree, but I'm pretty sure she's referring to the Virgin Mary."

"Like she's talking to her? And she doesn't explain?"

"I haven't asked her to. It seems intrusive. She'd tell me if she wanted me to know, wouldn't she?"

"You should ask her next time." He paused. "I wouldn't put it past you to follow her, but I'm not suggesting that."

Cora chuckled. "Maybe I will. If the time seems right. We'll see."

As with every morning call between them, after it ended, Cora realized how much she missed Cisco. The quiet of the convent, welcome at first, wasn't as comforting as the background noises of home while she worked: the roar of the vacuum, running water and clattering dishes from the kitchen. She even missed the frequent curse words Cisco uttered after some minor mishap or in reaction to TV news. Phone calls were soon over and didn't quite cut it. Well, it would only be another week.

She remembered how their friendship began. Meeting through work, they discovered they had both recently ended relationships. Over lunch or coffee, Cora found confiding in Cisco more helpful than talking to her women friends. There was something reassuring about talking to a man who understood her feelings, rather than a woman taking another woman's side. Cisco really listened and empathized. He, in turn, explained his fear of marriage, the bitter arguments he'd witnessed between his parents, and the painful betrayal during a short-lived marriage of his own that left him crushed and vulnerable. She heard his story with compassion, as he heard hers.

She came to value his casual approach to life, his undemanding appreciation of her, and his decisiveness, elements that had been missing from her old relationship. Over years, they shared the intimate details of each other's lives, until they realized they meant more to each other than sounding boards and their mutual sympathy and fondness developed into romance.

She tore herself away from memories and took a few minutes to straighten the stacks of materials on her desk, sorting out what she had accomplished so she could plan her day.

After a week at the convent, Cora's life, like that of the sisters, had fallen into a pattern: get up early, skip Lauds but join the sisters for daily Mass, chat with Cisco, eat breakfast. When the sisters went off to their jobs or chores, Cora spent the morning circulating—perhaps more accurately, snooping—getting to know the sisters, what each of them did, gaining some sense of their personal lives. Often, she saw Agnes, Bernadette, and, less enthusiastically, Fatima. After lunch she did research or worked on an outline of the book in her room, unless she had appointments at St. Marija's, St. Joseph's, or Assisi Hill.

Most days she had lunch with Maryam at Assisi Manor, a little escape from convent life. Usually she returned to work on the book when the sisters returned to their jobs and community prayer in the afternoon. Other than lunch, Cora took her meals with the sisters, ate dinner in the convent before returning to her room, and chose not to join the nuns for Compline.

Evenings, she could watch television or join the sisters in a common room if she liked, but she found the absence of television noise a welcome break from home, where Cisco had it on most of the day, whether he was watching it or not. Sometimes she just relaxed and read on her Kindle, but more often she felt compelled to finish some writing task or research. The books she had initially placed at her bedside were replaced by books Sister Elizabeth had loaned her. One was a translation of writings by Mother Josepha that she hadn't found time to start yet.

The longer hours and increased activity were rejuvenating. She stayed up later and woke up clear-headed. She felt more energy than she had at home, or since her cancer treatment, and was getting significantly more work done.

At her desk now, she reviewed her to-do list. Her accomplishments were significant—online research, tours, interviews. With Sister Lorita's go-ahead, she had formulated an outline that had some real teeth to it while waiting for Sister Lorita to gather information on the building of Assisi Manor.

She turned to her computer and opened a folder named "Religious History," gratified by the long list of files the folder contained. On paper, she underlined items on her to-do list that had no folder yet and starred items to tackle next.

Then she launched One Note, where her online research data was stored. There were pages for all three Catholic institutions she had researched thus far: Assisi Hill, St. Marija's, and St. Joseph's. She reviewed each page to determine what remained undone.

Two hours later, stiff from sitting, she walked down the hall for coffee, remembering a conversation she'd had with the courageous Winnie Garth. They had set a date for Cora to speak to Assisi Manor's reading group about her novel, *Wawetseka's Tale*. Winnie, who had no self-consciousness about her speaking handicap, had developed clear ways of communicating with concise words and hand motions.

In the kitchen, Cora poured a cup of coffee, heated it in the micro-wave, and returned with it to her room.

It seemed to be a day for focusing on Cora's past. Thinking of Win-nie and Wawetseka triggered a memory of Cora's cancer treatment, one that had made her self-conscious: her radiation mask. To protect vital structures in her neck, it was important that Cora stay motionless while radiation was delivered to specific areas of disease. To guarantee she re-mained still, a form-fitting plastic mask had been made that covered her from head to mid-chest.

She would lie on the radiation table while technicians placed the mask over her head and shoulders and fastened it to the table. It was very tight. She couldn't fully open her eyes, but she could see a little through the slits and the holes in the mesh of the mask. It pressed against her nose and she could barely wiggle her lips, but she could breathe and part her lips enough for her voice to be heard. Her shoulders were tight against the table, but her arms were free.

She heard that some patients thought the experience claustropho-bic, but Cora had found the confinement comforting, comparing it to how a swaddled infant must feel. The comfort was reassuring once the machine began doing its thing, exuding a loud rattling sound as it cir-cled around her head. It made Cora think of an Indian shaman, danc-ing around her, waving a rattle in ceremonious noise-making to frighten demons away. The image probably occurred to her because just before her cancer diagnosis, she had finished writing *Wawetseka's Tale* about the Potawatomi that once lived in Lemont. She pictured a short, scantily clad, dark-skinned man conducting a healing ritual to cure her cancer.

Her technician later told her the noise she heard was from the opening and closing of the gears in the bore of the therapy machine that directed radiation beams to each precise programmed location in her neck. He had laughed when she told him about her "witch doctor."

Now Cora pushed the memory from her mind and forced herself to review her detailed notes about the history of the sisters' order and the photos she had taken with her cell phone.

Like the friars at St. Marija's, the sisters at Assisi Hill were a Slovenian-Austrian order of Franciscans. The Franciscan Fathers at St. Marija's had sent a request to Slovenia for sisters to support their mission. The

Sisters of St. Francis of Christ the Teacher responded, established Assisi Hill, and the connection between the two institutions had lingered to the present day. Although the nuns arrived in the United States as early as 1909, they didn't come to Lemont until 1925.

A few days ago, Cora had toured Assisi Hill Academy, the order's former high school building on the northeast side of the property. The school had been forced to close in 2014 after over sixty years of educating young women. Today the building housed two establishments: a day school for first to eighth grade students with learning disabilities, and a retreat center. The school's gym and acres of outdoor space could be rented for sports or other activities.

A secretary, currently in charge of the facility, had shown Cora around.

"It's sad that the school had to close," Cora said. "I had a friend who went here in the 1970s and she loved it." Cora remembered fondly her own college years at St. Xavier, a women's Catholic college in Chicago that was now co-ed. She had been happy there. She thought young women who attended high school at the Academy would have had a similar pleasant experience.

"Yes, it is sad," the secretary said. "Sister Fatima took it especially hard."

"Sister Fatima?" Cora said. "She was a teacher here?"

"She taught English, but only one class. She was dean and assistant principal. She gave a lot of her life to the girls, devoting herself to their problems, and she was good at her job. She doesn't think her work these days is as fulfilling. She's rather bitter, I'm afraid."

That explained a lot. Not that understanding made it any easier to get along with her, but Cora could be a bit more charitable now.

"What about Sister Agnes and Sister Bernadette? Were they teachers too?"

"Sister Agnes was a biology teacher, but she retired long before the school closed, although she continued to come to lab classes and help out. The students loved her. Sister Bernadette taught first-year algebra and geometry."

Cora forced herself to stop woolgathering and returned to One Note. Since her visit with Sister Elizabeth at St. Joseph Convent, she had copied extensive material from the order's website and downloaded the pictures she took when visiting Heritage Hall, the sarcophagus, and the chapel. *Too much information!* She'd rather be reading what Sister Elizabeth had given her about the life of Mother Josepha—books, pamphlets, and promotional materials about the woman's life.

After browsing a small pamphlet about Mother Josepha and reviewing a translation of her writings, *The Chronicle*, Cora's imagination was captured by the story of the young Josie, who had reluctantly left her native Poland to establish a new life in Chicago at the age of twenty. The young woman had remained devout despite hardship in her native land, only to witness poverty in her adopted country. Cora was struck by her simplicity, shyness, devotion, clear thinking, and courage, and found herself identifying with the young Josie instead of the mature Mother Josepha.

But she would organize her research now and read more that night.

She closed the St. Joseph's file and opened St. Marija's. She had been back to the monastery only once since her initial tour with Father Bozic. On her second visit, he had showed her around the print shop archives and walked her through the contents of the monastery's library, piling a stack of resources on the large oak library table.

"I'm sorry to say that these are the only documents written in English. Most of our records are in Slovenian, including all the newspapers in the print shop. I don't know how we're going to do this. I wish I had the time to sit by your side and translate, but I'm afraid I can't."

Although disappointed, Cora said, "I wouldn't expect you to do that. You've been more than generous already."

"Maybe once you have a sense for how you want to proceed, I can find a lady from the congregation who will be willing."

"That would be wonderful!" she had said.

Actually, she thought now, compared to the two institutions of nuns, dealing with a single place that had only two buildings, both of which saw limited use these days, seemed like the least of her tasks.

She sighed and picked up a paper folder, titled "Other." Before opening it, she looked at the stack next to her laptop with dismay, feeling a chill in the pit of her stomach. Maybe Sister Lorita was right about limiting herself to Assisi Hill. She had a sudden fear of being unable to organize the project into a manageable common theme. She'd only looked at three places so far and the material was vast already.

In addition to One Note pages for the three institutions—St. Marija's,

the Franciscan Sisters of Our Lady, and Assisi Hill—she had accumulat-
ed extensive files titled "Sisters/Nuns," "Saints," and "Sister Josepha".
Another page titled "Maps and Buildings" served to keep perspective.
When she had felt a need to answer some questions about Slovenia and
Poland, she started other pages. There was a "Miscellaneous" page, and,
unable to restrain her curiosity about the unusual material that composed
the stations and prayer valley monuments, she'd compiled a "Stone"
page. Now she opened a page titled "Other Religious Institutions".

A formidable, so far untouched, list appeared of nearly a dozen places
in the Lemont area—retirement homes for priests, seminaries and religious academies, nursing homes and senior residences, and a Carmelite
priory. The priory grounds included the St. Theresa National Shrine
that honored St. Theresa of Lisieux, called The Little Flower, a Carmelite sister.

Saints. Up to now, saints had had little importance in Cora's life, although of course she had grown up knowing about some of the more
popular ones, said prayers to patron saints, and had a few books about
saints. Now here she was, tangentially involved with the canonization
of Mother Josepha, and Father Bozic had mentioned another saint-to-
be, Bishop Frederic Baraga, the first Slovenian missionary to come to
the United States in 1830.

She felt the blood drain from her face and lowered her head into
her hands. What was she doing? If Cisco was here, he would have said
she was once again filling her plate to impossible heights. She hadn't
even begun studying other area institutions. Why punish herself with
so much more?

Because she had a nagging feeling that there was a bigger picture, some
reason why all these orders gravitated to the same place. Cora's approach
to any project was thorough, and she couldn't give up without a try.

Cisco had warned her this was a big job. He seemed to be right again.

"When did you know me to take the easy way out?" she'd asked him
before.

"When did you know me to do things the hard way?" he'd countered.

She smiled at the thought, wishing again that Cisco was here now. Perhaps this was why they worked together so well. After all, she believed,
if two people thought the same, one of them wasn't necessary.

No, she wasn't ready to give up on what she thought was a really good idea. And she knew where to go for help.

She picked up her phone and called her friend and previous partner-in-crime, Frannie Berkowitz. Frannie had grown up in a blue-collar black neighborhood in Chicago, but after she married a white Jewish man, she spent her married life in a predominantly white community. After her husband's death Frannie returned to her roots, moving back into her mother's old two-flat. Cora had given her a job in the office she managed at the time, but had to fire her after less than a year because of Frannie's unorthodox manners and inability to control her tongue, which generated complaints from co-workers.

Oddly, they had remained friends, and in fact the two women got even closer after both had retired, finding a common interest in mysteries, especially those that involved historical events. Although Frannie's outrageous personality and appearance took some getting used to, her loyal friendship and excellent internet skills had proved helpful on more occasions than Cora could count.

Frannie answered the call right away.

"Wondering when I was gonna hear from you, gal," Frannie said without a hello. "What's up? How's it going in Sisterland?"

"It's going," Cora said.

"But you need help, right? Got yourself in too deep in crap and Frannie's got to save your ass again?"

"Could you?" Cora said. "You got time?"

Both women knew the question was facetious. Frannie liked nothing better than to use her computer research skills and was bored out of her mind when she didn't have projects to work on. She and Cora had been involved in a number of adventures, but nothing since Cora's cancer diagnosis. Frannie would be champing at the bit. Cora pictured her friend's eyes lighting up while she put on a sacrificial attitude.

"Lord, lemme just see now…" Frannie said. "Huh. Got my work duds on, sitting here on my black butt working on a cup of coffee, watching *The Talk*. You know I hate to miss Sheryl Underwood and those other hosts are pretty entertaining too. Yeah, I guess I got time. My magic fingers itching to be doing something other than picking my nose. You got something serious happening in that convent? I know you attract weird stuff, gurl. What you got going on?"

Frannie liked excitement and especially anything that smacked of mystery—like their previous escapades—but she was jittery about contact with the supernatural. Although writing the book about Wawetseka had started off innocently enough....

Cora said. "It's all I can do to keep the facts straight on three places so far. I could be missing something important at other organizations, or heading in a wrong direction. I'm just afraid if I stop to gather data to get an overview, I'll lose track of what I'm doing here or go off on a tangent."

"So, you need me to do a down and dirty on other places on your list? Do I got that right?"

"Start with a down and dirty, yeah. Then I'll tell you where I'd like you to dig deeper. Do you mind that we're looking at religious institutions? I mean, I know you're Catholic, but this isn't as exciting as the other things we've worked on together."

"Excuse me. You got me wrong, there, gurl. I got pretty content these last few years, you not dragging me into some supernatural world. Seriously, what makes you think I want to go back there? At least if we stay in them churches I can feel safe we won't be conjuring up no ghosts or funny stuff like we did before. Count me in."

Cora smiled. With her trusted friend on the hunt, it was almost a guarantee that things would start happening. Based on past experiences, the question was whether or not things would happen in a good way.

# Chapter 12

Relieved that Frannie would be taking part of the workload, Cora was a little sorry she hadn't kept the Poor Clares for herself. A contemplative order, the Poor Clares were founded by Clare of Assisi, a close friend of St. Francis. The nuns did not leave their convent and followed very strict rules, praying in their rooms or communally. Cora wondered about that sort of life. Frannie would surely find interviews tricky.

She was also reluctant to hand over the religious institutions that once existed near her house, on land occupied today mostly by private homes. Cora often walked down the streets, remembering a night when abandoned buildings still stood on the properties. The National Guard had staged a practice assault on the buildings that were slated for demolition. They hadn't forewarned residents of the drill. Cora and her neighbors gathered in the street, horrified by helicopters, planes, loud noises, and flashes, thinking they were being invaded.

Well, she couldn't do all the research herself. Frannie was up to the task, and would undoubtedly enjoy the challenge.

The morning had left Cora feeling overwhelmed and a little squirrelly, in need of a change of scenery. The afternoon was sunny and warm—as good a day as any to try the shortcut to St. Marija's that Sister Maryam had suggested. Cora packed up her laptop, a notepad, and her phone. Why was Mother Josepha's biography on her desk, though? She thought she had left it on her nightstand. She intended to read it when she got back—she didn't need a reminder. She picked it up, returned it to the nightstand, and left her room.

With a light step despite carrying her heavy purse and laptop, she found the little bridge. Father Bozic had told her that the pond at St. Marija's was filled from a stream that ran underground from Assisi Hill. Maybe that stream coursed under this bridge in wetter weather, going underground at some point.

Past the bridge was a field through which ran a faint path. She crossed the field and pushed through a thin strip of woods, to come upon, as promised, the Lourdes Grotto, the pond, and the surrounding Stations of the Cross. She was enchanted! What other mysteries were hidden in these places?

Two hours later, Cora was still in the monastery library, intently making notes, when Father Bozic walked in.

"You're not wasting any time, are you?" he asked. "Have you found anything of interest?"

She smiled and leaned back in her chair, thinking how fond she was becoming of the gentle priest. What a relief it was to escape the scandals about priests that had been in the news and explore the good done by the church.

"Oh yes! Your website and Facebook pages were very helpful. I'm going through the newsletters and references you left." She gestured at the books that lay open around her on the library table. "I mentioned it before, but I'm still curious about the stone used for the grotto and the stations. Some of it looks like crystal, with bubbles like little geodes." As she said this, she reached into a pocket and fingered her crystal rosary. "It's so unusual, I can't help but think there has to be some significance to it."

"All I know is, it was ordered from a stone company in the late 1930s." He laughed. "It must have been a huge order. The stone craftsmen here at the time just kept using it up until it was gone. All the monuments were finished by about 1940, before we built the guest house in 1946."

"Why would they go to all that trouble and expense instead of using stone quarried nearby?"

"Good question, but the answer seems to be lost. If you find out, I hope I'm the first to know." He chuckled, then shrugged. "I sometimes wish they had made a different choice. Mosquitoes breed in those little holes in the stone."

She leaned back in her chair. "I doubt I'll be able to spend much time at St. Marija's for a while. I'm expecting a lot of material from Sister Lorita, and I'm reading Mother Josepha's literature at night."

"Did you know that we're involved in a cause for sainthood too? Our deacon is active in the cause for Bishop Frederick Baraga, who came to the Midwest in 1830. He worked with Native Americans, rebuilding missions in northern Michigan that were abandoned by the Jesuits after the French and Indian War."

Cora hadn't known any details. "I have to get over being amazed by all I'm learning. That being said, I'm trying to get as much done as I can while I'm still at the convent. I'll be devoting more time to St. Marija's after I get home."

He sighed and sat in a chair across from her. "Hopefully we won't all be shut down in the meantime."

She looked at him inquisitively. "What do you mean, shut down?"

"The pandemic. It's been officially declared now. Travel is being discouraged, and I've been told to expect restrictions on gatherings. We may have to wear masks, like they do in China. Or even be ordered to stay at home. The Cardinal is trying to figure out how this is going to affect our services, or if we can even have Mass."

"Really! There's no television in my room and I haven't had time to read news since I arrived." She grinned at a sudden thought.

"What's funny?" Father Bozic asked.

"I was just remembering—a month or so ago on television I saw a Chinese policeman arresting a woman who refused to wear a mask. Nothing like that could happen here, of course."

He smiled. "Let's hope not."

She frowned. "I hope it won't interfere with my husband's return home. He's on vacation in Arizona. He's due back next week."

"Surely they'll contain it," he said.

"Yeah." A little worried, she took an opportunity to get his opinion on another matter. "Can I ask you about something that's been bothering me?"

"Of course."

"You know Sister Maryam? At Assisi Hill?"

"Not well, but yes," he said.

"She goes barefoot sometimes, even outside when it's cold. None of the other sisters do that. Do you have any idea why she would?"

"Well, going barefoot is a sort of penitential practice, a self-mortification that contemplative orders believe makes prayer more effective. But we're not contemplative communities." He frowned. "I had no idea she was doing that. Could be to achieve a sense of intimacy, or perhaps for a special intention or a penance? You know, like when people bargain with God for something they want?"

"I've been known to do that. Not very often, though—only nightly!" Cora laughed, and then grew serious again. "Sister Maryam also says Our Lady tells her things. I think she's referring to the Virgin Mary."

"Of course, as Catholics we believe that Mary has appeared on earth, but I think it's more likely Maryam is speaking of Mary figuratively. Meaning Mary would want that, and so she says it as if Mary told her."

Cora thought it went deeper than that, but perhaps she was making too much of her observation. Father didn't seem to think it unusual or important.

The priest leaned back, stretched out his long legs, crossed them at the ankle, folded his arms over his chest, and looked into her eyes. "I don't know much about you as a person, Cora. What makes you want to take on such a big job, especially since you're not heavily involved in the church? Is there something I don't know?"

She avoided his eyes, looking down at her hands on the table in front of her. "I'm very interested in the history of Lemont, and the religious communities here are a big part of that history, yet few people know about them. I think that story should be told. Some say I have a gift for the written word, but I don't know..." She chuckled self-consciously.

"So, it's all about history to you?"

"Yes..." she said, choking on the word. "...No." She paused. "I had cancer, Father, almost five years ago."

"Would you like to tell me about it?" he said.

Suddenly Cora did want to talk about it with this man. She spoke at length, the words tumbling out, about finding out she had cancer, her shock and disbelief, her treatment, and her emotional reaction to the experience.

"I did a lot of pretending," she said. "Not only to family and friends, but to myself. I thought keeping a positive attitude would get me through, and perhaps it did. Everyone kept telling me how brave I was. I didn't think of myself as brave—I just wanted to live and did whatever it took to increase the odds and make the journey as easy as I could.

"Friends kept saying they hoped I'd get a little better every day. But that's not how cancer works. You start off feeling well, and the treatment makes you sick. You get worse every day, not better, because that's what it takes to kill the cancer. And it continues long after the treatment itself is over, sometimes years after. For some people it never ends.

"One day the treatment is finished, and you want to celebrate. But it's the biggest letdown. No matter how many times your doctors told you the effects are cumulative, that you will still get worse, that it will take time, you fool yourself. You completed treatment, you're proud of what you did, and now you'll be well. But you aren't, and in fact you may be worse than ever."

The priest said, "Most people don't think of that."

"On top of that, you've come to depend on your doctors and technicians, and on seeing them every day. But when treatment ends, you don't have an appointment for a month. You feel deserted, and lonelier than you ever felt in your life.

"There was a time, months after treatment, when I still could only eat oatmeal and Ensure, and my nausea and pain were still getting worse instead of better, and I didn't think I could make it after all."

She reached into a pocket for her handkerchief and blotted her eyes.

"I got up in the middle of the night and found my rosary." She touched the beads in her pocket when she returned her handkerchief to it, and left her hand there. "I prayed to God for patience and strength, and said the rosary over and over until I finally fell asleep. I don't know if God heard me, but I had to do something and there was nowhere else to turn."

"So, you turned to God. Were you angry with Him?" Father asked.

"Not angry, no. I always felt responsible for my own life. I don't know if it was Him, or me, or the doctors, or just because it wasn't my time yet. But whatever, I got better." She grinned weakly. "As you can see, I'm here."

"But you were frightened."

"I was." Up until then Cora had remained composed, if a little wet-eyed, almost as if she was talking about someone else, but now her voice broke. "I must confess—I mean, not formally confess, I haven't done that in years and I'd want to prepare…" She gave a nervous snicker. "I know, this isn't funny."

She composed her thoughts while he said nothing, watching her with his warm brown eyes. It was a relief to be telling her fears to someone, someone she didn't feel she had to pretend with, instead of struggling with her thoughts alone.

She took a deep breath and looked down at the table. "I don't know if I believe, I mean really *believe*, in God. I follow the rules, for the most part, not going to Mass so much, but I pray and I try to be a good person, and I don't think I'm committing any big sins. That counts, doesn't it? I find it hard to believe that we won't be judged on the good life we led in its entirety, not whether we dotted all the i's and crossed all the t's.

"But is being a good person enough? I can't *feel* Him anymore. I can't *believe* that there's really someone out there taking care of me."

She rubbed her cheeks with both hands, then lifted her head to meet his gaze. "I *want* to believe! I talk to Him all the time, as if He *was* there. But it's more like something I should do, or just in case. Prayer is the habit of a lifetime, but I'm not sure how meaningful it is."

The priest smiled gently. "Prayer is not a bad habit to have. So, if you can't believe in God, you can't believe in life after death, and that frightens you."

She closed her eyes in relief. He got it. "Yes. Exactly."

"It's quite characteristic for miracles to begin with doubt about faith, you know, especially Eucharistic miracles."

"I didn't know that." She reached for her handkerchief and blotted her eyes again, then touched her rosary another time.

"The purpose of miracles is to bear witness to some truth. Catholics are not required to believe in any particular miracle, but are asked to believe that God *can* intervene in some extraordinary way. Extraordinary as in unexplainable by the laws of scientific fact and human reasoning."

"Miracles are always about belief in some way?"

He nodded. "For example, there are many instances when a miracle occurs during consecration. A priest feels doubt about the real presence

THE MIRACLE AT ASSISI HILL


of Christ in the host, and then the host will bleed or change to living flesh and blood in his hands."

He cupped his hands in front of him as if holding something precious. "Did you know that fragments of those hosts hundreds of years old have been documented to be still intact today, verified by contemporary scientists? Samples containing intact heart muscle or blood cells have been found that appear as if they were taken that very day from a living person. One such example from 750 AD has been confirmed by the advisory board of the World Health Organization as recently as 1971."

She let what he told her sink in and then said, "What do I do?"

Instead of giving her an answer, he asked a question. "Can you remember a time when you *did* believe?"

A specific memory stood out and she nodded. "It was embryology class, when I was in college, working on my bachelor's degree. We were studying human fertilization. Did you know that as soon as the man's sperm penetrates the woman's egg, the egg's lining hardens and becomes impermeable? If the egg was entered by more than one sperm, there would be chaos in the embryo, upsetting the signals for division and growth into a new human life. This all happens in an instant. When I heard that, I had a moment of wonder. How could this level of complexity, indeed all the complexity of life, especially human life and reasoning, be due to mere spontaneous survival of the fittest, evolution, pure chance? There had to be a guiding hand in it, a superior all-powerful being. There had to be a God."

"So how did you lose that logic?"

"The logic is still there. But so is the doubt. Sometimes I feel foolish thinking that there is anything after death. To me, one follows the other. If there is life after death, there is a God, but if there is no God, then there is no life after death. It should be easy for me, because I've had certain experiences. But I'm so grounded in science and the material world, I always think there must be an alternate reason for the unnatural things I've seen. I just haven't been smart enough to find it yet."

"What experiences are you talking about?"

Cora hesitated. She'd had odd experiences most of her life—things that moved unexplainably, disappeared and then appeared again, an encounter with a ghost at St. James Cemetery, and an adventure with a friend who said he had met a ghost. But she had not linked her super-natural experiences to religious experiences. Did she want to admit any of this to this priest?

Before she could decide, Father stopped her. "I don't think you're going to get more work done today. Let's go downstairs to the kitchen for some coffee. Maybe the ladies left some bakery goods."

Relieved to break the growing tension, Cora followed him downstairs. On the way, she told him about the ghost that had taken revenge, not on her, but on her friends. When she was finished and they were seated at a table in the church hall, Father said, "I'm not going to comment on your experience, but certainly, providing you believe it was real, that should be enough to convince you there *is* life after death."

She shook her head. "You'd think so, wouldn't you? But my life is practical, material. I feel that I control my own life, and it's up to me to fix things when they don't work. It's hard for me to let anyone else, even God, take care of matters for me. When things don't make sense, I just don't let myself believe what they indicate, even though the experience really happened. I'm like St. Thomas, Doubting Thomas. I trust only what I see, hear, or feel."

"Maybe that's at the heart of your disbelief, Cora. It's not a matter of God's existence, but your inability to trust Him fully, that's standing in the way of your peace."

"What do I do about it?"

"You're tied to the conventional world. You think of existence in terms of making the most of the life you're in now, not in terms of preparing for another life. That's very common. Your desire to do good works is a start, but you would benefit by thinking about how to rely on God in-stead of your own actions. That's the way to peace."

Cora smiled. "Like the hymn. 'Take my yoke upon you, I will give you peace,' or something like that."

He returned her smile. "Sort of. The hymn can serve as a reminder, surely."

He was right that her focus was on the natural life. She was so con-fused! The concepts of ghosts and miracles and communicating with God or the saints were mind-boggling. How could she believe in one thing and deny another? How did it affect her life, her death, her preparation for life after death, if there was such a thing?

She'd been here a week and her research wasn't leaving her time to work out her objective of getting closer to God. She was allowing commitments to be an excuse and procrastinating once again. Or was the fact that she was so easily distracted from her desire to make God a focus of her life telling her something? Would she ever take the time to make it happen?

Thinking about these matters was not only frustrating, it was frightening. Her mind felt saturated. She had to think about it later. Right now, she had things to do. Tomorrow was another day.

# Chapter 13

Cora's eyes flew open in the darkness. She was terrified, consumed by a feeling of doom. Her heart beat wildly, a charge passing through her as if mind and body were disassociating, making her feel weightless, floating, watching herself from a distance at the same time that she fought to remain within her physical body.

Is this what it felt like to *not* be here? To be dead? When dead, would she still be able to reason, even if her thoughts were lost in panic? Would her mind, her memory, stay with her soul after it left her body? If there was such a thing as a soul, surely God would let her keep her mind.

No! If these thoughts continued, she might really die. She must regain control, think of something else, get up, move around.

As if crawling out of quicksand, she hauled herself upright and stood next to her bed, tingling from head to toe, clutching the edge of the mattress for support. After a moment she pulled herself together, then reached for her phone and checked the time. Four in the morning. The chapel should be empty at this hour. *Do something active. Move!*

Deep breaths slowed her panic attack. She threw pants and a sweatshirt over her pajamas and added a heavy sweater. If she tried to go back to sleep, her terror would return. Better to face her fears with a clear mind, not a panicked one. She left her room, closed the door with a faint click, and walked softly down the hallway, feeling a bit like a criminal even though the sisters' rooms were in another wing and she wasn't disturbing anyone.

She reached the chapel and went in. A soft glow from a side chapel was the only light in the room. She sat in a back corner, turning her chair to view a statue of Mary and the infant Jesus there. Cora was fond of this statue because, unlike most artists, the sculptor had portrayed Mary as the young teenager she was when Jesus was born. The Virgin sat with baby Jesus standing on her lap, her cheek resting against the toddler's soft hair, a loving expression on her girlish face.

"Mary, help me," Cora whispered, burying her own face in her hands.

After a moment she raised her eyes and stared into Mary's stone ones. Cora sensed her pleas were being heard. In her mind, Mary was not in the statue in front of her but looking down from heaven with compassion, her arm extended as if reaching for Cora's hand.

Cora thought she was in the right place. The solemn silence felt tangible, as if the world was focused on her words, if she could only use the right ones. She glanced around to be certain she was alone. For her, religion was a very private matter, not to be shared with others. Yet her thoughts began to come from her in whispers, as if speaking instead of silent prayer would prompt a reply from Mary.

"You know, Mary, I usually go direct to God the Father with my requests. I'm praying, as our catechism promises, that you will put in a word for me. I know I've been neglecting you, that I don't know God as well as I should, or your Son, nor do I even know you. But I pray to you because, like me, you are a mother, and I need a mother tonight.

"Help me to not be so terrified of death. I didn't think much about death when I had cancer. It was too near and I was chicken. Then when the cancer was over, I had faced the beast, and I wanted a break from unpleasant thoughts. But cancer left its scars—oh yes, it did. Because now I keep fearing the cancer will return, or some other disaster will strike, like the hand of doom hovering over me. I know I can't live forever, but I don't feel prepared!"

She heard a sharp crack and looked around the chapel again. Nothing. Probably just night-time noises, building settling or radiator popping. Although she felt a bit silly about talking in an empty room, she crossed hers arms over her chest and persisted.

"Like Father Bozic said, I'm tied to this conventional world. If I knew what life after death was like, it would be easier. But I have no confidence in my guesses. Help me to trust in God that there is life after this one and that it will be good. I've always believed I have to prove my worth in this life in order to be happy in the next. But Father said I have to transfer my confidence from myself and trust in God completely. But

I'm so used to doing everything myself, it feels wrong to let God solve my problems. I don't think I can detach myself from this world. Can you help me regain the trust I once had? That moment in college I described to Father Bozic?"

The words she had said to Father Bozic came to her again. "Take my yoke upon you...I will give you peace." The melody and lyrics echoed in her head. She was calm now, but did not yet feel she could leave the issue in Mary's hands. Her prayers turned to silent ones.

*I try to get closer to God, and I try to be compassionate. But it's hard to think in terms of preparing for another life when all I've ever done is struggle to make the most of this one!*

*I wish Cisco could help me, but he doesn't believe. How can I help him believe if I'm doubtful myself? I know, I'm making excuses and using Cisco as an excuse too. I keep taking on too many projects, keeping myself too busy to think about my faith.*

*But even if I wonder if God's really there, I pray, because I'm not sure. I follow the dictates of the church, too chicken to believe there's no God or after-life. But sometimes I feel like a hypocrite, silly me, preparing for something I can't fully believe in. I truly want to believe in my heart.*

If only Cisco was here now! Maybe he wouldn't understand her fear, but he would somehow make her feel better. If he was here, maybe she wouldn't feel so alone or even be having these thoughts.

Cora heard rustling behind her. Someone entered the chapel, and Cora turned to watch Sister Fatima walk up the center aisle. Fatima must have seen her sitting there, her chair askew, but the nun didn't acknowledge Cora's presence. Instead, she passed by and took a seat at the far end of the row immediately in front of the altar. She wondered if the nun had been in the chapel long enough to have heard her whispers.

*How embarrassing! She's probably annoyed to find me sitting in the place she wanted to go,* Cora thought. *Well, I'm annoyed too, that Fatima of all people interrupted my solitude. I wonder what she has to pray about that brings her here in the middle of the night.*

Attempting to ignore the nun's presence, Cora tried to resume her conversation with Mary. *What haven't I done that I feel I need to accomplish in this world?*

She had been a good wife to Cisco, loved and cared for him, raised their children and loved her family, saved her money to leave them comfortable. Even though she got bitchy now and then, surely they understood.

She volunteered in her community, donated time and money generously. She was loyal to her friends and helped them when they needed it. People liked her well enough, she thought. There were projects, like the books she'd written and the one she was working on. Would she feel like her life was a failure if it ended before she finished her projects?

All of this was the be-good-and-get-rewarded belief. It hadn't brought her closer to God.

How had the saints done this? What was it about saints that allowed them to put everything on earth aside and think only of God? *Nothing in my life resembles the lives of saints. I can understand and admire saints who proved themselves through good works, like Mother Theresa of Calcutta. And now Mother Mary Josepha. Have I done enough good works? But, if I were to devote myself to helping the poor and needy now, or some other charitable work, how would that affect Cisco and others in my life?*

Her thoughts were interrupted by a soft cough from the front of the chapel. Turning her head a little, Cora saw Fatima from the corner of her eye. The woman was still sitting in the same spot, looking at the floor, unmoving.

What had brought Fatima to the chapel this early? Apparently, she had been a kind and sympathetic counselor for students at one time. Why was the sister so judgmental and critical now? Why did she have such a poor opinion of Maryam? Maybe it was because, now that Maryam was the only young religious living at Assisi Hill, Fatima struggled to bridge the superior-student relationship and treat Maryam as an equal. Perhaps she thought today's young women were too secular-minded to embrace religious life. Or maybe Maryam did something that prompted Fatima's disdain. Something beyond the misunderstanding over a cat blocking the convent doorway.

The nun's presence at this hour could be coincidental, but maybe she was snooping. Had she been watching Cora ever since Cora arrived at the convent? Irritated by Cora's friendship with Maryam, perhaps?

Cora hadn't come to the chapel to think about Fatima. Whatever the reason the nun was here, there was no peace here any longer. Cora took a final look at the statue of Mary, made the sign of the Cross, stood, and left the chapel. Fatima never looked up.

Cora Tozzi, *History of the Religious Institutions of Lemont*
(Chicago, Madonna Press, 2024), 35–41

*"It is always so: God allows sadness in our lives,*
*but He also consoles us. As much as I was able to,*
*I reassured myself with the thought that whatever*
*I did, I would do it for the greater glory of God."*
—*The Chronicles of Venerable Mother Josepha of Chicago*

### Josie's Journal
### Chicago, November 28, 1886

My heart is heavy this evening. I am too sad to sleep, but perhaps I will be more accepting of God's will after I write down my thoughts.

The evening began well enough when we entered our apartment. Mama looked at me with suspicion, eying the ragged old woman at my side. She tapped her foot rapidly on the floor, like she does when annoyed. "What is this, Josie?"

"Father Vincent says Busia needs a place to stay." I looked at Mama with what I hoped she would understand was an appeal to her usually generous nature.

"Always a place to stay," she said, and then closed her eyes and drew in a deep breath. "And always our house." But she stepped aside and waved toward the bedroom off our dining room.

Busia and I went into the bedroom, my hand on her arm. Her stringy gray hair was matted, tangled, and obviously had not been washed in some time. I would not be surprised to find lice. She had an unpleasant odor, too. Perhaps she had soiled herself. Before anything else, I would give her a bath.

I helped her remove her coat, which was too thin for November in Chicago. I piled it on a chair next to the bed and placed my own scarf over the coat. I can easily knit myself another.

Busia began to cough, doubling over with the effort, her cheeks flushed. She might have a fever. I would have to tell Mama to watch that she did not get sick, too.

"Let us get you washed up and comb out that hair, Busia. Then I will make you some soup and hot tea," I said, when the coughing had ceased. "Soon you will be well, with a warm bed and good food."

The hope and gratitude in the old woman's eyes were as clear as her desperation had been earlier that afternoon.

I thought we were done with poverty when we escaped persecution in Poland. I believed our troubles were at an end, and indeed, for our family, we are very fortunate. But many in Chicago, indeed throughout the country, face economic disaster. Things have gotten no better on the streets in the past few years. Homeless elderly women and young girls are not uncommon. Father Vincent knows we have space in our three-bedroom apartment now that only Mama and I live here.

Much has changed in our lives since Papa died this past August. Theo is married and lives in his own apartment with his pregnant wife, and of course Frances and Katy live in their convents in Milwaukee and San Antonio. Rosalie and Adam live nearby, but are busy with their many children and church responsibilities. So, Mama and I are alone.

Dear Papa is greatly missed, but now we have room for the unfortunate women who otherwise would walk the streets, cold and hungry. Helping the needy gives me great joy, to see their faces light up when I serve their favorite foods or patch or sew new clothes for them, or bake a cake, much of which would go to waste with only Mama and me to eat it. I teach them to love Jesus, how to pray, and I find ways to get them things they need. These things strengthen my own love of God. It is a circle: love for Jesus leads to love for people, and loving people increases love for Jesus.

Mama only grumbles a little, and then becomes quite welcoming to our guests. But often there is dismay and reluctance on her face when I come home with a new unfortunate in tow, or when there is not enough space for our visitors and she has to share her bed with me to make my room available. Perhaps she thinks we have done enough, that it is time to let others take care of the needy, or she fears it could get to the point that we must live in corners of our own home and stumble over children sleeping on our floors, like our life had been before we left Poland. This memory is sad for her, and she must be lonely now that she has only me for company. And I am busy, of course, busier than ever with my activities at St. Stanislaus and my dressmaking shop.

Mama is no longer young, and after all these years of helping others, she probably feels she deserves quiet comfort as she grows older. I think she gives in because she knows how important helping the needy is to me. I feel the misery and sufferings of others and it seems to me that I could not love Jesus or expect Heaven if I were concerned only about myself and my mother. I feel a persistent urge to sacrifice myself for others.

But tonight, Mama went to the kitchen without a word while I took Busia to our bathroom and filled the tub with hot water. While she bathed I took her soiled and smelly clothes to the basement and put them in a washtub to soak. They would have to be boiled.

I went into the kitchen where Mama was making dinner. I held a nightgown of hers. "Can Busia wear this tonight? She is near your size and has nothing except her dirty clothes soaking."

Mama looked at the nightgown. It used to be her favorite but she had newer ones. She sighed, and then she nodded. "Do not do her laundry tonight. I will look for some clothes to replace hers, if you have not given all of mine away," she said.

Busia had little to say during dinner, eating with her gaze fixed on the table. "You are not only kind but a good cook," she said to Mama after she finished. She returned to the bedroom and soon I heard snores, although it was still early in the evening.

Mama and I went into the living room. Mama had mending to do, and I had to finish some fancywork on a dress I had promised Mrs. Stolarski would be ready for her son's wedding that weekend. John Grabiec had told Mama he would come to visit and to expect him at eight this evening, after the finance committee meeting at St. Stanislaus. John was a well-to-do businessman, a generous widower who was head of the finance committee. And he wanted to marry me.

I had already put John off. At another wedding two months ago, John led me onto the dance floor and proposed to me. I like John well enough and should be grateful for his attention. He is not only handsome and wealthy, but a kind and generous man, devoted to his religion, with two sweet young daughters who need a mother. The single women in the parish think him the best catch.

"John," I had said. "If there is any man I would want to marry, it would be you. But my heart is devoted to God, and it would not be fair to your daughters. I cannot give you or them the attention you deserve from a wife or mother. My mind is only on God and how I can serve Him. And I have my mother to care for."

"Your mother can live with us," he protested. The expression on his face told me he realized his argument was weak.

"Mama does not want to live off others, but to make a home with me. Theo would welcome her, and so would Rosalie and Adam, but she does not want to disrupt their young families. Even before Papa died, it was Mama and me together," I said. Katy in San Antonio had come into my mind then, how my sister and I shared a bond like Mama and I did. A pain stabbed my heart. How I missed Katy!

"But, Mama aside, it is not good for me to marry any man, John. You deserve better," I told him.

Since that occasion we had remained friendly, but it was awkward when we met. I wondered why he wanted to see us tonight. It seemed Mama was just as baffled as I was. John had left word at the church that he needed to discuss something with me, but had not explained what that was.

I was also a little apprehensive, wondering if I had made my feelings clear. I hoped he was not going to press his offer of marriage, or that he and Mama had not cooked up some plan. Surely John would not make things difficult.

There was a knock on the door. When I answered, it was not John but a man with a telegram addressed to Mama.

"It is from the Sisters of Charity," I said, my hand shaking a little as I held the envelope. Telegrams often do not tell good news. But I did not want to alarm Mama, so I said, my voice light, "Maybe they are planning some surprise for Katy and want us to participate. Perhaps some special award. I bet that is it. She must have done something that she will be recognized for, out there where the wind turns around and blows back."

Mama did not believe me. "Why did they send a telegram, instead of a letter, for such a thing?"

"Maybe they just realized they left it too long to tell us."

Katy wrote to us every week, long letters full of enthusiasm. She had finished her training as a nurse and delighted in this calling, giving herself unselfishly to corporeal works of mercy. Her letters told not only about her hospital activities in the city of San Antonio, but how she tended the sick on farms in surrounding areas. In one letter some weeks ago, she confessed that she sometimes stopped to visit a small village of Indians who lived some four miles outside the city, and how sad their existence was.

*"Mother Superior is not too happy that I stop to see them. She says we cannot be sure it is safe. But these people need me more than any other, and are so grateful for the little things I can do and bring to them, like bandages and simple medicines."*

"Is she not worried about Geronimo?" Mama asked at the time. "Did I not read that he is to be tried for his crimes in San Antonio? His friends might cause trouble."

"Mama, you worry too much," I told her. "The Indians are friendly now, and Geronimo no longer a threat. Besides, you know how sweet and lovable Katy is. Surely the people in this village are grateful and love her for her cheerful nature."

Most recently, Katy told us she had selected her religious name. She would be known as Sister Catherine Marie. It was unusual that a novice was allowed to keep her given name, but Katy had presented her argument with much passion.

*"They finally agreed when I convinced them I wished to take the name of Catherine of Siena, who, like me, devoted her life to God at the early age of seven, instead of Catherine of Alexandria, for whom Mama named me."*

With these thoughts in our mind, we both stared at the unopened telegram.

"I bet it's an announcement about taking her final vows. They might send a telegram for that reason," I said.

Mama smiled proudly. "It is too far for us to go, of course."

"The imp! They should have known her when we did." I forced a short laugh I did not feel, and saw my own fear in my mother's face.

I sat on the davenport next to Mama and tore open the envelope.

*"We are extremely sad to tell you that our much-loved Sister Catherine Marie has left us. She had been tending a sick farmer, and on the way home her buggy struck some obstacle and Sister was flung to the ground. She was brought unconscious to the convent, where she died of her injuries several days later. Sister Catherine's funeral will take place on December 1 and she will be buried in our community cemetery. We take some consolation in knowing that she is now with her beloved Jesus."*

"Why?" Mama cried, tears streaming down her cheeks, clutching her chest in agony. "Katy is only eighteen years old! Why did God take her so young? What is happening to my family?"

I knelt in front of Mama and wrapped my arms around her, but I was just as devastated. We cried together until no more tears would come, and still my throat and chest burned, my mouth filled with bitter fluid, my head pounded with the repeated question Mama had asked. "Why?" Over and over, the only word we could say.

My mind was full of questions the telegram did not answer. Was Katy alone when the accident happened? Who found her, and how long had she been lying there? Was she unconscious or in pain? Had she made peace with God before she died? Would I ever know the answers to these and other questions?

As I write this now, my mind is full of images of Katy as a young girl. Many times, we sat together gazing out her bedroom window at church steeples in the distance, Katy bubbling with happiness as she conversed lovingly with our Lord. I take consolation that Katy died like a saint, serving a sick person. I picture San Antonio surrounded by barren plains, Katy driving a buggy, alone and happy, and then the buggy jolting and turning over, and Katy flying to strike her head, perhaps, on some rock. Sweet little Katy, now with her Lord in Heaven. I should be happy for her but it is too painful. I will never see her in this world again.

As I tried to console Mama, we heard another knock at the door and I remembered that John was coming. He immediately saw my distress and reached out to hold my hands. "What happened?" he asked.

I could not look at him. "The worst possible tragedy. Katy, my sweet sister, the daughter of my heart...we just found out she was killed in Texas."

John pulled me into the parlor, where he went to Mama and hugged her. Then he turned to me and took me in his arms.

"I cannot find words," he said, his lips against my hair and his voice breaking. "It is, as you say, the greatest tragedy. Let me think how I can help."

Presently he released me, and we sat next to each other on the sofa, me in the middle holding Mama's hand on one side and John's on the other. I passed the telegram to John to read, since I was too upset to read it to him.

When the story was all told and we had regained some composure, John said, "Let me bring Rosalie and Theo here, so you can tell them. Then I will arrange for a carriage to take all of you to San Antonio."

"What good will that do?" I asked, my voice shaking. "We could never get there in time for the funeral, even with a relay of horses. It is too far."

"Then I will talk to Father Vincent. I will ask him to arrange a requiem service here at St. Stanislaus on the day of Katy's funeral. We will not be present but we will be united in spirit. I am sure Father will agree."

"Yes, I am sure he will. But Sister Frances, my sister in Milwaukee. She must be told, and she must come too."

"Certainly, I will arrange that. Do not worry about any details. You have only to ask and I will be here. Now let me get your family." He stood and reached for his coat.

I followed him to the door. Compelled to speak my mind, I put my hand on his arm to stop him from leaving. "I do not know what Mama and I would have done if you had not been here. I cannot tell you how much your kindness means. How fortunate we are that you asked to visit this particular evening." Suddenly a thought struck me. "Did you already know about Katy, and that is why you came here to help us?"

The surprise on his face was honest. "No, it was a different matter entirely, but that is of no consequence now. Another time."

I still wondered if he had wanted to talk to me again about marriage. I looked away for a moment and then directly into his eyes.

"You are a good man, John. The best man. I am so sorry I could not be more to you."

He touched my cheek fondly. "I know that, Josie. It is not right for you, and I am sorry too. But we will always be friends."

"Why did you come tonight then?" I asked.

"I have some ideas about how to help the unfortunate, the people you take in from the streets. I wanted your opinion."

I had forgotten Busia. How could I care for her now with our family in mourning? I sighed. Perhaps she would distract me from my grief.

# Chapter 14

"I'm going over to St. Marija's this morning," Cora told Cisco. She had gotten a little sleep after returning to her room from the chapel, but felt sluggish. "Father Bozic found a woman from the center who's willing to translate for me. I'm going to meet her and we'll set up dates to go over old records."

"That's good," Cisco said. She thought he sounded tired this morning too. Maybe the visit wasn't working as well as when it began. He wouldn't have wanted to tell Cora that, since the golf trip was her idea. Then again, maybe she was imagining it because she was down this morning herself.

"How about you? Where are you golfing today?" Cora put her phone on speaker and tossed it on the bed while she rummaged through her voluminous purse, irritated that everything dropped to the bottom, making it difficult to find anything easily.

"Oh yeah." Cisco paused. "We're going back to Barney's club. Maybe we'll just play nine holes today."

"Nine? Is Barney pooping out on you? You always want to play eighteen."

"Maybe it's for the best. I'm kind of tired."

"Really? Do you feel okay?" Cora stopped checking her purse and searched the closet for a top, chose one pretty much at random. Physical complaints rarely bothered Cisco, but he had cardiac stents.

"Don't worry, I'm fine. Guess I'm not sleeping as well as I do at home."

"That's probably it." Cora had wanted Cisco to get checked for sleep apnea, since he sometimes breathed irregularly at night, but he insisted he didn't need that. She'd bring it up again when they got home.

The call left her missing Cisco tremendously. She felt close to tears, thinking about how much she wanted to be home with him again. She had come here to be alone and work out personal issues, but she'd spent little time doing that. The convent was not her life.

She shrugged into the top, then frowned. It didn't look right with these slacks. She changed to the dark grey ones, closed her purse, slung it over her shoulder, and left her room.

The day was sunny and unseasonably warm, and Cora felt a need for physical activity. She decided to take the pleasant walk to St. Marija's. She paused at the grotto in front of the statue of Our Lady of Lourdes, with only a silent "hi" and "goodbye" to the Virgin Mary. Not wanting to restart her earlier disturbing thoughts, she moved on quickly toward the monastery.

She spent the morning in the monastery library reviewing additional materials Father Bozic had left. Her spirits lifted as she worked. Before she knew it, it was nearly one o'clock. She quickly ate a sandwich and bag of potato chips she'd brought with her.

When the translator arrived, Cora was delighted to meet her. Fifty-ish, tall and mildly obese, with dishwater-blond hair and the shadow of a mustache, Janna spoke Slovenian as well as un-accented English. The two women found common ground with shared interests in history and choral music.

"This is exciting," Janna said. "I've never met a writer, and I love old records and looking for answers. This is going to be fun." They agreed to meet at St. Marija's every Wednesday afternoon.

"If this pandemic situation will let us," Janna said. "Did you hear? They're talking about suspending international travel and closing theaters and restaurants. Can you believe it? They may even ask everyone to stay home and work from there. It's like some disaster movie come to life."

Cora shook her head. "I've been a bit out of the loop." Maybe Cisco should come home right away, before he got stuck in Arizona. She'd call him when she got back to her room. She reached for her phone to check for date conflicts, but couldn't find it.

She rummaged in her purse, then emptied it on the table. No phone. She patted all her pockets—pants, top, jacket—then did it twice more. The phone wasn't in any of them, or on the table, under books or papers.

Janna double-checked the numerous piles of research materials, looked on chairs and the floor.

"What's your number?" Janna asked, pulling out her own phone. Cora told her. She entered the number, but no ring tone sounded close by, and the call went to voicemail.

Cora tried to remember everything she did before leaving her room that morning. She had the phone when she talked to Cisco, then she had changed her pants. The phone must be either in a pocket in the original pair or she had set it on the bed and not picked it up again.

"It's like missing an arm," she joked, though her pleasant mood was ruined. "It must be in my room, but now finding my phone is all I'll think about. Does that happen to you?"

"Absolutely," Janna said. "It's hard to imagine life without it. If I'm not checking email or texts, I'm making notes or playing games. Wasting way too much time!"

"Isn't that true? It's essential but it's also a curse. Without it you feel like you're cut off from the world."

"And how did it ever get so crucial that people have to be able to reach us every minute of the day? No wonder we've forgotten how to relax."

A few minutes later, Cora was walking back to Assisi Hill. As she passed the grotto and went through the strip of woods to enter the field, she realized this was the same field where she had first met Sister Maryam, before beginning cancer treatment.

She crossed the field and started over the little bridge, then paused as something below caught her eye: a large pile of stones along one side of the slope. Scrutinizing both sides of the dry watercourse below, she noticed more piles at intervals. Some were barely noticeable, overgrown with weeds and other foliage, and wouldn't be seen once the branches leafed out. Beyond the curve of the gully, it was impossible to tell how far the piles extended.

Reminded of the monuments in the gardens at St. Marija's, Cora felt compelled to investigate. She reached for her phone to check the time, then laughed. She didn't have the phone, which was why she was hurrying back to her room. Despite her sense of urgency, curiosity nagged. Did this property belong to the convent, or to the monastery? Maybe neither, but it was certainly private. She was a guest at both places and didn't want to reward their generosity by trespassing.

She wrestled with herself for another minute, but curiosity won out. Tomorrow's forecast called for rain, and she had appointments after lunch. It might be days before she could get back here. A swift glance around confirmed that she was alone. No one would know if she investigated. She returned to the foot of the bridge, looking for a way to safely descend into the steep, wild ravine.

At some distance, leaning on its side and almost covered by grasses and weeds, was a small signpost. *Grotto & Stations*, the sign said. *Warning. Enter at your own risk! Dangerous walkways. Not responsible for injuries.* There seemed to be no pathway in the thick weeds and brush, but Cora pushed through, working her way to the bottom, grabbing branches of scrub brush now and then to steady herself.

Once at the bottom, she spotted an overgrown path and followed it. Eventually, she discovered a rough monument composed of rocks and stones of many sizes and types, brown, yellow, and gray, some moss-covered. The structure was about eight feet tall and six feet wide, shaped like a "C", with a stone crucifix on top. A copper plaque was embedded at eye level, weathered to blue, depicting Christ carrying the cross.

Cora doubted these Stations of the Cross were still being visited. It was likely the sisters at Assisi Hill found it easier to visit nearby St. Marija's and had stopped maintaining the hazardous ravine. She wondered if there were snakes. Nonetheless, she followed the ravine further, curious to see if other stations remained intact or had crumbled. If she had her phone, she would have been snapping photos to study in more detail later.

The footing was tricky, but the ground was dry. Before long, her pants and jacket were covered with tiny burrs from brittle, dry weeds. It would be a job to get all of them off. Maybe she'd just throw these clothes into a plastic bag until she got home. Maybe Cisco would remove them for her when he got back, an even better idea.

She kept walking along the base of a ravine, dwarfed between steep walls twenty-five feet tall. Looking up, the feeling of isolation from the outside world was enhanced by a cloudless blue sky. The valley was more than a hundred feet from one side to the other at its top, about forty feet across at the bottom, filled with a wilderness of dry, leafless shrubs, weeds, and grasses, and a mere trickle of a stream down the center. More Stations of the Cross came into view on both sides, but it was impossible for Cora to cross the rocky, muddy stream bottom for a closer look. Unless she came across a better spot ahead, she would have to retrace her steps. She opted to continue in the same direction. The ravine would have to end somewhere, because Main Street and St. Marija's cemetery both lay in the direction it was running.

Moving north, each station was about a hundred feet from the next. After the fourth station, the ravine curved to the left and ran west. Here was a small bridge over the stream and a more defined path that led up the east slope, bordered by rows of cantaloupe-sized rocks. But Cora wanted to see where the ravine ended. Her sense of urgency about the phone was gone. She was caught up in a spell that was at once captivating, mystical, magical, ethereal.

Beyond the curve were two more stations, and still another could be seen ahead. To her surprise, Cora realized she was no longer alone. Someone was kneeling on the rough ground in front of the next station. As she got closer, Cora recognized Sister Maryam.

How appropriate. Cora grinned. Who else would be down here but the mysterious Sister Maryam? It was surely after 3:00 P.M. now—this must be the secret place Maryam ran off to in the afternoons. What was she doing, though?

Cora's inclination was to either draw back and watch unseen or leave, but again curiosity drove her on. As she approached, she noticed that Maryam was barefoot today despite the chill and the rough, muddy ground. She wasn't wearing a jacket either. And she wasn't doing anything except staring at a spot above the station, where a small tree, no more than a shrub, grew. Was she praying? Did this station have some significance for her?

A thick branch of the tree seemed to be encased in pale fog that appeared slightly brighter than the surrounding area. Why would fog appear on such a sunny afternoon? The branch was bent as if a heavy weight sat on it, yet nothing was there. A low buzzing, in a cadence resembling speech but without words, seemed to originate from that spot.

Maryam gave no sign of having noticed Cora, despite the fact that she hadn't concealed her approach and was now only ten feet away. The nun's hands were pressed together in prayerful pose, fingertips touching the base of her chin, a smile of total delight on her face, her eyes bright, her attention on the tree and foggy patch absolute. She nodded her head and murmured, "Of course. I will always do anything you ask."

Maryam wasn't talking to her, Cora realized. Then who was she talking to? No one else was here. Cora scrutinized the tree. It looked the same: the bent branch, the puzzling fog. What was going on?

As Cora watched, feeling a little dizzy, Maryam continued to respond as if she were in conversation with some unseen being. Cora was mystified. Perhaps she, and not Maryam, was delusional. But no. A truck rumbled past on the road near the top of the ravine. Trucks would not appear in a delusion.

Although she didn't look ill, perhaps Maryam needed help. Cora hung back, unsure what to do, not wanting to leave her friend here by herself. But what could she do, other than physically drag Maryam away?

She moved closer and spoke quietly. "Maryam, this is a wondrous place, but I'm surprised to find you here. What are you looking at?"

Maryam didn't seem to hear her. Was the nun having a spell of some sort? A little frightened now, Cora glanced again at Maryam's bare feet. Should she go for help? But she'd have to leave Maryam here alone, and anything could happen while she was gone. What if Maryam collapsed, or needed CPR? Weren't you supposed to seek help first, then give CPR while waiting for help to arrive? Cora couldn't remember. And she didn't have her phone to call for help.

She went to Maryam's side and touched her shoulder gently. "Maryam? It's me, Cora."

Still no response. Her friend looked so delighted with whatever was happening, her expression adoring as she gazed at the patch of fog. If she was distressed, there was no sign of it. She appeared to be in a trance.

A gentle breeze blew through the quiet ravine, moving nearby branches and grasses. But the tree and the fog remained motionless. It was as if Cora stood between two separate worlds, one that moved around her and the other that stayed still—only Maryam, the fog, and the quiet buzzing within it.

Maryam continued her odd conversation with nothing. Between nods and verbal responses, Cora heard continued buzzing originating near the tree.

As Cora tried frantically to decide what to do, Maryam's smile faded. "Oh, how sad," she said. "I'll tell her."

And suddenly it was over. Maryam extended both arms as if giving a blessing, reverently made a sign of the Cross, and stood.

Cora looked at the tree. The fog was gone, the branch no longer bent, and now it swayed in the breeze.

She turned back to Maryam. The young woman's eyes were shining with tears. Despite her lack of awareness earlier, she didn't seem at all surprised to see Cora.

"I'm so sorry! The lady gave me a message for you," Maryam said, her voice full of sympathy as she moved toward Cora and reached for her arm. "We have to hurry back to Assisi Hill. Someone is trying to reach you. It's about Cisco! There's been an emergency."

# Chapter 15

There on the bed was Cora's phone, where she had apparently left it after talking to Cisco on speaker that morning. There were four messages and two texts, all but one from Barney in Arizona, the remaining call from an unknown Arizona number. No calls from Cisco. If Cisco had an emergency, why hadn't he called her?

Her stomach dropped and she looked at Maryam with panic in her eyes.

"Calls and texts from Arizona, but none from Cisco. I have a bad feeling."

"Sit down, Cora." Maryam guided her toward the desk chair. "Do you want me to stay?"

Cora dropped into the chair. She picked up a pen to keep her nervous hands busy.

"I'd rather be alone to talk to Barney. I'll find you afterward and tell you what's going on."

Maryam nodded, squeezed Cora's shoulder, and left the room, closing the door softly behind her.

Cora closed her eyes tightly. A huge lump had formed in her throat, and her head was ringing. She swallowed hard and forced herself to place the call to Barney.

"Cora, thank God. Where are you? Are you sitting down?"

"I'm in my room, Barney. And I'm sitting. What happened?" Her mouth felt dry, as if she was peeling her jaw apart with every word.

"Are you alone?"

"Yes, I'm alone. What happened?" she said again.

"Cisco is okay, but he's at the hospital. He had some sort of blackout or

123

seizure, I don't know. He was talking again by the time the ambulance arrived, so I think he'll be fine—he walked out with them supporting him. But he's still in the emergency room."

Cora took a deep breath, her eyes moist with relief. He was alive! Cisco had a history of seizures, although he hadn't had one for over twenty years and he took his medicine regularly. Maybe he forgot to take his pills. If so, he might be released as soon as the post-seizure effects wore off.

"You should call the hospital right away. They're waiting to hear from you," Barney said.

"Aren't you there with him?"

Barney hesitated. "They wouldn't let me in, Cora. No visitors are allowed, because of that virus. They want you to call."

Cora opened a drawer and pulled out a notepad. She stared at the blank page. "Did you reach Joe? Didn't Cisco tell you to call him?"

He hesitated again. What didn't he want to tell her?

"He wasn't all that coherent, Cora. This only happened a little over an hour ago. I thought I should reach you first."

"How did it happen, Barney?"

"Well, he was fine this morning. We played nine holes and came home about an hour before noon. Connie was out shopping. Cisco said he was a little tired and wanted to lie down. I thought that was strange, but he went to his room. Around noon I knocked on the door, but he didn't answer so I went in. He was rolling around on the bed. His eyes looked glassy, unfocused. I don't think he knew I was there. I called for an ambulance right away. Before it got here, he was trying to get up, but I could tell he was confused. I made him stay in bed so he wouldn't fall."

"What do you mean, confused?"

"He listened to me when I told him to lie down, but he didn't talk to me. I thought he understood me, though. And then the ambulance came and the paramedics took over. He started to talk a little, mostly yes, no, I'm okay. But he couldn't answer a lot of their questions."

Her heart skipped a beat. "What kind of questions?"

Once again Barney paused. "He couldn't say his name, or my name, or where he was."

Did that happen with a seizure? Maybe. She didn't know. It had never happened before. Cora felt sick.

"I talked to a nurse at the emergency room. Fortunately, Cisco had information about his stents in his wallet, and a list of his medications. That helped. But you need to call as soon as you can."

"Okay, give me the number." She wrote down the name of the hospital, the phone number, and the nurse's name. "I'll call you back after I get this sorted out."

After Barney rang off, she sat still for a moment, gathering herself. Then she sent a text to Joe. *Dad went to the hospital in Arizona by ambulance. I'm calling there now. Will let you know as soon as I can.*

The hospital number rang eight times before it was picked up. Fortunately, a live person answered. Cora asked for Stacy, the ER nurse Barney had said was in charge of Cisco. She waited two endless minutes on hold, her alarm growing, and then Stacy came on the line.

"You husband's been here about an hour, and he's stabilized," Stacy told Cora, whose fear immediately lessened. "We still don't know what happened. He's down in x-ray getting a CT scan now. Hopefully we'll know soon. He has a history of seizures, is that right?"

"He hasn't had a seizure for ages, more than twenty years. Controlled on Dilantin all that time."

"And how long has he been in AFib?"

Cora was stunned. AFib? Atrial fibrillation? Cisco had four cardiac stents and was under the care of a cardiologist, but... "Never! I mean, he's never had that."

"Well, he's in it now. We're monitoring him, of course. AFib isn't life-threatening, but it can cause a stroke. According to his list of medications, he's not on a blood thinner, right?"

"No, he's not. He was after he had his stents, for about a year. Then his doctor took him off. Just aspirin since then."

"Well, as soon as we get the results of the CT and know that he isn't bleeding in the brain, we'll start him on heparin to prevent a stroke from the AFib. Hopefully this is just a seizure from his known epilepsy. We've given him some IV Dilantin to bring his level up. We've also called a neurologist and cardiologist. We'll know more soon."

"I'm in Illinois," Cora said. "It will take me a while to get there."

"Before you make plans," the nurse said, "we're not allowing visitors now, due to restrictions from this coronavirus. There's no hurry for you to fly here. He's doing well, and we can talk to you on the phone just as easily in Chicago as in Phoenix. Maybe in a few days...."

"I can't see him?" She was devastated. How would he know she was involved? He'd feel alone. They were always together—did everything important together. He had been with her every moment of her cancer treatment. How could she not be there?

The nurse's tone was compassionate. "Look, when he gets back from radiology we'll call you, okay? We'll do a FaceTime visit. It's almost as good as being here, and the best we can do right now. You'll feel much better after you talk to him. We'll make that happen as often as you like. But..." She paused.

Cora held her breath, trying to maintain her composure. The details were coursing through her brain, unpleasant possibilities offering themselves unbidden: what if his heart was failing, or he'd had a stroke instead of a seizure? *No! This isn't happening. I refuse to think the worst!*

"Mrs. Tozzi, the most likely things to have happened are either a seizure, or a stroke from his AFib. In either case, your husband's brain hasn't recovered yet. He's responding to us, talking, and moving all his limbs. But he's still confused. What I'm trying to say is that you shouldn't get upset if he doesn't seem himself. He's going to need time."

"My cousin told me he didn't know his name or where he was before the ambulance brought him in."

"Yes, that's what I mean. He may know who you are, but he may not. You can't let him know you're upset if you want him to stay calm and cooperative. That's important."

"Do you mean he isn't cooperative?"

"He pulled out his IV, and took a swing at me when I tried to stop him. He doesn't seem to understand why he has it."

Another blow. "That's not like him. He's a really sweet guy. He's always cooperative and would never hit anyone."

"I'm sure you're right. But his brain isn't telling him that right now. Do you understand?"

Cora's eyes filled with tears. "Okay. Let's try the FaceTime call as soon as he gets back. I'll handle it."

Immediately after she hung up, she placed a call to Joe, who picked up right away.

"I'm in the room with a patient—give me just a minute," he said.

A few seconds later, he came back on the line. "Okay, I'm where I can talk now. What happened?"

Cora filled him in and answered all the questions she could. She struggled to remain composed as tears coursed down her cheeks and her voice broke. Her heart thudded so loudly she asked Joe if he heard it over the phone, but of course he didn't.

"I have to go to Phoenix," she said. "I have to be there with him, but they tell me I can't. He needs me! How can I not go?"

"Mom, listen. We're all limiting visitors now. From what you told me, his condition isn't life-threatening, he's in the right place, and they're taking good care of him. Your being there won't make any difference."

"But it will! He'll know I'm there! He needs someone he loves to get him through this, not a bunch of strangers."

"Mom, we're in a pandemic. The hospital has no choice about allowing visitors. They're not making exceptions right now. Look, let me call there. Hold tight. I'll get back to you in a few minutes."

It was only about fifteen minutes later that Joe called back, but it seemed an eternity.

"Okay, Mom, I spoke to his ER doctor. All the right things are being done, and he's in no immediate danger—like they told you—but he has to be watched closely. Whatever happened is over, but they have to prevent complications and help him recover. He's in good hands."

"Did you talk to him?"

"He wasn't back in his room yet. They've already ruled out bleeding in the brain, but what he experienced could be from a clot caused by the atrial fibrillation. They're preventing any more damage by starting him on heparin right away. So, they've got a handle on this thing."

Cora let out a slow deep breath. "That's good, isn't it?"

"So far, yes. It's also a good sign that he's responsive and moving his extremities on command. But he's still confused, not clear where he is or why. They can't move him from the ER until they know if he has to go to a stroke floor or a cardiac unit. He'll need a telemetry bed."

"Are you saying he had a stroke? You remember when Grandma had one. She wasn't responsive for days."

"It's too early to say, but it's possible—maybe likely."

"But his signs are good? He's responding already, and moving every-thing?"

"Yes, that's all good. But Mom, he's got a way to go. We don't know the whole picture yet. It's only been a few hours."

Her deep breath stuttered out this time, audibly. In her mind, she was seeing her mother eight years ago, lying comatose in a hospital bed while Cora sat in a chair beside her, holding her hand and singing "Happy Birthday" over and over. The nurses had said familiar tunes would be comforting. But now she couldn't even hold Cisco's hand.

Joe interrupted her thoughts. "But there's a good thing. They're not allowing visitors, but since I'm a doctor they'll let me into the hospital. I can keep an eye on things and I can probably see him. I'll fly out tonight. Does that sound okay to you?"

"Oh, God, Joe! Can you really do that? At least until I can get there my-self? I would be so relieved! But don't you have appointments scheduled?"

"I'll get my office to reschedule my face-to-face appointments for the rest of the week. With this virus everyone is canceling anyway. I can do phone visits from Arizona just as well as from home.

"I'll make it happen, Mom. Listen, do you want me to call Pat and Marty? You should stay off the phone while you wait to FaceTime with Dad."

"Could you call them? Tell them I'll call later. There's a call coming in now—must be the hospital. I'll let you know how it goes."

The first thing Cora saw when the FaceTime call connected was the ER nurse, a pleasant thirty-something woman with a neat appearance and light brown hair tucked behind her ears. She reminded Cora of Helen Hunt. Her face bobbed up and down regularly. Apparently, she was walking toward Cisco's room as she talked.

"Your husband is back in his room, sitting up, and expecting your call." Stacy smiled, and her voice was warm but professional. "Let me show him to you." As she moved the phone, Cora caught glimpses of an all-too-familiar emergency room set-up, a cramped space jammed with monitors, IV stands, and medical equipment surrounding a hospital bed.

Cisco lay in the bed in a semi-reclining position, attached to an IV. He looked surprisingly normal, strong and healthy, but unhappy. More than unhappy, he looked angry. She felt her eyes sting with relief, but remembering Stacy's caution, she wiped them quickly before he saw her face in the phone and caught her distress.

"And here's your husband," Stacy said in a cheerful tone. Cisco's face moved around on the screen again as apparently the phone was placed in his hands.

"It's your wife on the phone," Stacy said softly. "I bet you're glad to talk to her! Now just hold this a little higher so she can see your face. You see her okay, don't you?"

"Hi, hon," Cora said, trying to sound optimistic. "I understand you've had quite the day. How are you feeling?"

He knit his eyebrows. "I'm fine. Get me out of here."

"They need to be sure it's safe before they let you go. Be patient, hon."

"This is bullshit. There's no reason I can't leave now."

Clearly, he was in denial. What should she say?

"Give it a little while, hon. You blacked out. They have to be sure you didn't have a stroke or something else is going on. You wouldn't want to go back to Barney's too soon. He'd have to take care of you, and you'd hate that, wouldn't you? Let them check you out first, and then we'll bring you right home."

"Bullshit! Who's Barney? I can take care of myself. They can't stop me. I'll just put on my clothes and leave."

"Please don't do that! Joe is on his way. He'll get in sometime tonight. He'll talk to them tomorrow and bring you home when you're ready."

"Joe? Why will it take so long for him to get here? He can take me home today."

"It's not that simple. He has to get a flight out and arrange for a car. But he'll be there as soon as he can."

"A flight? What are you talking about? He can drive here in two hours. Why can't you come get me?"

"It's more than two hours to Arizona. And things are complicated because of that virus that's got everyone worried. The hospital has new rules…"

She saw the muscle in his jaw jumping, the one that told her arguing would do no good. "Stop confusing me. What does Arizona have to do with anything?"

"Hon, you're in a hospital there."

"I'm not!"

"Then where are you?"

"I don't know! What difference does it make? Stop asking stupid questions."

Cora didn't know what to say, then asked, "Do you know who I am?"

"Of course! You're my wife! The nurse said so."

"What's my name?"

"What kind of crappy question is that? Cisco."

"My name is Cisco?"

"Of course!"

"No, *your* name is Cisco. What's mine?"

"Cisco, I said. Weren't you listening? Just get me out of here!"

Cora felt herself tearing up. She had to keep it together.

"Wait for Joe, hon. He'll get there as soon as he can. And listen to the doctors and nurses meanwhile, okay? I love you, and I'll do my best, but you have to be well first."

"You bitch! Why are you doing this to me? I'll get home myself. Go away and leave me alone!"

He began to thrash around the bed. The screen tilted, and abruptly showed a wall. He must have dropped the phone. But she could hear what was happening.

"Don't pull on that," Stacy said. Her voice rose. "Help in Room 119, stat!" Cora heard other voices and a flurry of activity.

After a couple of minutes, someone picked up the phone, and Stacy's face appeared. "Sorry," she said. "We've given him a sedative and he's calmer now. I thought talking to you would help, but he's still confused. It was worth a try. I'm so sorry you had to go through that, but give him a little time."

Cora swallowed and nodded, and thanked the nurse before ending the call. She had no idea Cisco's personality could be affected like this. When her mother had a stroke, she was impaired and confused, but her personality remained the same. This was a shock. Cisco just wasn't acting like himself. What if he didn't get better? What if the change was permanent? She had to keep reminding herself that her mother had gotten well again.

# Chapter 16

Cora wished she could lie on her bed, bury her head in her pillow, and try to escape in sleep. But Sister Maryam was waiting for her. She wiped her eyes, went into the bathroom, bathed her face with cool water, and then studied herself in the mirror. Her expression was frightened, her eyes red but dry now, at least for the moment. Feeling a sudden weakness in her knees, she sank onto the closed toilet seat and took three deep breaths. Finally, she stopped stalling and went in search of Maryam, careful to take her phone with her this time.

She found Maryam seated at a table in the convent's dining room, which was otherwise empty. Cora took a chair, trying to control her trembling chin and voice.

"Cisco's in the hospital," she said.

Maryam pressed both hands to her cheeks. "Oh, my goodness! What happened?"

"He had some sort of episode, a seizure or blackout," Cora said.

Reaching across the table, Maryam laid her hand over Cora's. "What do you need me to do?"

Cora smiled weakly. "Company would be good right now." Her face crumpled and her voice broke. "He swore at me, Maryam. Called me a bitch and told me to go away. That isn't like him!"

"Of course it isn't!" Maryam said. "He's not himself. He's angry, and probably scared. He needed to lash out, and you were there."

Cora nodded. "I know, but it still hurts. I can't stand the thought of him like this!"

Maryam rubbed Cora's hand. Haltingly, Cora told her the details of Cisco's condition.

"And I can't…be there with him. Because of this damn virus. No visitors. He has no one!" With these words, the whole situation descended on her and she broke down, unable to hold the tears back any longer. "I'm so frustrated!" she sobbed.

Maryam shook her head sadly. "This can't get much worse for you, can it? I'm so sorry."

"Joe, our son—he's a doctor—he's going. But I have to be there, Maryam! Cisco will want *me*."

"Maybe you should be patient, just for now. Cisco's angry, but he'll figure things out on his own. Maybe—"

"No! I have to help him! I have to!"

"Cora, you can't help him today. Even if you got on a plane right now, you wouldn't get there until the middle of the night, and the hospital won't let you see him. He's safe and he's where he needs to be. You said they have him sedated. I'm sure he'll be fine through the night. In the morning, Joe will be there, and I bet things will look better by then. You can talk to your husband again, and then I'll help you make travel arrangements, whatever we need to do. Give it the night."

"I'll never sleep. Just…pray for a miracle!"

"I will." Maryam smiled. "Count on it."

Perhaps her mind just needed relief, but at the word "miracle," Cora remembered what she had witnessed in the ravine. What *did* happen there? What was that strange fog, and the voice-like buzzing sound? And how did Maryam know Cora had missed an emergency call? Urgency at the time to get back to the convent had driven the questions out of her mind, but now she seized an opportunity to divert her frantic thoughts.

"In the ravine, Maryam. How did you know there was an emergency call? Who told you?"

Maryam turned her head away and stared at a wall. After a moment she seemed to come to a decision. She looked at Cora and took a deep breath.

"A miracle—you used the right word. Yes, a miracle." She paused, searched Cora's face, then fixed her gaze on her own hands, resting on the table. "For a long time now, Our Lady visits me. I was talking to her earlier. I didn't know you were watching, but she told me." Her eyes flickered back to Cora, as if looking for a reaction.

Cora knit her eyebrows. Our Lady. Was Maryam saying she was being visited by the Virgin Mary? From heaven? Surely that wasn't true. But a look at Maryam's face confirmed her friend was serious. She looked absolutely radiant. Whatever was going on, it was obvious Maryam believed it.

"She told you what? What did she actually say?"

"We were talking, like we always do, about sin in the world, about the need for people to pray more, how I can do more for the elderly, other things. And then she said my friend Cora had come—that you were there. She told me to take you back to your room because you didn't have your phone and there was an emergency with your husband. She said we should hurry, and then she smiled at me, raised her hands in blessing, and left."

Stunned, Cora stared at her. Was Maryam delusional? That was her secret? She'd been spending time in that ravine, where she'd go into—what? A self-induced trance? Surely the Blessed Mother wasn't really visiting her!

"Does Sister Lorita know about these—what do you call them—visitations? And the other sisters?" Maybe this was the reason some of the sisters shunned Maryam—they thought she was making things up. Or did they believe her and were jealous?

Maryam shook her head. "Sister Lorita is the only person I've told, until I told you just now. It's not time to make the visits public, we decided. We don't want to start a media circus before Mary tells us why she's here and who she wants to know. I told you because Our Lady gave me a message for you, so I believe she wants you to know. I do think someday she'll ask me for something."

Her friend's belief might be easier to relate to if Cora's religious doubts didn't make her skeptical. She didn't know what to say. She settled for, "What do you talk about?"

"It's just like close friends having a conversation. I tell her my problems. She listens and gives me advice. A lot like praying, only she's a real presence instead of in my head. I always feel better after talking to her."

"You're calling her Our Lady. Has she revealed herself as the Blessed Mother?"

Maryam shook her head again. "No, but this is the same way Mary came before, at Lourdes and at Fatima. Who else would it be? Those other times, her message was about sin in the world and saying the rosary. She's been giving me the same message, only she says to pray the Franciscan Crown. Do you know what that is?"

"Yes, I just learned about it. It's a seven-decade version of the rosary, the Seven Joys of Mary that Franciscans pray, instead of the five-decade version most Catholics say."

Cora reached into her pocket for her own ever-present rosary, and as she touched it, her chest ached with grief and her eyes grew shiny again. What if Maryam really did see a visitor from heaven—Mary, or an angel, or someone else? Improbable as it seemed, if there was an ounce of truth in Maryam's claims, maybe Cora should take advantage of that at such a desperate time. Was this providential? Perhaps it was the answer she had been seeking when she came to the convent to resolve her doubts.

She was so confused! Afraid to pursue the opportunity, but equally afraid to disregard it. Cisco's health could be at stake.

"Maryam, you have to ask Mary for me. Will she make Cisco well? Will she save my husband?"

"I'll ask her, of course. But you can just pray to her yourself."

"I already include Mary in my prayers. I'm afraid she won't hear me. But she'll respond to you."

Maryam hesitated. Cora waited anxiously, assuming the nun was remembering their discussions about Cora's conflicted beliefs. Finally, Maryam said, "Well, I'll try...."

Cora had a sudden idea. *Why am I finding out about Mary's visit at this particular moment if I'm not meant to contact her?* "I want to go with you to the ravine. Will she talk to me?"

Maryam looked doubtful. "I've never tried to bring anyone, even Sister Lorita. I could ask her—"

"There's no time for that! Can't we just go? Now?"

Maryam was shaking her head. "It doesn't work like that, Cora. It's certain days, certain times. She tells me when to come. I've gone other times and she's not there."

"Can't we try? Please!"

Maryam still looked dubious. She glanced at the clock on the wall, which read ten after four. "Cora, you need to think everything over, at least a little bit. Cisco's condition, Mary's visits, it all just happened.

Think it through. Evening prayer is soon, and then dinner. After dinner, if you still want to go, I'll take you."

Elated, Cora said, "Oh, thank you, thank you!" There was nothing further to think about. She had Maryam's promise.

Maryam held up a hand. "We'll have to be careful, though. You saw how treacherous the ground is, and it'll be dark. I've never met her at night. I don't think she'll come, but I'm willing to try for your peace of mind. Please promise me you won't be even more upset if nothing comes of it."

Cora clasped both Maryam's hands in hers. "Thank you, Maryam. I can't tell you how grateful I am, grateful to you and grateful to be here in the convent when this happened. I don't know how I could have dealt with everything if I was all alone at home. Just to have someone to talk to, someone who cares, it means so much." *Let alone we may be taking my problems directly to the mother of God tonight!*

As they got up to leave, Cora noticed Sister Fatima sitting in a far corner of the room. She must have entered from the kitchen, unnoticed, while Cora and Maryam talked. Fatima glanced their way. She said nothing, but the usual scowl was on her face. *That woman is everywhere! Has she been watching us all this time? How much did she overhear?*

Cora turned away. She had enough problems. She wasn't going to let Fatima be another one.

# Chapter 17

A moonless night had descended by the time Cora and Sister Maryam left the convent. They stopped at the thick woods on the ridge to allow their eyes to adjust. Through the blackness, their flashlights faintly disclosed the path over rough stones and dirt, covered with dry leaves from last fall.

"Walk carefully, Cora. The ground's uneven here, and after we pass the statues we'll be going downhill."

Cora didn't have to be told. She tested each step before taking another. Shapes loomed on her left, and she directed her flashlight there. Topping a pile of large, moss-covered rocks were life-size, white stone statues. A sculpture of Jesus knelt on the ground, gazing at a winged angel, the scene depicting Jesus in the Garden of Gethsemane. The spot was in a wooded area that couldn't be seen from Assisi Manor.

"The surprises here never end," she said, as she swung the flashlight beam back on the ground. The path turned to the right and ran downhill, clearly outlined with grapefruit-sized rocks, the ground leaf-covered, stones stepping downward every few feet. The creepy atmosphere was accentuated by cold, darkness, rustling branches, and skittering night-time creatures. The air smelled earthy and damp, hinting at slippery footing. As soon as the thought entered Cora's mind, she slid a few inches, but caught herself.

"Let me go first," Maryam said, grabbing Cora's arm. "I haven't been here in the dark either, but at least the way is familiar to me. I know these woods so well I could walk through them with my eyes closed."

Cora was resistant. "I'm more comfortable leading. I don't like empty darkness at my back. I'm afraid you'll get ahead, and something could sneak up behind me."

Maryam gave a snort. "So instead it's behind *me*. I wouldn't do that, you know. You can trust me."

"I didn't mean you'd go far ahead on purpose, but...oh, I know you wouldn't. I'm more confident if I can set my own pace. You can just as easily *tell* me where to go to find your visitor." Cora realized she was being a control freak, and she didn't feel comfortable calling the person they were trying to contact "Mary." Since her identity hadn't been confirmed, it felt more right to use the term "visitor."

"How long have you been seeing her?" Cora asked.

"Since I was a teenager. When my dad used to bring me here. Mary often visits children, you know."

"That's why you joined the convent then?"

"It was a big part of my motivation, yes."

They crossed the stream that was only a trickle and followed the path on the far side, passing a number of Stations of the Cross. Their bobbing flashlight beams enhanced the spooky atmosphere. Sometimes objects seemed to be moving closer or farther away, or they became more or less distinct, dimmer or lighter. The slightest noise seemed ominous and threatening. Cora wanted to call out, "Who's there?"

They finally neared the area where Cora had found Maryam earlier that day. Maryam stopped.

"We're close." She played her flashlight around, judging the distance from the last station, and focused the beam on a small tree near the top of the ravine. "This is it."

"What now?" Cora whispered.

"I don't know," Maryam whispered back. "Why don't you lean against this little tree right here and wait. I never call her—I just come, and so does she. I'll kneel and pray. I think we should turn off our lights, though." She looked into Cora's eyes. "I don't think she'll come."

With the flashlights off, the night seemed even colder. There was no appreciable wind, but Cora shivered anyway, standing with her back against the thin tree her friend had indicated while Maryam walked about fifteen feet away and knelt.

A rushing sound startled Cora. An area behind her brightened, casting shadows that raced through the trees. She realized it was a car passing on Main Street, a short distance from the woods and ravine. It brightened the area just enough to highlight Maryam kneeling on the cold ground, facing the top of the ravine, her hands folded in prayer. Cora wondered if Maryam's knees hurt. At least she was wearing shoes tonight.

In the darkness, Cora's hearing was exceptionally sharp, but she strained even harder to pick up the slightest unusual sound. Amid the rustling of branches, leaves, and night creatures, she heard the sibilants of Maryam's whispered prayer. Cora's anxiety built as nothing else happened. The sound grew monotonous, and her thoughts returned to Cisco's condition. She leaned her head against the tree trunk and shut her eyes. Even if she couldn't see Cisco at the hospital, she wanted to be in Arizona. She couldn't just stay at the convent, waiting.

The voice, when it came, was Maryam's, and it was joyful. "You're here!" she said, and then nothing.

Cora's eyes flew open. Her friend was staring toward the top of the ravine, hands still in a prayerful attitude. Cora followed her gaze.

Was there a spot near the top of the ravine that was brighter than everything around it? A patch of fog, maybe only imagined, seemed to hover there. She couldn't pull her eyes away. Her acute hearing focused at that spot, but strain as she might, all she heard over the pounding of her heart was a low buzzing that rose and fell in a cadence of speech, like earlier today. That time, too, could have been her imagination.

She heard Maryam's soft voice again. "You must know why I'm here, why I came at night to find you—to ask your intercession on behalf of my friend and her husband."

The skin on the back of Cora's neck prickled. She heard no response, saw no change, except that Maryam nodded.

"It's God's will, of course. Is there something I can tell her?"

A long period followed, in which Cora heard only the low buzzing and the occasional nod or comment from Maryam: "Yes" or "I see." *Something* was happening! Something Maryam believed, but Cora couldn't clearly see or hear. Some*one*—who might be a visitor from heaven.

Cora wanted to call out, "Please help him!" or "Make this go away." She opened her mouth to form the words, but none came. If she interfered with the promise of heavenly help, it might be denied. Was she speechless for this reason or did some other force keep her frozen, unable to utter a sound or even move? Her legs trembled with weakness and she clutched the thin tree for support.

She trusted Maryam to beg for a miracle, to promise that Cora would do anything in return, anything the visitor asked. But she didn't hear Maryam say any such thing.

And then, a feeling of calm fell upon Cora. Warmth spread through her, and she forgot the cold. She felt weightless, as if she were floating. The feeling was so strong she looked down, but her feet were firmly on the ground. She was filled with resignation, peace, and trust, as if responsibility had passed from her hands to someone else's. A voice in her head told her to take a step back, have faith, and let what was to happen play out.

She remembered once again the words from Handel's *Messiah* that she had sung with her choir and mentioned to Father Bozic: "Take my yoke upon you. I will give you peace."

Was this what Father Bozic had meant? But her inner self, her grounding in the physical world, was too ingrained, and after a moment, confusion returned and the meaning of the Biblical words seemed reversed. She was accustomed to bargaining with God, asking for favors as reward for her actions or a sacrifice. Was she now to simply trust in God's compassion and let Him work out the details? It was tempting, but it went against what she had done all her life.

In the end she was left with hope and a feeling that she had done all she could—for now.

She heard Maryam say, "I will tell her."

With those words Cora found herself released from her immobility and she went to Maryam's side.

Maryam looked up at her, beaming with happiness, and then stood, brushing debris from her knees and skirt. "Did you see her?" she asked.

Cora shook her head. "I only saw you. Maybe a little fog. And I only heard you speaking. But you saw her?"

"Oh, yes, even in the dark! She was so sweet, so loving, Cora. I wish you had been able to see her. She would have made you feel so much better."

"What did she say? Is Cisco going to be okay?"

Maryam turned on her flashlight and started walking back up the ravine. Cora followed anxiously.

"I didn't ask a lot of questions, but she knew what we wanted. It's in God's hands, of course, but she will add her pleas to yours. She said to trust in God. You are doing the right thing. Stay in the convent and wait for a sign. Cisco is in good hands. You should not expect an immediate answer, but in time. She did not promise a miracle. She said God prefers to act in more natural ways."

"So, in other words, she's saying I should stay here, trust the doctors and God, and Cisco will get better? To do nothing. That's going to be hard." Cora's chest felt empty and she wanted to weep with conflicting emotions of disappointment and hope.

"When visitors come to us from heaven, they always ask for something hard, Cora. They ask for things that make people saints because they've done something hard, not easy. Didn't Sister Elizabeth talk to you about that?"

Slowly Cora was leaning in a more logical direction. If a visitation had taken place, at least she had done everything she could for the moment. Perhaps help from heaven was on the way. She had covered her bases. In the morning she would see what else developed. What else could she do?

They walked a while in silence, crossed the stream, and stopped again in front of the statues at the edge of the woods.

"The Agony in the Garden of Gethsemane," Cora said. "I feel that despair tonight. Jesus was asking his Father to spare him from what was to come. Just as I'm asking for Cisco to be spared and come home to me."

Cora remembered another quote from the Bible: *Father, if you are willing, take this cup from me; yet not my will but yours be done.* It hadn't worked out so well for Jesus.

Maryam reached for Cora's hand and held it but said nothing.

"I didn't see or hear her," Cora said again. "Only an indistinct light spot, and what you were saying to her. You saw more than that?"

"Oh, yes. I always see her as a woman in the flesh. And I hear her voice clearly."

"What does she look like?"

"She's small, about five feet tall, and slender. She doesn't have an exceptionally attractive face, but her eyes are lovely and filled with compassion, and that makes her beautiful. She's very gentle. She dresses simply in a dark brown shirt and skirt with long sleeves and a shawl that covers her head and shoulders. She holds her hands up in prayer, the same posture I take when we're together."

That was not what Cora had imagined. Mary had usually been depicted in art and been described by those who claimed to have seen her as being dressed in white or pale blue, wearing a long veil, holding her hands out in welcome. She was also said to be very beautiful and radiant.

Cora glanced around her, avoiding Maryam's eyes. Something wasn't right.

"Wait for a sign, she said. Any idea what I should look for?" Cora asked.

"She didn't explain. I think she thought you would know when it happened. But she asked a favor from you, Cora."

"A favor?"

Maryam smiled. "Remember what I said earlier about how I expected her to eventually ask me for something? Visitors from heaven have a reason to come to earth, some mission to ask of us. Pray the rosary, or pray for peace, or build a shrine, that sort of thing. But she was more specific, and she asked that *you* do it, not me."

"Really? You mean like a bargain? She will help me if I do something for her?"

"No, she didn't put it that way. She said she would help you and Cisco, but that you were the person who could help her."

"What did she want?"

"She said that Katy was a saint, and you could get Katy the recognition she deserves."

# Chapter 18

Later that night, Cora fell asleep troubled by thoughts that Cisco's condition had been inflicted on him as a punishment for something *she* had done. She racked her mind trying to remember what that could be. Maryam would say that God didn't punish people that way, and Cora tried to believe it, but it was hard for her to toss off guilt.

If only she hadn't suggested Cisco go to Arizona. She could have spent more time with him instead of on her own projects and problems, been more understanding of his needs, thought more about him than her own concerns. She had been so sure she was always right. She should have recognized something was wrong and prevented what had happened.

And now she faced an impossible task, laid on her by the visitor—find out about Katy, whoever she was, and somehow persuade others that a woman Cora knew nothing of was worthy of sainthood. If the visitor could help Cisco in return, or was even real.

When she woke at four o'clock in the morning, she felt too restless to go back to sleep. She pulled on some jeans and a sweatshirt and went back to the chapel, which was again empty. This time she sat in the front row of chairs.

Praying made Cora feel like she was doing something proactive at times when she thought there was nothing else she could do. Mental dialog with a heavenly person helped her to deal with things emotionally, and sometimes she even figured out something she could do about the problem. She prayed to God and an assortment of saints, but didn't know them like Sister Maryam knew the Virgin Mary.

Could she rely on the promise made in the ravine?

It occurred to her that she was being hypocritical, praying despite her doubts about the existence of God. But Cisco's illness caused her to turn for help to the God she wasn't sure she believed in. She had been brought up Catholic, had followed her religion her entire life, and it was the only comfort she knew.

She stared through iron grillwork at the huge, arched stained-glass window beyond. In the wee hours before dawn, the brilliant colors were muted. She took a few deep breaths and sat erect, her hands clasped in prayer across her chest. Get her attitude and posture right if she expected God to hear her—that's what the nuns had taught her. She turned to glance at the statue of the Mother and Child in the back of the chapel. Mary's eyes seemed to look into Cora's with compassion, but perhaps only because she needed compassion so badly. Her prayers were silent tonight.

*Dear God, please give Cisco a good night. May he wake up this morning with a clear head, a strong heart, and all risk of complications over. May he be healthy and happy, and may he appreciate the care he's getting.*

*But if You can't do all that, dear Lord, then please at least keep him safe and restore his health.*

She closed her eyes and cradled her head in her hands. She felt so lonely without Cisco, so empty.

*Bring him home! My life is not complete without him! And give me the strength, the intelligence, and the patience I need to help him stay well and safe and happy. I'm willing to do what it takes, whatever that is.*

She paused for a moment, afraid she was forgetting something.

*Thank you, dear Lord, for saving his life and for getting him to the hospital in time. I know this could have been worse. But please, please, help him now!*

She sagged back in her chair, pulled out her rosary and prayed it. She couldn't think of any other prayers to say after that, or anything else to do. Later in the morning she'd start making calls. There was little point in returning to bed—she was wide awake now. She continued to hold her rosary, and her thoughts returned to whatever had happened in the ravine last night.

After a few hours distance from last night's "visitation," she was no longer certain of what *had* actually happened. All she really saw was

Maryam, appearing to be in some sort of trance. Aside from that, there was a bright spot that could have been anything—even a figment of her imagination, brought on by the spooky woods, the stress of the day, and her need to believe out of fear for her husband. Same for the buzzing sound; it easily could have been some early spring nighttime insect or unidentified animal.

Not having seen the "visitor" herself, she must rely on what Sister Maryam told her, and Maryam could be wrong, misled, or even inventing a story. Maybe Maryam was dreaming—not in a trance, not seeing a visitor from heaven, but delusional. Or she could be faking the experience. But why would she do that? To make Cora feel better? To make herself seem more important? But she claimed she had been seeing Our Lady for years, not just today.

Cora was cursed with the ability to see multiple sides of a problem. Some thought that quality an advantage, but Cora knew better. Seeing all sides raised doubts and got in the way of making decisions. Here she was again, Cora the questioner, looking for rational, conventional answers for experiences she could not easily explain, when the most obvious reasons seemed to be not rational or logical at all, but supernatural. Would following the visitor's request be an effort to cover all the bases again, do *something*, ignore her doubts—like she was doing now, praying in the chapel?

What she *had* directly experienced last night, though, were two overpowering sensations. While Maryam was in her trance, Cora had been incapable of going to Maryam's side. And that warm, peaceful feeling came over her, albeit only for a few moments, but so real, so comforting, as if she was being taken care of by someone who loved her. Where did that come from? She snorted quietly. And where did it go? She still needed it!

Despite her doubts, Cora *wanted* the apparition to be real. And if Cora believed what Maryam told her and her own gut, then she now had a mission: to find out who the visitor was, who Katy was, and what made her worthy of being a saint. And do it in time to help Cisco. She snorted again. *That's all. Just solve another mystery, with a ticking clock attached to it.*

Someone entered the chapel, but Cora kept staring ahead. It must be nearly 5:00 A.M., still too early for the sisters to gather. Someone else needing a favor, perhaps.

She heard soft rustling as someone approached. She looked up. It was Sister Fatima. Was the woman following her?

Surprisingly, Sister Fatima sat beside her, reached out, and clasped Cora's hand without looking directly at Cora. In a soft, kind voice she said, "I thought I might find you here."

Cora glanced at her but said nothing.

Fatima squeezed Cora's fingers. "You're suffering, not only from worry and sorrow, but from doubt. You don't know if God will answer your prayers. But I have faith, so let me pray along with you. Remember what Jesus said: '…if two of you agree on earth about anything you ask, it will be done for you by my Father in heaven. For where two or three are gathered in my name, I am there among them.'"

She looked at Cora, smiled gently, and squeezed her hand again. "I'm here to give you a quorum."

# Chapter 19

Fatima hadn't asked questions or offered advice, only kept her company and listened when Cora talked. Word must have gotten around about Cisco, but how Fatima knew about Cora's troubled relationship with God was puzzling. Neither Sister Maryam nor Father Bozic would have told her. She must have divined it somehow, just as she must have suspected Cora would return to the chapel, having seen her there before.

Whatever the reason, Fatima's compassion was exactly what Cora needed. Cora found it easier to talk to people she didn't know well, able to speak freely, her words not tailored to the opinions of well-meaning friends. Fatima only held her hand and listened, and they prayed together.

Of course, Cora told Fatima nothing about Maryam's visitor.

Just after eight o'clock that morning, right after he saw Cisco, Joe called. His words relieved her, but she wanted details.

"So we don't know yet what caused his blackout and confusion?" Cora asked.

"Well, he could have had a seizure, since he's had them before," Joe said. "But it's unusual that confusion would last this long afterward. AFib isn't likely to cause confusion, either. Not impossible, of course. Symptoms like his could be from a stroke, but it's been less than twenty-four hours, yet he has no muscle weakness and he's moving everything normally. He'll get a CT scan in a day or two to be sure."

"He already had a scan, and it didn't show anything," Cora said.

"That scan was done without contrast, which doesn't show as much detail. It wasn't safe to use contrast until they were sure he wasn't bleeding in the brain."

"I can't believe your dad has AFib. He didn't have any symptoms, and he's been seeing his cardiologist regularly. He has been tired lately, though."

"That's good—we know he hasn't been having the arrhythmia for a long time, then. But fatigue is a symptom. We can treat AFib if we have to. It's pretty common. A lot of people live with AFib and don't even know they have it. The important thing is to prevent complications, the most serious of which is stroke. But he's doing okay, Mom. So that's where we are now."

This was only partially reassuring. "But if he's still in AFib, he could still have a stroke."

"No, he can't. They started him on a blood thinner as soon as they knew he wasn't bleeding in the brain."

"There's no chance he can have a clot, then?"

"Very unlikely. The blood thinner prevents clot formation."

She'd have to settle for that. From her medical background, she knew there were no absolutes. One depended on odds, and those seemed good.

"Could his symptoms be from something else?"

"There are less likely things, like infections. But let's not go there. He's physically strong, he's awake and alert. We're going to get through this, but it could take some time."

"What did you think when you saw him?"

"Well, like I said, he's talking. He's moving his arms and legs equally and well, he can get up and walk, although with the monitor and IVs that's difficult, so he'll only get up once or twice for the next day or so."

She knew when Joe was being evasive. "What about his confusion? His anger?"

"He knew me, as I said. Follows directions pretty well. Still has trouble answering questions. And he wants to go home."

"What kind of questions doesn't he answer?"

"It's complicated and all over the place. He knows his name, my name, your name. He knows his Social Security number. He can repeat things back to you, even two or three items you ask him to remember. But he doesn't know what state he lives in, and when I asked him who the president was, he insisted it was Howard Hughes. You can point to something and ask what color it is, like my hair, and it'll take him a few times to get it right. Questions annoy him. He doesn't understand why he's in the hospital and keeps insisting he's fine. He can't describe things very well, even if they're right in front of him. And he can't operate the remote control for the TV, just keeps pushing random buttons impatiently."

Cora gave a little laugh. "That's nothing new. He's always impatient with the remote, but he gets it figured out."

She heard a long indrawn breath. "Well, he's not figuring it out now." Joe paused again. "And he pulled out his IV during the night. He bled on the sheets and they had to be changed.

"Mom, listen. I don't want you to worry needlessly, but right now Dad has a definite cognitive problem. It's really early, and the brain does funny things. There could be some pressure or swelling, from whatever insult his brain had, but *something* happened and we can't ignore his symptoms. We can only keep testing, treat what we find, and wait for him to get better. Tincture of time. We'll know more soon. I'm here, and the staff is giving me free access to him despite the virus restrictions. Try to think positive."

"How can I do that? I'm scared, Joe. I don't want to face life without him. And he'll want to know I'm nearby." Her words were sticking in her throat and her eyes burned.

"Look, why don't you check the airlines for flight information, but don't book anything yet? Let's see what develops today. Mom, please. Give it a little time. These things get better. Just stay where you are until we know more."

Another voice in her head reminded her that last night's "visitor" also told her to stay in the convent. She didn't know why, but if heaven was telling her to stay put, she supposed she could wait a few hours.

"I'll try," she said. She cleared her throat. "When can I talk to him again?"

"How about in a few minutes? I'm downstairs getting some coffee from a vending machine. Ghastly stuff, but the cafeteria is closed due to the virus. As soon as I get back to his room I'll call and put him on. Do you want to talk or FaceTime?"

"FaceTime! I want to see him."

The call went well at first. Cisco looked strong, not sick at all, nor did he seem confused. He wasn't smiling, though.

"Hi, hon," she said. "You look better today. How are you doing?"

"I'm doing just fine. I don't know why they're keeping me here." He waved his arm, probably to show her the IV stand or monitor. Like a stereotypical Italian, he couldn't keep his hands still while he talked. She smiled and waited for him to hold the phone back up to his face. She heard Joe in the background: "Let me help you. You have to hold the phone in front of you, here."

"I can do it! Let me alone!" Cisco replied. His face appeared again.

"They won't let me get up." His eyes started to wander. "There's something in my arm."

The picture tilted and his face vanished. She heard Joe again. "Don't touch that, Dad. You have to leave it where it is."

Cisco's face reappeared. "They're trying to tell me there's something wrong with my heart."

"That's why you're on a monitor. Because your heart isn't regular—it's beating too fast. They need to watch it to see if they have to give you medication."

"Bullshit! There's nothing wrong with my heart!" She saw the rigid jaw that meant he was trying to control his anger.

"Hon, you know that's not true. You've had stents and now your heart isn't beating regular."

"Bullshit! I have to get out of here! Ask them where they hid my clothes. Even my own son won't tell me. It's a conspiracy."

She lost his image and heard a thud as the phone fell to the floor. Only the ceiling was visible now. She heard sounds of a struggle, and Joe trying to calm Cisco and then calling for help. *What now?* She paced her room, scared and frustrated because she couldn't watch what was happening. After a time, Joe picked up the phone. "I'll call you right back."

Minutes later, her phone rang—a call, not FaceTime. "I'm sorry, Mom," Joe said. "I thought the call would go okay. They had to sedate him again to calm him down. He tried to pull his IV so he could go home. He and I had that conversation this morning and he seemed to accept things then. I don't know why he got so upset now, but he's fine on the sedative."

Cora knew why. She remembered when her grandmother was in a nursing home. Although Cora's mother visited regularly, she didn't have a car, but Cora did. So, when Cora visited, Grandma wanted Cora to drive her home. "Please," she'd beg. "Take me home, Cora." She would cry and get so upset that Cora knew her visits were doing more harm than good. In an effort to keep her calm, Cora missed the last few weeks of her grandmother's life.

Now it was happening all over again. Cisco knew Cora would do anything for him and had the power to check him out of the hospital, but was refusing to do so. It made him angry. Like with Grandma, Cora's calls could be doing him more harm than good. Maybe what everyone was telling her was right: it wasn't a good idea to go to Arizona yet.

"Joe, perhaps it's better if I talk to him tomorrow. Meantime, you're my eyes and ears. Call me tonight, or immediately if anything happens."

Cora Tozzi, *History of the Religious Institutions of Lemont*
(Chicago, Madonna Press, 2024), 62–66

*"I was overcome with a kind of misgiving, thinking
that it would not be an easy task to teach myself and others
as well to be good religious. I had no spiritual training and
my education was limited. I submitted to God's will with this
thought: I would allow Him to do with me as He pleased."*
—The Chronicles of Venerable Mother Josepha of Chicago

### Josie's Journal
### Chicago, November 28, 1893

It is hard to believe that today is seven years since the day Katy died.

We wrote to the Sisters of Charity of the Incarnate Word in San Antonio shortly after her death, but they had little more to tell us, only that she had been found unconscious by an overturned wagon. She died at the convent a few days later. That was all we were to know.

My mind still envisions horrible images to fill in the scant details: Katy, beautiful as always, blood oozing between the pale brown braids wrapped around her head, one leg crushed beneath a wagon wheel, another wheel still spinning. The horse, still in its harness, thrashing and screaming in pain. Someone would have to put the horse out of its misery. Bloody wounds, birds and insects, maybe black ugly vultures poking their sharp beaks, too awful to comprehend. Then a kindly soul chances by, makes the sign of the Cross, and notifies the sisters, who bring her to the convent.

In truth, why do we need to know details? We know what is important: our beloved Katy died as a martyr to her religious generosity and
her profession as a sister and a nurse; she had been a good, devoted
young woman, and loved by all; and she was gone from us forever, taking a place of honor next to her beloved Jesus in Heaven.

There are still moments I ask why God had to take Katy from us so
young. Some say in my place they would be angry with God, and, in
truth, I have been tempted to anger. But we cannot know what God
has planned for us, and I always return to my faith that He knows best.

Still, my heart aches, not only for our loss, but with guilt because of
my part in allowing Katy to go to San Antonio. Mama had fought against
the move, fearing the very thing that had happened. What if I had sided
with Mama and against Katy's wishes? Would she still be alive today?
Or would I have deprived her of her greatest desire and three years of
perfect happiness? Some say God should not have allowed such a thing,
but I cling to the knowledge that she died happy, doing what brought her
joy and fulfillment. This is some small comfort.

Mama and I live quietly now, as I promised Papa. I am a spinster of
thirty-three years, busy with church activities and my dressmaking business. My biggest fear now is that no one will be able to alleviate the
suffering of the poor and homeless that surround us.

Today Chicago is crowded with nearly two million people. The Colum-
bian Exposition provided work for only a short time. Only five days after
the fair opened, there was a great stock market crash, and once again
jobs were lost and homeless people roamed the streets. Bankrupt railroads not only put men out of work but destroyed the businesses that
depended on them, hitting Chicago, a railroad hub, especially hard. Then
an even more severe crash came in July, and by the end of the summer
we were in the worst depression we have ever seen. The homeless are
housed in public places, in empty railroad stations, government buildings, fire stations, and libraries.

Father Vincent is sending poor women, widows, and the sick to me
and Mama. We care for them in our home until we find places for them.
Recently, others have been sending needy women to us as well. Now
winter is almost here and the problem is urgent.

There are too many. Today we have two elderly women in our spare bed-

room, two sisters in my bedroom while I share Mama's bed, and a pregnant woman sleeps on our sofa. Father is sending over an old woman
who has a terrible cough, and we will put a cot for her in our dining room.
Others we have had to refuse.

I have been thinking of buying a larger house and gathering a willing
group of women to help, but I do not know where we will find the money.
And would other women be willing to join me?

I told my idea to Adam, my brother-in-law, who is experienced in real
estate matters, for his opinion.

He was enthusiastic. "Not only is a shelter desperately needed, but
you and Mama could have your home to yourselves. What does Mama
think of the idea?"

"I have not told her yet. I did not want her to count on it until I knew it
was sure to happen. You are the first person I have told."

"Well, I think it is wonderful, and of course I will be more than happy
to help you find a building. Where will you get the money? Or your 'little
band of willing apostles,' as you called them?"

"I think I need to find devoted women first, and they can help me raise
funds. I will work out what it will cost to house twenty persons, if you
can find out the cost to purchase or rent a home of the right size. Then
I will talk to Father Vincent and get his support and blessing. My friend
Sophie Wisneski will help present the plan to the Third Order of St. Francis. I am sure some women will join us."

Adam looked thoughtful. "If you intend to buy a home and recruit others, you will need the support of the business community. Have you
thought about that?"

Approaching the community was, I instantly realized, an excellent idea,
but I would have to fight my natural shyness and reluctance to ask others for donations. I did not know how this would be done but I saw the
value of including the idea in my plans.

The next afternoon I left the dressmaking shop early and went to the
rectory to talk to Father Vincent. He, more than anyone else, knew the
urgent need.

"What to do with the homeless, who are now sleeping in the church
vestibule, parish hall, and school hallways, and who roam hungry in the
streets by day?" he said. "I have had many sleepless nights trying to

answer the question, and you present me with an answer! It is a good cause, Josie, and one I would be happy to help bring to fruition, but..."

My eyes searched his, and a wave of fear struck me.

"Josie, I know how dedicated you are to helping those in need. I know too that you finish what you start. But opening a home for the homeless is a big commitment, and if we begin it, we must guarantee its perpetuation. What if something happened that made it impossible for you to continue? It could all fall apart."

I was dismayed. Was he going to refuse permission? "Does that mean we should never start? These people need help, and—"

He held up a hand. "You mistake me, Josie. What I am saying is that if the church is to support such an endeavor, it needs to be done under religious obedience."

I felt my hands grow cold. Religious obedience. He meant he would give permission only if a religious order was founded for our purpose. A religious community had never been part of my idea. If that was the condition, I had to consider it, but the thought frightened me. What did I know about being a nun, or founding an order? I had left that to my sisters while I took care of things at home.

I resolved to investigate this, and proceeded to look for volunteers.

For the past seven years I have been the mistress of novices of the Third Order of St. Francis, single lay women devoted to the church and charitable activities. I thought that among the hundreds of women some would be interested in supporting my plans and excited about forming a new religious order, since their dedication implied more than ordinary love of God and His church.

After the Rosary Sodality meeting the next night, I asked my friend Sophie Wisneski to stay and talk. She tried to excuse herself, as her ailing parents were waiting for her at home. I thought uncharitably that not only did I too have a mother at home, but our apartment was filled with needy women. But I said nothing and Sophie stayed.

I not only sought Sophie's opinion, but hoped she would become involved. Sophie is ten years older than I am, a superior of the Rosary Sodality. I explained my plan and expressed how important she would be to the plan's success.

To my great relief, Sophie approved. She wanted to join, but said that her ailing parents and invalid sister made that difficult. I suggested she bring her family along, as I planned to do with my own mother. Sophie agreed to think about it.

A few days later, When Sophie and I presented the plan to the Third Order, almost a hundred women signed their names as volunteers. After the excitement died down, one woman asked if we would start right away. Then the unexpected happened.

I assumed we would begin to organize and raise funds immediately. Sophie and I had discussed the plan in detail, so I thought we were in complete agreement. She had not voiced any doubts other than her family situation, and we had resolved that. But now she advised the women that such an important undertaking should not be rushed into. We should take a year to evaluate and pray for God's blessing on the proposal.

A year! The room full of women met this suggestion with silence. The harshest months of winter were upon us. Already there was not enough space for all the people seeking shelter. What would these people do?

But some heads nodded. Perhaps we were being carried away by passion. It would be disastrous to jump into something that was not well thought out and perhaps not part of God's plan. So, when we polled the women again, the majority agreed to postpone the start date.

It occurred to me, not for the first time, that Sophie might be jealous. Her behavior was very strange. I had gone to her in trust. Why did she wait until this moment, when we had so many eager volunteers, to suggest a delay?

I pushed the thought from my mind as unkind and undeserved. Sophie had helped me for years. I am a quiet woman and dislike conflict. I look for good in people and usually find it. Sophie, however, is the superior of this group, and I am only the mistress of novices. What we plan to do is a big leap, and Sophie has much more experience. So, reluctantly, I yielded to the presumed wisdom of Sophie's suggestion.

I confess I also wondered how we would live as a community without a permanent home, but St. Francis himself had no permanent home when he founded the order that bears his name. The thought of following his example brings me peace of mind.

Despite my doubts, I am eager to begin. I remain convinced my plan is God's will, and whether it is to happen now or a year from now, I am ready for whatever my part turns out to be. It seems to me that with the help of God I will be equal to any task.

This may be the hardest thing I have ever done, but what would be harder for me to accept? To give up and see poverty persist, knowing I could have made a difference? Or to move ahead regardless of the personal sacrifice required?

If there must be delay, then that is God's will too. I placed my trust in Him and maintained my happy disposition, seeing the will of God in all life's events. But part of me fears that delay will bring disaster.

# Chapter 20

After the disturbing calls with Joe and Cisco, Cora knew if she didn't keep busy she'd continue to stew about Cisco's health until she made herself sick.

It wasn't yet nine in the morning. She started to sort papers on her desk until she realized she had already done that. To avoid staring at the walls in angst and self-pity, she kicked off her shoes, grabbed a composition book, picked up a biography titled *Josepha of Chicago*, and propped herself up in bed to read and make notes.

The writer, a devoted and scholarly man, was clearly extremely knowledgeable about Mother Josepha and brilliantly insightful. But the structure of the book was hard to follow, rambling and redundant, jumping back and forth in time with inconsistent continuity, as if each chapter had been written as a work of its own and then pieced into this volume. Cora knew she was being overly judgmental, but the biography needed more concentration than she had today.

Nonetheless, she tried. One chapter concerned the exhumation of Josepha's remains from St. Adalbert Cemetery in Niles and their transport to the chapel of the mother house in Lemont. The process involved many participants and meticulous documentation: priests, sisters, doctors, a bishop, members of the Tribunal, postulators, and a representative from Rome sent by the Pope. The next chapter described the economic environment of the city of Chicago in 1881, when Josie Mrozek, later to become Mother Josepha, arrived.

Cora got through two chapters. By then it was ten o'clock, so she set her work down and went to the kitchen. Finding the large room empty, she fixed herself coffee and toast, then moved to the dining room. Her stomach felt jittery, making it hard to eat even that much.

She found herself wishing Sister Fatima would walk in. Just why Fatima had decided to be nice to her was mystifying, but she believed the woman's compassion was genuine. According to what she'd been told, Fatima had been well respected and effective as dean of the high school and much beloved by students. Perhaps she blossomed with opportunities to touch the life of another person and now saw Cora as the recipient of her kindness. Whatever the reason, Cora's feelings toward the woman had changed.

But Fatima didn't come, and Cora's thoughts returned to the previous evening and the visitor. Assuming there really was a visitor, was she the Virgin Mary, as Maryam believed? In the light of day, Cora's gut told her something was off. For one thing, Maryam's description didn't fit. From Cora's prior research, Our Lady's physical appearance and manner of dress had been fairly consistent—blue and white garments, not brown, a face of radiant beauty rather than plain unremarkable features. Also, Mary always came for a greater reason—to show the world its error, to give instructions to prevent a dire fate for humankind, to bear witness to some universal truth. But Maryam's visitor wanted someone to tell the world about Katy, whoever that was.

If the visitor wasn't Mary, then who was she? Cora had already decided to look into the visitor's request, despite her doubts. But first she had to determine who the visitor was, who Katy was, and why the visitor cared enough to come to earth with a mission that involved Cora.

She went back into the kitchen, washed her cup, and went to find Sister Maryam.

When she got to Assisi Manor, the secretary at the door asked her to wait in the lobby while she notified Sister Maryam.

"I'm sorry," Maryam said when she appeared. "Because of this pandemic, we're being asked to limit visitors. We don't want the whole residence to come down with this bug. We're going to have to wear facial coverings, and we may have to close to visitors completely before long."

Cora looked over her shoulder. The secretary was out of earshot. "Well, it's *our* 'visitor' I came to talk to you about. Can we go somewhere private?"

"Let me grab a sweater. We can go for a walk."

They left the building and strolled through the parking lot, toward the old school.

"Before you tell me what you came for, how is Cisco doing?" Maryam asked.

"There's not much change. Our son Joe, who's a doctor, is there with him now. Cisco's still confused. He has atrial fibrillation and the doctors think he may have had a stroke. I'm worried sick. But there's nothing I can do."

"I never met your husband. What is he like?"

"He's what you could probably describe as an average good guy. Average height and build. The little hair he has left is dark, and he wears glasses. He's easygoing, but we bicker good-naturedly a lot. He's kind and helpful. He lets me take the lead and never gets upset over my craziness. And he's very supportive. I mean, how many guys would take over a good deal of the housework so I can sit at my computer or run off on projects? He even steps in to give me a hand—a hand he notices I need without asking—and he never complains. Well, he rarely complains." Cora grinned, then her mouth trembled. "We complement each other, Maryam. I'm a better person because of him, and I hope I can say that he's a better person because of me." She swiped her hands across her eyes.

"You have a storybook marriage, it sounds like," Maryam said.

"We don't often think that way, but perhaps we do."

They had passed the entrance to the old school and turned south to head past the convent and into the sports fields at the rear of the property. They walked awhile in silence.

"It shouldn't come as a surprise that I've been thinking a lot about last night," Cora said. "If I understand what happened, some things don't make sense to me."

"What do you mean, 'if'? I told you what happened," Maryam said.

"Maryam, please understand. I saw nothing with my own eyes. The experience is all new to me, and you have to admit it's hard to believe. I'm trying to make sense of what happened. I'm sorry, but it puzzles me why you're so sure it's Mary who's been visiting you. You said she never revealed herself as the Blessed Mother, and the description you gave isn't like other times Mary appeared, is it?"

Maryam smiled. "Leave it to you to bring up a historical element! Mary can appear any way she likes, can't she? She's done the unexpected before, appearing to children like she did at Fatima, or to people of limited intellect, such as Bernadette at Lourdes."

"But she never appears in dark colors. Always white or pale blue, isn't that right?"

"Usually. Why does that make a difference?"

"She's always described as radiant. Light, bright colors go with that. Not dark brown, like what you said she wore. And what's her message? When Mary appeared in the past, she always had a message for the world. But not this time?"

"No, not at first. She just made contact and asked for prayers."

"You've been seeing her for years, Maryam. Has she ever hinted at a message? Something that would have an impact on all of humankind? Isn't that what Mary did when she came to earth before? Something like this pandemic. In fact, isn't this pandemic exactly the kind of warning that Mary would give? But she hasn't mentioned it, has she?"

Sister Maryam eyed Cora suspiciously. "Didn't you say you came here hoping to get closer to your religion? I'm the religious person, but you're doubting my judgment in religious matters. What are you suggesting?"

How did Cora answer that? She understood she was casting doubt on a very important belief of Maryam's. Of course the young nun would be irritated, even offended. Then again, maybe Maryam was being defensive because she was unsure herself.

Or had she made the whole thing up and was annoyed that Cora had seen through her act? Clearly this was not a good time to suggest that Sister Maryam may not have had a visitor at all. Whatever the answer, Cora didn't want to damage their friendship. Too much was at stake. She had to get to the bottom of the matter, in case someone from heaven really could help Cisco get well.

A light breeze was blowing. Maryam pulled her sweater closer and wrapped her arms around her shoulders.

Cora stared at the ground ahead of her. "Maybe the reason she asked me for a favor is because I'm so grounded in earthly matters, and that's the sort of person she needs to get something done. I must sound like I'm challenging you—I don't mean to do that. I'm just using logic and trying to get an extraordinary experience clear in my head. Assume for a minute that this isn't Mary, but some *other* visitor from heaven. Who do you think it could be?"

Maryam closed her eyes for a moment, then shook her head. "I have no idea. I never thought she was anyone but Mary. Who do *you* think she could be?"

"Maybe her clothes are a clue?"

"A plain, modest dark brown shirt and skirt. Something you'd expect a religious woman to wear," Maryam said.

"So, let's start there. Then let's ask why she's appearing here, in the ravine at Assisi Hill. She could appear anywhere. Why here?"

"She could be attached to the place from her life on earth, I suppose."

"Yes, I thought that too. But what about why she appears to you, instead of someone else?"

Maryam laughed. "That one's easy! Because I'm a loner and a dreamer, not particularly good at anything, and susceptible to suggestion."

Cora chuckled. "I'd debate that 'not good at anything' part, at least."

A rumbling noise caught Cora's attention. Off to her left, a worker was using a leaf blower to clear the tennis courts.

Sister Maryam said, "Maybe we'd better head back." The women turned around.

"Okay," Cora said, "the most crucial question is, *why* is she here? What's her purpose? What's so important she leaves heaven to talk to you? Mary, or whoever it is, wouldn't come to earth without a good reason, right?"

"She hasn't told me yet. I'm sure she will when the time is right."

Cora looked off in the distance, thinking. "Maybe she has."

"What do you mean?"

Cora took in a deep breath and slowly let it out. "I'm figuring it out as I go here, so be patient. A deceased woman, a saintly or religious person, leaves heaven, comes to Lemont, and communicates with you. Just like ghosts who can't rest if they've left behind something unsettled, maybe there's something really important on earth that your visitor wants resolved. She wants me to reveal information about someone named Katy."

"So, not something of universal importance to the world—she's here for something personal?" Sister Maryam said.

"Why not?"

"Well, certainly with God all things are possible. But what am I supposed to do with this notion?"

"Maybe nothing, except what you already have. Last night, our visitor told you to have *me* find out about Katy. How did I get in the picture? And who's Katy? A saint who deserves to be recognized, isn't that what she said?"

"Yes. I did wonder why she didn't ask me to do that instead of you."

"I don't know. Maybe because I'm good at digging up information. Maybe she wants someone who isn't a religious person. Or maybe she wants us to be a team."

Maryam laughed wryly and glanced sideways at Cora. "So now I'm only the messenger? I was perfectly happy talking to Mary. Now all of a sudden, we're chasing after an unknown woman named Katy. Another mystery from the past has just landed in your lap."

But Cora didn't laugh. She hoped Sister Maryam wasn't angry about all the questions, but she just couldn't accept the young nun's interpretation of events.

"I didn't bring Katy or me into it, Maryam. Your visitor did. I'm really sorry. But I have to figure this out. Cisco's life could depend on it."

# Chapter 21

At lunchtime, Cora's appetite was as bad as it had been during her radiation treatment. After the first few weeks of therapy, her sense of taste had gone wacky, and putting anything in her mouth was like a game. She remembered telling Cisco, "Sweet things taste salty. Salty things are sweet at first but turn bland right away. Peanut butter tastes like applesauce and applesauce tastes like eggs." Before long, the only foods she had been able to tolerate were oatmeal and Ensure.

Her radiation oncologist had told her, "Your throat and other internal structures are experiencing the same burns internally as you'll soon see externally." It was the beginning of a worsening ordeal that lasted the better part of a year.

Cisco had been with her every step of the way then. How could she not be with him now?

Today, after only a few bites of a peanut butter and jelly sandwich, Cora returned to her room, lay on her back in bed and closed her eyes. She hoped to throw off the fogginess left from her restless night and escape her problems in sleep, but an aching pain across her shoulders persisted. *Must be tension. As if I don't have enough to worry about.* Surely, she wouldn't be cursed with her own health crisis on top of everything else! Her heart beat hard and fast. She heard the rhythmic pounding and swishing in her ears and forced herself to breathe slowly and deeply. She had to stay healthy.

Cora had developed what she called her three-P method of coping with stress—pity, prayer, and plans. She allowed herself five minutes of pity, tears if necessary. This was followed by ten minutes of prayer, handing her worries off to a greater power. If she had not relaxed sufficiently by then, she started planning what to do next, finding action took her away from her funk.

Now she got through the pity part and the prayer part. She had just started planning what to do that afternoon and evening when her cell phone rang. It was Joe, earlier than expected. *Is this good news or bad news?* She took a deep breath, sat up, and answered the call.

"Well, Mom, I wouldn't say this is good news, but we know what we're dealing with now and that's a step in the right direction."

"Go on." Her face felt flushed, her hands cold but damp with sweat.

"The second scan *does* show that Dad had a stroke. It's in the frontal part of his brain, the part that controls language, emotion, and reasoning. That explains why he's having trouble understanding what's happening to him, why he's angry and less rational."

Cora let the words sink in. Her mother had a stroke and recovered. But it had taken a long time. "He's going to get better, right?"

"He's gotten better already, but there are no absolutes here, Mom. It depends on how well the brain recovers. It's only been a day."

"I know. The brain is swollen and needs time to shrink before he makes progress." That was what she'd been told about her mother's stroke.

"That's the simple explanation, yes. It's early." He let out a long breath. "Look, Mom, this was not a small stroke. Quite a large area was involved. Frankly, his neurologists are amazed at how much function he has already. He has no muscle impairment at all, and he understands fairly well. These are really good signs, but you have to understand that there was damage."

Her eyes were burning. Would Cisco ever be the same again? Would it be like living with a new person? She wanted the man she had fallen in love with!

"I have…to be there, Joe." Her voice didn't sound like hers, thin, breaking, and squeaky.

"Mom, there's no point." Joe said it gently but firmly. "They won't let you in. There are absolutely no visitors allowed, no non-medical people. What's the point of you sitting alone fretting in a hotel room and talking to Dad on the phone when you can stay comfortably where you are among friends and still do that?"

"I'd see you. Maybe Barney and Connie."

"Very little of me. When I'm not at the hospital, I'm trying to cover my practice remotely. I'm sure Barney and Connie don't want the responsibility, and even if they did, air travel is restricted now. What are you going to do, drive out here by yourself? Or risk getting this virus on a plane, even if you could get a ticket? No. I don't need to worry about you, too. Please—I really don't want you to come now."

Joe meant well, but his words hurt. She swallowed hard. "Is he calmer today? Less angry? Less confused?"

"Some. He's still getting sedation, and he's more cooperative, a little more anyway. He wants to go home, of course. Still hates being asked questions, which happens all day long. Questions irritate him and he gets pretty mouthy. At least he's not pulled his IVs out so far today. He's not exactly the favorite patient on the floor, but the nurses are being good to him. They know what they're doing, Mom. Nonetheless, I'm sure they'll be relieved to send him home when he's ready." He chuckled a little. "You know how stubborn Dad can be."

"And outspoken."

"Well, expect him to be even more outspoken, at least for a while." He paused. "It's not his fault, you know. He can't help it—it's how the stroke affected him. But what if he gets really agitated, or even violent? Are you prepared for that?"

"What are you saying? That he could be dangerous to me? That's crazy! Never."

"Mom, it's not him, remember. It's the stroke. His behavior is not his fault, and it's not your fault. But I have to think about you, too. That's one of the reasons I want you to stay right where you are, where you're safe."

*Safe? From Cisco? Is that what he means? Surely, he means safe from the coronavirus.* She knew Cisco would never hurt her.

"Do you think I should talk to him? Can we try that again, or would that be a mistake?"

"He's calm now, but I'm not on the floor. I've got some work to do. Let's leave it until tonight, after dinner. About seven Chicago time. And let's do a phone call. We can FaceTime tomorrow if tonight goes well."

She lay back down for a while after Joe's call, staring at the ceiling. Despite what her son had said, she knew Cisco was not a violent man.

Assuming he would get better—and she had to believe he would—would their life be the same as before? She desperately hoped so, but could only wait and see.

Again, she was struck with feelings of guilt and regret. Why did she suggest Cisco go to Arizona? Perhaps if she'd been a better Catholic, this never would have happened.

With what seemed like an endless afternoon looming ahead, she had to keep busy—keep her mind from running wild with everything that could go wrong. Tincture of time, Joe had said. Time would cure Cisco. Believe it—for the next few hours, at least.

Work or go for a walk? She sat up. She'd try work first, leaving the walk in abeyance in case work failed. Of course, if she walked, she would think. But walking always helped her deal with stress.

She picked up *Josepha of Chicago* again, and read the added material before returning to where she'd left off. She set the book down and Googled the author, Reverend Henryk Maria Malak, then located him on the Franciscan Sisters of Our Lady website.

Born in Poland in 1912, the Roman Catholic priest had been incarcerated in Nazi concentration camps during World War II. After liberation from Dachau in 1945, he emigrated to the United States in 1950. In 1960 he read a copy of Mother Josepha's journal, *The Chronicle*, and developed a devotion to her.

He moved to the convent in Lemont in 1963 and opened the Mother Josepha Museum in the old Walker Mansion on the property. In 1972 he was appointed postulator for her cause and was present when her body was exhumed and placed in the sarcophagus in Lemont. He had *The Chronicle* translated from Polish into English and wrote two biographies about Mother Josepha, the first in 1975 and a revised version in 1982. The latter was probably more readable, but the 1975 book, with almost twice the material, was the version Cora had on hand. She dived in again, despite knowing it would be like sifting mud. So far, she had only gotten to page 25, the end of Chapter 2.

She turned the page. The bold heading struck her immediately: *Chapter 3. Katy.*

Katy! Her heart beat faster. It could be coincidence, though. Katy was a common name, even more so when Josie Mrozek was alive.

Cora began to read. Josie Mrozek was becoming increasingly involved with caring for Chicago's homeless and destitute, moved by their misery and sufferings. Some three years previously, at the age of fourteen and recently graduated from school, her beloved younger sister Katy had joined the Sisters of Charity. The superiors eventually sent Katy to their novitiate in San Antonio, Texas, where she trained as a nurse. Then one day, a telegram arrived. Katy had been killed in a tragic accident. The telegram read:

*"We are extremely sad to tell you that our much-loved Sister Catherine Marie has left us. She had been tending a sick farmer, and on the way home her buggy struck some obstacle and Sister was flung to the ground. She was brought unconscious to the convent, where she died of her injuries several days later. Sister Catherine's funeral will take place on December 1 and she will be buried in our community cemetery. We take some consolation in knowing that she is now with her beloved Jesus."*

The following chapter, "Her Adopted Daughter," described Katy's life in greater detail, including the close relationship between her and Josie. Cora let out a breath. Maryam's visitor was Josie, later to become Mother Josepha. A hunch, but it felt right, and Cora had learned to trust her instincts.

She flipped through the book, searching for photos of Josepha. She found a few, depicting a short, average-appearing woman dressed in dark clothing of the period. The photos were consistent with Sister Maryam's description of her visitor.

It made sense. Mother Josepha's appearance to Maryam, a nun who would be receptive to her, had not been coincidence. She came to this place searching for someone who had the skills to look into her sister's death and life, to find whatever it was that made Katy deserving of sainthood—starting with Sister Maryam, until Cora became Maryam's friend. Cora, with her experience solving historical mysteries.

She went back to the book and jotted down a few details. Then she called Frannie. The call went to voicemail, so she left a message.

"Frannie, drop everything else for the moment—this is urgent. Find out everything you can about a woman named Katherine Mrozek, that's

M-r-o-z-e-k, Katherine with a "K", born in Poland in 1868, moved to Chicago in 1881. In 1884 she joined the Sisters of Charity of the Incarnate Word and moved to San Antonio, Texas, where she became Sister Catherine, with a "C", and was killed in an accident in 1886. Find out what you can about her life as a nun, how she died, and about the sisters. Call me if you have questions, but please start as soon as you can. Thanks!"

She ended the call, jammed her phone into her pocket—she wasn't going to be caught without it again—and grabbed her jacket. She'd tell Maryam—no, not yet. She might have offended Maryam during their last conversation and wanted to be better prepared. Maryam was going to resist, and Cora couldn't blame her. Not only did Cora have no real evidence to back up her hunch, but she had no absolute evidence other than Sister Maryam's word that a heavenly visitor even existed.

Her car keys were in her purse. She'd try to catch Sister Elizabeth at St. Joseph Convent. If the sister didn't have time to see her—no, she *had* to have time to see her! Cora would make it happen somehow. If she could plead Katy's cause on earth, then perhaps Josepha would plead for Cisco in heaven. Supposedly she was doing that anyway, but Cora's actions might make Josepha grateful enough to work harder.

Cora checked the time. She was on a roll but she had to get back for the phone call with Cisco tonight. Should she tell him what was going on? Hell, no! He had enough to deal with, and would never believe in what she was doing. Better keep this to herself for now. She picked up her purse and left.

# Chapter 22

When Cora arrived at St. Joseph Convent, the secretary left her desk to talk to Cora through the locked glass door. No visitors were allowed due to coronavirus restrictions. Cora begged the woman to call Sister Elizabeth, and she finally agreed.

Cora alternately leaned against a wall or paced the tiny entryway while she waited, mulling over the implications of her recent discovery. She wished she could reveal her suspicion that the visitor in the ravine was Mother Josepha, but she had to keep Sister Maryam's confidence. Mother Josepha herself might not want her appearance known. If she did, wouldn't she have said so, or appeared to someone at St. Joseph's instead of only to Sister Maryam? More than anyone, the appearances would be important to Sister Elizabeth, but Cora couldn't tell her yet.

Perhaps she had been too hasty, running over here before thinking this through. She almost rang the bell again to ask the secretary to tell Sister Elizabeth to forget it, when she spotted Sister Elizabeth approaching from within the building. The nun, wearing a face mask, unlocked the door and stepped outside. She handed another mask to Cora.

As Cora pulled the mask straps over her ears, Sister Elizabeth said, "They're calling this virus a pandemic now. Aren't they taking precautions at Assisi Hill? Their situation is similar to ours. We can't allow the virus to spread through the community or into the residences. Our seniors are so vulnerable."

"They've been trying to figure out how to handle the situation—I'm sure they'll decide soon. There's a lot of meetings going on, but I've been too busy with personal problems to notice the details." She reached out to lay her hand on Sister Elizabeth's arm, then thought better of it. "Can we go to the museum and talk there? Something has come up. I have different questions than on my first visit."

Sister Elizabeth glanced into the lobby, then back at Cora, her eyes doubtful. "The museum is closed—the whole building, really—to visitors. But I can make exceptions, if we keep our distance and wear masks." She shook her head. "Who'd have thought we'd be doing this, in this day and age? It's like some disaster movie, isn't it?"

Cora followed Sister Elizabeth back into the building. When the receptionist came toward them, holding her hand up in warning, Sister Elizabeth waved her away. "I've got it, Barb," she said. They proceeded the short distance down the hall to the Mother Josepha Museum. Sister Elizabeth unlocked the door and turned on the lights. They went to the back of the room and sat on either end of a long armless bench in front of a display case.

Cora gazed at the case without really seeing its contents as she told Sister Elizabeth about Cisco's hospitalization and her frustration over her inability to join him in Arizona.

"I'm desperate," she said. "The last time I was here, you and I talked about Mother Josepha's need for documented miracles, and I thought...."

"You want her to intercede and heal your husband?"

"Yes." Considering her personal doubts, and knowing she wasn't being completely honest, Cora avoided looking at Sister Elizabeth. "I've never been this close to a saint before. The idea came to me...it seems like the right thing to do. I hoped you could tell me the best way to go about it."

There was a long pause while Sister shifted position.

"I don't know what to say, Cora." Another pause. "I wish I could give you a hug. It's so sad that with this pandemic it's dangerous to touch. God wants us to offer comfort to each other. But words will have to do today."

Sister Elizabeth's mask moved a fraction. Cora imagined a smile behind it—the nun's eyes appeared gentle. "So, pretend I'm holding your hand now. How does it feel?"

Cora was relieved. This was going to be okay. "Warm and soft."

Sister Elizabeth gave a short chuckle. "Your thoughts are kind, but my hands are rather rough. I'm glad you think of them as soft."

The women sat in silence for a while. Then Sister Elizabeth said, "We all wish for miracles at one time or another, don't we? Of course, they rarely happen, and when they do it's often in an unexpected way or an unlikely place, not how we imagined."

"I just wish the whole business would go away, like a bad dream."

Sister Elizabeth sighed. "I wish I had advice to give you, but the only thing I can say is to pray as often as possible, and ask Mother Josepha specifically for what you wish."

"Pray how? Are there special prayers?"

"The prayers you know, I'm sure. Say rosaries. Do you know how to make a novena?"

"Pray nine times, yes."

"And the materials I gave you last time included a card with a prayer Mother Josepha wrote. Include that."

"Can you tell me anything else? Something that will make her want to help me? I'm just getting to know about her and haven't done anything to support her cause yet."

"It's not in her nature to be selective about who she helps, Cora. Do you realize what's in that case in front of you?"

She hadn't paid attention, but now she looked. In the center was a tarnished crucifix about six inches tall, in a glass and antique gold container that rested on a piece of handcrafted needlework of some sort in deep purple and silver. She remembered that the young Josie had been skilled in embroidery and there were samples of her work elsewhere in the museum. She leaned forward and peered at the note card. It said the crucifix was from the Franciscan Crown—or the Seven Joys of Mary Rosary—worn by Josepha. Among other items were Josepha's prayer book, fragments of wood from her casket, and a lead casket plate inscribed *Spoczywaj w Pokoju*, translated as *Rest in Peace*.

"Relics. Josepha's relics."

"Yes. These are second class relics. Do you know what that means?" Sister Elizabeth said.

"Not really. Not at all, actually. Just that relics are something left over from a person's life."

"Second class relics are things that were owned and closely used by a saint or venerated person. Third-class relics are items physically touched to either first- or second-class relics."

"And first class?"

"Physical remains."

Bones, or parts of Josepha's body. The idea was discomfiting. "Are relics supposed to have some sort of magical power?"

"Not magical. That would be the wrong word. It's more like a tangible memorial, but there are documented reports when a relic was thought to have protected the person who possessed it, or to have caused a healing or miracle."

If only she could tell Sister Elizabeth the whole story. Mother Josepha appearing in the ravine must be the ultimate miracle!

Cora sighed. "I wish I had one of those. Are there any first-class relics of Mother Josepha here?"

Sister Elizabeth laughed. "All of them—in the chapel, in her sarcophagus. Her body was exhumed, remember?"

Of course! Mother Josepha's remains were right here. The same woman may have come down from heaven, and Cora had witnessed Maryam's conversation with her. *She even sent me a message!* A chill ran across her shoulders and down her spine as the impact hit home.

"This is a big deal, isn't it?"

"A really big deal." Sister Elizabeth smiled again.

*If only she knew!*

"Take something personal and hold it while you pray," the nun said. "Maybe take some petals off the flowers on her sarcophagus."

Cora remembered Winnie visiting the sarcophagus and wondered if she took any petals. "Can we stop for some when I leave?"

"Certainly."

Cora stood and walked a few steps away to another display on her right that contained an almost life-size photo of Mother Josepha in her habit. Hanging from her waist was the Franciscan Crown rosary and a heavy white cord with three knots. Sister Elizabeth had said on her previous visit that the knots represented vows of chastity, obedience, and poverty. Cora had seen this same photo in books, pamphlets, and on the order's website.

Surrounded by her white wimple, eyes behind rimless glasses, Mother Josepha's unsmiling face had not appeared especially compassionate, the quality for which she was so well known. But when Cora looked at the photo now, the eyes seemed to connect deeply with her, as if she and Josepha shared a secret. As indeed they did, she realized. With that realization came a conviction that the events in the ravine were real and that the heavenly visitor was Mother Josepha.

A feeling of comfort filled Cora, as if she were in the warm embrace of a kind-hearted woman who would take care of her troubles. She understood in that moment why it had been so important that she come here, to the museum, immediately. She had to test her theory in the place she felt close to the saint—to get vibes from the spaces surrounding her. Her instinct had been correct: she felt energy in this room, with the woman's life all around her, more than she did standing by the sarcophagus. It was the woman's life that intrigued Cora, not her death.

Suddenly she felt afraid, and let her gaze slip from Josepha's photo to the floor. *If her presence is real, now I have to do as she asks. I have to admit there is a world beyond the physical world I'm so tied to.*

But now was not the time for cold feet. She hadn't asked Sister Elizabeth the most important question. She returned to the bench and sat back down. "In his book, Reverend Malak writes at length about what he calls the mother-daughter relationship between Josie and her sister Katy. Does that agree with what you know?"

"It does."

Cora glanced at Sister Elizabeth. "He's not always clear in his writing, but he's always passionate."

Sister Elizabeth chuckled. "That's true. He tended to be subjective, but he did a lot of research and there isn't anyone who knew more about her than he did."

"So, there are no other clues to what happened to Katy, or what she did in San Antonio, except what's in his book."

"I don't know that anyone ever looked any further. The assumption was that if there was any more to the story, Reverend Malak would have mentioned it. I know none of us has searched for additional information since he died."

Frannie would be doing that by now, Cora thought. But it wouldn't be easy to find out what Katy was doing, why she deserved to be a saint, and exactly how she died, let alone to prove it and get the church to take on another saint candidate.

Cora pressed both hands to her cheeks, feeling overwhelmed, not for the first time. "I haven't gotten too far in her biography yet. I only know the basics of Josepha's life—she started by taking the poor, homeless, and elderly into her home, then founded the Franciscan Sisters in 1894, and they opened St. Joseph's Home in 1898. She would have been 38 years old then. Did she just continue with works of mercy after that?"

"It's not a happy story, Cora."

Cora looked at Sister Elizabeth in surprise. The nun elaborated. "People don't get to be a saint by leading an easy life. They do remarkable things, but they confront adversity."

"Okay...like what?"

Sister Elizabeth took a deep breath. "She was replaced as Mother Superior. It happened right after the St. Joseph's Home was officially blessed and the sisters moved in with their first residents."

"You mean as soon as she fulfilled her dream, she was fired? Why?"

"I think the best way of saying it is that despite her many virtues, Mother Josepha was not the most effective leader. She was expected to set and follow rules, but not everyone agreed with her. There was a lot of dissent and complaints from the sisters, and some left. She was too kind, found it hard to discipline others, and was awful at herding cats. It seemed she couldn't do anything right. If she was lenient, she was accused of being lax, but if she was strict, she was accused of being overly harsh. She relied on the priests and her best friend, Sister Anne, throughout her term as superior. When the new home opened, a change had to be made. Sister Anne was a take-charge person who brought people together, so she became the new superior."

"So, Mother Josepha came up with the idea, persevered over tremendous difficulties, gave up everything she owned to help the poor, and as soon as she succeeded she was denied the satisfaction of enjoying her own accomplishments?"

"Some put it that way. In fact, you'll find that Reverend Malak was one of those people. But that opinion doesn't make sense to me. Sister Anne was not only Josepha's best friend and mentor for many years, but they shared common experiences and problems, including needing to support their families. I can't believe there were hard feelings between them. Mother Josepha was such a compassionate person, she would prefer to think well of others. I also think she may have been relieved to give up the responsibility, especially to someone she loved and who she thought would handle the situation better than she could. She was very humble, Cora."

Cora felt skeptical. Wasn't it like a slap in the face, to see all her efforts disregarded? Josepha must have felt humiliated. "So, she did what, then? Assisted the new superior?"

"She ran the laundry and the embroidery shop, and taught others fancy needlework. She planted a garden and did most of the garden labor herself. As the years went on, the newer sisters never knew she founded the order, but gave the credit to Sister Anne. All Mother Josepha did was forgotten. She was just the little old nun they called Sister Gardener."

"And then she died? In obscurity?"

"And then she died. Of stomach cancer. In pain but without complaint until the end. She was 58 years old."

Cora was moved. "And she never knew what happened to her beloved little sister."

# Chapter 23

On her way back to Assisi Hill, Cora passed St. Marija's. On a whim, she returned to the entrance and drove up the hill. It was midafternoon. She wouldn't call Cisco until seven. With the Franciscan Crown rosary and its significance to Mother Josepha fresh in her mind, she felt like exploring the Rosary Valley at St. Marija's in greater detail.

Walking down into the valley, she noticed that the steps were bordered with concrete and studded with pieces of bright blue and red glass that caught the sun. The builders had taken every opportunity to ornament the garden.

On previous visits to the valley, Cora was so taken with the uniqueness of the setting and especially of the unusual reddish stone that she had spent little time examining the sculptures individually. The sculptures depicted the Seven Joys of the Blessed Virgin Mary. From her religious education as a child, Cora remembered some of the milestones of Mary's life, the theme of the Franciscan Crown rosary.

The first monument was on her left. A round, bas-relief plaque of cast concrete set into the stone depicted the Annunciation, when the Angel Gabriel announced to Mary that she was to be the mother of God. Cora whispered Mary's reply in this silent, isolated place. "Be it unto me, according to your word."

With her phone, she snapped a picture of the monument and then a close-up of the plaque, and moved on to the next stop, the Visitation. This image showed Mary's visit to her cousin, Elizabeth, who was soon to give birth to a son who would be John the Baptist. Cora, who performed with a classical choir, remembered a line from the "Magnificat," the words said by Mary when she greeted Elizabeth: "My soul doth magnify the Lord, and my spirit hath rejoiced in God my Savior." The words, long forgotten, struck her with fresh meaning. She conjured an image of the two mothers-to-be, women about to have an experience that would change not only their lives but the world, the wonder and fear they must have shared. Mary was only fifteen years old at the time, Elizabeth elderly but miraculously with child.

Next was the Nativity, the birth of Jesus, followed by the Adoration of the Child Jesus by the Magi after his birth. Cora photographed each plaque with her phone.

Rounding the bend and continuing back toward the entrance to the valley, the first monument on that side commemorated the Finding of the Child Jesus in the Temple. Then came the Resurrection of Jesus after his death, and finally the seventh joy, the Assumption and Crowning of Mary as Queen of Heaven.

Reaching the beginning of the path again, Cora was about to leave, but realized with some amazement that she had just demonstrated how ingrained her religious beliefs were. Did this mean she was getting closer to her intention to strengthen her belief in God?

Impulsively, she doubled back to take another look at the Finding of Jesus in the Temple. Of the important events in Mary's life, this story, rather than the Nativity, resonated most with Cora. To her, it signified the relationship between Jesus and Mary—their life as mother and son. If she remembered right, Jesus was twelve years old and the family was returning home from a festival. Having raised two boys, Cora thought this age was an especially precious time. By twelve years, mother and son had gotten to know each other very well. The child was becoming independent, but was still Mama's little boy. She could only imagine Mary's panic when she realized Jesus was lost. And it took three whole days to find him! How distraught she must have been, thinking the worst.

Cora put herself in Mary's place. Three days of terror, and then there he was, acting as if nothing was out of the ordinary, chatting with teachers in the temple, astonishing them with his own knowledge. What would Mary have been thinking, feeling? Relief, of course. Happiness. Astonished to find her son holding court among the most brilliant scholars of the day. She would have seen her little boy in a new light. Their relationship would have been changed from that day on, by the glimpse of the great man her child was to become. She knew she had given birth to God's son, but this could have been the first time she fully realized what that meant. This indication of the future would have made her proud, but at the same time frightened of more changes to come.

What was it Mary said to him? "Why have you treated us like this? We've been looking all over for you, and feared the worst." Or something like that. Just like a mom. And he replied, seeming puzzled at her distress, "Why? Didn't you know I'd be in my Father's house?" Wouldn't she have been heartbroken, foreseeing in that moment the time when Jesus no longer belonged to her but to the world? And the kingdom that was not of this world?

Cora's thoughts turned to Mother Josepha, Mother Superior of the convent she founded, and mother-like to her sister Katy, who called her Josie. How heartbroken Josie must have been at Katy's death, to have to let go of her baby sister, the girl she had raised like her own child. Her worst fear had come to pass—she would never see Katy again. How very sad. And just like Mary knew about Jesus, Josie was clearly convinced that Katy was a very special person in God's eyes.

But unlike Jesus, Katy's goodness was never made known to the world. Was Josepha now depending on Cora to do that? And what was it that made Mother Josepha think there was more to Katy's death than she had been told—something that marked Katy as saintly?

The sun seemed suddenly too warm. Cora opened her coat and felt an urge to cool her hands against the stone, that very unusual stone that so captured her imagination. She had never actually touched it, but she did now, placing one palm on each side of the plaque, feeling the abrasive surface, the sharp crevices and embedded crystals. Although the stone itself was warm, the effect it had on Cora was of coolness and calm. She felt glued to the stone, sensing that if she tried to remove her hands, she wouldn't be able to.

But she didn't *want* to remove her hands. She felt somehow a part of the stone, even her mind no longer her own. She lost awareness of her surroundings, staring into the image on the plaque, yet not seeing it. Instead, a scene played in her mind, the stone like a conduit.

What she sees is an open-bed buggy drawn by one horse, hurrying along a dirt road. The area is sparsely covered with scrub-like trees. A young woman, dressed in black, is driving the horse at a fast trot. The horse's bay coat is dark with sweat, and the woman keeps glancing behind her, a black shoulder-length veil whipping around her head. From her dress, Cora thinks the woman is a nun. Someone, wrapped in brown blankets, lies unmoving, seen through the open sides of the buggy bed. Dust billows behind the vehicle.

After a final backward glance, the woman flaps the reins sharply, urging the horse into a gallop. The horse appears to be struggling, its eyes wild with fright. Cora feels fear and urgency as if she is sitting next to the driver, the trees flashing by as the buggy flies down the road. Then the trees clear and the landscape turns flat, dry, and rocky. Ahead is a short, flimsy-looking bridge without railings that crosses over a thin, dry streambed.

A panicked horse, a driver hauling on the reins, straining to stay in control. The images like random snapshots flashing on a screen, sometimes so quickly that Cora has no time to notice details, other times stopping still for longer, some repeating over and over. The thundering of hooves accompanies the images, an odd echo, pounding in Cora's ears like a heartbeat.

Then silence.

A new scene: a woman lying motionless in the dry creek bed and then the sound of a horse screaming. A man riding up, a very large man on a tan-colored mount with a black mane, tail, and stockings. The horse appears too small for its rider. The man has dark skin and straight black hair that reaches almost to his waist. He wears a dull red shirt, open at the neck and tied at the waist with a blue band, tan pants, and brown knee-high moccasins.

Holding a rifle, he moves slowly, sliding off the buckskin and heading to the upturned bed of the buggy. He examines the man who is still inside, nods, and then goes down into the gully. He leans over the woman and stands for a moment, rubbing his face with both hands. Then he walks over to the struggling horse still caught in the buggy harness, studies the animal, and shakes his head. He aims his rifle at the horse's head and fires. The flailing and the screaming stop.

He returns to the buggy, lifts the man in it onto his massive shoulders, then sets him on the ground. The man from the buggy appears frail. The big man then takes a blanket from the buggy, goes to the gully, wraps the blanket around the young woman, picks her up, and places her in the buggy. He arranges her carefully and shades her from the sun, then returns to the man on the ground and lifts him onto the buckskin's saddle. The man slumps over the horse's neck, either unconscious or too weak to support himself. The larger man climbs on behind him, supporting him with his arms. The small horse seems unfazed by the weight. The rider touches his heels to the horse's sides, and the horse walks away.

The images stopped, even though Cora's hands remained on the stone. Gradually she became aware of birds, a breeze, dry leaves and twigs rustling around her. Feeling unsteady on her feet, she pulled her hands free, walked a few paces away from the monument, sank down on a large rock near the side of the path, and buried her face in her hands. When she lifted her head, the valley looked the same as when she entered it.

What had just happened?

Many years ago, Cora had read tarot cards for a few months, despite the church's advice against such practices. After a time and some experience, she developed an intuition and just let the cards "speak" to her. She discovered she was hitting a lot of things on the head.

She stopped reading tarot when a frightening experience came too close to home. She had been practicing, having Patrick, her older son, shuffle the cards before she spread them out. The death card kept coming up in the present position in the spread. She looked for alternate meanings, not wanting the cards to indicate her son's death, but it happened seven times in a row. The next day she learned that a priest at her church with the same last name as theirs had died while hearing confessions, at the same time she had been reading the cards. She never touched a tarot deck again.

The experience she'd just had while touching the stone felt similar to, but much more intense than, her previous experiences with tarot.

But what were the images telling her?

Cora got up, went back to the monument, and placed her hands where they had been before, hoping to bring back the visions much as she might try to return to an unfinished dream. As before, the stone was rough and warm, but she remained attuned to the real world around her, noticing birds in nearby trees, the droning of a plane high above, a train horn in the distance.

After fifteen minutes, she gave up and walked slowly back to her car, bewildered and overwhelmed.

# Chapter 24

After leaving the Rosary Valley, Cora considered going to the ravine. Perhaps Maryam's visitor would appear to her, now that she had sent a message to Cora.

She decided against it. She was tired. Her thoughts fluctuated wildly based on facts and events that changed every few hours. If she didn't clear her mind she was likely to make mistakes, and she couldn't take more stimulation today. She had to digest the events of the past two days and what had just happened in the Rosary Valley.

When she was in college, Cora once dreamed that God spoke to her and gave her His phone number. The dream had felt so real that she got up and wrote the number down. She expected it to look like gibberish in the light of day, but it didn't: it looked like a valid phone number. When she told her friends, they wanted to know what happened when she called the number. She had no intention of calling it. What would she do if God answered?

That was how Cora felt about the visitor. She hadn't *proved* the visitor existed, but she now thought that Sister Maryam was meeting Mother Josepha, and Cora feared personal contact with the would-be saint. Anyone who called her chicken wouldn't be far off.

Back in her room at the convent, Cora sat at her desk, pencil in hand. Was this afternoon's experience a message or an illusion? It could be overactive imagination, from bits and pieces of what she'd been learning about Josepha's life and family. Had her personal stress led to hallucination? Her exhaustion to a waking dream, her mind trying to resolve subconscious thoughts. If so, what was her mind trying to tell her?

Whatever it was, her "vision" had seemed to portray the death of Katy, Mother Josepha's sister, with details added to the general story that Cora already knew. It made sense based on known facts, but also generated new questions.

She opened her notepad and began writing down parallels and differences between her imagined version and the one in the biography she had read. Assuming Katy was the woman driving the buggy, another person had been with her. That person, a frail man, wasn't mentioned in Father Malak's biography. Who was he, where was Katy taking him, and why?

A stranger took the frail man away. The same stranger laid the injured Katy back in the upturned buggy, handling her respectfully. He also shot the dying horse. Who was he, and why did he do what he did? The stranger resembled an American Indian more than a farmer, based on his dark skin and hair and manner of dress, especially the moccasins. Did Indians still live in that area of Texas in 1886? And Katy, or whoever drove the buggy, had urged the horse into a reckless gallop after looking behind her, as if running from someone. Why was she running, and from whom?

Cora glanced at her night table, where the biography lay with a bookmark stuck in it. The telegram received by Josie and her mother said Katy had been visiting a sick farmer and his wife. Was he the frail man in the buggy bed? What happened after Katy left the farm until the accident occurred? How long was she lying in the creek bed before she was discovered?

The buggy had been traveling through a lightly forested area. Cora didn't think of San Antonio as forested. She thought instead of vast barren plains, rocks, and brown hills. Not the kind of place she'd expect farmland to be, either. Had her vision been of San Antonio or somewhere else?

She slumped back in her chair. The only reason to think her vision took place in San Antonio was because of what she knew from Josie's biography. The images could have been entirely unrelated, but then why had Cora had the vision at all? It felt so real! Perhaps her mind was filling in the sparse facts with details based on imagination, history, and guesswork. Was she blowing the whole experience out of proportion because of her emotional state, fatigue, and obsession with the unusual rock she'd been touching at the time?

Did the rock have anything to do with the vision, or was that just another coincidence? No one seemed to know what kind of rock it was or where it came from. She would ask Janna to track down its origin, if possible, from the Slovenian records at St. Marija's.

Restless, she got up and began to pace. If there was a connection between her vision and Mother Josepha's beliefs about Katy's saintliness, Cora didn't see it. Katy was a nurse with a self-sacrificing and cheerful nature, but that didn't seem like enough to warrant sainthood. What might Katy have done to elevate her to that level, at least in her older sister's view? After Katy left Chicago, Josie only had letters to tell her what Katy's life was like, and Cora's knowledge was diluted by what historians had written. None of Katy's letters seemed to have survived. So what made Mother Josepha suspect there was more to Katy's story?

And the vision itself. Why did it happen when and where it did? In the Rosary Valley, when Cora was thinking about the challenges of being a mother, and while touching a monument celebrating an important event in the life of Jesus's mother? Josepha was actually called "Mother," as leader of an order of religious sisters. Before that, Josie Mrozek had been a second mother to her kid sister. And Maryam, Cora's new friend, believed she was seeing the mother of God.

*Here we go again*, Cora thought. *Another motherhood mystery.*

Since Cora's retirement, events that related to mothers and their children had kept cropping up. First, she had nursed her own dying mother. Then she had been haunted by the spirit of a young mother who was grieving the death of her child. Cora had written a biography of an Indian mother who sacrificed all she had to save her only son. And shortly before Cora's experience with cancer, she had helped a friend locate the mother who deserted her as a child.

Now here she was again, solving another historical mystery involving mothers, with another paranormal component. Only this time she was following the orders of a heavenly visitor and channeling an illusion brought on by high stress levels and some odd rocks, not clearly understanding why, but afraid to disregard the clues.

Fortunately, she had friends who wouldn't think she was crazy—

Frannie, for one, and another friend, Dan Mahoney, who loved digging into this kind of thing. They would understand and help her.

She glanced at her wristwatch. It was almost six o'clock. Joe would be calling from Cisco's room in an hour. Enough for today. She'd talk to Frannie and Dan tomorrow, hopefully after an encouraging call with Cisco and a decent night's sleep. A *good* night's sleep was a lost cause.

# Chapter 25

That evening, Cisco was calmer and seemed happy to hear from Cora, although still angry and in denial about his medical condition. He was on only mild sedation, and no longer tried to pull out his IVs. He was more polite to hospital staff, but rude to specialists and therapists who asked too many questions. Still, it was progress.

"You don't need to call me every few hours," Cisco told her. "I don't know what all the fuss is about. As soon as I convince the doctors I don't have to be here, I'll be home. And Joe should go home. I don't need him, either. I'm not a baby. I can get home myself."

"You're in Arizona, hon," she reminded him. "You don't have a car. When the time comes, Joe will pack up your things and take care of it." She paused. How could she explain pandemic-related travel restrictions when Cisco kept forgetting he wasn't in Chicago? He'd think he could rent a car and drive 1,800 miles home alone, even though, before his stroke, she always took the role of navigator. However, she wanted to avoid arguments tonight—keep things upbeat and pleasant.

"We'll deal with the details when they release you," she said instead.

"When's that going to be?"

"I'm not sure. Your doctors said you're doing very well. Surprisingly so, in fact. But they want to be sure they're not missing something before they let you go."

"Covering their asses."

"That could be, but it's to your benefit. Don't forget you're in AFib now, and that has to be managed. With your history of heart disease and stents, I should think you'd want to be sure that was under control."

"I suppose. But I still feel fine."

"Joe says you feel good because you're only lying in bed, not doing anything. If you were trying to do everything you normally do, you'd be tired. Remember, you were getting tired golfing. That never happened before. It's probably because of the AFib."

"I'll be fine once I get home."

"Don't be in such a hurry. Think of it as an extended vacation. Just relax, watch TV, check the news on your phone."

"My phone doesn't work right in here. The remote is crap, too. I push the buttons, but nothing happens. There's nothing on this television I want to see anyway."

She suspected he was being impatient, and that the fault was his, not the remote's. He had always been impatient. Joe had warned her he was more so now, but…. Maybe she wasn't giving Cisco enough credit. Maybe the remote didn't work well. She felt like a traitor. Her eyes started to burn and she blinked hard.

"All these people keep coming in and asking me stupid questions, treating me like some sort of idiot," he muttered. "I wish they'd just leave me alone."

"They're just doing their jobs, trying to evaluate you and make you better." She paused. "Play nice."

"I don't need to be better—I'm perfectly fine. It's stupid. I don't need them."

"You could be right, hon. But maybe they can help, if you give them a chance."

He was getting annoyed, she could hear it. "How many times do I need to say I don't need help?"

"Okay. But they don't know you like Joe and I do." She paused again. "Your doctors think the stroke made it harder for you to do some things, but you feel the same so you don't realize it. Sometimes, when they ask you questions, you don't know the right answers."

"The questions are stupid."

"Then you should be able to answer them, right?"

"Bullshit."

His refusal to accept his condition was maddening, but also familiar. It wasn't much different than when she refused to believe she had cancer, was it?

"Hon, Joe knows about these things. He agrees with the doctors, and I'm sure you know he wants the best for you. We all want the best for you, including the doctors and therapists. Please be patient."

"Sure, Joe agrees—he's a doctor himself, so he thinks like them."

"He loves you, hon. I'm sure he's watching them like a hawk. When he thinks you're able to go home, he'll work it out. This just happened yesterday. Give it a little time."

Cisco said, "Okay," probably not because he agreed with her, but because he was tired of arguing. It was a baby step, but in the right direction. She'd take that for the time being.

"I love you, hon. I'm so sorry this happened. I wish I could be there."

"I love you too, but stop worrying about me. I'm fine. I'm glad you called."

"I'll call again tomorrow, sometime in the morning, okay?"

"Sure. If that's what you want. Bye, hon."

She ended the call, feeling a tiny bit better. All in all, she thought, at least Cisco didn't sound angry with her today—that was good. But he hadn't told her to take care of herself, which he normally did. In fact, he hadn't shown any concern for her, which was unusual. It had to be because he wasn't thinking clearly yet. Didn't it?

*Joe says Cisco's pretty unpopular with the nurses—he's surly and doesn't cooperate. That's not him! Everyone knows he's sweet and thoughtful. I wish I could convince them what a nice guy he really is.*

*What if he comes home a different person?*

She took a deep breath. Just like her husband, she had to be patient and take baby steps. Be content for now with the fact that he was controlling his rage. Hopefully that wasn't entirely due to sedation, but due to healing.

Cora Tozzi, *History of the Religious Institutions of Lemont* (Chicago, Madonna Press, 2024), 77–82

*"My doubts disappeared after I submitted myself to the will of God."*
—*The Chronicles of Venerable Mother Josepha of Chicago*

### Josie's Journal
### Chicago, January 31, 1894

When I arrived at St. Stanislaus, I had to struggle to pull open the heavy church door against a bitter wind and driving sleet. I was starting to think I did not have enough strength when someone pushed the door open from the inside. John Grabiec held the door while I slid through.

I caught my breath in the vestibule. "John, thank God. But why are you here this afternoon?"

"I just finished the Sunday collection accounting," he said. John is the church's treasurer. He studied me for a moment as I stamped my dripping shoes and removed my wet head scarf, shook it out, and retied it under my chin. Wet or not, a woman's head must be covered in God's house. "There is much talk in the parish about the wonders you have done for the poor. But I look at you and see a woman with a drawn face, about to fall asleep on her feet. You are killing yourself."

He was not wrong. I was at the brink of exhaustion, but I do not like to act the martyr. We did our best, Mama and I. Mama could no more turn away the poor women and children in desperate need of shelter than I could, but she was no longer young. The hardest work was left to me.

I reassured myself that what little I did was for the greater glory of

God. But this winter is surely a test, and even I wonder in weak moments why God has allowed such misery. Then I tell myself it is always so: God allows sadness in our lives, but he also consoles us. Would we truly appreciate the joys of life if we did not have the opposite to compare them to?

"I have found that I must have a spirit of prayer, John, or I will find it hard to continue. Pray with great faith in God, and He will take care of everything."

John smiled at me. "I do not think God gets all the credit, Josie. Do not minimize what you do. Go home and sleep."

I smiled at him and shrugged. "I have a nice bed but some do not. Someone must care for those who have no one. There will be time for me to sleep later, I think."

"The poor will always be with us, Josie. Jesus Himself said that. I admire your compassion, but you are no good to anyone if you kill yourself."

We could have done so much more if we had moved ahead immediately to raise funds and locate a building to shelter many. It was hard to wait a year, but that had been the decision, and I had reluctantly agreed. "Fortunately, I am not there yet, John."

I turned to enter the church, thinking the conversation was over, but John put his hand on my arm. At first, he said nothing, and I saw indecision on his face.

"Come," he said presently. "Sit with me. I want to talk to you."

He led the way to a pew at the rear of the empty church. I opened my coat and slid across the seat, leaving room for him. What was this? I was afraid he was about to confess to still having feelings for me. But Father Vincent had told me John was happy with his new wife and daughters. What did he have to say to me now?

It seemed as if he did not know how to begin. Finally he said, "I never did tell you why I came to see you, the night we heard Katy died."

The thought of Katy still strikes like a blow to my stomach. My eyes filled with tears. I blinked rapidly to keep them from falling.

"I...I will never forget all you did that night, John. Everything would have been so much harder without you."

He looked down at his hands in his lap. "You know I have been fortunate to keep my wealth during these hard times. I am not as dedicated as you, but I can help. I know successful and influential people, and how to organize men and women. I wanted your ideas about the best way to help your cause."

I looked at him in amazement. "John, we are a house of women." I shook my head. "I had not considered men—"

Before I could finish, he interrupted. "With money, Josie. I want to help you raise funds. I have heard about your plan to establish a shelter for women and children. You need money. I have money. I have friends with money. I am offering my services to you when the time comes."

It is not only God who answers prayers. But then again, perhaps it was God who sent John to me.

### October 7, 1894

Tonight, I renewed my plea to the ladies of the Third Order. I took it as an encouraging sign that the date fell on the feast of Our Lady of the Rosary.

My heart thumping, my mouth dry, I addressed the gathered women. "A year ago, we resolved to band together and establish a shelter for poor women, the elderly, and children. After a year of contemplation, it is my opinion that this is what God wants us to do. How many of you are still in agreement?"

I saw blank looks on the faces of many. Apparently, some had forgotten completely, and others had lost their resolve. My face burning and my heart thudding, I went on. "Father Vincent gave his approval on the basis that we operate as a religious order. I have also had promises from some businessmen in the community to help us raise funds."

The blank looks turned to doubt, as if some now felt they had been hasty at first, not realizing they would be giving up their secular lives for lives of religious devotion. One woman raised her hand tentatively and asked to speak.

"This may have been the worst winter we have seen, and the deepest depression," she said. "Yet we managed to get through it. Perhaps the need to provide for others was not as great as we thought."

Some women nodded. I found it hard to believe they had not seen with their own eyes the women and children sleeping in hallways at night and wandering the streets by day. Did they not know that the parish could do nothing because of the enormous expenses to maintain the church, the school, and the orphanage? Collections were low and donors few in these difficult times. The treasury was empty, the parish had fallen into debt, and banks were unable or unwilling to help. The sight of starving masses outside his doors greatly distressed Father Vincent, but he was powerless to assist.

For a moment I thought of telling the ladies how Mama and I not only shared our home but the countless times we used our personal savings to buy medicine or clothing. But I remained silent. Telling of our personal suffering would serve no purpose if these women no longer possessed compassion.

Then Angelina Topinski raised her hand and shyly rose to her feet. "Josie, I am overjoyed to hear that we are finally ready to help these poor people. This morning I saw Mrs. Przewoznik sitting on the corner with her three children, one still a baby in her arms, begging for food. The children were shivering. I would have sent her to you, but I knew your home was full. It tore at my heart to pass by a neighbor I had called friend, but our family has nothing left to give."

Angelina paused to wipe tears from her eyes, and there was some whispering among the women. Then she lifted her head proudly and looked around the room. "I for one remember my commitment, and I am ready to join you immediately." She smiled gently. "My own family will be glad, I am sure, since once I am out of their house they will no longer have to feed me."

Angelina's comments had some effect, so I allowed the women to talk among themselves for a time. The discussion was spirited, but none wanted to address the group.

After five minutes of chatter, I held up my hand and asked for attention. "Let us see where we stand," I said. "There is Angelina, and there is me. Are others willing to join now and devote their lives to serving the poor?"

My friend Sophie Wisneski, who had advised the group to wait a year, got up and came to stand next to me. "You all know I am needed at home to care for my elderly parents and my sister, who is mute. I cannot live with the group, but I believe in Josie's plan and I will support it insofar as I am able."

I was disappointed, of course, that I did not get from Sophie the commitment I had expected, but at least she endorsed the cause, and that apparently had an effect on some of the others as well. By the end of the meeting, I had the names of seven volunteers, which made eight women including myself.

A year ago, nearly one hundred had been willing. I had never been convinced that the delay was needed, but the women had voted and I had no choice in the matter. Now, the outcome was not what I had hoped for, but it was a start. I was heartened by my conviction that the volunteers were all strong in their devotion, and we could build on our beginnings.

The next step will be to seek guidance from Father Vincent for the founding of our new order. In my mind, this is another matter entirely, about which I have much misgiving. If Sophie had given a stronger endorsement, and if Father Vincent had supported the plan without the requirement to found a new order, I believe there would have been a greater response. But I reminded myself that they had more experience than I in matters of the church. I only hope I am up to the task. My biggest fear is that those who are in need will be left on their own.

### November 9, 1894

Father Vincent was away for a time, summoned by the Resurrectionist Fathers in Rome to represent the American province. The poor man is burdened not only by vast responsibilities at St. Stanislaus, but matters of a worldly nature. It was two weeks before I could speak with him, on November 2, All Souls Day.

Word must have reached him, since before I could open my mouth he said, "Come to the parish office, where we can talk undisturbed."

When we arrived there, I told him there were eight women prepared to proceed, that John Grabiec would help with funds, and that we could also expect support from my brother Theo, my sister Rosalie, and her husband Adam.

Father said he was impressed with my progress. "I hoped you would have a larger number of volunteers, but it is a start. You will remember, though," he said, "that I can sanction the project only if you are prepared to live under religious obedience."

Of course I remembered, since that part of the plan gave me the most concern. It would not be easy to teach myself and others as well to be good religious.

It was not as if I had no experience at all. For the past twelve years I have held the position of Mistress of Novices for the Third Order, guiding young women to a life of prayer and performing works of charity and teaching. But the Third Order is a secular society, and my limited education in Poland and absence of formal spiritual training weigh heavily upon me. Still, it never occurred to me to ignore Father Vincent's conditions. I submitted to God's will with this thought: I would allow God to do with me as He pleased. With His help, I would find a way.

And so, the fear of living under religious obedience gave way to joy at the thought of starting the project at last. My heart was full to bursting with warmth and gratitude.

A week later the volunteers gathered in Father's office. He opened a new notebook and interviewed each woman in turn, asking her full name, date of birth, address, family, and if she was committing to religious life of her own desire. After enrolling all eight of us, he gave a ten-minute lecture on the expectations of religious life. Then he spoke about the group's mission, which was to serve all those in need, especially women, children, and the elderly.

His next question surprised me. "How much money will each of you contribute?"

I felt my face drain of color. I looked at each woman for her reaction. It seemed to me the question was a blatant demand to test our devotion, to see just how serious we were, and I thought it might scare some away. Depth of commitment was important, but I wished we could have eased into the realization.

Some of the volunteers looked baffled, others frightened or hesitant. Only Angelina looked excited, as if she were bursting to speak. Sophie's face wore an expression I read as, "I told you so," but immediately I thought my suspicion was unkind.

I felt compelled to speak first, to set an example. I said I would give the entirety of my savings, my living quarters and all furniture, and my sewing machines. It was everything I had, but Mama would live with our new order, so she and I would have no further need for material things.

My instincts proved right, as each woman after me named the assets she would bring to the project. One had a change of heart. Unwilling to sacrifice her possessions, she withdrew her application.

We now numbered seven devoted sisters-to-be.

# Chapter 26

Whеn Cora joined the sisters for breakfast the following morning, Sister Agnes handed her a pale-blue paper face mask. "We have to wear masks now unless we're alone or eating." Sister Agnes rolled her eyes. "Seems excessive, but the order came from the cardinal, and we follow his dictates."

Cora set her food on the table, noticing that everyone in the dining room not actively eating and drinking wore a facial covering. She also noticed that tables were now farther apart and only two sisters sat at each table instead of four. She pulled the elastic straps over her ears, crimped the strip of metal across her nose, and sighed. At least they hadn't asked her to leave the convent, although that would probably be next. She missed home, but now, facing the prospect of being there without Cisco, she didn't want to leave. Friends within reach were comforting. The alternative, home with only her cell phone and her worries, depressing. Not only would Cisco's absence be overwhelming, but Cora had never lived alone and never wanted to.

"I'm sorry to hear about your husband," Sister Agnes said. "We're all praying for him."

"Thank you," Cora said simply. "He seems to be getting a little better, but this is only his third day in the hospital."

"Oh my—I'm so glad to hear he's better."

Cora lowered her mask, then sipped coffee and took a nibble of the scrambled eggs. Thank God Cisco had been more calm and cooperative last night, which relieved her stress somewhat. Thankfully Sister

Agnes didn't ask for details. She really didn't want to talk about Cisco's condition.

Back in her room later, Cora wondered how Frannie's research was going. It wasn't likely she'd gotten far in half a day, but Cora wanted to talk to her anyway, to share the previous afternoon's experience and discuss priorities. She felt disorganized and at loose ends, like she should be doing something, but she couldn't focus or start anything productive.

Frannie picked up on the third ring. "These nuns you sicced me on are a big deal in San Antonio," she said. "They founded the city's first hospital, during a cholera epidemic some few years after the Civil War. Twelve thousand sick and dying, and no hospital, so they went there to start one. Then the sisters opened schools and started teaching all over the country, including Chicago—that must be how Katherine Mrozek got involved with them. They run a university—the University of the Incarnate Word, what else? Now the good sisters got the university and five hospitals in the San Antonio area."

Frannie was babbling. Cora suspected she was anxious to show off, or excited by the thrill of the chase. Cora smiled. Typical Frannie.

"I got puzzled about that Incarnate Word business. Heard the term, but didn't know what it meant. Comes from John in the New Testament. You know, 'And the Word was made flesh, and dwelt among us...' Meaning the moment the Son of God became human in the Virgin Mary. You following this lingo?"

"Uh, yeah. A bit hazy—I haven't been sleeping great—but yeah."

"You didn't tell me much, gurl. Just to drop everything and start researching this nun. So now I'm trying to find a news article about this woman's death. It's pretty tedious—"

Cora interrupted. "Frannie, listen. I know you're working hard, and I called to explain, but..." She wasn't sure how to begin. "You're gonna say I'm nuts—that this is a waste of time."

"Huh. Wouldn't be the first time, gurl. Lord! You been dragging me through weird stuff for years, I don't have to tell you."

"Well, yeah. But...okay, I had a sort of 'revelation' yesterday. There's a monastery next to the convent, and they have a secluded outdoor statuary area. The shrines are made of this really odd stone—yellow, gray, reddish-brown, with bits of crystal in it. I put my hands on the stone yesterday, and as soon as I did, a scene started playing in my head—you know, like when you close your eyes and try to imagine something? The images came on their own, though."

She stopped for a moment, realizing she hadn't actually spoken to Frannie since before Cisco's hospitalization. So much had happened in such a short time, it seemed impossible Frannie didn't know about Cisco's stroke. But of course she wouldn't, because Cora hadn't told her.

"Let me back up. Sorry for starting at the end instead of the beginning, but I'm not thinking straight today. Cisco had a stroke two days ago."

"Oh, crap! Is he okay?"

"Depends on how you define 'okay.' He's recovering, and the doctors are optimistic, but you know what a worrier I am."

"Yeah, I know that about you. But why aren't you with him instead of yakking with me?"

"He's in Arizona, and the hospital isn't allowing visitors, and this coronavirus makes travel almost impossible, and—" Cora's voice broke. "Oh, Frannie, the nightmare just goes on and on."

Once started, the whole story poured out, about Cisco, about Maryam's visitor, about Mother Josepha and her sister Katy, about Cora's vision when she touched the stone, about her belief that Maryam's visitor was actually Mother Josepha. For once Frannie had little to say and let her friend talk.

When Cora finally stopped, Frannie said, "Lord! You got some serious problems, especially about Cisco. You sure you can't go to Arizona?"

"I want to. But everyone tells me to stay put."

"Well, I ain't telling you that. And when did you ever listen to what anyone else says? Huh. But I got no answers about how that gets done." Frannie paused. "Always got to be some supernatural business with you. A saint appearing this time instead of a ghost? I guess they're not the same thing, since a saint is in heaven and not between worlds. Should be used to this stuff by now.

"As for the rest—you got some wild imagination in that statuary garden. Like you said, could just be your head acting on its own, putting stuff together from the back of your mind. Can't say what it all means, but I'll study on those details you told me. So, you want me to check things out, right? Find out what this nun, Katy, was doing—if there was any connection between her and some Indians, and who she had in the back of that buggy, and how she died?"

Cora drew a long breath. "Yeah. I don't even know what we're looking for anymore. I just sense it's important to know what Katy was up to, and whether Indians had anything to do with why she died. Maybe the sisters didn't know, or maybe they knew and covered it up. This vision I had could be a clue, but it's probably a wild goose chase. I can't get it out of my head until it's checked out, though, and you're faster and more thorough with online research than I am. Especially now, with Cisco...." Abruptly, she couldn't go on.

"What makes you think finding out about Katy will make Cisco better? Did this Mother Josepha, if that's even real, make a deal with you?"

"No, but it makes sense to me that if you do a big favor for someone, they're more inclined to help you in return. It's supposed to be different with heavenly beings, but I only know how things go on earth."

"That could work. You can't run to Arizona, so we might as well give it a go. Well, I'm in. Huh. Maybe your Indian was Apache, that'd be interesting. What about that rock type you mentioned? You want me to find out about that too? Can you send me some pictures of it?"

"Don't worry about it, Frannie. I'm calling someone else, an archaeologist, about that. You have enough to do. I know it's nuts, but I feel like I have to...like completing this investigation for Maryam's visitor will affect Cisco's getting well. Like fulfilling a promise."

"Okay. Tell me why Sister Katy had to go all the way to Texas. Weren't there nuns in Chicago she could have joined up with?"

"From what I read, the Sisters of Charity ran the school at St. Stanislaus, the parish Katy and her sister belonged to. When she joined them, she intended to stay there, but the sisters decided to leave Chicago and go back to their mother house in San Antonio. Katy was committed by then."

"Well, I'll get on it. Say, you think Katy's death was really an accident? Any notion she could've been murdered? Maybe by some Indian, or cowboy?"

Cora had avoided that idea. "I hope not, Frannie. But if she was, it's about time somebody found out, don't you think?"

"Well, you know you can depend on Frannie and her flying computer

fingers. Hope your archaeologist friend understands about how you attract the supernatural—which I'm not too cool about, I shouldn't need
to remind you. But maybe this time it's okay, being there's a saint and
heaven and all."

"Oh, he does, Frannie. Dan has a serious interest in the occult. He's
also grounded in reality, though. Trust me, Dan's the right guy."

# Chapter 27

Dan Mahoney and Cora had met through a mutual friend who was an expert on ghost lore. An archaeologist and noted expert in American Indian culture in the Chicago area, Dan followed personal interests and was a popular lecturer. He had been impressed by Cora's book about Wawetseka, an Indian woman who lived in the early 1800s. He had contacted Cora, and they'd built a friendship on their shared interests in the paranormal and American Indian history.

Standing together at business functions, they made an incongruous pair, Dan young, tall, and strong-looking, Cora everyone's image of the white-haired little old lady. Neither of them was seriously involved with supernatural pursuits, but both had had enough experiences to keep an open mind. They were neither skeptics nor fanatics, preferring to remain in touch with reality while admitting that there was enough oddity in the world for the possibility of supernatural phenomena to exist.

Dan was always available when Cora called him, as he was that morning. "A favor?" he said. "Sure! What's up?"

"I know this isn't really your field, but I'd like you to identify some rock for me."

"Rock like music, or rock like stone?"

Cora chuckled. "Like stone. I'll text you some pictures. I should ask a geologist, but I don't know one. I thought you might. Or maybe you know enough yourself to tell me what it is and where it came from—anything you can about it."

"I'll try. Do you think it's local?"

"I doubt it. It was ordered and delivered back in the late 1930s, but the records are either lost or they're written in Slovenian."

"Bummer. Lots of luck finding someone who reads Slovenian. Well, send me the pictures and I'll see what I can do. Maybe something will ring a bell. If not, I have friends I can call. Can I ask why you need to know this?"

How much did she want to explain, even to Dan? She took a deep breath and plunged in. "I had a strange fascination with this stone the first time I saw it. It's kind of ugly, actually, but it stuck in my mind, and I wanted to know more about it. Then yesterday I touched it and had a weird experience—like a waking dream, playing out in my head. I felt like I couldn't take my hands off the rock while I was having this vision, or whatever. When it was over, I *could* pull my hands away. Weird, huh?" She paused. "I have to know more about the stone."

"Tell me about the vision."

She described what she'd seen, knowing the presence of an American Indian would hook him. When she finished, he asked, "Is there anything going on that would make you imagine this? Anything significant about a nun or an Indian you can think of?"

Another deep breath. "Well, I've been staying at this convent for a while, and the stone is at St. Marija's, a monastery next door—"

"What? Why are you staying at a convent?"

Dan would understand. She told him why she was staying at Assisi Hill, about Sister Maryam and the visitor, and the visitor's request, and how she'd linked the visitor to Mother Josepha and her sister Katy.

When she was done, all Dan could say was, "Wow. A saint appearing from heaven!"

They were both silent for a time. Then Dan said, "I'm glad you called. I'll help in any way I can, even if you just need to talk. You know...."

"Yes?"

"Just thinking if I know anyone near San Antonio. I studied there some years ago—there must be someone. Maybe—yeah, there is somebody, actually. I'll see if I can track her down, if she's still in the area. Even if she isn't she'll probably know people...."

"That would be great! But I have another researcher working on Katy's history. First let me see what Frannie finds out. I wouldn't even know what questions to ask right now. I'll get back to you—it shouldn't be long."

"Okay. Send me those pictures, and I'll check out your rock. What's your time frame? How soon do you need an answer?"

"I think it might be important. Can you find out in a day or two?"

"That fast? What's the rush? This Mother Josepha has waited for a hundred years."

She told him then about Cisco's condition. "It's not like there's a deal or anything, but I can't help but feel that if I answer Mother Josepha's questions, it will make a difference in Cisco's recovery."

"Whoa. This is a lot more than idle curiosity. I'm so sorry for both of you."

"Thanks, Dan. I have to do *something*. I can't just sit and pray. What if I could have helped him and didn't? I'd never be able to live with that."

After ending the call, Cora reflected on how fortunate she was to have friends who not only wanted to help, but understood her situation and weren't frightened off by bizarre circumstances. She worked best as the head of a team, and now her team was in place, moving forward with their objectives. Almost. She had one more person to enlist: Maryam.

Thinking of the young nun brought guilt. She'd betrayed Maryam's trust, telling Frannie and Dan about the visitor. But they had to know in order to clearly understand what they were doing. Frannie and Dan would keep confidence, and she'd explain to Maryam somehow. She had to. Maryam was not only a friend but Cora's conduit to Mother Josepha. She had to settle any misunderstandings as soon as possible.

But first, before it got too late, she called Janna and asked her to search St. Marija's records for any information on where the strange stone came from.

# Chapter 28

"I just got back from seeing Dad. I think the staff is making an exception for me because Dad's calmer and more cooperative when I'm around—and professional courtesy," Joe said that afternoon.

There was little change so far, but that was to be expected. Cardiac workup had been done that morning, but the results weren't back yet. Joe had talked to a medical school friend, an electrophysiologist who specialized in cardiac rhythm disorders—the electrical component of heart disease.

"The heart works more effectively in sinus, or normal, rhythm," Joe told her. "When the heartbeat is irregular, some people just don't feel well. If that impacts their lives, there are things that can be done to return the heart to sinus. So, while he's recovering from the stroke, he'll be evaluated to be sure the heart is otherwise healthy and there's nothing else going on. Once we know how serious his situation is, we can talk about options or interventions, if needed."

"Like I said, the only thing he ever complained about was being tired. That's a good sign, right?"

"It is. But the tiredness probably meant something was wrong. He may not need anything else. He'll have to take a blood thinner, though, so he doesn't have another stroke."

"So, the AFib caused the stroke?"

"Not for sure, but it's highly likely." He paused. "Now don't go worrying about another stroke, Mom. The blood thinner is taking care of that, remember. He's on it now and will stay on it when he goes home. He's been on it before, when he had his stents. Nothing to worry about there."

Cora closed her eyes for a moment and took a deep breath. "What cardiac tests did they do?"

"A stress EKG and a cardiac echo. Of course, he's on a telemetry monitor and he gets resting EKGs a few times a day. So we know when he's in or out of AFib."

"How's it been?"

"He's in AFib most of the time."

That was worrisome.

Joe interpreted her silence correctly. "This isn't life-threatening, Mom. I told you, remember—lots of people live with AFib?"

"I just…because of the stroke…how much of this does he understand? I mean, you said the doctors will discuss options with him. Can he make those decisions by himself? I still feel like I have to be there."

Joe sighed. "Well, that is a bit of a problem. For the most part, he understands when we explain it to him. But then later, when someone comes in with questions or medication, he seems to forget, gets resistant, and we have to start all over again."

"But he does understand?"

"He seems to, yes. I'll be here to make sure."

"And he agrees? He's being cooperative?"

"I think you could say cooperative, but reluctant. He's not convinced."

"He still thinks he doesn't need to be there? That this is all a waste of time?"

"Unfortunately, yes. Look, Mom, today seems to be a good day. Why not talk to Dad now?"

Cora wouldn't go so far as to say Cisco was in good spirits, but most of the conversation was rational, as long as she didn't ask him any complex questions.

"They let me walk to the bathroom now, but I have to get the nurse to unhook me from the monitor and I have to drag the IV. It's a pain in the ass. And people keep coming in asking stupid questions all day long. It's ridiculous."

She was glad to hear they were starting therapy already. "Be patient, hon. They have to find out what's going on so they can help you recover."

"Yeah, right. Recover from what? How many times do I have to tell you, there's nothing wrong. A couple more days and they'll let me out of here.

I should be out now, but I promised Joe I'd cooperate. And what's with this fucking phone? I push the button to change the channel and nothing happens—instead the nurse comes in and says I called her. Nothing works right around here."

He'd always been somewhat impatient, pushing any old remote button. She told herself it was nothing more than that and calling the remote his phone. But he had a way to go if he couldn't distinguish between the buttons for the TV and the nurse call.

"Hon, I miss you. I wish I was there."

"I miss you too, but there's no point in you flying out. There's nothing you can do, and I'll be out soon, probably before you could even get here."

At least he knew he was in Arizona now.

Her hand tightened on the phone. Every time she ended a call, she had an irrational fear it was for the last time.

"Well, bye hon," she said.

"Bye."

Cora sat a few minutes, swallowed a lump in her throat, blinked her burning eyes, then forced herself to stand up and paced the room. There was nothing more she could do for Cisco right now, and handing over research to Frannie and Dan made Cora feel left out. She was used to directing the show, but she hadn't left much for herself to do.

Once she'd decided that Sister Maryam's visitor was Mother Josepha —not Mary, the mother of God—she was driven to feel closer to Josepha. One way to develop a more personal relationship was to get to know the saintly woman based on what she did while she was alive. Another was to work with Sister Maryam to determine why Mother Josepha was visiting earth. She would do both.

Sister Maryam believed that her visitor was the Blessed Virgin, and only Sister Maryam had direct contact with the visitor. Whatever else was going on, Cora had to stay in Maryam's good graces. Maryam had to be an active participant on Cora's team. So, she prepared for a heart-to-heart with Sister Maryam, who didn't know yet that Cora believed the visitor was Mother Josepha, nor about Cora's vision in the Rosary Valley, let alone that she'd told Frannie and Dan about the visitations. Maryam wasn't going to be happy about that.

She had to bring Maryam up to date, confess, and clear the air. She hoped her vision in the Rosary Valley would help convince Maryam.

When Cora arrived at Assisi Manor, she found the entry door locked. Through the glass she could see Maryam seated at the front desk, intent on some papers before her. When the nun didn't look up, Cora knocked on the door frame. Maryam reached for a face mask, drew the loops over her ears, and got up to let Cora in.

Cora took a deep breath through her own mask. "I hate wearing these stupid things already. I have a lot to tell you, and I really wish we could see each other's faces."

"Maybe it's better we can't." Sister Maryam pointed to two straight-backed chairs in the deserted lobby, and they sat down.

*Uh-oh. This isn't promising already.*

"How's Cisco today?" Maryam asked.

"He's calmer, more rational. They're still doing tests. It's complicated."

"How are you handling it? It's got to be hard."

"It is. I'm really tired and empty. Painful whenever I think about him. I'd rather *not* think about it…or talk about it. I have to distract myself and keep busy with other things. That's why I'm here."

True as her words were, Cora didn't want sympathy from Maryam now. They had to work things out as if Maryam's visitor was the only problem.

Cora leaned back and crossed her legs at the knee. She swallowed, realizing that her posture didn't reflect sincerity and leaned forward instead. "Maryam, please don't think I don't respect your opinions. I know you're the one having the experience, and I know how important it is to you. Nothing could be *more* important, and here I come, and it must seem like I'm trying to burst your bubble. I wish I didn't have to do that. But what if you *are* wrong? You'd want to at least consider what could be the truth, wouldn't you? Won't you hear me out?"

"Cora, I know it's hard for you to believe Mary is visiting me. It's not every day we have visitors from heaven. But I believe the visits are real, and you must think so too, since you asked me to take you to her. If anyone is going to come from heaven, who would it be but Mary? I'll listen to your thoughts, but that doesn't mean I'll agree with you." Sister Maryam's words sounded friendly enough, but firm.

Cora nodded. "That's all I ask."

Maryam looked up expectantly. Cora hoped she could present her thoughts well. She leaned back in her chair again. "I think I know who Katy is. And maybe why your visitor wants me to investigate."

Sister Maryam stiffened. "That didn't take long."

"Yes. We talked about this yesterday. But already a lot has happened."

Cora told Sister Maryam about Mother Josepha's little sister, and the relationship between them that she'd learned about in Josepha's biography. How she went to visit Sister Elizabeth at St. Joseph Convent and found out more about Mother Josepha's life, then the experience she'd had in the Rosary Valley. Finally, she explained that she had contacted Frannie and Dan to help gather information, and what their plans were.

Maryam looked upset. "I thought you understood no one else was to know, Cora. You botched that already, didn't you? I wish you had consulted me before you told anyone else. You may know these people well, but I don't know your friends at all."

"I know. I feel sorry about that, but it's done," Cora said. "They won't tell anyone else, and they needed to know."

Maryam crossed her arms over her chest. "We'll get back to that. You think Mother Josepha wants to find out what happened to her sister, Katy. For some reason she thinks Katy did something saint-worthy that no one knew about. If that's true, why didn't she appear to someone from her own order, where her main supporters are? Why has she been talking to me for years, when she really wanted you? It was just a coincidence you happened along? It's a roundabout way of doing things, don't you think?"

"It seems so—you're right. Maybe she came here because the ravine is so isolated. Or maybe because she thought a young nun would be more receptive and the nuns at St. Joseph's are old. Or she didn't know who could help her, so she started a relationship with a receptive person until the right circumstances and the right person came along."

"Me being the receptive person, and you being the right person?" Maryam's words sounded sarcastic, but Cora detected humor in her eyes above the mask. That was a bit encouraging.

"Yes. She doesn't see the past, before she arrived in heaven, only what she experienced during her own life. Who knows if souls in heaven even have the same sense of time as we do? She might not know any more of what happened to Katy now than she did when Katy died. Maybe she hoped to come across someone with the skills to find out. Or maybe she wanted us to work together."

"If Katy is in heaven too, why doesn't she just ask her?"

Cora shook her head. "That's a good question. I don't know. Does anyone know how souls communicate in heaven? But if she did ask Katy, how does that get Katy recognized as a saint on earth? Maybe Mother Josepha can't find her. Or maybe Katy's not there yet—"

"Come on, Cora! Really? Katy isn't in heaven because she's in the spirit world or something? Or purgatory?"

"I don't know all the answers. I just think I'm right about this." Cora met Maryam's gaze. "Your visitor needs someone who will find out the circumstances of Katy's death, someone who will look at it from the viewpoint of a person grounded in earthly matters, with earthly logic, who can fully understand Katy's death as a natural mystery and pursue it to a conclusion. That's not you. You would look to heaven for answers." She lowered her gaze and rubbed her forehead with both hands. "I'm guessing here, Maryam. This is all new to me and it's happening so fast."

Sister Maryam's eyes appeared to soften. "You're under so much stress, Cora. Are you seeing things clearly? Are you grasping at straws for answers that you think may be a way to help Cisco, or a way to resolve your doubts about faith?"

Shaking her head again, Cora said, "I really can't answer that. You could be right. But if you aren't, then I'm ignoring an opportunity that could save Cisco, isn't *that* right? I have to act on what my head and my gut are telling me to do. I could ask you the same question. Why are you reluctant to consider you've been talking to Mother Josepha instead of the Virgin Mary?"

"Mary has been an important part of my life for many years. When she first appeared to me, I was just a kid. It never occurred to me that she could be anyone else."

Cora could understand that. Wasn't part of her own belief based on the relationship she was developing with Mother Josepha?

Maryam shook her head. "Mother Josepha, wonderful woman that she was, in the annals of heaven is not a very important saint, or even an official saint at all yet. Why would she have the authority to visit earth?"

"I don't know," Cora said again, her eyes moistening. "Her own authority? I don't know how these things work." She fidgeted in her seat. After a moment she asked, "If it is Mary, what's her message? What does she want to tell the world? When she appeared to others, she always came with a message. After all the time she's been seeing you, you still don't know why she's here, do you?"

"I was waiting for her to tell me when to let others know and what she wanted me to say and do. She's always revealed herself to innocents over time, and eventually delivered her message to all, along with a miracle to ensure she was believed. She hasn't told me yet, but I'm sure she will." Maryam leaned back, folded her hands and placed them under her chin. "If you happen to be right, and she is Mother Josepha, what do we do now? What's my place, then? Why don't the two of you just talk to each other?"

The question hadn't occurred to Cora. After a moment's thought, she said, "I don't know why, but I think she still wants to talk to you. If she wanted to talk to just me, why didn't she reveal herself to me when we were there together?"

Maryam ran her hand through her hair and released a long breath. "The ways of heaven are not to be understood by us mortals, it seems. Even when God wanted Mary's approval to be the mother of His Son, he sent an angel to get her consent. Never could figure out why He didn't just ask her Himself."

Cora chuckled, and soon so did Maryam.

"So, what do you want to do, presuming you're right, which I'm not agreeing to yet," Maryam said.

"We have to do what Josepha asked. Find out how Katy died and why Josepha thinks Katy deserves to be a saint. Whatever it takes to find out about the parts of Katy's life and death that Josepha never knew."

"And you think the clues may be in your vision in the Rosary Valley?"

"Yes."

"And you'll be doing what?"

"I'll put together what everyone else gathers. Look for answers and identify new areas of inquiry. Follow my intuition. Hopefully it will all come together. Juggle the balls and somehow save my husband in the process." She couldn't just sit on her hands and wait for everyone else.

"Maryam, my friends are a good team. But things are likely to come up that only you can do. I really hope you'll be willing to participate, no matter how you feel about what we're doing."

Sister Maryam sighed. "If you are right, then it doesn't make much difference if your friends are included. I'm not convinced, but I see no downside to helping you. Your theory about Katy does make some sense. I guess I can act as intermediary. Mary will tell me if we're wrong."

# Chapter 29

Frannie's desk was a blond wood dining room table with two leaves. She had inherited the table from her mother, along with a two-flat building constructed in the 1920s on a narrow lot in a reasonably safe, inner-city Chicago neighborhood. Her living room windows looked out onto her street, and an enclosed back porch overlooked a tiny yard and alley. Bedroom, kitchen, and dining room windows revealed only brick walls of adjacent two-flats a mere six feet away, one beside her improvised desk. Windows were important, for things like staring and thinking.

Which was what Frannie was doing now. She had pulled her comfortable orange-colored sweatshirt over her 44 quadruple-D bosom and squeezed into the brown leggings—the outfit that Cora said made her look like an orange sherbet cone—and was sitting with her feet propped on a dining chair, cup of coffee in hand, plenty of milk and sugar, staring through the window at a brick wall and wondering where to start.

Although Frannie thrived on the sense of accomplishment she got from solving mysteries, it wasn't only about the chase. She also had a soft spot for people in trouble, and Cora was the closest thing she had to a best friend. Now Cora wanted to know what Katy Mrozek, a nun, the sister of an about-to-be saint, was doing that led to her death, how she died, and if Indians were involved. In 1886.

Frannie was a Midwest, big-city girl, born and raised. What did she know about Indians in Texas in the late 1800s? Only what she saw on TV and in the movies. Dusty, open plains, mountains on the horizon, the Alamo, and scantily clad dark-skinned men, wearing headbands with feathers, galloping their horses after a stagecoach or surrounding a wagon train. That was Frannie's American West.

Her knowledge was largely based on a TV series she'd been addicted to as a child. She searched her memory for the details. Yes—it was called *Broken Arrow*. She slid her feet off her chair and googled the name, and it came back to her. Cochise, an Apache Indian chief, played by Michael Ansara. The series took place after treaties had been signed, but one side or the other was still causing trouble. Chiricahua Apaches—she had loved to say the word. Cheer´-a-cow´-wah.

Besides Apaches, what other Indians lived in Texas? Comanche. Cheyenne, maybe. Or was that Wyoming? How much did she need to know? Had to start somewhere....

She opened Google Maps. She guessed the convent where Katy lived in 1886 would have been near the center of town. She found San Antonio and zoomed in on the Alamo, figuring the mission would be near mid-city. She switched to satellite view. Of course, it looked different today. But if she was traveling by horse and buggy to a farm outside the city, what was the farthest reasonable distance she would have gone? Ten miles?

Frannie printed the map and drew a ten-mile perimeter around central San Antonio. Using that as a guide, she zoomed in again, trying to get some sense of the terrain and comparing it to the image she'd formed from Cora's description of her vision. As expected, business, industrial, and residential areas occupied most of the area now. In 1886, where might farms have been? Indian villages? Near water, she guessed. Follow the river and tributaries. The San Antonio River.

Frannie saw a lot more trees than she'd expected. She switched to topographic maps on Google Earth. The landscape looked green and hilly to the north. East was lush with a lot of trees. West appeared dry and flat, while southwest looked like desert.

This was not going to be easy.

Next, she browsed historical websites. Wikipedia yielded mostly Spanish-Mexican settlement and indigenous people prior to 1700. Too early.

After a series of misses, she found the Historical Society of San Antonio and called the number listed. The person who answered the phone referred Frannie to a number of sources, and, when Frannie mentioned that she was looking for a nun, suggested she call the Sisters of Charity directly. Frannie had already explored the order's website extensively, but she might call later.

She watched a video about building missions in San Antonio and discovered that, prior to the early 1700s, the area had been inhabited by Coahuiltecan Indian Nations. Missions were built on their villages, and the Indians converted to Catholicism and lived on the mission property.

Coahuiltecans got along well with the Spaniards who built the missions, but their numbers were severely reduced by diseases the priests brought in. Then Apache and Comanche, hostile tribes, came and competed for food, water, and living space. Coahuiltecans had no option but to work in mines and on mission ranches. Eventually they married Spaniards or Mexicans and were assimilated into the local population. A few scattered bands continued to survive traditionally, living off the land. They became farmers and merchants who appeared regularly at plaza markets to sell produce, livestock, and birds.

Frannie decided that if Katy had contact with Indian tribes, it would have been traditional Coahuiltecans. Considering Cora's vision, the logical place for the accident was within ten miles south of San Antonio. She wondered again if Katy's death was an accident. Cora's vision, if it meant anything at all, hinted otherwise. Previous projects Frannie and Cora had worked on involved historical murders. Was this another unsolved murder case? Gleefully, Frannie rubbed her hands together.

Her stomach was talking to her. She glanced at her watch—almost dinnertime. She took a sip of cold coffee and made a face.

She'd start interviews tomorrow. On her list of leads were: American Indians in Texas, Institute of Texan Cultures, Indigenous Cultures Institute, the history department of the University of the Incarnate Word, the Texas State Historical Association online, and now the Sisters of Charity of the Incarnate Word.

~~~

Cora was one of Dan's favorite people. But no matter who made the request, after their conversation that afternoon he'd be champing at the bit. Her questions hit a host of his hot buttons: Native American culture, geologic and historical elements, the unusual and mysterious, and a paranormal component. Hallelujah!

Now that his wife and tween daughter had gone to bed, he could devote time to the project. Feet up in his recliner, on the table beside him a cup of strong Kenyan coffee from the coffee plantation he co-owned with an African archaeologist friend, he lit an imported South American cigar and sighed with pleasure. The photos of the rock Cora had sent were displayed on a laptop on the coffee table, magnified to actual size. He thumbed through a heavy illustrated book in his lap and compared the photos on the pages to the images on his screen.

He stroked his neatly trimmed dark beard and thought for a few minutes. He was pretty certain Cora's photos showed a number of different rocks, not a single composition. Some was sedimentary limestone, distinguished by the presence of many unusual cavities that indicated karst limestone, formed in ancient seas and weathered through exposure. Karst was found on surface landscapes but also in quarries and cave systems. Dan was sure the rock also contained igneous quartz, crystals, and geodes. How these sedimentary and igneous materials came together was a mystery, but nonetheless that's what they were.

"How cool!" he spoke the words aloud, excited because limestone, quartz, crystals, and geodes were all said to have paranormal properties. In particular, they were reported to hold spiritual imaging to an unusual extent. Primitive peoples and a variety of cultures often viewed these rocks as sources of energy, kept them in sacred pouches, and used them in religious ceremonies. The combination found in the rock Cora photographed could be enormously potent.

Years ago, while working on an archaeological dig in Kenya, Dan had been disturbed by images that mysteriously came into his head. The experience was similar to what Cora had described, so real and startling that he was driven to conduct a study of residual haunting. His research revealed what paranormal investigators called "stone tape theory."

The theory proposed that certain rocks have the ability to imprint, or "record" energy and store images and events from the past. An event imprinted itself on the environment where it took place, the rocks capturing its energy like a big magnet or battery, much the same as film or magnetic tape records and replays voice or images. The energy remained but changed form, and could discharge, or "replay" itself as a psychic impression at any time. It could be visual, or sounds, smells, tastes, perhaps touches—and the rocks could hold this potential for years, decades, even centuries.

The phenomenon was especially notable in areas where there were large deposits of limestone. It could be experienced by anyone, but especially by people who were more sensitive to psychic phenomena. Emotional or traumatic events were most likely to be captured, due to the high energy generated when such events took place. *Like what Cora experienced when she touched the stone?*

Cora had said the monastery received the rock in the late 1930s as a single shipment, but she didn't know where it came from. An internet search revealed that although karst deposits could be found throughout the world, significant deposits exist near San Antonio, where Katy had died. The Spaniards had used quarried limestone as early as the 1700s for construction of missions along the San Antonio River.

Dan remembered reading about a system of limestone caves in St. Louis, Missouri, and checked Google. As early as 1838, the Lemp Brewery had stored and lagered beer in their naturally controlled-temperature, refrigerated caverns. A tunnel through the cave system connected the Lemp Mansion, a Gothic castle sitting on five city blocks, to the Brewery and caves—a mansion that was reputed to be one of the most haunted places in America. This strongly suggested a connection between karst limestone and paranormal activity.

Had the stone at St. Marija's come from nearby St. Louis? It would have been a straight shot along old Route 66 when the rock was ordered, the major highway in the 1930s and '40s that passed through Lemont.

Or had it come from as far away as San Antonio?

Regardless, Dan was convinced the combination of rock that composed this stone had the ability to cause what Cora had seen—if any stone could cause a residual haunting, this would be it.

But what Cora really wanted to know was how Katy actually died. If the answer lay buried in Indian culture and history, who better than Dan to pursue it? Cora said her friend Frannie was working on that information. Dan had never met Frannie, but Cora often talked about her and had given him Frannie's contact information today.

Dan had pertinent connections in San Antonio and a good working reputation with indigenous people—resources unavailable to Frannie—who would welcome him and share their knowledge. This wasn't a given for white people, who were still viewed with an element of distrust. Of course, Frannie wasn't white, but she wasn't Indian, either.

His old dig buddy, Maria Garcia, lived in Austin. Maria could tell him what tribes inhabited the San Antonio area in 1886, and perhaps give him the name of a Native historian knowledgeable about those tribes. He wasn't going to sit back and wait for Frannie to stumble her way through Texas. He'd call Maria tomorrow morning, after he reported his findings to Cora.

# Chapter 30

**D**an called the next morning, just as Cora got back to her room after a hasty breakfast. She found his information about the stone fascinating, especially the stone tape theory.

"So, if I understand what you're saying," she said, at her desk reviewing the notes she had taken, "the scene I saw in my mind actually could have happened, and was captured by the stone before it was quarried in Texas? Like filming a movie. And now that the stone is here in the Rosary Valley, it can replay that event, and that's what I saw?"

"Yes, potentially. We already know you have a stronger sensitivity to paranormal phenomena than the ordinary person. If the stone actually came from Texas, that is. Can we find out?"

"I've already asked Janna to look for a record of the purchase. She's been translating St. Marija's records from Slovenian for me. I suspect the information is going to be hard to find, though." A sigh escaped her. "I don't know what to think. Isn't this stone tape theory a bit far-fetched?"

"I can't argue with that. But what other leads have you got?"

Her elbow resting on the desk in front of her, she propped her chin in her hand. "I'd hate myself if I didn't at least try to follow the clues in my vision, wouldn't I?"

"I wouldn't let you *not* try—or hate yourself."

She laughed. "Okay then, what should we do, in your professional opinion?"

"Let's assume the stone came from Texas, the woman driving the buggy was Katy, and your vision was the 'recording' of her death. If that's true, what questions come to mind?"

"Who was the man in the buggy? Why was he there? Who was the rider that took him away? Where did he take him, and why? Did Katy know those men? What was she up to?"

"Exactly. The man on horseback is a clue. Was he chasing them? Why? And what did he do after he left Katy and the buggy behind?"

Cora thought this over. "In my vision, Katy kept looking around while she was driving. I think she spotted the man on the buckskin following her, recognized him, thought he was dangerous, and whipped her horse to go faster."

Dan picked up the questions. "You told me Josepha's bio said Katy went to tend to a sick farmer and his wife. Was the farmer the man in the buggy with her? Was she bringing him back to her convent?"

"Maybe. But the man on the horse...why was he following them and why was she afraid of him? He could have been a relative of the farmer, but I thought he looked Native American. That's why I told Frannie to find out what she could about Indians living in the area."

"I made pretty much the same guesses, Cora. I know you said Frannie's researching this, but I think I can help. I've worked with Native Americans on digs and I've presented my findings in ways that have been helpful to them. They respect that, and some have become good friends. Now, that doesn't necessarily mean anything in Texas, but I know another archaeologist who lives in Austin and works with local Indian organizations. Why don't I contact her and see if she has any ideas?"

"Oh, Dan! Would you?"

"Of course."

"I bet, with you and Frannie working together, we might make some sense of all this."

"Um...work with Frannie? I don't know. I thought I'd be going it alone."

"We don't have time on our side here—we have days, maybe. Two heads, you know. You'll like Frannie. She's a straight shooter. I'll reach her now and get her on board. I'll call you. Stay tuned!"

Cora rang off and took a minute to finish her notes, then punched Frannie's number into her phone and put the call on speaker.

"Hey, gurl!" Frannie said. "Just about to call you. Things is going pretty good. Made a dent, got a shit-ton of leads. Only I can't pronounce the name of the tribe I found." She spelled it out for Cora. "C-o-a-h-u-i-l-t-e-c-a-n-s. How the hell am I supposed to say that? Huh. Texas Tecans, I'm gonna call them, so you best know that."

Cora had learned to let Frannie ramble. It actually turned out to be faster, and a little easier than trying to herd cats.

"Seriously, got your paper and pencil, Cora? I know you're gonna want to make notes, unless you want me to package everything up and email it to you?"

"I've got a notepad, but if it isn't too much trouble, email would help too." She had already written down *Coahuiltecans*.

Frannie explained how she narrowed down the indigenous cultures around San Antonio to the probability of 'Tecans.' She'd left voicemails and sent emails to every contact person she'd identified. "Must be near a dozen people, and not heard back from one yet, but it was late yesterday. Still, I might have to get pushy. You know I'm not afraid to do that."

Cora laughed. "In fact, you're good at it."

"I'll get on the phone today, follow up, and zero in on 1886. I'll find newspapers from right before and after Katy's death, look for articles about her accident and what else was going on around that time."

"You're amazing, Frannie."

"Huh! You already know that. Just another example of Frannie and her magic fingers at work. Gotta be old hat to you by now." Cora pictured her friend with a big grin on her face. Frannie loved to show off.

"So now, you called me, gurl. You would've just waited for me to call *you*, unless you got something on your mind. Get down on it."

Cora told Frannie about Dan's findings. When she was done, Frannie asked, "This is your archaeologist friend, right? The one who did all that work with the Indians near Chicago?"

"Yes, right. He's worked a lot with indigenous people, and they like him. He has contacts in Texas, too." She paused. "I'd like it if you two worked together on the Indian research."

"Excuse me! You know damn well I work best alone. Why you gotta stick me with someone else? It'll only hold me back."

"We've worked as a team before, Frannie, and that went fine. This time, you and Dan can decide who's going to do what without me in the middle. Like I told him, two heads, you know?"

"Huh. So, he needed convincing too, you're saying?"

Cora said nothing, pretending the comment didn't need a response.

"I got it, Cora. He's some hotshot professional guy with connections, and I'm a nobody with balls, never mind I'm a woman." She gave a deep sigh, the long-suffering Frannie act. "And I was having so much fun just going my own way...."

"You're going to do that anyway, Frannie. You always do."

"Right. And it always works. So what's this Dan guy's phone number? He might as well take some of my to-do list."

"Frannie. Play nice. Okay?"

"I always play nice." The chuckle that followed sounded a bit sinister.

Well, that probably went as well as Cora could have expected. Both of her friends had already provided valuable information, and her theories stood up so far.

Now to figure out what to do with the rest of the day. If only Cisco was here to help and give his opinion. Of course, she was doing all this *because* he wasn't here to help her. But damn, she missed him!

She pulled out her rosary and prayed to Mother Josepha for Cisco's recovery.

# Chapter 31

"First things first," Frannie mumbled, staring at her computer with the essential cup of coffee beside her. "Let's find out what this Katy Mrozek's life was all about, and who was around when she died."

Looking for an obituary, she typed *Katherine Mrozek, San Antonio, 1886* in Google's search field. Many of the sites that popped up required paid accounts or trial subscriptions, but on Myheritage she found nineteen entries with variations of the name. One of these was Katarzyna Mrozek, date of birth 1867, parents Jan (John) and Agnieszka (Agnes). The sibling names also matched the data Cora had given her. Unfortunately, there was no additional information. "At least we know the woman existed," she said under her breath.

Other genealogy resources, including Family Search, Ancestry, and the website for Texas state records, turned out to be a waste of time. "Nothing but dead ends, literally," she grumbled.

Katy had been buried on convent property, so funeral parlors were of no use. She studied the website of the Sisters of Charity of the Incarnate Word, viewing video clips and timelines for a while. The order had played a dominant role in the history of San Antonio, even owning the property that contained the headwaters of the San Antonio River. She found a photograph of the hospital that existed while Katy was there. She had imagined a primitive, barracks-like building, but the Santa Rosa Infirmary was a large, three-story wooden structure with balconies. It would have been the only hospital in the area at that time, serving a population of perhaps 30,000. The building probably also housed the sisters.

Searches for Katy came back "not found." Which of the huge number of medical and educational institutions affiliated with the order might know if and where records about Katy existed? Frannie clicked the "contact us" button and sent an email to the director of vocations, a Sister Barbara Marie. If she didn't get a response by tomorrow morning, she'd pick up the phone and keep going until she reached the right person. She knew it was unreasonable to expect an answer in one day, but patience was not one of Frannie's qualities.

She left the sisters' website and searched for news articles about Katy's death. The free search on Newspapers.com yielded only one likely newspaper, *The San Antonio Daily Light*, from December 1886. A quick scan left her disappointed; there was nothing in it about a young nun's death, or even an accident involving a buggy outside of town.

She tried the website for the University of Texas at San Antonio, and a pop-up opened offering a chat with a librarian. Frannie accepted, but the helpful librarian who entered the chat couldn't find any useful references. He suggested she contact special collections at the university library and the Sisters of Charity. Again.

Laborious exploration eventually led to a site named *Portal to Texas History*, where *The San Antonio Daily Light* was digitized online. Her initial search gave almost 33,000 results. Adding filters, first for 1886 and then for Bexar County, narrowed it to 335 results. Articles in each four-page edition appeared randomly, major events mixed with political matters, local gossip, and ads. After an hour, she'd read only three papers and found nothing about Katy's accident.

"Huh," she muttered. It made no sense. The *Daily Light* freely reported who was visiting in town and similar trivia; they wouldn't omit something as newsworthy as the accidental death of a young nun. The death should have been on the front page, Frannie figured. Unless it had been covered up. *Come on, Frannie. who'd bother doing that?*

Her eyes were crossing. She'd take a break before trying to locate someone who knew about the Coahuiltecans. Cora's friend Dan would surely have some ideas about that, but she wanted to get a head start so she didn't sound dumb when they talked.

She skipped lunch but started a fresh pot of coffee. When it was ready, she poured a cup and added extra cream and sugar. She glanced at the kitchen clock, then reached into a cabinet and added a dash of Hennessy's cognac. "Just for the taste," she rationalized. "It's near enough afternoon. Might as well enjoy my work."

She picked up a notepad and pen. "Don't you even rag on me 'bout making notes like you, Cora," she mumbled.

How could she find out what sort of presence the Coahuiltecans had in San Antonio in 1886? She already knew that most of the Coahuiltecans had either died off or were assimilated into the population by the early 1800s. The Spanish left, and the French left after the Louisiana Purchase in 1803, and then the flood of pioneers came from the eastern United States. The missions had shut down, but a few traditional Coahuiltecans had remained in small clusters, and that was what Frannie was looking for. Who might know about those little groups today?

Historical societies. History departments at local universities. Museums? Were there any Coahuiltecans left that might have some record of their own history? She went back to Google, and before long developed a list that once again included the University of the Incarnate Word's history department.

She took in a deep breath, let it out, and wiggled her fingers in the air. Too much information now. She worked steadily until her cell phone rang at two that afternoon. It was Dan.

"Cora told me you'd call," Frannie said. "I got to tell you, I work best alone. Snooping and following my instincts, wherever they take me."

"So do I," Dan replied. "But Cora has a point. She's in a hurry for answers, and if we split the work, we'll get answers in half the time. We can let each other know about dead ends so we don't both waste time on the same useless resources."

"That don't work for me. I get hunches from what other people *think* are dead ends."

Dan sighed. "Look, I'll tell you my best guess about the Indian link we're looking for. I think it's the Coahuiltecans. They were pretty well assimilated by the 1800s, but—"

"Not all of 'em were. Yeah, I found them too. And I agree with you. Got calls in to some folks who ought to know more, but I haven't heard back yet."

"Um...great. Why don't we send our to-do lists to each other, then?

I'll let you know which places I have contacts at, and you can take the remainder. We'll work on the lists for—what? Two hours? You jot down your findings, I'll do the same. Then we'll talk and update the plan. Does that work for you?"

"We need to be looking for the same thing. What exactly do you think we're looking for?" Frannie asked.

"What Katy was doing, who she was involved with at the time of her accident. We might find a small group of traditional Coahuiltecans that Katy interacted with. We can approach this from the standpoint of history, or records at the convent, or the Indian connection. We want to find a living group of historians knowledgeable about Coahuiltecan history. If we're lucky, we'll locate a tribal archive and someone who will be willing to talk to us and look for a tie to Katy. I can tell you now, that last part won't be easy."

"Because?"

"Because Native Americans remain suspicious. They don't even like the term Native American, because they don't identify themselves as American, but as members of a nation or tribe, like Cheyenne, Lakota, and so on. Historically, outsiders have not respected or treated them well. They aren't likely to talk to us unless we gain their trust and convince them that what we're doing will benefit them in some way."

"I can be convincing—just you wait and see."

"Well, it's taken *me* years, but I hope the trust I've developed among other tribes will open some doors. Hopefully we'll get lucky. I suggest you start by learning something about the Coahuiltecans so you don't offend them to begin with."

Frannie figured she already knew more than Dan was giving her credit for. But she also knew some people found her brusque manners objectionable. Maybe it did make sense to let Dan handle personal contacts with Indians while she covered historical societies and universities. She'd keep that in mind, but she wouldn't promise to hold back if she got the bit between her teeth.

After exchanging and reviewing their lists, Frannie noted that she and Dan each had exactly seven sources to research. Good. Let him earn his keep. She'd still beat him to the chase.

~~~

Despite the fact that it had been Dan's idea to make the Indian contacts himself, much of his list turned out to be an exercise in futility. The history of the Coahuiltecan people was interesting enough, but the pressing issue was to see if any archives existed and who the gatekeepers were.

To start, he selected the Institute of Texan Culture and the Indigenous Cultures Institute for deeper dives. He intended to make direct contact, but, as he told Frannie, he would pave the way by having an insider make the introduction and request. His good reputation in Chicago and the Midwest mightn't mean much in Texas.

He searched a variety of websites, looking for personal connections. He found a single Coahuiltecan site, the Tap Pilam Coahuiltecan Nation. Their website was current, but didn't name anyone he knew. Nor did it mention archives, and its activities seemed to focus on current issues.

Next, he browsed websites of Apache and Cherokee tribes. Again, he didn't recognize any names.

Finally, on the *Institute of Texan Cultures* site he found his old friend, Maria Garcia. He dialed the number listed and got a recorded message: "Due to Covid guidelines, no staff are currently in our office. Please leave a message and we will return your call as soon as possible. We pick up messages Monday through Friday." Dan left a message for Maria, stressing that the matter was urgent.

He was lucky. She called fifteen minutes later. "You'll need someone at Tap Pilam Coahuiltecan Nation, most likely. Or the American Indians in Texas at the Spanish Colonial Missions," Maria said.

"Don't any of your organizations have shorter names?" Dan asked.

Maria laughed. "Seems to go with the territory, doesn't it? Unfortunately, I don't know anyone at either place. But do you remember Ramon Gomez? That night we all went bar-hopping in Austin? The guy that tried to get the bartender to leave with him?"

Dan chuckled. "How could I forget? He stuck eagle feathers in his hair and pretended he didn't know they were there. Once she caught on to his charm, she gave in."

"Ramon works at the Indigenous Cultural Institute now. Their members are from Mexican-related tribes, including the Coahuiltecans. What they do is more ceremonial—getting the descendants together for tribal dances, traditional food, things like that. But he can probably introduce you to someone at Tap Pilam, or point you in the right direction. Here's his number." She read it out, and Dan copied it down. "Tell him I said hello. It's nice hearing from you, Dan. Don't be a stranger."

Dan called Ramon immediately and, as expected, left a message, since everyone was working from home now. He shook his head. Who would have thought a pandemic would interfere with doing a favor for a saint? Who would have even put a saint and "pandemic" in the same sentence? That came from knowing Cora.

While he waited to hear from Ramon, he wondered if Frannie was having any luck.

# Chapter 32

Frannie sighed. This pandemic thing was frustrating. Getting a single callback on the same day, or within any reasonable time, seemed impossible, but it would be a lot harder to work her interview tricks via email.

Librarians, though, had already developed ways to assist patrons from home. Frannie spent some time in online chats with librarians who found contact names, phone numbers, and email addresses. She left voice mail messages where she could, emailed, bit her tongue, bounced her leg, and waited.

Meanwhile, she kept hunting for material relating to the Coahuiltecans in 1886. Most of what she found was written in the 1950s through the 1980s, but one article was recent—September 26, 2019. She copied a quote to her clipboard:

*A majority of Coahuiltecan names disappeared from the written record during the seventeenth and eighteenth centuries as epidemics, warfare, migration, high infant mortality, and general demoralization took their toll. Missions and refugee communities became the last bastions of ethnic identity. The Indians caused little trouble and provided unskilled labor, working at plantations and mines. Ethnic names vanished with intermarriages. By the end of the eighteenth century, the missions closed and Indian families were given small parcels of mission land. Descendants of some aboriginal groups still lived in scattered communities in Texas as late as 1981.*

The last two sentences confirmed that a small traditional group living around San Antonio in 1886 was not only possible, but likely. With Cora's theory on solid historical grounds, Frannie stuck a forefinger in the air and shook it in celebration: One!

What could Katy have been doing with the Indians? Did anyone at the convent back then know? The newspapers had no accounts of Katy's death that Frannie could find, so the story the nuns had told the Mrozek family was suspect. Maybe there was something the nuns didn't want known. A cover-up might not be so far-fetched after all. Frannie rubbed her hands together. It was high time she got to the bottom of things.

How much of Cora's paranormal vision in the Rosary Valley might be real? This could be a wild goose chase, but Frannie didn't think so. Cora's instincts were always right on. She'd trust Cora's gut in a minute. If there had been a cover-up 135 years ago, could she find out the truth now? Even if anyone today knew the secret, would the sisters still want to protect it?

"Okay, sisters," she mumbled. "Your turn. Show Frannie what you got."

She opened the Sisters of Charity website and sent another email to the director of vocations. Earlier, she had reviewed the order's history timeline. She scanned it again, noting that the order had opened Santa Rosa Hospital in San Antonio five years before Katy's arrival. There was no relevant information for 1886. "Sister Works," described as a collection of materials produced through the years by the nuns, looked interesting. Maybe Katy had contributed to it. The archives were open for visits. With Covid, that was out of the question, but maybe someone would search for her.

She leaned back in her chair to think. She had two phone numbers —the director of vocations and an archivist from the Heritage Center. But how would she explain that something that happened 135 years ago was urgent enough to require immediate handling? *Yes, I know there's a pandemic, but you see, this saint from heaven is visiting near Chicago and I need to know about her sister so my friend's critically ill husband will be cured, it's a matter of life and death. That'll work! Yeah, right. In my dreams.*

Frannie wasn't reluctant to stretch the truth when necessary, but she was more convincing when she embellished instead of telling bald-faced lies.

A deadline—that was it. She could claim she was gathering infor-

mation to flesh out Mother Josepha's life. That part was true. Frannie
Googled "procedure to become a saint" and took some quick notes so
she'd sound convincing. She'd say the Congregation for the Cause of
Sainthood for Mother Mary Josepha was to meet in less than a week
and they wanted to know about the candidate's relationship with her
beloved younger sister, Katy, who had become a Sister of Charity. The
panel wanted to know if any records had turned up since the last investigation was done, when the cause was opened in 1962. That should do
it. If she could get to the right person, she'd wing it from there. Frannie
was proud of her bullshit skills.

Then she felt a glimmer of doubt. How big of a sin was it to lie to
a religious person? Her story was only a little fib, wasn't it? Frannie
shook it off and left a voicemail message for Sister Barbara Marie, stat-
ing it was vitally important to talk to her immediately. She looked at the
time. It was already after one o'clock. She wondered if she'd reach Sister Barbara today.

A secretary got back to her within fifteen minutes, and Frannie made
her case.

"I'm sorry, the coronavirus changes everything," the woman said. "Everyone is working from home, I can't put you through—"

"I don't expect you to do that, but surely you can call her, tell her how
urgent the matter is, and she can call me. Let me give you my number,
and that's Berkowitz, B-e-r-k-o-w-i-t-z."

"I've got it, but will the Congregation even meet because of the coronavirus?"

"We can't take the chance. They'll expect us to be ready, or maybe
they'll have a conference call or something."

The woman sighed, sounding overwhelmed. "Zoom. That's what everyone's doing now. One more thing to learn. I'm not looking forward
to it." Then after a moment, "Okay. I'll call Sister Barbara and give her
your message, but I can't promise when she'll get back to you."

Luck went Frannie's way. Sister Barbara called in a matter of minutes.
The secretary had been suspicious and protective. Sister Barbara was
suspicious, but sharp. After Frannie told her story, the nun threw around
a lot of terms like Servant of God and Venerable, and when she asked
the name of the postulator, Frannie almost confessed.

"Sister, I'm sorry—but I'm helping a friend here," she said. "I don't know all the specifics, only that we're trying to find records on Katherine Mrozek. I'd be happy to answer your questions, but I don't know any more than I've told you. I can put you in touch with my friend if you like, but she's had a family emergency. Right now, all I really want is the name, phone number, and email of the person who can look into the matter for us." *How's that for pussy-footing?* Frannie rolled her eyes and grinned.

"A family emergency?"

"Yes. Her husband had a stroke."

Sister Barbara's voice held a note of compassion now. "How sad, and what a bad time for it to happen."

Frannie held her breath.

"Sister Mary Dorothea is our archivist," Sister Barbara said after a pause. "But, due to this virus, I can't guarantee she can do any research for you, and I'm reluctant to put her on the spot by giving you her contact information. If she's not going to the center, she'll have limited access to records. Why don't I call her? I'll explain what's going on and ask if she can help. One of us will get back to you by the end of the day."

Frannie didn't know whether to cheer or hang her head in shame. Lying to a nun. Was that a sacrilege?

# Chapter 33

By midmorning, Cora was squirrelly. "How I can be exhausted and hyperactive at the same time!" she mumbled.

In her room, she found herself looking at the same notes over and over, piling and then scattering them again. A lot of irons in the fire but nothing was clicking yet.

She'd spoken to Cisco and Joe, and there was nothing really new. This was Cisco's fourth day in the hospital, and he was taking a step backward, if anything. No violent outbursts, but he remained sullen and disagreeable, still refusing to cooperate with therapists, doctors, and nurses, still insisting he wasn't sick. "They're all making mountains out of molehills," he complained. "Get me out of here."

"Soon, hon," she had told him. "You've got nothing to do while they're getting your heart checked. Why not just go along with them? What have you got to lose?"

"It's stupid. All bullshit."

Angry, yes. But at least he was relatively calm. She didn't know if he was still getting sedatives, but she could rely on Joe to do the right thing and let her know anything important.

She placed a call to Janna, wondering if the woman had found out where the unique stone in the Rosary Valley had come from. Janna hadn't, but would keep looking.

"I checked with Father Bozic yesterday for access to the library and print shop files. No one goes there, so there's little chance of picking up or spreading this crazy virus, he said. How are things at the convent?"

"We're being careful. Wearing masks, distancing ourselves. Visitors are limited, especially in the senior residences. I keep thinking they'll ask me to leave, but they haven't so far."

"Don't go anywhere you don't absolutely have to, that's my advice. I'll reach you on your cell if I find anything."

After the call, Cora couldn't sit still. Everyone had tasks, but she had nothing to do. She didn't want to wander around the convent, calling attention to herself, risking reminding the sisters she didn't have to be here. She paced her room, feeling inadequate, worrying that there was something she should be doing, something she was missing. She wasn't used to sitting around and letting others do the work. If she wasn't busy, she felt like she was doing something wrong—akin to committing a sin.

She'd finished reading about the life of Mother Josepha. She knew from experience the information needed to incubate in her subconscious before the full impact hit. Forcing it would be nonproductive, perhaps even detrimental. But she wished she knew Josepha better. It was difficult to get into the head of a woman whose entire life had been about loving God and compassion for others. Cora thought she was compassionate herself, but not anywhere near Josepha's level. It would be easier to find Katy if she understood Mother Josepha, wouldn't it? If she could connect and find motivation outside of her own needs?

She'd had two opportunities to meet the saint-to-be, but hadn't seen her either time. Maryam had been there then. What if Cora went to the ravine alone? Josepha might appear to Cora if she went without Maryam.

Why not try? Pandemic restrictions didn't include walking alone outdoors. She glanced out the window. The day was overcast, the trees swaying vigorously in the wind. She checked the weather on her phone. Current temperature 38 degrees, with a high of 48 and rain predicted that afternoon. The day wouldn't get any better. She should go right away.

Cora dressed quickly in sweatpants, a long-sleeved T-shirt covered by a sweatshirt, hiking boots, leather jacket, knit scarf, gloves, and knit hat—that should do it. She slid her phone into her pocket and headed out.

The lawn surrounding the convent was wet. It must have rained during the night or earlier in the day. The ravine would be muddy, but it would be worse later. Reaching the top of the ravine, the leaf-covered path looked slick but firm. At least it was daylight.

She tested each foothold as she stepped down the slope, not switching her weight to the next leg until she was planted solidly. Wherever she came across branches, she grabbed them for support. A few puddles lay at the bottom of the steep incline, but the ground was firm enough to support her. The wind was brutal, coursing through the ravine like a tunnel, blowing dried leaves to obscure the path here and there. But she persisted, knowing that if she stayed to the right wherever the path divided, she would eventually come to her destination. She hoped she would recognize the spot.

She knew right away when she got to the place, even though she was distracted the first time she'd been there and the second time it was dark. But there at the top of the ravine was the little tree, and at the base the area where Sister Maryam had knelt and Cora had watched and waited. Behind her she heard, as before, noise from the road up above. Fortunately, the ravine was deep here, with thick brush that partially blocked the wind, and after it veered to the left the ravine no longer funneled the wind down its course. The air was damp and cold, but Cora had dressed warmly. She found a branch to sit on, facing the tree where Maryam said her visitor always appeared.

A few minutes passed, and Cora began to doubt herself. Why had she felt compelled to come here? She crossed her arms over her chest and gazed at the visitor's tree. To make personal contact, to be reassured that she was on the right track, that Mother Josepha wanted her to investigate Katy's story. More than that, she wanted to feel Josie, to know her, to develop empathy as between friends.

She wanted Josie's approval.

"Are you here?" she called. She waited—heard nothing, felt nothing unusual, absolutely no change in atmosphere.

"Am I right? Is it you, Josie?"

She paused. She felt silly. "I'm trying to find Katy, find out what happened to her in San Antonio. That *is* what you want me to do, isn't it? That's what you told Sister Maryam?"

She jumped at a sharp cracking sound from the foliage on her right, but saw nothing when she looked. Was someone watching her? No, that was crazy. No one would be here, especially in such weather. No voice or buzzing sound came from the tree either, so she took a deep breath and went on.

"I'm guessing here. I'm assuming you haven't been able to connect with Katy in heaven for some reason, and her death haunts you. You believe she must have been doing something important that led to her death. Finding out what that was may even lead you to her. I don't know how these things work. But you think I can help here on earth. Am I on the right track? Is that what you want?"

There was no indication anyone was there. Cora longed for the peaceful feeling that had possessed her when Maryam last talked to her visitor, but no such feeling came. Overcome with hopelessness, Cora covered her face with her hands and rocked her body from side to side. Then she composed herself, wiped tears from her face with her gloved hands, and looked at the tree again.

"If you're there, please, please! Help my husband! I can't imagine my life without him! Bring him home! Help him! Please!"

But there was no sign of any kind. It grew colder, the wind stilled, and fog filled the ravine. Whatever small shelter the gully had provided was gone. Cora shivered in misery, stood up, and started the hike back to the convent.

Almost immediately the fog gave way to a steady rain, blowing in sheets from the northwest. Cora struggled into the wind, walking carefully but hurriedly on the slippery, muddy path. At times it was difficult to see through the rain, but she sensed a presence and stopped to examine the brush. Had someone been lurking when she tried to talk to Josie? She looked around her, but saw no one. There was no shelter either, no option but to keep going.

With relief she reached the final ascent. She had only to climb out of the ravine, through the thin patch of woods, and then it was an easy walk back to the convent. In her discomfort, her desperate need for relief from the elements, and her fear of being watched, she momentarily forgot the need for caution. Her right foot came down hard and crooked on a tree root. Pain shot up her leg. She stumbled and pitched to the side of the trail, where she grabbed a thin branch that gave just enough support to break her fall.

Her ankle, however, was not so fortunate. Placing weight on it was excruciatingly painful. She must have twisted it badly. It would support her, but she was afraid to transfer all her weight to it. Walking the remainder of the way on her own was impossible. She could call for help, but what if someone had been following her, someone with evil on his mind? She was too far away to be heard even if anyone else were out in the rainstorm. No one would have missed her or be looking for her.

She had her phone. She could call the convent—but that would put someone else at risk, and she felt too humiliated, unless she had no other choice. Stupid, stupid to come here!

She lowered herself to her hands and knees and scanned the debris for anything she could use as a crutch. Eventually she spied a broken branch, near enough to the path to reach. It was an inch thick, crooked, and much too long. Unable to break it to a shorter length, she gave up and just grabbed it near the middle. It brought to mind Moses with his extra-long staff, but it was enough to allow her to hobble slowly up the incline and limp toward the convent.

# Chapter 34

"I won't bore you with the details," Dan told Frannie when they connected again late that afternoon. Dan tended to give lengthy explanations, but they were fighting the clock today.

"I've narrowed the possibilities to the Tap Pilam Coahuiltecan Nation. If any archives exist, these people either have them or know where they are. There are other organizations that work with them to some extent. I have a friend at one of those, and I'm waiting for a call from another friend who can probably introduce me to the right person at Tap Pilam to help us. Roundabout, but should be a sure thing."

"Already? That's good," Frannie said, more quietly than in their last conversation, and Dan got the feeling he had impressed her. "Did you have any luck?" he asked, trying not to sound condescending. It wasn't likely Frannie would have been able to make such contacts.

"A bit. Mostly I sent out a lot of emails and left a lot of voicemails. Who knows when, or if, I'll get called back. This pandemic sure screws things up, doesn't it?"

"Don't feel bad. I'm finding that, too. But it is what it is."

"I did have a little luck at the Sisters of Charity, though," she said, her voice a little stronger now. In fact, Dan thought she sounded a bit smug. "I got the name of their archivist and talked to another sister. Her *boss*, I think it was. She promised one of them will get back to me today."

It was Dan's turn to be impressed. "That's great. How did you do it?"

Was that indistinct sound a chuckle? Frannie definitely sounded amused. "Huh. That's for me to know and not to let you know."

"Well, I'd say we've both been pretty productive. Hope the rest of the day goes as well."

"Oh, I got a feeling it will. We be on a roll." This time Frannie laughed out loud, and Dan found himself joining her. Maybe working with this woman wasn't going to be so bad.

"What happens, though, if we get through to all the right people and still can't find answers? What if there are no records of Katy Mrozek? That's a real possibility, you know," Dan said.

"I'm not worried about that. You ever worked with Cora before?"

"Not on a project, no."

"When you've worked with Cora long enough, you'll know. Just mark my words. When the clues run out, somehow the next clue gets provided. Could even be something supernatural involved. Count on it."

~~~

Shortly after talking to Dan, Frannie received a call from Sister Barbara at the Sisters of Charity. Sister Dorothea, the convent's archivist, would look for records pertaining to Katherine Mrozek and call Frannie with the results the next day.

"Did she think there was anything to be found?" Frannie asked.

"We should have a record of Katy Mrozek's arrival, her vows, and her burial. There may be little else, but I'm sure Dorothea will check our Sister Works, a collection of our sisters' writings, artworks, and other accomplishments." She let out a long breath. "Don't get your hopes up, Mrs. Berkowitz. From what you told me, Sister Catherine was here less than three years. She probably hadn't taken her final vows yet, and any writing she may have done might not be considered important enough to save in the Sister Works. We would have had no idea at that time of her older sister's potential for sainthood, of course."

Frannie thanked Sister Barbara profusely and signed off.

Since she wouldn't hear from Sister Dorothea until the next day, and other callbacks or email responses might or might not come, Frannie had the afternoon free to read old newspapers. This time she would be more thorough, and look not only for articles about Katy's accident and subsequent death, but also get a sense for what was happening at the time, especially if it involved local Indians.

She selected a few issues of the *San Antonio Daily Light*. The local
section had several articles, a few with headlines, many short three-line,
gossip-type entries, all in random order. There were many ads for medical remedies and testimonials for such products. Another page was a
serialization of some popular novel of the day. Crime items had headlines in bold type.

### Bold Burglary

*The burglary reported yesterday of Mrs. Theo. Zopis's residence on Pros-
pect Hill was committed about 12 o'clock. Mrs. Z. was absent from home and
returning noticed one of the windows open. Suspecting something wrong, she
asked Mr. Johnson, a neighbor, to accompany her, and they saw a Mexican climb
out of the window. The Mexican without turning aside, threw his hand on his
hip pocket as if to draw a weapon, ordering Johnson to stand aside, and then
escaped gracefully to the mesquite brush and disappeared. They discovered that
the Mexican had stolen a good watch and chain and two pairs of earrings, but
had been in too great a hurry to secure a sum of money that lay on the mantel
shelf, or to break open a trunk containing other valuable jewelry.*

*Huh*, Frannie thought. *Nothing like telling the world where your valuables
are hidden. Wonder how long they lasted after the paper came out.*

The language throughout the paper was colorful and completely inap-
propriate by today's standards, but entertaining. Frannie continued a
tedious search, not finding any mention of American Indians, but plenty
of bias against Mexicans and blacks. She was about to give up when she
struck gold in an issue from December 17, 1886.

### Tobacco Farmer Dies

*If you frequent the market at San Antonio Plaza you will be familiar with
Jose Sanchez, known for selling a tobacco that is much favored and felt to be
superior to any other tobacco available.*

*We are sad to report that the son of Jose Sanchez, Rafael Sanchez, has noti-
fied us that his father will no longer bring his fine tobacco product to our market, due to his untimely death some weeks ago.*

*The Sanchez family is part of a small group of Coahuiltecan Indians who
were granted a tiny farm on mission property nearly a hundred years ago after*

*the missions closed. They have continued to farm the land and live peacefully there, preferring traditional culture to our way of life, and eking a small profit from their farm sufficient to ensure their bare survival.*

*Mr. Sanchez had developed pain and swelling in his belly and trouble breathing some weeks before his death that was unresponsive to the best efforts of the shaman. It may be wondered if our Sisters of Charity at Santa Rosa Infirmary might have been able to effect a cure, had the family not relied on the chants, sweating, and sucking cures of the native culture.*

*Rafael Sanchez has informed us that the family will no longer participate in our markets. It seems the tobacco-growing process involved secrets that died with Jose, and his relatives have decided to seek other work. Therefore, if you have any of the fine tobacco left it would be best for you to use it wisely, as it will no longer be available.*

Frannie sat back with a satisfied smile. She had confirmation of a group of Coahuiltecans living in the area, and the dates made sense. A connection, and a name! Now she had proof such a group existed, the next step was to connect it to Katy. They were on the right track, she was sure of it!

# Chapter 35

Ramon Gomez called Dan that afternoon. "Hey, Mahoney! Y'all still serenading the ladies these days?"

Dan laughed, remembering an escapade the two had shared. Ramon had talked Dan into singing at the hotel room door of a mutual lady friend at two in the morning, their voices echoing throughout the hotel's atrium.

"Sorry, pal. Takes two wild and crazy guys for a good serenade," Dan said now.

They got down to the reason for the call and, after hearing Dan out, Ramon brought up a complication. "I wish I could help, but Tap Pilam doesn't have staff or resources for archives. We all value our history, of course, but it's as much as we can do to manage tribal citizenship and protect our rights. Revitalization of culture is important, but mostly done through social gatherings."

"I guessed that. But I thought you'd preserve your history in some way and that you might know where archival material could be found. Specifically, Coahuiltecan history."

"We've outsourced much of our archives to institutions with better resources. We own the items, of course, and the programs fall under our direction, but universities handle the collections now. Why don't you tell me what you're looking for, and I'll see if I can direct you to the right place. Why do you need this?"

Disappointed, Dan explained. "It's for a good friend who's in a bind. She's writing a book and—"

"No, no, stop. They're all writing a book, my friend."

"This one is different—"

"They're all different. Look, if you were doing this for yourself, I'd feel better about it. You have a track record with us—we know we'll be represented fairly when we deal with you. But for someone else...."

"Ramon, I can guarantee this. It's as safe with her as it is with me. She's looking for information about a Catholic nun, a woman we think was known to your people. Only good can come out of this, I promise."

Ramon was silent, apparently thinking.

Finally, he said, "Why don't I point you in a direction I think will help. If you actually find what you're looking for, and if it turns out to be a protected tribal matter, we can talk again. Maybe you'll be lucky and no special access will be needed."

"That would be great."

"So, give me some details, names, dates, places, whatever you know of the story. Slow, so I can make notes."

Dan did as requested, telling Ramon what Cora had told him. After a moment of consideration, Ramon said, "Written histories of indigenous peoples dating back to 1886 are highly unlikely. Some effort has been made to collect *oral* histories, though. However, certain collections are protected and require approval from the Coahuiltecan Nation to access, and approval is only given through the Tap Pilam Tribal Council. That's the procedure, I'm afraid."

Dan wondered whether Cora would want to go through all of this before she even knew whether such a document existed. Also, did she want him to inquire on her behalf or did she want to be directly involved? If she did, that could mean serious delays.

"I'll have to discuss this and get back to you," Dan said. Ramon promised to send him contact information for university people, as well as someone at Tap Pilam.

After the call, Dan searched university sites to get ahead of things on his own. He made an educated guess that a department that had created an oral history archive would be most likely to also have a more complete collection. He identified four such collections, and after reading the small print narrowed it down to two. He was in the process of deciding which to approach first when Frannie called.

"Hold everything," she said, excitement clear in her voice. "I think I found the guy in the buggy!"

After she told Dan about the article she'd found, he was skeptical.

"Go with me here," Frannie said. "Cora would tell you—you got to trust my hunches. This article never would have called to me if it wasn't meant to be. Here's the thing. There wouldn't have been many Indians around San Antonio in 1886. We were looking for a sick dude, could be about to die, who Katy could have known. The date fits, and the location fits, and the circumstances fit. Seriously, we got nothing else to go on. We got to find this Sanchez family. What could it hurt?"

Dan sighed. "Well, it's pretty thin, but it is the first actual name to come up. It wouldn't hurt to add the name to our search criteria, providing we ever get an opportunity to do that."

"I already looked for death notices or anything else on both of those names. You'd never believe how many Jose Sanchezes there are, but none in San Antonio in 1886, so that's another one of them dead ends."

"Indians had rigid burial rituals, but they didn't include announcements in the papers. So yes, I wouldn't have expected you to find a death record," Dan said. "But at least we have confirmation that our logic is sound as to the existence of Indians that could have interacted with Katy. That's encouraging. Now we need the rest of the story. Honestly, I wasn't sure we could do this. Here's how my afternoon went." Dan filled Frannie in on what he had learned from Ramon.

"Hurry up and wait again. So, what now?" she said.

"I think it's time to get some input from Cora while we wait for Ramon to call back. Bring her up to date and let her decide who does what from here."

"Well, what you still talking to me for, then? Get talking to Cora. Don't you forget to tell her about my part, ya hear?"

~~~

Sitting upright in bed, Cora watched while Sister Fatima attached metal clips to the three-inch wide elastic bandage she had just finished wrapping around Cora's ankle.

"Thanks, Sister. I could have wrapped it myself—I just needed the bandage," Cora said.

Fatima shook her head. "It's no problem. It's awkward to wrap yourself. Is it very painful?"

Cora slid her feet to the floor and tentatively put some weight on the ankle. "I can hobble, but I won't be running marathons anytime soon."

Fatima grinned. "And do you usually run marathons?"

Cora laughed. "Not usually, no."

Fatima tested the clip to be sure it wouldn't come loose. "You really should have an x-ray. But with COVID-19 increasing every day, the emergency rooms are packed with infected people. You don't want to catch the virus in the ER."

*Or bring it back to the convent, I bet she's thinking.* "I think we're good with the bandage—that's probably all they'd do at the ER anyway. It's pretty swollen—can you send me some ice? If it doesn't get better, I'll get it checked tomorrow."

Cora gingerly moved back to the bed and put her feet up. What she wanted to do was take a painkiller and go to sleep. But she had to keep her phone turned on in case she got a call from Arizona.

Fatima pulled the chair out from the desk and sat down uninvited. *Here it comes*, Cora thought.

"So, what were you doing out in this weather?"

Lying to a nun felt as bad as trying to lie to God. But she couldn't break Maryam's confidence. "I remembered something I saw in the ravine and wanted to check it out before the rain destroyed it." *Misleading, but not really a lie*, she told herself.

Fatima shook her head again. "That ravine is dangerous. It's crumbling, full of poison ivy and snakes. No one, especially people as old as us, should be roaming around down there."

*Poison ivy! Snakes! Yuck!* "I'll certainly think twice now," Cora said. From the beginning, she knew she was trespassing into areas where she didn't belong, abusing the sisters' generosity, and look what it had gotten her—punishment for her transgressions.

The door to Cora's room stood open, but Maryam knocked on the frame. A look passed between Maryam and Fatima that Cora couldn't interpret. *Are these two still on the outs or are they in collusion?*

"I see Fatima's taken good care of you," Maryam said.

"Yes, I was just finishing." Fatima got up and moved to the doorway.

"If you need any help later, let me know. I'll send some ice, and I'll tell Sister Cook to send you a tray for breakfast in the morning."

"Oh, no! I'm too much trouble!" Cora said.

Fatima grinned. "Sisters are devoted to helping the needy, remember. It's our life. Don't think twice about it." With that, she glanced at Maryam again and then left.

Sister Maryam carried a cane in her hand. At least, Cora assumed it was a cane. The stick was made of light-colored wood with many knots along its length and a crook at the top like a goose's neck, its shaft twisted and tapering to the tip.

Sister Maryam held it up. "I'm going to loan this to you. Now don't laugh until you hear the story. Have you ever heard the legend of the dogwood?"

"Um—no," Cora said.

"You've seen a dogwood tree, though, right?"

"Actually, I have two of them in my yard. I love them. They're small—"

"Yes, but supposedly dogwoods weren't always small. Once, they were large and stately trees. It was said that the cross Jesus was crucified on was made from dogwood. After his death, a curse was put on the tree. It would thereafter be thin and twisted. Also, dogwood flowers have four petals arranged in the shape of a cross to remind one of Christ's agony, the tip of each petal indented as if a nail were driven in it, with reddish stains that resemble drops of blood. The center of each flower is rough, signifying the crown of thorns."

"Is that story supposed to be true?" Cora said.

"No. Like I said, it's legend, but a beautiful one, don't you think?"

Cora smiled. "I love it. So, this cane, I assume, is made of dogwood?"

"Absolutely. It's been in my family for years. Dad called it a shillelagh. He got it in Ireland, and it's supposed to be centuries old. The handle looks uncomfortable to hold, but it actually isn't. This will do the job well enough for the time being. Better than that wobbly thing I heard you came in with."

Cora pictured a shillelagh that her Irish father had owned, which had once hung on a wall in a guest bedroom in her parents' home. She had never thought she'd actually use one.

"Thank you, Maryam. You're too good to me. The bandage helps, but the cane will keep me from falling."

Maryam took a seat in the same chair Fatima had vacated and released a slow breath. "Yes, well, do you want to tell me what you were doing in the ravine?"

Cora gave her a lopsided smile. "I wanted to see if Mother Josepha would talk to me."

"I suspected as much. And did she?"

"No. All I got out of the excursion was this bum ankle. A pointless 'trip,' you might say."

"I might also say it serves you right." Maryam snickered, then looked at her seriously. "But you're only doing what you think you must, aren't you? To help Cisco?"

Cora nodded.

"You only have to ask for help from heaven, you know. You don't have to earn favors. That's not the way saints work," Maryam said.

"But it's the way I work. I'm used to taking responsibility for my problems in some way. Won't she be grateful if I do something for her?"

Maryam let out another long breath. "It's already been quite a day, even before your fall."

"Really? What's going on?"

"I was still in bed this morning when Winnie called, before six. She didn't sound herself, in fact, she spoke much more clearly."

"What did she want?"

"She wanted to show me something, to meet me right away. I made time for her, of course, prayed my morning office, dressed, and met her half an hour later."

"What did she show you?"

"Only herself." Maryam paused. "Her disfigurement was unchanged, of course, but her face had an expression of peace and happiness that was so captivating you almost didn't notice the damage. It happened late last night. She said an extreme sense of well-being came over her. She got up and looked in her mirror. Nothing was really different, but she *felt* different, she said, and spoke aloud in her room. She said, 'What's going on?' The words came out clear. The first clear words she had spoken since her accident."

"And she was speaking clearly to you, too?"

"She was. Physically there was no difference, but functionally—remarkable. She still has an impediment, of course, but she's not hard to understand at all. No drooling, and she tells me she can eat much more easily. It was beautiful to see, Cora."

"What does she—what do you—think happened?"

"She says it was through the intercession of Mother Josepha. That's who she prays to, you know."

"Yes, I saw her at St. Joseph's chapel one day."

"And that's not all, Cora. As I said, an eventful morning."

"Go on."

"I thought about what you said and what happened to Winnie, and I went to the ravine early this morning. I wanted to ask my visitor directly who she was. So, I went there, and she appeared. I think she was expecting me."

"And?"

"You were right. She is Mother Josepha."

Cora was stunned. Even though she had convinced herself it was Mother Josepha in the ravine, the admission made the experience real. Everything she said and did became more important.

"I would have thought you'd tell me right away," Cora said, her voice weak.

"I wanted to, but I had appointments I couldn't change, and then I closed myself in my office to think it through. This was a radical adjustment for me...I'm sure you understand. All those years thinking I was talking to Mary."

"I don't know what to say," Cora said. "Knowing for sure...."

Maryam nodded, staring at the floor. "It changes everything." She exhaled and then raised her head and met Cora's gaze. "I don't suppose you've had time to get any new information yet—it's only been a day."

"Actually, my friends have discovered quite a bit already." Cora brought Maryam up to date about the unusual stone in the Rosary Valley, and the Coahuiltecans, and wondered whether Frannie and Dan had made any more progress while she was out wrecking her ankle.

Maryam looked thoughtful. "I still wish you hadn't told your friends about the visitations. But maybe because it's Mother Josepha and not Mary after all...."

"They had to understand why what they're doing is important. They won't say anything. You can trust them."

"I know. You're right. I'm just so afraid of turning a miraculous event into a media circus if word gets out." She sighed. "Well, I was reluctant to give up on Mary, but it would be exciting if I can actually help get Mother Josepha declared a saint, wouldn't it."

Cora Tozzi, *History of the Religious Institutions of Lemont*
(Chicago, Madonna Press, 2024), 86–93

*"I became accustomed to their murmuring. When it*
*was necessary to sacrifice myself in order to bring about*
*peace, I did not hesitate; I trusted in God and He came to*
*my aid. In spite of any adversity, I maintained my happy*
*disposition since I saw the will of God in all life's events."*
—The Chronicles of Venerable Mother Josepha of Chicago

### Josie's Journal
### December 1, 1894

Oh, beloved and immaculate Mother, obtain for us from your Divine Son one thing, just this one thing, that this little band, attempting the new work, may remain forever yours and through you, your Son's, I pray.

I understand now that Father Vincent was wise to require that our mission be achieved through the foundation of a religious order. How else could we measure the commitment of our members and ensure that service to the poor would not be abandoned if the work got hard?

But I remain full of misgivings. How can I lead others when I myself am simple and uneducated in spiritual matters? Am I a fool to think I can do this? Yet, I wish only for God's will to be done. I will place my trust in Him, confident that He will tell me what to do, and proceed with our plans.

A new candidate has presented herself, and we are back to our original number of eight. Father Vincent gave us an outline: we are to have a six-month trial period as postulants, then receive the habit and instruction on religious life. We are to work out the details among us.

"Since you have no home of your own," he said, "I suggest you choose the home of one of you as a temporary arrangement."

We had looked at each other blankly. Then Angelina, who was living with her brother's family, suggested, "Perhaps we could live in Josie's home?"

I had to admit my home was the best option. Our apartment had a parlor, kitchen, dining room, three large bedrooms, a bath, and there was also a full heated basement that could be converted to more rooms. My brother-in-law Adam would allow us to use the building until a permanent home could be arranged. So, I agreed.

But would Mama still have her comfortable chair, where she sat to read and pray the rosary? She was accustomed to privacy. How many women her age, 64 years, would agree to share their home?

I need not have worried. "I want to be with you Josie, as we have always been," Mama said. "I can cook, keep the house, or help in other small ways. It will give me some purpose. It will be more like the life I am accustomed to than any other choice."

I remembered the words of Ruth in the Bible: "Where you go I will go, and where you stay I will stay. Your people will be my people and your God my God."

My heart burned, whether with pain for forcing this situation on my poor mother or with joy for her acceptance and the gift of her in my life I could not tell, nor did it matter.

### December 8, 1894

The founding of the Franciscan Sisters of Our Lady took place on the feast of the Immaculate Conception that honors Mary, the symbol of women's instinct to protect and guide loved ones. The life I chose will not bless me with children of my own, and I had lost Katy, the sister I thought of as my adopted child. Instead, I devote my life to fulfilling the physical needs of others.

And so, we gathered around the dining table, eight serious but joyous faces, having moved into our new rooms. Sophie Wisneski was there, although she would not be living with us, since she is needed at home to care for her family. I was pleased she was joining the community even in this way, as her experience was valuable.

As I listened to the idle conversation, I gazed at the wall across from me, where a family portrait hung, the last remnant of our private lives. The portrait had been taken the year we arrived in Chicago from Poland. In the back row stood Rosalie, Theo, Frances and me, and sitting in front of us was Katy in the middle with Mama and Papa on either side of her. The serious expressions on our faces did not reflect the happiness we felt in being together in this city and this country, although I did think that my lips were curved just a little bit. We had shared many meals around this very table when Papa and Katy were alive and before Frances and Theo left.

Now we will have a full table again every day.

With some reluctance I interrupted the women's happy chatter, and handed a pencil and paper to each. "Father Vincent says we are to choose a superior. To be sure this is done freely, write down the name of the person you wish to lead us," I told them. I then led them in invocations to the Holy Spirit and to the Mother of God.

When the votes were passed in and Sophie Wisneski counted them, six of the eight women had selected me to be the first superior of our group.

### December 24, 1894

Father Vincent came tonight to bless our temporary quarters. He walked from room to room, carrying a brass pot of holy water, blessing each space with his aspergillum. When he walked out into the night, snow was falling thick and fast. Beyond the snow we saw the new towers of St. Stanislaus Church proudly shining against the sky. It seemed a magical moment.

Our table was piled high with traditional Christmas Eve dishes. We crowded elbow-to-elbow, laughing as we jostled each other for space, with the two mothers also at the table. We said grace, and then Angelina held up the Oplatki, thin white wafers stamped with Christmas images.

"As the youngest member, I will begin the Oplatki tradition by asking

God to bless us with health, success, and happiness during the coming year." Angelina broke off a piece of an Oplatek and passed the wafer to me. I broke off a piece and said, "May the joy we all feel today sustain us." I passed the Oplatek to Mama.

Mama had tears in her eyes. "We are thankful that God has brought us all together to do His work." The piece she broke off was larger than the others, and everyone laughed.

Sophie took the wafer and considered for a moment. "I pray that we have the strength to accomplish the challenges ahead."

When the last piece was passed to the last woman, and all had made their blessing, the women began to exchange tiny pieces of their portion with each other, accompanied by a personal blessing. As each piece got smaller and smaller, the blessings became less serious and general hilarity broke out until Mama asked, "Are we ever going to eat all this food? It will be cold."

I am filled with happiness for the devotion of my colleagues and that God has brought us all together. But my mind is already arranging the beds, preparing for the needy and the poor, and converting one of the bedrooms to a dressmaking shop, which will be a major means of our support. There will be hard work ahead, but I believe that, with the help of God, I will be able to accomplish what I have set my heart on.

### July 7, 1895

We have become comfortable with new routines, although life is harder than any of us had anticipated.

We rise at four thirty to take turns washing and dressing in the single bathroom. We say morning prayers, then at seven we go to St. Stanislaus for Mass. At eight we have breakfast, and then we work. After work we return home for supper. One of us reads aloud from a book of spiritual writings. Then we have a short period of personal time, before saying the rosary, evening prayers, and then dropping into bed.

From the beginning our house was filled to capacity with sick and elderly women, and continued to be full even after we took over the second apartment and converted the basement.

Father said we were unlikely to raise sufficient funds to build a home for the aged without going door to door to beg, but I prefer to earn what we need. Everyone is suffering from hard times, and I do not want to ask our neighbors to deprive their families further by giving us what little they have. So, my skills as a dressmaker are put to use, and Angelina joins me in the shop. We sew night and day to earn money for food, clothing, medicine, and supplies for ourselves and our residents.

The other sisters go to St. Stanislaus, where they receive a modest salary to run the parish laundry and tend to housekeeping. In addition to washing and ironing clothes, mending church linens, cleaning the rectory and taking care of the priests, they care for our residents. Sophie is unable to partake in the work, since she is needed by her own family. Our earnings go into a common fund to be used to build a more permanent home.

I did not realize at first that not everyone's dedication was the same as my own. Sister Bertha began to complain because she had to do hard physical work at the rectory while I got to stay home and sew.

I was reluctant to make decisions that displeased my fellow sisters. Perhaps I was too timid and gentle to be a good superior, but I was uncomfortable with harsh discipline. My solution was to take the toughest tasks myself, and I switched jobs with Sister Bertha. It was not long before Sister Bertha complained that work in the sewing room was too hard, and then one day she announced she had made a mistake and left.

After a while, some of the other sisters felt the same as Sister Bertha. Again, I took on harder work myself. Some sisters took offense at my inability to take a firm hand, and before the six months was over there were only three of us living together, plus Sophie.

Sister Bertha's parting comment was hurtful. She accused me of using the money we earned for my own pleasure. I offered this pain as a sacrifice to Jesus and hoped for the best.

Life was even harder with only three of us to do the work previously done by seven. But somehow, I never felt completely exhausted. My greatest joy was kneeling down to say the evening prayers and rosary with the residents. It seemed to me that God was pleased with the little good that I could do.

And so, our six months as postulants completed, tonight all four of us became novices and took first vows as Franciscan Sisters of Our

Lady. Our little group was made up of myself, Sister Angelina, Sister Sophie, and a quiet woman in her forties, Sister Clare.

Up until now we had used our given names, prefaced by "Sister," but when taking first vows we would choose a religious name to represent our birth into a new life. We also elected to wear a formal habit. As postulants we had dressed simply in long black skirts and long-sleeved white blouses. By wearing a habit now, instead of later as most orders do, our manner of dress would be our badge of identification, and we would be accepted more readily as religious.

I had designed a habit and spent countless nights closed in my room sewing, planning to reveal the new habits at tonight's celebratory dinner before we took our vows. Each sister would don her habit for the first time and reveal the name she had chosen. In most orders, religious names are selected by the superior, but I let each sister make her own choice.

"I wish we were having our surprises before supper instead of after," Angelina said. "I am too excited to eat."

Clare also had a broad smile on her face. "I am sure Josie has done a good job. Have you ever known her to fail in her dressmaking skills?"

"It is not her skill we are nervous about, but whether or not we will like what she has come up with," Sophie chipped in.

"Our mothers worked hard to prepare this pork roast and make pierogi," I said. "We cannot disappoint them."

"Well, yes, but eat fast then," Angelina said.

After eating, I slipped away and placed a new habit in the sisters' rooms, leaving it on the bed. Let the sisters see themselves the first time in privacy, I thought.

The habit I had designed was traditional, as the sisters had requested. It was a dark brown, floor-length tunic, with long, loose-fitting sleeves. The headwear was of starched white fabric and consisted of a cap, a wimple around the neck and cheeks, and a rounded guimpe to cover the upper chest and back. The veil came below the waist and was of the same dark fabric as the tunic, but lined with a white under veil. The cincture worn about the waist was of heavy white cord, with tassels on each end and three knots representing the vows of poverty, chastity, and obedience.

I finished dressing first and waited in the parlor for the others.

When Angelina arrived, her face was glowing. "It is perfect!" she said, and then burst into tears of joy. "I cannot believe this is me," she said, when she could continue. "I am really a bride of God now. This makes it real in a way I never felt before."

Just as she made this comment, Sister Clare arrived. She was smiling, too. "It is just the right thing," she said.

I went to them and checked the wimples to be sure they were not too tight, made sure the guimpes were centered, and the cinctures hung just so. Sophie had not joined us yet and I was nervous about her reaction. Would my friend approve?

When Sophie entered the room, she looked serious. I thought she looked like someone who had worn the habit for a lifetime, it suited her so well. Our eyes met and she smiled.

"I could not have done better, Josie."

I sighed with relief and gave Sophie a hug. Usually she bore hugs rather stiffly, but this time I could feel her soften in my arms. I took her hand and pulled her onto the chesterfield beside me, and waited for Angelina and Clare to take their chairs.

"Before we announce our professed names, I have gifts from Father Vincent." I reached for a small box I had placed on the table next to where I sat and took out four chains with a crucifix, four inches in length, suspended from each. "We will wear these around our necks at all times to complete our habit. The cross will lie just below the guimpe. It will be attractive and identify us quite clearly as belonging to Jesus."

Each sister took a crucifix and hung it around her neck. Nothing was said, but Angelina had tears in her eyes once again, and I saw similar emotions on the faces of Sophie and Clare.

"Now," I said. "Sophie, please go first and tell us what your professed name will be."

Sophie's face softened. "I will be Sister Mary Anne," she said. "Anne with a 'e' for St. Anne, the mother of the Blessed Virgin. It signifies for me the relationship I have with my own dear mother."

I thought her choice was very fitting. Sophie devoted much of her life to caring for her mother, which must be very difficult. Yet she did so without complaint. Well, with little complaint.

"I will be Sister Mary Martha," said Angelina. "St. Martha was a close friend to Jesus and often looked after Jesus in her home. She is a patron of housekeepers and those who care for others. I have devoted my life to others, and so I wish to be known by her name."

Sister Clare said quietly, "I will be keeping my baptismal name, Sister Mary Clare. As a follower of St. Francis of Assisi and founder of the first order of Franciscan Sisters, the Poor Clares, she is a fine example of a woman who gave up worldly matters to live in poverty, as we have done. There is no better choice for me, I believe."

And then it was my turn. I found it difficult to speak for a moment, my heart so filled with joy for the blessings that had led us to this night, warmth and gratitude for the women who surrounded me. My eyes filled with happy tears that streamed down my cheeks.

"I also have decided on a name similar to my baptismal one. I will be taking the name Sister Mary Josepha," I said. "You all know how important the Blessed Mother is to me. Although I am not a mother, my little sister Katy was like my own child, and I cherish my heavenly mother as well as my earthly mother." My eyes sought Sophie's. "You know from your own experience how important our mothers are."

I let my gaze fall to my hands, which were folded in my lap. "Although the name Josepha is similar to Josephine, that is not the reason for my choice. In taking the names of both Mary and Joseph, the foster father of Jesus, I am honoring the Holy Family. Our community is my family now."

# Chapter 36

The next morning, the swelling in Cora's ankle was down a little. The aching was tolerable if she kept her foot elevated.

Early last night, after Fatima and Maryam left, Cora surrendered to the pain she had tried to hide, reluctant to let them know how bad it really was. She took two Tylenol and went to bed. When the phone rang about seven o'clock, she checked the caller ID. It was Frannie. She let the call go to voicemail. She did the same with a call from Dan a little later. She didn't have the energy to deal with anyone and was embarrassed by her clumsy accident. She'd call them both in the morning. There weren't any calls from Arizona.

Now, sitting on the side of her bed, she moved her ankle tentatively. Pain caught her when she tested the range of motion. Carefully, she stood. She couldn't put full weight on her leg, but could hobble cautiously with Maryam's cane.

*I won't tell Joe or Cisco about this. They'll want to know how it happened and then what will I say? They have enough to worry about.*

Fatima knocked on her door at eight o'clock, bearing a tray with coffee, scrambled eggs, and toast. "Thought I'd save you a trip," she said.

"Thanks, I've already had one," Cora said with a chuckle.

"Oh, that was a joke."

"Yeah. A tired old one—sorry."

"How was your night?"

"Uncomfortable, but I got some sleep. My ankle is less swollen this morning. It will probably get worse through the day."

"If you stay off it, maybe not."

*Yeah, right. With a sick husband and the search for Katy. I really want to languish in bed.*

Fatima sat on the side of the bed and touched Cora's sleeve. "You're in good hands, Cora. You'll get through this."

Cora just nodded.

"I can't stay long," Fatima said. "I'm sorry to say, Sister Agnes is very ill. Sister Bernadette is afraid she may be our first case of COVID-19 and Sister Lorita is hoping it doesn't sweep through the convent."

"How awful! Poor Sister Agnes!" *Oh my God, what if the pandemic does run through the convent? What if I get the virus? I can't think about that on top of everything else.*

After Fatima's departure, Cora left most of her breakfast untouched but kept the coffee within reach. She took a deep breath, picked up the phone, and punched in Cisco's number.

Cisco sounded distant and sullen this morning. Cora tried to cheer him up with aimless chatter, but she could tell he wasn't listening. "When are they going to let me out of here?" he grumbled. "It's been weeks!"

It was only his fifth day in the hospital, but she understood how that time might seem longer. He demanded his release from the hospital again, and she gave him the now-customary spiel about needing to get his heart stabilized first. She made an excuse to end the call before he noticed how upset she was, fearing the effect her breakdown would have on him.

Joe's news wasn't much better. "Dad's electrophysicist is considering a cardioversion," he said. "He's staying in AFib. They'd like to shock his heart back into sinus rhythm."

The procedure sounded dangerous. "How do they do that?"

"It's not a big deal. They put him asleep for a few minutes and administer an electric shock. It's not as drastic as defibrillation, like you see on TV. They monitor his heart rate the whole time, of course."

She closed her eyes. "I should be there."

"Mom, it's not a sure thing and they could do it at any time. You'd never get here in time, even if they let you in, which they won't. I'll be there. There's very little risk, trust me. They do this all the time."

After the call, Cora let her tears fall, taking deep breaths to control her own breathing and heart rate. She didn't need to suffer a cardiac event herself. When she was composed, she washed her face, changed into jeans and a sweatshirt, and took another Tylenol. She grabbed a notepad and pen, piled pillows against the headboard of her bed, and eased herself against them. Damn, her ankle hurt!

She returned the calls from Frannie and Dan. So as not to distract them from their main objective, she minimized her injury. After hearing their updates, she was pleased with their progress but felt more than ever like a bump on a log. All she had done personally was manage to turn herself into a cripple and make a difficult task even harder—nothing *useful*.

But she wondered if she was on a wild goose chase, looking for Indians in faraway San Antonio, hoping they'd lead her to a nun who died over a hundred years ago. Maryam had confirmed that the heavenly person appearing to her was Mother Josepha, but did they know for sure what the saint-to-be wanted? And would any of their efforts affect Cisco's recovery? Although logic said otherwise, Cora felt in her gut that they would. She sighed. Where Cisco was concerned her hands were tied for the moment, but she had to stay busy or she'd go crazy with worry.

She reviewed her friends' progress. What could she do, that others weren't doing already? She had questioned Sister Elizabeth extensively and read all available materials about Josie Mrozek. She thought of going back to the Rosary Valley and trying to conjure up another illusion, but after yesterday's disastrous trip to the ravine she wouldn't be able to drive there, or limp on her injured ankle from the parking lot into the valley.

Best let Dan and Frannie follow up with the Coahuiltecan and Sisters of Charity contacts. But she could dig deeper into university websites, even if she was duplicating her friends' efforts. Another set of eyes on a project never hurt.

Cora opened her laptop and clicked on the website that listed the four cultural programs Dan had identified. She studied each one, and some others. Oral histories of indigenous people were the best places to explore, especially since Frannie had found a name that might narrow the results. It was too much to hope the materials were digitized online, but perhaps a willing archivist would help her.

The program that interested her most was at the Institute of Texan Cultures, through the University of Texas at San Antonio. At 969 interviews, conducted between 1967 and 2011, this oral history collection was not only the largest, but covered the longest period of time. The interviews weren't limited to Indian culture, but surely Native history would be a major component. Maybe she'd get lucky.

With some difficulty, she found contact information for the program director. Dan had warned her that, due to COVID-19 work-at-home guidelines, getting someone knowledgeable to pick up the phone was likely to be a challenge. And she would need good reasons to request immediate answers. Taking a page from Frannie's playbook, she prepared a backstory to sound convincing. She glanced at her phone—almost an hour before noon. She needed to eat something, but not cold eggs and toast.

She struggled upright, grabbed the shillelagh, and limped to the kitchen.

The cook looked up from stirring a pot. "Coffee's fresh. Can I get you a cup?"

"I'd love that, but I'd never be able to carry it to my room." Cora nodded at her cane.

"That sucks," the cook said. Cora dumped a few health bars and an orange into a tote bag and slipped the straps over her shoulder, then carefully turned and left.

Back in her room, she called the institute. As she'd expected, she had to leave a voicemail. The time in San Antonio was the same as Chicago —11:30 A.M. Central Standard. The institute might still be clearing their morning messages.

Cora nibbled at a health bar while she waited. A secretary called twenty minutes later. Cora had rehearsed, and was prepared for battle. "I live near Chicago, and I'm researching the history of an order of nuns in San Antonio back in 1886. I'd like to know if someone is available to search your archives for a particular oral interview in your collection."

The secretary sounded apologetic and overwhelmed. "Ordinarily I would connect you, but everyone's working from home because of the pandemic."

"I'm aware of that, but isn't there a way I can reach someone? I really need the information today. Could somebody at least tell me if what I'm looking for is likely to be there or if I should look elsewhere?"

"Well...I'll see what I can do." The voice was doubtful now. "I'll see if anyone has access to our tapes from home or is planning to come in. I can't guarantee anything."

"I understand, and I appreciate your trying."

"If you don't get a callback within an hour, call me again." She gave Cora a direct number.

Cora's phone rang less than fifteen minutes later. A woman on the other end introduced herself as Amelia Santos, the Director of Oral History Collections at the Institute of Texan Cultures.

"I hope I have the right place," Cora began.

"And I hope I can help you." The woman laughed. "It's actually rather frustrating trying to find work-arounds to do the same things at home that I usually do in my office. Your request sounded interesting. I welcome something as simple as a phone discussion."

Cora sighed with relief. She remembered what Frannie had said about the helpful people at university libraries. Maybe she was getting a taste of Texas hospitality. She put her phone on speaker so she could take notes.

"What are you looking for, and how do you plan to use the information?" Santos asked.

"I'm writing a book about the history of religious orders in Lemont, a suburb about thirty miles from Chicago. A nun here is about to be named a saint, and her sister died in San Antonio in 1886. The circumstances are sketchy, and no one has given it a fresh look for almost fifty years. I was hoping that the oral interview program your institution conducted would fill in that story."

"And what's the urgency? I was told you need a fast response."

Cora crossed her fingers on both hands. "There's a meeting coming up in two days to decide whether or not this story is going to be included. If there's no new information, we'll have to scrap it. I think it's an important story, and I'd hate to do that."

"Two days? That's not much time."

"I know. But if there's something there, I can get the decision postponed. That buys more time to dig into the details."

"I see. So, you don't actually need the entire story right now, just to know if a file on it potentially exists. And if we have nothing?"

"Then maybe you can point me in another direction, to some other organization that might help."

"Well, that depends on the specifics, of course. Let's get to that."

"Okay. We're looking for interviews pertaining to a woman, Katherine with a 'K' Mrozek, or Sister Catherine with a 'C', from the Sisters of Charity of the Incarnate Word. She died in 1886 in a horse-and-buggy accident after rendering medical attention to a farmer. We suspect her death is connected to a Coahuiltecan man named Jose Sanchez, who died a short time after she did."

"Let me stop you right there. Have you contacted the Sisters of Charity?"

"We have. But we have reason to believe their information is inaccurate, and we want to verify it through other sources."

"Hmmm. Inaccurate. That's interesting."

"Yes. We believe Sister Catherine visited a Coahuiltecan village where Jose Sanchez lived. We'd like to confirm that and find out more about the village and its residents."

"So, you also want to know about this Coahuiltecan community?"

"Yes. Exactly. We're trying to establish contacts at Coahuiltecan organizations too, but that hasn't been easy. Of the other places we're looking at, your program seems to be the richest and most comprehensive source."

"Well, thank you for that, but therein lies the rub. Our organization has over 900 interviews classified into nineteen categories. A very small number pertain to Native Americans, but we can't rule out less-specific categories such as ranching, San Antonio, sharecropping, general—you get the idea. And our program isn't the only one archiving oral histories. At our university alone, there are four independent studies, and other Texas universities have their own collections. Also, not all our histories are digitized yet. Some are still on audio cassette or disc."

She paused. "Here's what I can do. I can search the digitized collection by dialing into the database. We digitized the oldest material first, and since you're looking into an incident from the 1880s, there's a good chance the information is there. I can search by names, dates, and other keywords and see what comes up. That won't eliminate the need for a more extensive search, but maybe we'll get lucky. If anything looks promising, we can discuss it and go from there."

Cora let out the breath she wasn't aware she'd been holding. *Thank you, Lord!* "Ms. Santos, that would be wonderful! How soon can you do this?"

"I've got one of those confounded Zoom conferences in a few minutes, which will probably go until about two. The search itself shouldn't take more than an hour. I think I can call you by late afternoon. But don't get your hopes up. And I have to warn you, I don't have staff, especially now, to listen through files that are hours long. I can find and send you MP3 files, unless they require a release, but you'll have to do the listening yourself. It could be a pretty big job."

"I've never been known to tackle easy projects. But thanks for the warning. Why would a release be needed, though?"

"Well, you're looking into Indian matters. Sometimes the tribes want to keep the material private. If the file is protected, you'll need to get that release on your own."

*Thank God for Dan,* Cora thought. "I'll cross that bridge if I have to. I'm more worried that you won't find anything. It's much harder to know when to stop if the information you're looking for just doesn't exist."

"You got it. Say your prayers and cross your fingers. I'll get back to you later."

Cora not only crossed her fingers again, but knocked on her wooden desk for good measure. She also said a prayer to Mother Josepha. Once again, covering all the bases.

# Chapter 37

**W**orking from his home office, Dan found a host of special and private collections, but it soon became apparent that his search criteria were inadequate. Even with more details he would need someone intimately familiar with the collections to narrow his search. By the time Ramon called, he had pages and pages of ideas but no home run.

"Hey, buddy," he said when he picked up the call. "I seem to have taken on a monumental task. I hope you can help me cut to the chase—being as we're old friends and all."

Ramon chuckled. "Well, there is that. So, what's up?"

Dan described his frustration. "There's beaucoup information—too much to plod through. I need to narrow it down. I have a lead, though—a slim one—to a Sanchez family." He related Frannie's discovery of the newspaper article from late 1886.

"This may be easier than we thought," Ramon said. "The Sanchez family are influential members of Tap Pilam. I can put in a word for you with Luis Sanchez. He's a good guy—you'll like him. Not as good as me, of course, but who is?"

"That would be great, Ramon. We really need to fast track this."

"I still don't get why something that happened so long ago is so urgent now, but I should be able to get him on his cell. Should I have him call you back or just tell you what he says?"

"I'd like to talk to him, if that's okay."

When Luis Sanchez called a little later, the conversation was short and definitely sweet. Luis's uncle, Carlos, had been one of the first people to give an oral interview at the Institute of Texan Cultures. Luis thought it was in the early 1970s.

"Uncle Carlos died...oh, it must be close to thirty years ago. He'd been entrusted with the oral history of the tribe, passed down through our ancestors, and he recorded many of our legends. My aunt used to tell me some of the stories when I was a kid. I seem to recall there *was* an incident involving a nun. They gave our tribe copies of the interviews, but it would be easier to get your information from the institute. Their archives are more organized and accessible than ours."

"That's great! Is there a particular person I should talk to?"

"Amelia Santos is the director of the program. She knows me slightly, mostly through my family's reputation. You can use my name, but it shouldn't be necessary. That's what they do—connect people to archives."

"Will you help me get permission to access the file if we find it?"

"You won't need it. Although most of our history is proprietary, the tribe signed an agreement with the institute that shared archives are open to the public. We wanted help, and that was one of the conditions." He chuckled. "Of course, we were careful about what we gave them. You'll find the number of interviews is limited. But I can guarantee you that, in a spirit of cooperation, no lies were told—this time."

~~~

"I'm sorry, Dan. I never thought we'd end up finding the same woman. I should have called you right away to save you some trouble," Cora said. "But I just talked to Amelia Santos this morning."

"Well, the important thing is that she's researching for you. I have to admit I was looking forward to talking to her, but direct is better, I guess. Is there anything you want me to do now?"

"Just stay tuned. I have a feeling Luis Sanchez is going to be important, and after I talk to Amelia I'll need someone to bounce ideas off of."

"Great. I definitely want to be involved."

He sounded disappointed. He must have felt proud of finding Amelia Santos, only to have Cora beat him to it. "We must be on the right track if we both found the same person. Don't worry, Dan. I'm not done with you yet—I promise!"

He laughed. "You'd better not be!"

Cora heard a beep on the line. "Someone else is calling—I have to go. It might be Amelia Santos. I don't know how to pick up her call without disconnecting you."

It was Amelia. "I have good news and bad news," she said. "The good news is that our oral interview series on Native Americans *is* digitized and online. The bad news is that there are only three interviews in the series. One is about the Alabama & Coushatta Reservation, another about Black Seminoles, and the last about the intermarriage of Seminoles and Black settlers after the Trail of Tears. They're not what you're looking for, but I've given you a log-on and password so you can read the transcripts and listen to the audios if you like."

"Okay, I'll do that," Cora said, a lump of disappointment in her throat.

"So I browsed other series lists, such as ranching, general, San Antonio, even a topic called bad history—that's almost forty percent of our collection. I could run a keyword search to narrow it down, but I had a better idea. A graduate student is writing a thesis and has been reorganizing and updating the oral interviews as she goes. She's current with the entire collection. She'll talk to you, and has some ideas. What do you think?"

Cora brightened. "I think that's wonderful. Actually, a possible lead just fell in my lap. I already gave you the name of Jose Sanchez, but I just found out that Luis Sanchez, from Tap Pilam, had an uncle, Carlos Sanchez, who did some interviews early on, and Luis said the story sounded familiar."

"Well, that's interesting. Be sure to tell Evelyn. That's the grad student I mentioned. She'll call you after we're finished."

"I can't tell you how much this means." Cora's eyes suddenly burned. It took very little to make her emotional today. Her instinct told her they would be successful in finding Katy's whole story—but would their success help Cisco?

She wished once again that she could bring coffee back to her room. Food she could do without, but coffee kept her going. Maybe she could find a sealed container—if she didn't drop it while limping down the hallway.

As promised, Evelyn called a few minutes later. "I want to see how much I can get done today," she began, her voice youthful and enthusiastic. "I can't believe my paper is benefiting someone before it's even written."

"I can't tell you how much this means," Cora said, again. "I was lucky to find you—and Amelia. I'm impressed with your university."

"Thanks. I'm just glad I can contribute—it sounds fascinating," Evelyn said. "Do you mind going over what you're looking for and why you need it? Amelia told me, but I'd like to hear it from you. Something you say might ring a bell that wouldn't turn up using basic search terms."

"Ah, I see. Well, let me tell you the story, then."

Cora spoke at length, filling in more details than she had told Amelia. The only information she held back was about her vision in the Rosary Valley and Mother Josepha's visitations.

Evelyn's voice rose. "I can't believe I might actually help someone become a saint. I'm Catholic too, but I've never heard of Mother Josepha."

"It's even better than that. We have reason to believe that Mother Josepha's sister, Sister Catherine from the Incarnate Word in San Antonio, may be deserving of sainthood, too. That's what the search is really about, to see if her life warrants opening a cause for sainthood on her behalf."

"Wow! I hope we're successful. You've spoken to the Sisters of Charity, I assume? The convent and the University of the Incarnate Word both have impressive archives."

"Yes, someone else is doing that."

"Well, I've already gone over the reports Amelia ran. I'll add a few keywords—Carlos Sanchez, *San Antonio Daily Light*, tobacco farming, San Antonio Plaza, 1880s plaza merchants—" She paused. "You know…?"

"Yes?"

"Just something in the back of my mind. From the San Antonio file. I think there was an interview about a merchant from that time period. I didn't read the whole thing, but it stuck with me because I was surprised to read that tobacco was being grown and sold in the marketplace. No one grows tobacco in Texas anymore."

Could they have found what they were looking for already? Could it be that easy? "Can you find that interview again? Carlos Sanchez's ancestor was a tobacco farmer."

"I'll try. Shouldn't be too hard."

"You know," Cora added, "I can do some of the work so you can spend more time locating leads. When you find something that's online or digitized, why don't you shoot me an email and I'll read through what you've found?" *Something to do so I don't spend the whole day dwelling on angst.*

"I was hoping you'd say that. But not all the materials are digitized or are online. Some are still on cassette or CD. That's going to slow us down. I've got your email address here—let me check it with you." She read it off. "Is that right?"

"Yes. Text me if you email anything. And I can tell you what I read, so you can cross off dead ends."

"Great. Let's get to work."

# Chapter 38

Sister Barbara from Incarnate Word called Frannie just after one o'clock that afternoon, as promised. Clearly, these sisters took their vow of obedience seriously.

"The convent is in isolation," the nun said. "We don't have any Covid cases, but we want to be sure we don't get any. So we're not allowing visitors or leaving the convent."

"I hadn't planned to visit—" Frannie began.

"No, I know that—I'm just explaining. Fortunately, our archives are in the convent, but our lay staff is working remotely. Sister Dorothea has a private office, but most of our sisters are working from their personal rooms. Only a few sisters are allowed in the archives—social distancing, you understand—but she's found one who can work on your research."

"That's awesome!" Frannie said.

"I told Sister Dorothea your questions are urgent and asked her to call you directly with preliminary results. She should have those in an hour or so. I hope we find something for you."

After signing off, Frannie sprang from her seat. She wished someone was there to high-five with. Instead, she slapped her dining room wall soundly. A few seconds later, her cell phone rang. Did Sister Barbara forget something? But it was her downstairs tenant, disturbed by the wall-banging and calling to be sure she was all right.

Too excited to work, Frannie bustled around her flat clearing away clutter. She poured a fresh cup of coffee, adding an extra spoon of sugar. *Got to replace all this energy.* Then she checked emails and Facebook posts and rewarded herself by trying to increase her level on Candy Crush.

Her phone buzzed at exactly two o'clock. After introductions and thanks, Sister Dorothea got down to business.

"Sister Catherine came here from Chicago in the fall of 1884. She was sixteen years old at the time, and had lived with the Sisters of Charity in Chicago as a postulant since the age of fourteen. She came to San Antonio, to our mother house, to enter the novitiate when the convent in Chicago closed. Then she trained as a nurse."

That confirmed what Frannie already knew. "Did you find anything about her activities after her arrival or about how she died?"

"Yes. She died on November 28, 1886, and she's buried here in our cemetery. The notes said she was injured when her buggy overturned on her way back to the convent after tending a sick farmer."

"We know that, too. We were looking for more details."

"About the accident, or about Sister Catherine's life?"

"Both."

Sister Dorothea sighed. "We're going through our Sister Works from the late 1800s—our collection that preserves outstanding works of charity or art produced by our nuns. Sister Jude is beginning at the date of Sister Catherine's death and working backward to her arrival, but I doubt a novice who was here such a short time would have achieved anything noteworthy."

"That makes sense. Do you know anything else about how she died?"

"Only that the accident happened on November 25. A messenger reported it, and the convent sent a wagon to bring her home. She was unconscious when she arrived, but she must have regained consciousness at some point because she professed her final vows before she died."

"That must have meant a lot to her. But don't the records say who reported the accident? Or any other details?"

"Sadly, they do not. Which is strange, I have to admit."

The sister wouldn't like Frannie's next question. *Best be careful now.* "Is it possible the details were omitted on purpose?"

"You mean something was covered up? What reason could there be for that?"

"I don't know. Maybe something she was doing led to her death. Maybe it wasn't an accident."

"Are you suggesting Sister Catherine was murdered? Do you really think the sisters would hide such a thing?"

Frannie backpedaled, fast. "Not a murder, necessarily. Maybe someone just...left out a few things that could have gotten someone in trouble."

"Someone here at the convent?"

"*Any* someone."

"There's no reason to suspect that."

"Other than the lack of details about her death. Like you said, that's odd."

"It was 1886, Frannie. Even if something questionable did happen, do you really think we're going to find out about it after all this time?"

The nun sounded less annoyed now, even a little curious. Frannie pressed her advantage. "We have to turn over every stone."

"Well, we're doing that. If there's anything here, Sister Jude will find it. You're looking other places too, right?"

"Oh yes, everywhere we can think of. But you're the only place that has a record of her so far. Look, is there any way to know if Sister Catherine had contact with people outside the convent? I heard she may have been spending time with Native Americans."

"How did you get that idea? I doubt it. There were a few Indians in the area back then, but our work was at the infirmary and schools. Sister Catherine would have had nothing to do with education, and we worked at the infirmary unless someone asked us to go out for a visit. It's unlikely Indians would have sent for us, since the reason they stayed here was to follow their traditional ways, not what at that time was considered 'modern' medicine. It's unlikely we'd have given medical care to Indians."

"If she was visiting with Indians, is there anywhere else to look? Records other than Sister Works?"

"Our early Mother Superiors kept daily diaries of sorts. They could have recorded progress or problems."

"Can you look?"

Sister Dorothea sighed. "That could be a huge task. What makes you think Indians are relevant?"

Frannie couldn't tell the nun about Cora's vision, with no clear idea how the sister would take it. "There was an Indian man who died a week after Sister Catherine. I found it in a newspaper article."

"And that's related to Sister Catherine how?"

"It's a hunch," Frannie admitted, swallowing hard. "But I have a good track record with hunches."

The nun sighed again. "Why don't we see if Sister Jude finds anything that backs up your hunch. If so, I'll ask her to check diaries from 1884 to 1886. Really, I hope we find what you're looking for, but I think all of this would have come out long ago if there was anything to what you're suggesting. We'll help as much as we can, but under the circumstances...."

"I get it," Frannie said. "And thank you. Should I talk to you or Sister Jude then?"

"Let me see what she finds. I should know more tomorrow."

*Crap! This doesn't look promising. I hope Dan's having better luck.*

~ ~ ~

By four that afternoon, Evelyn had sent Cora several interviews of interest. Cora scanned the transcribed summaries from beginning to end, looking for clues even when the material seemed to have nothing to do with her quest. The attached MP3 files took longer, but there had been only two so far. They were also unrevealing.

And then Evelyn called. "Bingo!" she said, her voice excited. Cora held her breath, her heart thumping so loud she thought Evelyn would be able to hear it.

"Remember what I said about something ringing a bell? About the tobacco merchant?"

"Yes."

"It's the one, Cora. In the San Antonio file—one of our biggest files, so finding it took a while. It's the recording I remembered—the same news story you told me about, I'm sure of it. And get this! The interview is not only about Jose Sanchez, but Sister Catherine Mrozek, too. The first time, I only skimmed the recording to get the gist for my thesis, but this time I listened to all of it. It tells how she died, and a whole lot more. This is exciting, Cora. This woman has to be a saint, and we discovered her! I've got tears in my eyes!"

Cora was speechless. Then: "It's an audio file, you said?"

"Yes."

"Can I listen to it?"

"Of course. It's not online but I can make a copy and send it to you. I'll do that right now—it'll take an hour or so. There are quite a few stories on the tape. The one you want is the third, and it starts nineteen minutes in. Jump to that spot."

"I don't need permission from the tribe or anything?"

"Nope. We have clearances on everything in the collection. I won't say more—you should hear it yourself. But you have to promise me something, Cora."

"Anything."

"Whatever happens from now on, I want in on it. Okay?"

"Absolutely."

# Chapter 39

University of Texas at San Antonio
Institute of Texan Cultures
Oral History Collection

September 13, 1978
Oral History Interview: Carlos Sanchez
Topic: Deaths of ancestor Jose Sanchez and Sister Catherine Mrozek,
November–December 1886
Interviewer: Reynaldo Mendez

Interviewer: This is Reynaldo Mendez, and today is September 13, 1978. I am interviewing Carlos Sanchez, the great-great-grandson of Jose Sanchez, who died in Bexar County near San Antonio, Texas in December of 1886. The remarkable circumstances of the death have been included on the calendar history, also known as winter count, that was kept by the Payaya tribe of Coahuiltecans. The oral history has been entrusted generation after generation to direct descendants, the current keeper and storyteller being Carlos Sanchez. Mr. Sanchez is here today to make an audio recording as part of a project sponsored by the University of Texas, Department of Cultural Studies. Mr. Sanchez, I understand there are two people who are important to this story, is that right?

Carlos Sanchez: That is correct. I am here to honor my direct ancestor, Jose Sanchez, my great-great-grandfather. His death occurred a short time after the death of a nun from the order of the Sisters of Charity of the Incarnate Word. Her name was Katherine Mrozek, also known as

Sister Catherine. My great-grandfather, Rafael Sanchez, is also in the story.

Interviewer: I would like you to tell the story as it has been memorized and passed down through the Coahuiltecan people, specifically through your family of the Payaya band. I will try not to interrupt unless we need a clarification.

Sanchez: Thank you.

As you know, in the nineteenth century our people did not have a written language, but that did not mean they didn't preserve our history and culture, especially as our numbers became fewer due to assimilation and emigration to areas outside San Antonio and Texas. A few of us remained in our traditional home near the San Pedro Springs along the river that came to be known as the San Antonio River, where we had been given small pieces of land to farm that had previously belonged to the missions. The missions were abandoned at the end of the eighteenth century.

(Cough and short pause.)

Our land was only a few acres, but since it was previously mission land it had been improved by irrigation ditches, and therefore we were able to grow and harvest enough to support our small community. We developed a strain of tobacco that was highly superior to what was available elsewhere, and sold it at local markets that were held weekly in the Plaza in San Antonio. It was barely enough. We were quite poor, and some years, when the crop was reduced by weather or insects, we nearly starved and had to beg from other farmers or charities. But we were free to live in our traditional way, and preferred our way of life to any other.

Our little village had about forty people. We had built twelve modest homes and one larger structure for gatherings and religious ceremonies. Our homes were made from whatever materials we could glean from the land—wood plastered with mud, grass roofs, whatever we could obtain from the Anglos. Our dwellings surrounded a large open area where women gathered to work together and where our ceremonies—*mitotes*, traditional dances—took place.

In the winters we had little to do, and in the evenings our men gathered and talked about all that had happened during the year. We adopted a tradition from other native groups of recording important events by sketching images or symbols on a deer hide. Later, when paper became easy to obtain, we used that. We called our records 'calendar histories,' but other Native Americans now refer to them as pictographic calendars, ledger art, or winter counts. Regardless of what they were called, they served the same purpose—a means of remembering the sequence of events and retelling stories of our people while preserving our history.

Once an event was decided upon, an artist or recorder—usually one of our elders—would update the calendar. An oral version of the story would be developed and memorized by men chosen to preserve our history—our history keepers. We would gather and repeat the stories while smoking tobacco. In this way, the long winter evenings went by, and our history was passed down from generation to generation.

I am now going to tell you the story that was preserved for the year of 1886.

Interviewer: Thank you for that background.

Sanchez: (Clears throat.)

About a year before the events of this story, a young nun from the Sisters of Charity of the Incarnate Word started to visit our village. The sisters operated the only hospital in San Antonio, and Sister Catherine was a nurse. She was often sent out alone to tend people on farms. One day she passed our village and stopped to introduce herself and ask if we needed anything the sisters could provide.

This was remarkable to us because, although we were careful not to offend the Anglos in any way, we were not popular. In essence we were shunned by all, who likened us to other Indian groups that used to steal from them and attack their homes.

But Sister Catherine was different. She was young, not yet out of her teens, a beautiful girl of slight height and build. She wore a black habit with loose sleeves, a waist-length black veil, and stiff white cloth around her face and neck. She said she was not a sister yet, but still training.

She had bright blue eyes, a brilliant smile, and was so merry that we began to refer to her as 'Joy.' She did not shy away from touching our women and children, but freely hugged them and put her arm around them. She bounced and cuddled our babies and made them laugh with funny sounds. Our children clung to her skirts and screeched with delight. Her goodness and holiness were obvious to all. We thought her an angel.

She began to visit us whenever she could get away. She brought candy and trinkets for the children, medicines, cloth, thread and sewing needles, kitchen implements and tools. If there was something we asked for, she brought it.

At first some of our men were suspicious. They thought that, like the missionaries before, her plan was to get us to give up our traditional beliefs. We were all nominal Catholics, having been brought up by ancestors who were taught that religion by missionaries. We worshiped Jesus in our own way, and this respect coexisted with, but did not replace, our ancient traditions.

Sister Catherine, however, only set an example of kindness and charity. We knew of her own strong belief in God, but she did not pressure us in any way. We grew to love her and look forward to her visits.

As time went on, we appreciated especially her medical skills. We had our own shaman who healed by traditional methods, such as burning or sucking to heal wounds and sores, blowing on affected areas, chants, sweating, herbs, and the like. We believed our shaman was in touch with beings who possessed more than natural powers and had the ability to direct those powers to affect healing. Yet we had also seen that the simple medicines and advice given to us by Sister Catherine sometimes cured sicknesses and wounds more quickly and easily, and she believed praying to Jesus was better than the shaman's powers. Soon it seemed that someone wanted her advice just about every time she visited. Even our shaman came to adopt some of her methods.

Sister was especially fond of my great-great grandfather, Jose Sanchez, who was quite elderly at the time. She gave him a token she called a relic, a piece of pale blue cloth she said had once been owned by an important saint, Rose of Lima. Jose valued this fragment and wore it in a pouch on a strip of leather around his neck. He would squeeze it when he felt poorly, and he said it brought him relief from his pain.

And then one day in late November, Jose took ill with burning, a painful throat, aching of his whole body, and extreme tiredness. He could not rise from his bed and was struggling to breathe. Most of our men were out of the village that day, cleaning the fields and planning the next season's planting. When Sister Catherine came to visit, she grew alarmed. She told the women that Jose had a sickness, the flu, that was infecting many people that year, and he needed to go to the Santa Rosa Infirmary, as she did not have what was needed to cure him. The women helped her load Jose into her buggy and covered him with blankets. He was too weak to do more than sleep.

(Voice turns raspy.)

When the men returned, they were alarmed to find Jose had been taken away, and consulted the shaman. The shaman was very worried. He thought they might have cures at the infirmary that could help Jose, but what would happen if he could not be helped and died there? Once he was away from the village, no one could assure him our traditional burial ceremonies.

Our people greatly feared death. There was always a danger, if things were not done according to our rituals, that ghosts could enter our village. All sorts of bad things could happen. Jose's spirit could haunt the village, perhaps taking the form of a wolf or an owl. This is why our people never killed wolves or owls, because they could be spirits of our loved ones. It was well known that people so haunted would die soon themselves. No, Jose's body had to be buried, not in some place determined by the Anglos in San Antonio, but according to our own ways, at our sacred burial grounds, where care would be taken to bury the remains as the spirits demanded, and complex paths taken home afterward to be sure ghosts could not follow people back to our village.

The risk of what could happen if Jose died at the hospital was greater than the risk that he would die in his home. We had to get Jose back. So Jose's son, Rafael, was sent to retrieve his father.

Rafael set out on his buckskin horse. After riding for about half an hour, he saw Sister Catherine and the buggy ahead, and increased his pace. As he drew near, Sister saw him and whipped her horse to greater speed. He didn't know why she did this. Perhaps she didn't know who he was or why he was following her, or perhaps she recognized him but hoped to get Jose to the infirmary before Rafael could stop her. For whatever reason, she went faster, and he chased after her.

It did not end well. As the buggy approached a narrow bridge, the galloping horse cut the edge too closely. The buggy tipped and upturned in a ravine. When Rafael got there, the horse was beyond help. Sister Catherine had been thrown from her seat and lay crumpled at the base of a large rock, unconscious but breathing. Miraculously, Jose was unhurt, still cushioned in blankets in the overturned, broken buggy.

Rafael shot the horse and carried his father away from the vehicle. He wrapped Sister Catherine in one of Jose's blankets and laid her in the buggy, covering her carefully to protect her from the elements. All he could do was try to make her comfortable until he could get help. He returned to his village and sent another man to the infirmary to report the accident so Sister Catherine could be brought to the hospital.

All this was done but, despite their best efforts, Sister Catherine died a few days later and Jose a week after her.

But that is not the end of the story. Can I take a little break now before I finish?

(Sound of rapid swallowing, then a click. Then a second click; recording resumes.)

To honor our dead and to protect our village, loved ones remember their dead in elaborate rituals that take place a number of times a day for up to a year, and certain things must be done in an exact order to appease the spirits.

For three days after Jose's death, we held dances and chants. During that time a grave was prepared in the cemetery. To be sure the spirits would not follow and learn the pathways between the burial ground and our village, the grave was hidden and a different path was taken each time we traveled there.

On the fourth day, we arose early so the burial could take place before sunrise, because sunrise is the time when the holy spirits bestow their blessings upon the dead. Before Jose's body was taken to the cemetery, everyone in turn placed both hands over him from head to feet, then placed their hands in a similar way over their own bodies. Doing this allowed each person to communicate or send messages to other deceased relatives through Jose.

The grave had already been dug, in such a way that Jose's head would lie to the west, facing the rising sun. When the burial party arrived at the cemetery, they placed belongings Jose valued and wanted to bring with him—his favored clothing, tokens, and other items—in the grave. A bow and arrow were always included, as souls need protection on the way to heaven. Evil ones would line both sides of the narrow, difficult road each soul must travel, and would follow Jose until he crossed the small log over the big river and his soul was safe at last.

An arrow was shot into the grave to alert the spirits that Jose's soul had begun its journey. Then Jose was placed in the grave, lying on his back. All this was timed carefully so that by the time the sun rose and the holy people blessed his journey, the grave was filled and the loved ones were free to return to their village by stealth.

Among Jose's valuables sealed in the grave with him was the treasured fragment of cloth given to him by Sister Catherine. This is important to know, for it explains what happened next.

All had gone according to our custom, until the last of the dirt filled the grave and the grieved were saying their final goodbyes. Then, out of a cloudless sky, there was a flash and a crash, and some people saw a lightning bolt strike a nearby tree. The tree burst into flame and the people jumped back in alarm.

But this was no ordinary fire. It gave off no heat, and it did not burn even when some walked forward and reached a hand right into the flame. Nor was the tree consumed. The flames stopped as abruptly as they started, leaving the tree living and unmarred, except for the blackened shape of a crucifix, in the center of which was embedded the scrap of blue cloth that had been buried with Jose.

(Pause, then the voice of Sanchez resumes.)

There is not much more to say. The tree stands today in the burial ground of our ancestors. It is still alive and strong, and every year it bears leaves and grows just a little larger. The burned crucifix is still there, exactly the same in size and appearance, and the cloth is still there, both completely unchanged by nature or the elements, exactly as they appeared the day the miracle occurred, over a hundred years ago.

This is the reason this story was chosen for the calendar history for the year of 1886.

Interviewer: What did your ancestors think happened? How did they explain it?

Sanchez: My ancestors thought Sister Catherine caused the miracle. They thought it was a sign that Sister Catherine was loved by God, that her death and Jose's were intimately linked to each other, and that both of their spirits were safe and happy. The sign meant they were to believe and remember this. They believed Sister Catherine had magic powers that were given to her by her God.

To this day, people say that Sister Catherine returns now and then to give guidance or to grant a request. It would be interesting if you recorded some of those stories.

Interviewer: That's remarkable. And a wonderful story. Why isn't it better known?

Sanchez: Our people keep such secrets to ourselves. Also, because a religious person had died, they were fearful of consequences. This is the first time this story is being told outside our tribal gatherings.

Interviewer: Did Sister Catherine's convent ever find out about the miracle?

Sanchez: No. Only about the accident. You remember, Rafael Sanchez sent someone to the convent to notify them to come and get her. At first the story was told that someone had simply found her there. People assumed that the man who took Sister Catherine to the convent hospital shot the horse, and no one said any different. The sisters knew that if word got out that any of our people were present at the accident, we would have been blamed. At that time, people still said the only good Indian was a dead Indian. To protect us, the sisters agreed to accept the story they were told. Of course, Sister Catherine was still alive at that time, and so was Jose. It worked out well for everyone.

Interviewer: Except Jose and Sister Catherine.

Sanchez: Yes. Except Jose and Sister Catherine.

(Hissing sound for thirty seconds, a clunk, and recording stops.)

Cora Tozzi, *History of the Religious Institutions of Lemont*
(Chicago, Madonna Press, 2024), 114–121

*"As soon as I saw the skeleton of the
building, I was overcome with fear and happiness.
I ascended the ladder to the top of the building in
order to see the progress made so far and to pray.
No one saw me but God...I cried from joy."*
—The Chronicles of Venerable Mother Josepha of Chicago

### Josie's Journal
### March 22, 1898

My joy is complete! Tomorrow we move into the St. Joseph Home at last!

I spent this morning with John Grabiec and Tommy, shopping for last-minute supplies, decorations and treats to surprise the sisters and residents and celebrate our first day. Then we drove to the home to take a final walk-through.

Before we left, I carried Tommy to the edge of our property to view our building from a distance. I am used to Tommy's weight. He is no burden, but a sea of mud surrounds the home and I sank to my ankles a couple of times. It was chilly and windy, but Tommy and I shared our warmth with each other, and I thought as I walked about the good fortune that had brought us together.

Tommy Tokarz has been living with us for a year now. At first, I was reluctant to take him into our home since we had only elderly women and no experience with young boys. But Father Vincent said the orphanage was unable to give Tommy the special attention he needed. At the age of five, Tommy had lost both of his legs under the wheels of a locomotive. His family was desperately poor, and he was left an orphan who had received no education.

When I went to meet him, Tommy sat in a wheelchair in the orphanage parlor. What remained of his legs barely came to the edge of the seat. But his eyes were a clear, sparkling blue, his hair a mass of tousled pale brown curls, and the look on his face spoke of hope and of mischief, as would be expected of a nine-year-old boy. His situation did not seem to have weakened his cheerful disposition.

I stood smitten, a distance of ten feet separating us. "Hello, Tommy," I said, smiling.

Tommy grinned widely and held out his arms, like an infant wanting to be picked up. I walked slowly to him and lifted him, as I would a younger child. He weighed very little, and I bore his weight easily. He wrapped his arms around my neck and laid his cheek against mine, as my beloved sister Katy had done years ago.

"Would you like to come live with us?" I asked. "If you come, you will have to work hard to learn about God and about other things, so you can catch up to boys your age. Can you do that?"

"I am ready, Sister," he said. "I wish only to be like other boys."

I think Tommy filled some of the emptiness Katy's absence had left in my heart. I found him a bright, willing, and cheerful companion. I carried him everywhere, took him to daily Mass, taught him school subjects, and instructed him in religious matters.

Today I hugged Tommy again, then turned and stood still. I was moved to tears at the sight of our new building. Three floors, topped by a peaked attic, with tall windows to allow abundant light. We have spacious, bright and cheerful rooms! It was worth the effort and sacrifices, even though the project was more difficult than we could have imagined when it began.

"Sister Josie," said Tommy. "Why are you crying? Is this not a happy day?"

I smiled. "Indeed, it is. My tears are happy ones."

But then I remembered the months of struggle after we first happy four took our final vows.

At first our lives did not change much. We followed the same schedule of prayer and hard work. I felt humbled by the loss of four of our original sisters, who left because they were unwilling to conform to the rules of religious life. Perhaps nothing could have been done. This failure, however, did not shake my resolve to provide for God's poor and infirm. In spite of adversity, I maintained my happy disposition, since I saw the will of God in all of life's events.

So, I had watched for an opportunity to build a home for the aged. When the opportunity arose to purchase land, it came at a very bad time, but nonetheless I grabbed it. The lots were in Avondale, north and west some nine miles away in an undeveloped part of the city. Prairie and farms, with only a cinder road, the purchase was a bargain. Sophie and I used our own money, putting down $1000 to buy twelve lots for $5000. The remainder was due over time. We were certain we would find the money somehow.

Once the land was ours, I went to Father Vincent. Fearing he had lost faith in us due to our reduced number, I thought having the land would impress him, and it did. He pointed out, however, that we could not depend solely on him. The burden for the remaining payments as well as constructing the home was on our little group of four. He suggested I assemble a committee of influential leaders from the parish to guide and support the funding. It was a good idea, but once again, my shyness made me doubt my ability to assemble such a group.

"Do you have suitable people in mind?" I asked, swallowing my apprehension.

"Well, John Grabiec, and he will bring some prominent businessmen with him. Stan Pluta, chairman of the Catholic Union, and Father Staszewski from St. Hyacinth's. An attorney, perhaps Peter Urban. Adam, your brother-in-law, of course." He paused and looked me in the eye, as if wondering why I was not writing down the names. "You should invite these. They may have other suggestions."

I stared at my hands in my lap. When I spoke, my voice was weak. "Will they be interested in what I have to say?"

He sighed. "It will not be easy, but your faith has gotten you this far.

God respects your humble nature, but you must do the work yourself so they will be convinced they are supporting the right person. I also have another suggestion."

I met his gaze, hoping for any ideas that would make our path easier.

"You should conduct a collection throughout the parish. If you can tell these men that you already have a considerable sum, they will be more inclined to believe in the project."

My heart sank. I had always believed our own work should pay our way. Going door to door felt like begging, and I also loathed the idea of asking people who were already poor for money.

Hearing my silence as consent, Father Vincent went on. "I will announce the collection from the pulpit on Sunday, so all the parish will know I support you. They will give if they can."

I broke the news to the sisters that night. The burden would fall on me, because Sister Anne was still needed to care for her family at home, Sister Clare had not been well herself and could not go door to door, and Sister Martha was needed in the sewing room. So, after laundry and cleaning at the parish, I would spend an hour each day knocking on doors.

Sister Martha had an idea.

"My friend Sister Mary Joan has experience collecting for another parish. Maybe she can go with you, since she is used to talking to people. If there are two sisters at the door instead of only one, people may be more generous."

I was relieved to think I would not have to go alone.

Soon we had almost $500. With this impressive beginning, I visited the men Father had named, and they agreed to form a committee to build a home for the aged and infirm. I think they took pride in the fact that ours would be the first home for that purpose in Chicago. Father Vincent, John, and Adam also helped get their attention.

By then winter was upon us and we had homeless and ill to house. We had room left for only three people, and knew we would be asked to care for more. So, in November we rented a building with three apartments. Two apartments on the first floor housed our residents, along with a kitchen and refectory, and another apartment on the second floor held a large sewing room and rooms for our sisters. Three more women heard what we were doing, asked to join our community, and were accepted as novices. This greatly helped with our workload.

One night, I was awakened by pounding on our front door. Two men stood there, supporting a frail, elderly woman, who appeared half asleep or senseless. One of the men, tall and well-dressed, looked with distaste at her hand where she gripped his arm to keep from falling.

"We heard this is the place to bring people like her," he said.

I sighed. It would have been charitable if he had brought her to his own warm home for the night, fed her, and found her some suitable clothes, as I would have done even years ago. But at least he had not just left her in the street.

"Of course," I said. "Please bring her in."

Some days I almost despaired. The hard work had me on the verge of exhaustion. I worried constantly about bringing in enough money for support, for loan payments, and to keep the approval of the building committee.

And then the rumors started. My brother-in-law had at first withstood the economic crisis, but soon began to suffer like others. He lost some buildings and fell into debt. I had counted on his repayment of money I had loaned him to enable us to satisfy our debt for the Avondale lots. When the situation became known, people again began to say that the money I was collecting would be used to support my own family. Collections went down. The unjust rumors were humiliating, and there were times when I shed tears in secret so the others would not see. Yet other days I took simple joy in our progress toward the realization of our dream.

During that long, hard winter we took in and cared for fifteen elderly women. We also collected almost $1000, all of which was handed over to the building committee. Somehow, we made it to spring.

In April 1897, the committee approved the plans and hired an architect. Almost immediately this was followed by additional disappointment when the parish's bank crashed along with other banks in the community. The parish could not make promised contributions to the building fund and could not borrow. We did not know where to turn.

My old friend Sophie, now Sister Anne, came to our rescue again. "We should take our problem to the Rosary Society," she said. "They have known and trusted us for years. We have been remiss in not asking their help before now."

And so, we did. Some women gave of their savings, others raised money from friends and family outside the parish, and with their help we made the last payment on the property. Now we had only the building to contend with.

By the end of the summer the economic crisis had lessened somewhat, and Father Vincent arranged a loan for construction of the home. However, the loan had to be collateralized, and the only collateral that could be agreed upon was the property itself. Since St. Stanislaus Parish would be taking the loan, the property had to be deeded to the church. Sister Anne and I signed the property over.

"I do not think it is wise to co-mingle the church's property with yours. If the church falls into deeper debt or defaults on loan payments, it will be beyond your control to save it," John Grabiec cautioned me.

"What else can I do, John?" I said. "I cannot see any other choice if we are to avoid another cold winter in inadequate quarters."

He bit his lip and shook his head.

I put my hand on his arm. "This decision is consistent with our vow of poverty."

Construction began in September of 1897. The construction company promised the building would be finished before winter. When I visited in November, I was delighted to see the skeleton of the home and a storage barn, but there was no roof, and winter was almost upon us. We would be spending another winter in our temporary apartments. Yet, as soon as I saw the unroofed framework of the building in the distance, I was overcome by a mixture of fear and joy and overwhelmed with gratitude toward God. He understood me.

In the wake of these thoughts, another problem occurred to me. In this mostly unoccupied area of prairie, with only a few scattered farmhouses, unoccupied property was vulnerable to theft and vandalism. Who would protect the valuable tools and equipment, and care for the horses during the long winter when no workers were present?

Once again, it was Sister Anne who provided an answer. If the barn could be made habitable before the workers stopped for the winter, she could move there, bringing her family with her. Converting the building would also make it available for other purposes at a later time.

This was an excellent solution that not only solved our problem but saved Sister Anne's family rent on their apartment. Some spoke harshly about Sister Anne, saying she was not as committed as the other sisters and was concerned only with her own family. They said she rarely participated in our community's life or work in any real way. Her ideas were often contrary to others, and she was stubborn and bossy.

I did not share this opinion. Sister Anne had been my mentor since I came to Chicago. True, she had sometimes given poor advice, but that was not because she did not care. She was often torn between the very real needs of her family and her ability to contribute to ours, and she was not well herself. Yet she had always been there when I asked for her help, and much of her advice had been sound. I believed her faith and her generous nature were real, although she was by nature a bit more cautious than I was. She was my good and loyal friend, and I loved and trusted her.

Tommy rubbed his head against my neck, reminding me I had been thinking too long of the past. All these difficulties were behind us, and we would move into the St. Joseph Home for the Aged and Infirm tomorrow. But I would be a fool if I believed hard times were over.

I rested my cheek against Tommy's head. "You are sleepy and it is time to drive back. Tomorrow you will have a room of your own, if only for a short time."

"Sister Josie, why do you think I want my own room? I like living with others."

"Ah, Tommy. You will see, once you have tried it."

When we left for home, John's wagon was soon mired almost up to the axles. The horses were able to free us this time, but how would it be in the spring, with thicker mud from melted snow and rains?

Sitting in the wagon with Tommy asleep, his head on my lap, I turned my thoughts from our past to our future.

Tomorrow we will have eight sisters, two mothers, Tommy, and fifteen residents to transport, with all their personal belongings, furniture, supplies, and the contents of the sewing room. John has borrowed wagons and labor, but, once there, no one will deliver to us when conditions are poor. We will have to transport loads of coal and sufficient food, and do so without depending on others.

John donated a horse and wagon to the convent. Thoughtful as his generosity was, I do not know how to drive a horse and wagon, nor do any of the sisters. One of us will have to learn. I suspect that will be me.

We are used to streetlights, warmly lighted windows of nearby homes, and noisy street traffic at all hours. Tomorrow there will be only darkness and silence, with a few creatures to disturb the night. But when the winter and wet days are over, we will have blooming gardens, visiting birds, and know the peaceful beauty of God-given nature.

We will learn to use tools and do our own repairs. We will plant a garden, get some cows, pigs, and chickens to provide food for our tables. All this I believe we can do. It may be easier for Mama and me, since we grew up on a farm.

But with no access to nearby homes and families, there is nowhere to ask for donations. St. Stanislaus is too distant now, so we can no longer earn money in the laundry or by housekeeping. Our dressmaking customers will not come so far. We will have to look for other ways to support our community. Perhaps we can plant flower gardens and sell flowers in the city. Or plant more produce than we need, and sell it. We can make baked goods. In Poland I learned fancy needlework and embroidery. I can teach these skills to our sisters and we can sell embroidered items, especially linens that will appeal to churches.

We can expect only occasional visits from our priests, so we will no longer attend daily Mass. But we can make one trip a week for Sunday Mass and conduct our own religious devotions.

We cannot ignore the difficulties ahead, but I prefer to think we are beginning a wonderful new life. Already six more women have asked to join the Franciscan Sisters of Our Lady. They will arrive after we are settled, and for once we have abundant room for them. There are rumors that the orphanage will soon be closed and over a hundred orphans will be sent here. We have no experience with children, nor how to educate them. Maybe our attic can be temporarily converted into space for children until a proper home can be built. Another home, and we are not even finished with this one.

A beginning has been made. With God's help, we will solve these problems. We still have our building committee, the Rosary Society, and John. Ever-loyal John.

I had a premonition that my trials were not yet over, but I pushed it aside. We had accomplished great things and would deal with whatever challenges the future brought.

Today was a day for joy!

# Chapter 40

"It seems that Sister Catherine, Katy, created quite an impression. You were right," Sister Dorothea said when she called Frannie at ten o'clock the next morning.

"I knew it!" Frannie slapped her palm on the dining room table, instead of hitting the wall this time so she didn't upset her tenant downstairs.

"There was very little material in the Sister Works from the nineteenth century," Dorothea went on. "It didn't take long to realize I wasn't going to find anything there. Since Katy died so young, I searched the twentieth century for sisters who could have known her. There were 72 of them."

"Narrowing that down doesn't sound easy."

"No, but I applied guesswork and math. Looked for sisters I thought Katy would be close to, with a similar background, work, age, and so on. That cut the list to sixteen. I checked those names against sisters who had contributed to Sister Works, and found four. One left a compilation of artwork, another a collection of essays on a variety of religious matters. Two were memoirs, so I looked at those."

She paused. "Actually, I got seriously fascinated reading about what our sisters did in the early years. Katy came here only fifteen years after we arrived in San Antonio, so a lot was happening. But you want me to get to the point."

Frannie had been jiggling her leg under the table. "Maybe we can chat about this later, but yes."

Her phone chirped and a notification popped up. Someone else was calling. Probably a crap call, she thought. But no, it was Cora. She let it go to voicemail. Sister Dorothea was a priority.

"One memoir was written by Sister Cecilia in 1946, two years before she died," Sister Dorothea said. "She was a good friend of Sister Catherine, and what she wrote not only confirms your suppositions but opens up the possibility that Katy should be considered for sainthood alongside her sister from Chicago."

Surprised, Frannie cleared her throat. "What did the memoir say?"

"I think you should read it. It will have more impact that way. I took pictures of the pages with my phone. Give me your email address and I'll send them to you." The sister chuckled. "You won't have to ask me again to look for further documentation. This discovery could be very important to our order. I've already located the administrative books of Mother Madeleine, who was Mother Superior while Katy was here. I'll read those after we hang up and call you if I find anything else."

When Dorothea's email arrived a short time later, Frannie downloaded the photos and copied them to a folder named "Sister Stuff." Cora would want to know what was in the material, so Frannie read the pages before returning Cora's call.

The memoir was handwritten in dark blue ink in a clear, rounded script. Fountain pens or dip pens, Frannie thought, would have been used in those days, and nuns were known for perfect handwriting. In 1946, at the age of 78, Sister Cecilia had written:

*One of my most tragic memories is of Sister Catherine Marie Mrozek. Sister Katy, as we called her, was a close friend. We both came from Illinois, although I grew up in East St. Louis and Katy in Chicago. We both arrived in San Antonio on the same day in 1884. We were both sixteen, of Polish heritage, and we both sang in the choir.*

*Katy had a lovely contralto, but often said her older sister Josie was blessed with the loveliest voice. She was very fond of her sister who, Katy said, had practically raised her and was more like a mother than a sibling. Josie, she said, was gifted in many ways, especially sewing and needlework, and made lovely clothing and church linens. Josie was exceptionally devoted to God and to the poor, elderly, and homeless, showing great compassion and generosity. It was Josie who inspired Katy from childhood, not only to love God but to love God's poor creatures, and who was largely responsible for Katy's desire to serve the church as a nurse. I, on the other hand, chose to serve God by educating his children.*

*Sister Katy and I shared confidences. Sister Madeleine, our Mother Superior, sometimes sent Katy out to local farms to treat those who could not come to our infirmary, even before her training as a nurse was complete. Katy had a happy demeanor and pleasing ways that charmed difficult patients, and such trips became frequent, Katy driving out alone with the convent's horse and buggy.*

*One day Katy came to me privately. She was clearly sad and disturbed. A disagreement with Sister Madeleine had left her conflicted.*

*Katy had been visiting the farm of Santiago Espinosa weekly for over a month. She brought Santiago's mother soothing medications and performed massages that greatly improved the woman's severe pain from a deformed spine. On Katy's way home, she noticed a dark-skinned man—a stranger—leaving the dirt road to take a trail across the prairie and over a small rise. Curious, not aware of any farms in that area, Katy followed the man. When her buggy topped the rise, she was surprised to see a small settlement beside an irrigation ditch, composed of about a dozen very poor-looking shelters.*

*From her sister's example, compassion was part of Katy's upbringing and very much part of her nature, but she was also fearless and curious. She could not leave without seeing whether or not these people needed assistance. So, she approached three women who were bundling tobacco. The women were suspicious at first, but as she did with everyone, Katy set them at ease and charmed them.*

*She learned that these villagers were a few remaining members of the Coahuiltecan tribe that had once populated the San Antonio area, and were struggling to survive. They lived on what they could grow on a few poor acres and what tobacco they could sell at market, now that most of the wild game had left the area. Their homes were mere shacks composed, Katy said, of thin logs from the scrub trees that grew on the savannas, stacked upright and plastered with mud, the roofs made of whatever scrap materials could be found. The people wore tattered clothing, and some of the children were naked. She could only guess what their health might be. They had no medicines or medical care.*

*When Katy returned to the convent she spoke to Sister Madeleine and pleaded for the Sisters of Charity to support these poor people. Sister Madeleine was reluctant. She knew of the village, but the people did not want help, preferring to rely on traditional culture. Assistance had been tried and had failed. Did Katy have a specific plan in mind?*

*Katy did not have a plan. But she vowed to come up with one.*

*When Katy told me this, I asked if she wasn't afraid to be a lone woman among these people, who had a reputation of being treacherous. Didn't she fear they might harm her? She admitted that Sister Madeleine had cautioned her for the same reason, and that some of the men did look at her with suspicion, but she felt that was only to be expected because of how they had been treated in the past. In her opinion, they were only misunderstood because they had different customs and values.*

*We decided that until such time as a good plan could be devised, Katy would stop at the village on the way home from the Espinosa farm. She would get to know the villagers and bring them whatever she could to alleviate their needs.*

*Katy did just that throughout the spring, summer, and fall, and it brought her much joy. She never told me what she reported to Mother Madeleine. My guess is that Mother knew of the visits and gifts, but preferred not to be directly involved. Katy loved those people in a very special way, despite the possible danger she faced.*

*Then came that day in late November, when a man rode in to tell us Katy had been injured in an accident out in the countryside. We sent a wagon to bring her back to our convent, but sadly, she died a few days later.*

*Aside from Mother Madeleine and I, no one knew of Katy's visits to the Indian village. I often wondered how the people fared after Katy was lost to them. But I will never forget her and what she did. She had the true makings of a saint, sacrificing herself to do works of heroic charity.*

Frannie pondered letting Cora read the memoir like she had done, but she wanted to share Cora's reaction. She was rehearsing how to break the news to Cora when her phone rang. It was Sister Dorothea again, even though less than an hour had passed since her earlier call.

Sister Dorothea sounded excited. "This gets better and better, Frannie. I can't tell you how glad I am that you called us!"

"What?" Frannie said. "Don't keep me in the dark, Sister!"

"Okay. Mother Madeleine was Mother Superior here from 1881 to 1907, and her journal is even more revealing than Sister Cecilia's memoir. Many important decisions were made at the end of the nineteenth century and the beginning of the twentieth. It was a turbulent time, when pretty much all our goals were accomplished. I don't know why we never did anything with these journals. I can only suppose the stories were lost in the bigger plans that were happening at the time or perhaps more nationally important events. What really amazes me is that when we summarized and cataloged our archives, the journals' importance wasn't recognized. I can't imagine how something like this got overlooked—"

Frannie interrupted. "Sister, what?"

"All right. The notes in the journal confirm Sister Cecelia's memoir and take it a step further. Again, you should read this yourself, so I'll send photos. I guarantee this will get you your hearing." She paused. "But here's what I'd like in return. Sister Katy's story bears more investigation, but I think we should work together from now on. The information is important to both of us. I hope you have no objection. Once this pandemic is over, of course. Maybe this summer?"

"Of course," Frannie said. *I got no authority to make that promise, but what harm could it do?*

Sister Dorothea's photos were clear and legible, as before. The handwriting was still in dark blue ink, but spiky and angular this time, not rounded like Sister Cecilia's. *How sad that our schools don't teach cursive writing anymore,* Frannie thought. Then she got down to reading.

*November 28, 1886 was one of the saddest days during my tenure as Mother Superior. It was the day Sister Catherine Marie left us and went to live with God at the tender age of nineteen. Sister Katy was one of the sweetest, most blessed women to enter our order, and loved by all. She was an excellent nurse, known for her compassion and generous heart, as well as for her lively, fun-loving attitude and deep spirituality. Despite her young age at her death, I can think of no person more deserving of the title of saint.*

*For some time before she died, Katy had been actively assisting a Coahuilte-can village. I knew these poor people, but circumstances made me unable to support them. Although I feared for Katy's safety, I didn't order her to disassociate herself from the village. I wanted to avoid a potential conflict with Katy's vow of obedience, knowing she would go there anyway. I also turned a blind eye to the disappearance of items from our storerooms that I suspect ended up at the village.*

*It was not that I had no sympathy for these people, but our mission was to support the health and education of the larger community of San Antonio, not the traditional lifestyle of those who had chosen to set themselves apart. Had they requested our help, it would have been given. But they did not want our help and we were not in a position to force it upon them.*

*When Katy had a serious accident, we were greatly saddened, but it was necessary to keep the circumstances to ourselves. I asked those sisters who knew the story to pledge not to reveal the full events, even to Sister Katy's family. We told the truth, but omitted certain details for the greater good.*

*It was a Coahuiltecan villager who informed us of the accident. He was afraid to attempt to transport Katy to the convent on his own. Many people living in and around San Antonio still saw all Indians as troublemakers, and therefore they not only shunned the villagers, but blamed them for anything bad that happened. If it became known that Sister Katy had been bringing an Indian to our infirmary for treatment when her buggy overturned, it was likely that certain local people would have set upon the Coahuiltecans or their village in anger. So we sent our convent workman to fetch poor Katy, and people assumed he was the one who found Katy and shot the dying horse. We chose not to correct that error. So, the true story was never told, and the Coahuiltecans escaped unjust blame but also never got credit for coming to the aid of a woman they loved as much as we did.*

Frannie sat back in her chair, amazed at how quickly the Sisters of Charity had been able to find the vital information, even in the midst of a pandemic. Maybe God was taking a hand?

She wondered if Dan had any luck today. Then she remembered Cora had tried to reach her earlier. It was almost one o'clock. She picked up her phone and tapped out Cora's number.

The call went to voicemail.

# Chapter 41

After listening to Carlos's interview the previous evening, Cora had tossed and turned all night. She was desperate to talk to Sister Maryam. But when she called Maryam in the morning, she got the nun's voicemail and left a message.

She called Joe next, who told her there was little change. Cisco needed more time to recover before his cardiologists would recommend cardioversion, medication or surgical intervention.

"Then too, post-stroke therapy is multifaceted," Joe said. "He'll need cognitive therapy, speech therapy, occupational therapy, testing for sleep apnea, evaluation of his ability to drive, and psychological evaluation."

Cora cringed. "Enough doctor talk. How is your dad accepting all this?"

"It's confusing him—two conditions, two sets of specialists. He's still balking at the countless tests and therapists, insisting he's fine and doesn't need them. I'm not pressing him—he needs time to mull over the idea. Why don't you talk to him?"

She did. On FaceTime, Cisco seemed physically well, as before, and for a moment she wanted to agree with him that he didn't need to be in the hospital and should come home. But when she asked him if he was glad Joe was there, he seemed confused.

"Joe? What are you talking about? Joe's in Indiana."

It was obvious he would need at least some of the therapy he was refusing. He went on, getting even angrier. "It's all bullshit! I don't need a psychiatrist! That's crazy! Why won't anyone believe there's nothing wrong with me? It's insulting."

Cora kept as calm as she could manage. "There's nothing to worry about, hon, but you have to stay in the hospital to be sure your heart is stable. Since you have nothing else to do while you're there, you might as well go along with the therapy sessions. We can talk it over after you get home, and only continue if you want to."

It discouraged her, that Cisco's mental and emotional status seemed to be at a standstill, but she tried to convince herself that six days was too soon to expect much improvement. She felt empathy for Cisco, remembering her own reluctance to believe she had cancer. How could she convince him to go along with the program, as she had ultimately done?

She wished she could confide in Cisco about Mother Josepha and everything that was going on at home, but clearly that wasn't a good idea. Nor could she seek his sympathy in attempting to deal with his problems that he wouldn't even acknowledge.

She had another flashback to some thirty years ago, when she'd raced to a northside hospital after receiving a call that Cisco was in their emergency room. Not knowing more than that he was stable, she feared the worst. She arrived to find out that he had suffered a heart attack. After a harrowing few weeks, he did well. But the incident prompted a paradigm shift in their lives and radical changes to their diet, exercise, and activities.

What would their life be like when Cisco got home this time? How many doctor and therapist appointments would he need? After her mother's stroke, Cora had dealt with her medical appointments almost daily for months. Cora's own cancer treatment had taken over their lives for more than a year. Now Cisco's therapy would likely consume another one. The realization made Cora's head spin, but she would put her life on hold once again and do it gladly. Hopefully she could finish her commitment to Mother Josepha, but Sister Lorita's book would have to wait once more.

She tried to reach Sister Maryam again, but her call still went to voicemail. She left another message. Where was Maryam?

While waiting, she called Dan. Calling Frannie would take longer. Frannie always had to embellish. Dan didn't have much to say, having spent the previous afternoon in unsuccessful online searches, but he was thrilled to hear about the discovery of the oral interview.

"I'm surprised they didn't need permission from Tap Pilam," he said. She thought he might be disappointed that he wasn't taking a more active part at this stage. As Evelyn had done for her, she wanted Dan to experience the joy of discovery, so she emailed him the MP3 file without telling him too many details.

"I'm heading over to see Sister Maryam," she told him, "so don't be surprised if I don't answer right away. I want to hear your thoughts after you listen to the interview, but I've got to call Frannie now."

"I haven't spoken to her since yesterday. She was expecting to talk to the head of archives at Incarnate Word."

"I'll have her call you if there's anything important."

It was ten o'clock. Still no word from Maryam. Cora punched in Frannie's number and waited, but got voicemail again. Where was everybody this morning?

She left a message. "Frannie, I have news you're going to want to hear right away. Give me a call."

She sat around, scrawled some notes, bookmarked the start of the MP3 file on her phone to share with Maryam, and fidgeted until thirty minutes to noon, then decided to head over to Assisi Manor and find Maryam, wherever she was. She pulled on her leather jacket, grabbed the dogwood cane, and limped out the door.

The secretary at the manor recognized Cora despite her mask and paged Maryam, who rushed over from the direction of the assembly space, a little out of breath. "We've been in a meeting all morning, but it's just about over. We're trying to decide how to meet Covid guidelines and get all the staff and residents to cooperate. Can I finish and meet you back here in an hour?"

"If you can't do it any sooner. I've got a recording that gives all the answers we've been looking for. I want to play it for you."

Maryam blinked rapidly, then straightened her shoulders. "Give me five. I'll make excuses and let Winnie take notes for me. Actually, I think she'll enjoy that." She rushed off.

The secretary at the reception desk spoke up. "Isn't this pandemic simply awful? People dying all over the world. I never thought this disease could spread like it is. I'm so worried about poor Sister Agnes, and what happens if all our residents start getting it? Why isn't someone doing something to stop it? Our government should be protecting us."

Cora had been so involved in urgent personal matters she'd given lit-tle thought to the enormity of the pandemic. All she said was, "Some things are hard to fix, but I'm sure people must be trying."

When Maryam returned a few minutes later, she led Cora into an unoccupied office behind the reception desk and closed the door. Cora pulled her cell phone from her pocket, placed it on the desk, pulled down her mask, and grinned. "This is amazing. Wait until you hear."

She jumped to the bookmark on the recording and started it, then plopped into a chair across from the desk as they both listened. When Katy's name was mentioned, Maryam looked up in astonishment.

"Oh, wow!" she said.

Cora held up a finger. "S-h-h-h! Listen!"

About five minutes into the interview, Cora's phone rang. She looked at the caller ID. It was Frannie. Not wanting to interrupt Maryam's ex-perience of the recording, she let the call go to voicemail. Fifteen min-utes later, the recording ended.

Sister Maryam's voice was little more than a whisper. "It's all true, what you suspected—it happened just like what you saw when you touched the stone. The Indians were involved when Katy had her accident. And then the miracle at Jose's burial! Wow!"

Cora grinned and nodded, sitting on the edge of her chair.

Maryam looked enraptured, her eyes shining with delight. "But... oh, Cora! Don't you see? We've been looking for documentation for Katy's sainthood and we found a miracle. We have to tell Mother Jose-pha! Right away!"

She sprang from her chair and reached for her coat. "I only wish I'd been more involved in the discovery. Mother Josepha's appearing any time I go to the ravine lately. You should come with me."

Cora laughed. "Try to stop me." She picked up her phone, glanced at the red number 1 in the corner of the phone app, and put it back in her pocket. Frannie would have to wait.

# Chapter 42

The weather, overcast with a leaden sky, was dry at least and the wind calm, although the temperature was chilly in the forties. Cora negotiated the slope down the ravine carefully with the aid of her shillelagh. Thankfully, it wasn't as slippery as when she twisted her ankle. Outside, Cora and Maryam dispensed with wearing face masks.

"I don't know if what happened to me in the Rosary Valley was paranormal or if my mind played tricks on me. But I read that Indians from Midwest tribes treated dreams and visions seriously. It was basic to their culture. Maybe that triggered my subconscious," said Cora, a bit out of breath as she struggled with the cane.

"I don't suppose we'll ever know. But your vision did point us in the right direction, however it happened," Sister Maryam said.

"How are we going to do this?" Cora asked. "I mean, she's never talked to me. You'll have to tell her."

"Has it occurred to you that I may not have to?"

"You mean because *we* know, now *she* knows? She's been watching us?"

Sister Maryam shrugged. "We talked about this before. We thought she could only know what she experienced when she was alive, and then what she witnessed looking down from heaven. Neither perspective gave her the knowledge she wanted."

"Yes. She wouldn't know any evidence of Katy's sainthood existed; she only hoped it did. So, she needed us to find it and bring it to light. Something like that."

"I bet she's watching us from heaven, and knows we can make the truth about Katy known to the world."

Cora grinned. "Awesome, isn't it?"

Maryam grinned back.

Cora wanted to laugh with delight, but at the same time she feared what would happen in the next few minutes. Then there was that empty feeling of worry for Cisco in her stomach. If it were only sunny—bright sun might dispel her misgivings.

They came to a thick pile of leaves across the path and slowed so Cora could navigate through them. "Do you want me to hold your other arm?" Maryam asked.

"So, if *you* fall, we can both go down?" Cora chuckled. "I'll let you know if I hit a rough patch."

They eventually reached the meeting place, so familiar to Cora now. She found the same thick fallen branch she had sat on and sat there again, breathing rapidly, facing the small tree at the top of the ravine.

Maryam patted Cora's shoulder. "I don't know if Mother Josepha will communicate with you, but you're part of this now. After all you've done, you have to be."

Cora reached for Maryam's hand and squeezed. "Go do it, Sister. Be my voice. You know what to say."

Sister Maryam turned away, walked forward, and knelt in her customary spot, on a pile of soft leaves alongside the trail that cushioned her knees. Cora wondered if Maryam made the pile herself and replenished leaves when it got too thin for comfort.

Twenty feet from Cora's side, Maryam clasped her hands in prayer, her voice soft but clear. "Mother Josepha, it's me and Cora. We want to tell you something that should make you happy. Are you here?"

Maryam waited a few minutes, filling the time by saying three prayers: "Our Father," "Hail Mary," and "Glory Be." Then she repeated her request to Mother Josepha, and recited the prayers again. When nothing happened, Maryam turned to look at Cora, her hands still in prayer position. "Sometimes it takes a while, but I thought because we had such good news—"

She was interrupted by a strong warm breeze that rushed down the ravine from the east, contrary to the prevailing westerly winds. When Cora looked at the tree, she saw as before the pale, hazy spot. In fact, today the entire ravine seemed murky and gray, all edges in it somewhat blurred. Was that only from the sunless sky? But there was the drooping branch, weighted down by something unseen. The breeze ceased as suddenly as it came, leaving the ravine bathed in heavy, warm air, and Cora heard a faint buzzing like insects—but it was still too early in the season for insects.

Maryam gave Cora a beatific smile. "She's here. I see her." At Cora's nod, she faced the tree again.

Cora strained her eyes and her ears, but as before she saw no woman in dark brown clothing, heard no clear words except Maryam's. She had hoped—what had she hoped? She hoped Mother Josepha would show herself and speak to her. That Mother Josepha would thank Cora for her efforts, so difficult under the stress of Cisco's health. That Mother Josepha would raise her hands in blessing and tell her Cisco was healed, no traces of stroke and with a strong and healthy heart that beat in rhythm. That's what Cora hoped.

In her anguish she lost track of whatever communication was taking place between Maryam and Mother Josepha. Tears rolled down her cheeks. She reached into her pocket for the handkerchief she kept there, and her fingers brushed her crystal rosary. The image of Cisco filled her mind. Not the angry, bald-headed Cisco she had talked to this morning, but Cisco when they were first married, his thick head of dark hair ruffled by the breeze, his Roman nose, and his devil-may-care grin.

She clutched her rosary. And then, as before, she experienced that warm, calm, peaceful sensation, filling her chest and mind with trust. The feeling was overwhelming, and in her mind were words: "It may not be as you wish, but it will be okay. I am with you."

She wiped her eyes, and the tears did not return. Then Sister Maryam was pulling at her arm. "Did you see, Cora?"

Cora shook her head, speechless.

"She knows, Cora. She knows what we discovered, all of it. I told her, but I think she already knew. She was happy, Cora. I know she was."

"Is she gone?"

Maryam glanced over her shoulder, toward the tree. "I don't see her."

Cora, her eyes clear now, looked at the place where Mother Josepha should be. The haze was still there, the branch still drooped, and she heard the low buzzing. "Don't you hear the buzzing, Maryam? She's still here."

Sister Maryam looked confused. But then, Maryam always heard voices, not buzzing.

Cora picked up the dogwood cane and struggled to her feet. "No, Maryam! That cannot be all! I have to know Mother Josepha is happy with us, that we've done what she wanted!" She turned to face the tree and brandished her cane above her head. "Did we please you, Josie? I have to know! Please! If you can't tell me, at least give me a sign!"

The sun broke through the dismal clouds, and Cora felt a vibration like electricity pass through her arm and into her body, an energy that seemed to originate from her cane. She lowered the shillelagh and held it in front of her, and she and Maryam watched spellbound as tiny branches grew slowly from the centuries-dead dogwood. The branches grew and covered the cane, and at their very ends, flowers bloomed— flowers with four white petals in the shape of a cross, each petal with a red indentation at its tip, the petals surrounding a bright cluster that resembled a crown.

# Chapter 43

As they walked back, each lost in her own thoughts, at first Cora didn't realize that she wasn't using her cane—her mind was occupied by the miraculous event that had just taken place. Her ankle moved freely and without pain, and even her knees, which had troubled her for over twenty years, no longer ached. She felt like she could even run a little, should the spirit move her, unlikely as that was—she hadn't run in years. In fact, with the sun out now, she almost felt like running, it was that energizing.

"My ankle doesn't hurt anymore, Maryam."

Sister Maryam looked at Cora's right leg. "You're not using the cane."

"I don't need it."

They slowly worked their way through the ravine.

"It's good you're not using the cane," Maryam said, after a long minute. "You don't want to damage the flowers. It would seem a sacrilege."

Cora stopped. Maryam, a few steps ahead, turned around. Cora said, "If this was truly a miracle, the flowers will live forever, won't they? When I asked Josie for a sign, she used the cane to show her power over the rules of nature. The cane will never change, or decay, but stay exactly as it was when the miracle occurred." She chuckled. "Why am I telling you this? You're the religious person, the one who's been talking to someone from heaven. We did witness a miracle, didn't we?"

Maryam looked back down the ravine, although the place of the vision couldn't be seen around the bend. "Of course it was a miracle! The wood in that cane's been dead for centuries, and even if the flowers could somehow be explained, why would it bloom then and there?"

They resumed walking in silence. When they climbed out of the ravine, they stopped at the statues of Christ and the Angel in the Garden of Gethsemane and seated themselves on the surrounding rocks. Although neither mentioned it, Cora thought they were both reluctant to return to the secular world. They didn't want to lose the magic, or whatever label they would end up using to describe this day. Where they sat was shady, but a nearby sunny patch seemed to spread its warmth to them.

"Do you think she'll come back, now that we found out what she wanted?" Maryam asked. Her voice broke, giving Cora the impression she was not just sad but a little frightened by the possible loss of the visitor who had been such an important part of her life.

"Even if she doesn't return, she will still be *with* you, won't she?" Cora answered. "Surely, if nothing else, you and Sister Elizabeth will work together now for Mother Josepha's candidacy for sainthood."

"Yes, of course, I'll want to do that. Won't you?"

"Certainly." She blinked rapidly. "But there's Cisco, and Sister Lorita's book—how am I going to tell her I'll have to put that off again?"

"You'll find a way, Cora. I have faith in you."

"Speaking of faith…." Cora trailed off, knowing it was hard for Maryam to relate, since her own faith was so strong.

"Surely you can't still doubt your faith, after all you've seen and after what just happened. Isn't that proof enough for you?" Maryam said.

Cora sighed. "I wish it was that simple. It's not about proof or logic. It's about feeling, deep down, that my faith is *real*. I'm afraid something in my nature makes me resist sudden bolts of belief. My faith is more likely to grow slowly. Or rekindle, might be more accurate. I had no doubts in my youth. I wish…."

"You wish?"

"I don't know what I wish. It's all been so rushed, so new—it hasn't sunk in." She sighed, her eyes fixed on the trail ahead. "I can't deny I've been in contact with Mother Josepha, and she's in heaven. If I believe that, then God and an afterlife must be real—which is what I wanted, but—a nagging voice keeps saying this is all silly. I'll wake up from a dream, or a logical answer will suddenly explain it all." She gave Maryam a weak smile. "I'm getting there, though—I think."

Cora's phone chimed. It was probably Frannie, she thought, intending to let it go to voicemail yet again, but she fished it out of her pocket to identify the caller. When she saw it was Joe, she stood, accepted the call, and walked a few paces away, her back to Maryam.

"Mom," Joe said. "Good news. Dad's being discharged this afternoon!"

Her heart soared. "What? What happened? Why, all of a sudden?" She walked the few remaining steps to the lawn at the top of the ravine, and paced, the cane tucked under her arm, forgotten.

He laughed briefly. "I'm calling from his room, standing right next to him. You know how it is with hospitals, Mom. When they're done, they're done. His cardiac status is stable, there are no more tests to run, there's no point starting therapy here when he'll be having it at home. He can go back to Lemont and see his own cardiologist, specialists, and make therapy appointments. He did go through with his evaluations yesterday, by the way, so there will be reports to bring to his therapists. The nurses will take care of all that stuff before he leaves." Another chuckle. "I think a motivating factor was his reluctance to cooperate. He's promised to be more cooperative as an outpatient. I don't know if we can believe him, but—his change in attitude is like a miracle."

"A miracle," she said, laughing. *The miracle I worked and prayed for. If only he knew!* "Believe him, Joe. I won't let him get away with anything."

Cisco was coming home!

She wondered suddenly if the reason Mother Josepha told her to stay at the convent was that she could do more for Cisco from here.

Then a sudden fear struck her. "How are you going to get him back to Illinois? The pandemic. He shouldn't fly, right? The last thing he needs is to get this virus on top of everything else."

"I'm going to drive him, Mom. I'll rent a car. We'll take it easy, stop a few nights. I'm a doctor, remember? I know how to take care of him. We'll be fine."

"You'll keep me posted?"

"Of course. From the car. We'll be bored with nothing to do but drive. We'll call every hour or as often as you want. Now, I've got to finish my virtual appointments, pack up, check out of the room, rent the car, plan the route. You want to talk to Dad? He's right here."

"Yes, please!"

"Hello," Cisco said. His voice through the phone sounded flat, emotionless. *Why isn't he overjoyed, like I am?*

"You're coming home! Aren't you excited?"

"I'm glad, yeah. They finally listened to me."

"Well, whatever it took. I'm so happy! I can hardly wait to see you—I've missed you so much! Please listen to what Joe says on the way home, okay?"

"Why are you so concerned? I'll be home in an hour." He sounded confused.

"Hon, you're in Arizona, remember? Joe has to drive you all the way to Illinois."

"Illinois? Oh. So, two hours then?"

A momentary trickle of fear marred her joy. What was the message that flashed in her mind in the ravine? "It may not be as you wish, but it will be okay. I will be with you."

The fear ebbed. They'd get through this.

After trading "Love ya" and ending the call, Cora searched for a word to define how she felt. Elated? Cisco was coming home! It had been so long since she'd been this happy. She wanted to laugh, shout with joy, jump up and down. Trying to control her scattered thoughts, she took a few deep breaths. She had an overwhelming impulse to tell someone, share the glad news that mattered more to her than any miracle.

She hurried back to Maryam. "Cisco's on his way home!" she announced. Even now, Cora found it hard to demonstrate emotion. Her voice sounded flat and her wide smile felt forced, her cheeks trembling.

Maryam threw her arms around Cora and they swayed back and forth as they hugged, heedless of the pandemic guidelines. When they parted the cane fell to the ground and an eight-inch branch with a cluster of three flowers broke off. Maryam bent to retrieve it while Cora picked up the cane.

"Look," she said.

They watched as a fresh branch slowly grew at the point of detachment, forming a new cluster of three flowers.

Maryam stared at the broken branch still in her hand. "I'm going to take very good care of this," she said, smiling broadly before she pulled up her mask.

# Chapter 44

Cora was excited to tell Frannie about the miracle and Cisco's hospital release, but Frannie didn't give her a chance at first, bubbling nonstop about her discoveries at the Sisters of Charity—the memoir written by Katy's friend Sister Cecelia and the journal of Mother Madeleine that explained Katy's activities among the Indians and the full circumstances of her death.

Cora sat with her feet up on her bed, letting her friend talk herself out, wondering if Mother Josepha had observed all that Frannie revealed or if another trip to the ravine would be needed. Then it was Frannie's turn to listen while Cora shared her news.

"Cisco coming home? Gurl, that's the best thing I ever heard—I been so worried. Because, what I said, Cisco and I, we be kindred spirits, you know. Well, not spirits exactly, but you know what I mean. He just gets things done, no fuss, no push-back. I don't always love everything he does, mind you, but he does the footwork while I—"

"Frannie, I know. But let's talk more later. I've got to bring Dan up to date, too."

"I'm happy for both of you, Cora," he said when she told him. "You got what you were looking for. And you were right about Frannie—she gets results. Only...."

"You sound disappointed."

Dan sighed. "Not really. It's just that...well, the discoveries we made are all good, but what archeologists really get excited about is *physical* evidence. Things we can dig up that no one has seen for ages. It's silly to think about that in view of what we've just done, but from a personal standpoint, I wish I'd been more helpful or that we'd found some new material of cultural significance—wait! I forgot about the tree!"

"You mean the tree Mother Josepha stood on when she talked to Sister Maryam?"

"No, no—although that's interesting too. I mean the tree in San Antonio, in the Coahuiltecan burial ground, with the crucifix and cloth artifact. We have provenance now. This is exciting! And I'll come out to Lemont for a look at that stone that caused your vision—"

"That *might* have caused my vision."

"Whatever. Did you ever find out where it came from?"

"Not yet, but Janna's still looking."

"I want to meet with her, too."

"I'm going to be busy, Dan."

His voice grew serious, but Cora could still hear an edge of excitement. "Of course. I'll do the work. You take care of Cisco. I'll text you if I have questions. I may even ask Frannie to help. But thank you, thank you, thank you!"

Next, Cora asked Sister Elizabeth to come to Assisi Hill for a meeting.

"But we're under quarantine. I mean…it's not like we can't go out at all, but we're expected to cooperate with the guidelines."

"Wear your mask. We'll social distance. Anything you want, but come. You'll be glad you did—I guarantee it. Mother Josepha's candidacy for sainthood is just a matter of time now."

"It always was."

"Not like this. Come."

Sister Elizabeth came. She, Sister Lorita, Cora and Maryam sat in a closed room outside the chapel while Cora and Maryam revealed the entire story.

Sister Lorita sat stunned, unlike her usual exuberant self, her hand covering the mask over her mouth. Cora wished she could see the other women's whole faces, but she saw enough in their eyes to know they were awed by the immensity of what they'd been told.

"These discoveries are just as important to Incarnate Word as they are to us. We shouldn't do anything without them," Sister Elizabeth said. "But, of course, we can use this new miracle for St. Josepha of Chicago now."

She paused and rubbed her forehead. "The question is what path to sainthood this satisfies. The miracle wasn't a medical cure, which is what the canonization process usually looks for."

"My ankle and knees got better," Cora pointed out.

"That's not sufficient magnitude. The church is looking for big miracles, near life-and-death issues, not small ones. And, as happy as I am about your husband's condition, his improvement could have been from medical care or normal healing, not clearly beyond natural law or indicative of heavenly intervention that the cause will want to certify. As for the cane—God isn't about parlor tricks. He's about belief, about bearing witness to some truth. But surely the cane will have *some* effect on the canonization process, and it will certainly attract believers. Can we see it?"

"It's in my room." Cora said. "Should we move there now?"

"The tree," Sister Maryam said. The others looked puzzled.

"The tree in San Antonio. We have to find it, substantiate that part of the story, that it's still unchanged, and link it to our petitions."

"Yes—Dan's already looking into that, but isn't that Katy's miracle—for her candidacy, not Mother Josepha's?" Cora said. "Is there enough reason to submit Katy for canonization?"

Sister Elizabeth thought for a moment. "There is a lot that would be attractive to the cause. The miracle, of course. Katy's young age at her death, her demonstration of heroic charity among the destitute, her persistence in the face of danger, her willingness to give her life to Christ. Some might even consider her a martyr. If the statement in the interview that she returns to grant favors can be proven, that will substantiate the condition that she's residing in heaven and acting on earth. And the time period, early in the settlement of both the order and Texas, should be of interest."

They decided that Sister Elizabeth and Sister Lorita would contact Sister Dorothea in San Antonio. The sisters at Assisi Hill and St. Joseph would be told the story, but asked to keep the matter confidential until they worked out details about making the information public.

"Are you sure they won't talk? You don't want this to turn into a media circus," Cora said.

"Need I remind you we take a vow of obedience," Sister Lorita said, laughing. "But it goes without saying that our book is going to take another detour, is that right?"

After the conference, Cora led the little party to her room to show them the cane. Sister Elizabeth and Sister Lorita stared silently at the branches and flowers, craning their necks to see the cane from every angle. No wilting or drooping had occurred since the blooms emerged. The wood appeared to be alive.

"Amazing!" Sister Lorita said. "You're sure it was dead wood before?"

"Absolutely," Sister Maryam said. "I've had it for years, and my father before that. It's always been dead wood."

Sister Elizabeth reached out a hand and then stopped. "Can I touch it?"

Cora chuckled. "I think it's decided to stay as you see it. We already dropped it and broke a piece off, and it just grew back. I don't think you can damage it."

"And so, the questions begin," Sister Lorita said. "Where does the cane belong? Sister Maryam owns it, which means it belongs to our convent, but it was in Cora's hands when the miracle happened, and Mother Josepha created the miracle, so the Sisters of Our Lady have a claim, too. We'll figure it out in time, I suppose."

At breakfast the next morning Sister Maryam told the entire convent about her visions and the previous day's miracle. Despite the masks, Cora sensed excitement and awe from most of the sisters, but doubtful looks passed between a few. She remembered that, thanks to Sister Fatima's bitter gossip, some of the women distrusted Sister Maryam.

Sister Bernadette was delighted. "I knew something special was happening to you, Maryam! How thrilling this turned out!"

Cora thought Sister Bernadette looked tired, despite her happiness at the news. She guessed that the nun was worried about Sister Agnes, who was having a difficult time battling Covid. The two of them were close friends. Cora hoped Sister Bernadette hadn't also caught the virus.

She pushed her worries aside. It was time for her to speak. She stood.

"I'm some distance from all of you. Do you mind if I take off my mask so I can speak more clearly?"

No one objected. Cora removed her mask, holding it in her hand.

"I came here," she said, "looking for certainty and peace with God. After difficult events in my life, I wasn't sure of my faith. Since I've been here, a lot has happened. I'm definitely moving in the right direction now." She smiled and met eyes around the room.

"My experience in the last couple of weeks has been indescribable. I met all of you and your peaceful lives rubbed off on me. The research we've done showed me your beginnings, and that history makes you special. But I never in my wildest dreams expected to be involved in the making of saints, and definitely not in what seems quite certain to be miracles.

"You have all been wonderful to me, allowing me privacy to deal with my husband's medical crisis, yet giving me the comfort of knowing your support was there for the asking."

Cora used her mask to blot her eyes. "Had I stayed home and not come here, Sister Maryam's visitor might not have been revealed as Mother Josepha, Katy Mrozek would still be unremembered, the candidacy of two saints would be slowed, and my husband might not have recovered so quickly. I can't thank you enough."

As Cora sat back down, she saw tears in some of the nuns' eyes.

Sister Fatima stood up. Everyone held their breath. "Ever since our school closed, I've been searching for something meaningful to devote my life to," she said. "I can't think of anything more meaningful than having these two women confirmed as saints. I want to help. Use me in any way you can." When she finished, she caught Cora's eye and winked.

*A winking nun,* Cora thought. *Sounds like a good name for a very special wine.*

Afterward, Cora and Sister Maryam were deluged with questions, ideas and offers of help. Most of the work would be shared by both Lemont convents and the sisters in San Antonio, so Cora only made notes and promised to pass them along.

Needing a few minutes alone, Cora escaped for a walk. She didn't go far, just stayed on Assisi Hill grounds. Although she might have headed for more remote fields, St. Marija's, or the ravine, she was too numb to chance another adventure.

As she reached the end of the gravel drive that led out to the fields, her phone rang. Irritated that even in the convent it was difficult to get away, at first she wasn't going to answer it. But it could be Joe, so she looked at caller ID.

It was Janna from St. Marija's. "I found it!" she said.

"Tell me!" Cora exclaimed, suddenly interested.

"I drew a blank with the accounts and paid bills. A number of years were missing, the crucial ones. Maybe they weren't kept or were misfiled or even hidden or stolen. Who knows? But whatever the reason, they couldn't be found."

"Tell me!" Cora said again.

"I don't know what possessed me to look there, but some records were stored in an old unused dumbwaiter in the print shop library in the basement. One of them was a newsletter. When the volunteers finished putting up the Stations of the Cross and the Rosary Valley monuments, they had a big opening ceremony, and the builder was interviewed to explain how it was all done. He said the statuary gardens were designed by a committee, but it was left to him and his assistants to craft them from the plans and obtain the materials. The decorative elements, the carvings and so forth, were purchased from a religious monument place. They used cinder blocks to make a form, placed the decorative elements, and then covered the remaining surfaces with the stone they had bought."

"Janna! Get to it!"

She laughed. "You're going to love this. Way too much stone was ordered, so once the Stations were done, they still had stone left. So they built the Rosary Valley, and they *still* had some left over to use in the grotto."

"But what was it, and where did it come from?"

"That's the funny part. The builder—a Slovenian immigrant, you shouldn't be surprised to learn—spoke very poor English. He found the stone in a catalog, and when he called the quarry he found out it was going out of business and the owner wanted to get rid of the entire stock they had left. Apparently, it wasn't very attractive and hadn't been popular. So, they offered him a deal to take it all. He thought he was buying holy stone—h-o-l-y, blessed by God—which he thought very appropriate, especially when he got such a good deal. He later found out it was named holey stone—h-o-l-e-y—because it was full of holes. His assistants had quite a laugh over the matter."

"But where did it come from?"

"A quarry called San Antonio Stone and Material Supply, a few miles southeast of San Antonio, Texas."

Cora Tozzi, *History of the Religious Institutions of Lemont* (Chicago, Madonna Press, 2024), 130–134

*"Now that the burden was taken away from me, it suddenly seemed as though a heavy stone fell from my head, and very often I perceived unusual happiness."*
—*The Chronicles of Venerable Mother Josepha of Chicago*

### Sister Gardener
### August 7, 1918

I have kept my old journal secure in a drawer next to my bed, never far from me, to read when I feel the need. Much has happened since my last entry many years ago. I have written of those events elsewhere in detail at the request of our archbishop. However, I want to end this personal record of my life with some thoughts while God allows me to do so. I have not decided what will become of it ultimately. I must think of a place where it will not be found for many years after my death. Or perhaps I will just destroy it.

The impulse to make a final entry came to me this morning. The weather could not have been more lovely, with a gentle breeze and puffy white clouds floating overhead. The fragrance of the rose garden was delightful, and the sun warm on my face. I thanked God for His blessings, for the favor He bestowed upon me by giving me the chance to work amidst the beauty of His creation, and for a life of accomplishments to His greater glory.

I was bent over, loosening the soil at the base of some climbing roses, when I heard soft footsteps and hushed voices. Between the foliage I saw that the voices belonged to three of our new postulants. "Sister Gardener must be here somewhere," one voice said.

"Yes. She is in the garden most days. Surely, she would not miss such a lovely day," said another. "But I do not see her."

They were, of course, talking about me. They must not have seen me behind the tall canes.

"I hear she is very ill and may not be with us much longer," said the third. "Perhaps she has taken to her bed."

"The older sisters say she has not had much education and does not speak English very well. That is why she works only in the garden, laundry, and sewing rooms. But they also say she is a hard worker and stubborn. She will come to the garden as long as possible, I think."

"Whenever I see her, she is always smiling. I have heard her humming, even secular songs. She seems quite happy in what she is doing."

"If gardening is all she does, it is good that she is happy, then. But I am sorry to hear about her illness. How long do you think she has?"

"Only God can tell us that."

The voices faded as they moved away.

No one is left now who remembers how our order began, or how the St. Joseph Home was built, or knows my part in our founding. They know me only as the humble, shy, and slightly mysterious nun they call Sister Gardener. It is not my nature to tell them otherwise. In fact, I thank God every day that He let me finish my ambitious goals and then allowed me the quiet life of obscurity that suits me so much better.

I was not a good leader. I worried about that very thing when I first went to Father Vincent, and he made it a condition that we could only proceed under religious obedience. My only education was a few years in Poland. I have no degrees, and my English is not easy to understand.

As Mother Superior, I was often criticized and rightly so. The sisters did not like the rules, thinking they were mine. They did not realize our rules came from the church. They complained that the life was too demanding. They quarreled and were suspicious of me, and although I did my best, I did not have the strength of character to discipline them. This weakness in me angered others, who thought I should enforce the rules more strictly.

What could I say? I could not speak in my own defense without criticizing others, and it was not my nature to do that.

These troubles, along with the cruel rumors that I was using the funds we raised for personal matters, gave us a poor image in the secular world. It became impossible to recruit women who might otherwise have wanted to join us. Therefore, it was no surprise when Father Vincent decided to replace me as superior, and as soon as possible.

I have only a small regret that my replacement happened immediately after our move into St. Joseph's Home. I would have liked a little time before dealing with more changes. But God's will was done, and was for the best.

The logical choice for our new superior was Sister Anne, who had the most experience. I was delighted with this choice. Although we did not always agree, Sister Anne and I were good friends and I respected her abilities to lead, which were much better than mine. I was not only happy to take a minor role in our community, but relieved by the transfer of responsibility. The important thing, the building of the St. Joseph Home and the perpetual provision for the care of the poor and homeless of this city, was done. My job was done. Recognition for the part I played was of no interest to me. There were better ways I could serve the sick, the poor, and my Lord, with much less stress and with better result.

Sister Anne assigned me to the garden, the laundry, and the sewing room, responsibilities I was familiar with ever since my life in Poland. I was perfectly content and fulfilled by these tasks, which left me free to worship God as I wished. Though that freedom did not happen immediately. Sister Anne was still preoccupied with her family or ill herself much of the time. With no one else to supervise, I had to step in, probably more often than anyone realized. However, as our image improved, eventually others took over and I became, with great happiness, full time Sister Gardener. Over time, the Franciscan Sisters of Our Lady grew. No sisters were left from our beginning days, and my role was forgotten.

For many years Tommy helped me in the garden, but I urged him to seek a life of his own, and finally he did that. It may seem strange, but he started working as a switchman for the very railroad that had been responsible for his injuries. He married and had three sons. His sons often bring him to visit me, visits I treasure.

Now, my life is near its end. The doctors have told me stomach cancer can be very painful and that I will suffer. I trust God will help me to endure and I am looking forward to seeing Him soon. Meanwhile, I am grateful He has allowed me to serve Him by providing for those who cannot help themselves, for the St. Joseph Home we have built in His honor, and for the opportunity He has given me to offer up my suffering for the greater benefit of the poor He has permitted me to serve during my life on Earth.

I have placed myself in God's hands. I look forward to meeting Jesus in person, when Mama, Papa, and Katy will be reunited with their beloved Josie for eternity. I am at peace and could not be happier.

# Epilogue

It was evening by the time all Cisco's orders, medical records, therapy reports, and discharge instructions were prepared. Too late to start for Lemont until early the next morning.

Joe told Cora that Barney and Connie had come to say goodbye. "Dad acted a little embarrassed. When Barney said, 'Sorry for how things turned out,' I shot him a look so he didn't go further down that road and told them it all turned out well, considering how it could have gone—thanks to Barney's quick action in getting the ambulance.

"I told Dad, 'You're a very lucky man. No physical weakness at all. We'll get everything back to normal once we get home, won't we?'

"Dad actually smiled at Barney then, Mom. He said he was sure the doctors in Chicago wouldn't put him through so many hoops, and he'd be back next winter for another golf vacation."

Joe sighed deeply. "At least, if he has to be in denial, he's looking forward to the future. Really, Mom, what I told Barney was true. It's amazing how much function Dad has. Considering the magnitude of his stroke, he should have had much more damage. Problem is, he doesn't really understand what he can't do, because the part of his brain that was damaged controls reasoning. Therapy and his cooperation are going to be very important."

"Let's just get him home and figure it out." Cora would deal with it somehow.

Joe didn't want Cisco to get overtired, so they would drive only as far as Albuquerque—seven hours—the first day. Oklahoma City was the next stop, and then St. Louis, getting them home by dinnertime on the fourth day. If all went well, they might arrive sooner.

This left Cora three or four days to get ready for them.

She stayed at Assisi Hill to organize the research she and Frannie had done, then took the materials over to Sister Lorita in her office.

"I'm so sorry I have to bow out again. Life keeps getting in the way. I still want to help with your book, but I just can't say when I'll be able to," Cora said.

"Of course, I understand." Sister Lorita gave a wry grin. "Thanks to you, we've been plunged into another project, at least for the next few months, so the book's been interrupted again anyway. Sister Maryam will do much of the work to get the two saints canonized, but we'll all be involved to some extent. We may have to train someone to replace her at Assisi Manor." She sighed. "Young women aren't exactly beating down the doors to join the convent these days, but maybe our lay volunteer program...."

"I've given you a copy of my research, so if I can't complete the writing, someone else will have a running start," Cora said.

"I knew you'd do that. We'll take over. But keep me posted."

"Of course."

Over the next couple of days Cora taught herself how to participate in Zoom calls and attended two meetings that included Sister Maryam and Sister Elizabeth from Lemont, along with Sister Dorothea, the graduate student Evelyn, Amelia Santos, and Ramon Gomez in San Antonio. They worked out schedules and discussed funding and volunteer programs.

Both Frannie and Dan offered their assistance. "I'll suggest you be invited to future Zoom meetings, so you can chip in if you see a place you can help," Cora told them.

Dan had already called Frannie with research requests. "Maybe that dude's all right after all," Frannie said. "He's talking about some field trip to find that tree. Huh. Wonder if he don't need an assistant. That's cool. I could do that."

Cora googled "Texas holey stone" and found photos that didn't look anything like the stone at St. Marija's. She decided the builder had been duped, as it wasn't even holey stone he bought.

She went home on the third morning. Joe thought he and Cisco would arrive about eight that night. They were a little ahead of schedule.

The house seemed strange, almost foreign, and even emptier than when she'd left it. Perhaps Cora's subconscious was telling her what a near call it had been for the home they both loved to be permanently lonely. She blinked away tears as she walked from room to room. She turned up the heat, but opened windows in the kitchen and bedrooms a crack. She couldn't welcome Cisco home to a stale-smelling and dirty house.

She made up a bed for Joe, wiped down the showers, sinks, and bathroom floors, set out fresh towels. She wiped away noticeable dust and spiderwebs. She had always hated dusting, joking to friends that her dust cloth was broken.

Cisco and her home would be her priority now, all other commitments set aside for the unknown future.

She made a shopping list of grocery essentials. Despite pandemic restrictions, she'd have to brave the stores at least once for milk, eggs, cheese, some fresh fruit and vegetables. Later she'd order online, delivery or pick-up. Or merely live off their pantry and freezer, which were well stocked and could actually stand emptying. Toilet paper, sanitizers, and paper towels were out of stock everywhere, she'd heard. They could use rags if they ran out.

The impact of the pandemic on Cora's personal life thus far seemed mere inconvenience in comparison to the enormity worldwide, which was only now sinking in. Experts warned that the tragic loss of millions of lives was only the beginning—they were to expect to live with death, isolation, job loss and financial hardship, perhaps for years.

Sister Agnes was hospitalized now and on a ventilator.

Cora went grocery shopping, wiped everything down with a soapy dishcloth when she returned, and put the food away. By then it was 4 P.M. Four more hours to wait. She was too keyed up to sleep. Cisco would want the television on once he got home, so she'd savor the silence for the last few hours.

She brushed her teeth and changed into pants and a top Cisco liked. As she was dressing, she remembered a discussion with Cisco during her cancer therapy, when she had been putting on her nightshirt for bed.

"Look at this," she had told him when he came into the room. She lifted her shirt and revealed her upper thigh. The skin had developed a scale-like appearance and was rough to the touch. "Didn't know chemotherapy would do this."

"Does it hurt?" he asked.

"No, but when I run my hand over it, it doesn't feel like *me*. It's like I'm turning into some creature. Snakewoman, maybe." She gave him a one-sided grin. "I wonder what sort of superpowers might go with this?"

"Maybe you can sneak up on a bad guy, coil around him, and swallow him whole."

"You'll be afraid to sleep in the same bed with me now," she said, slipping under the covers and curling up at his side.

"Sssssss…," he had said.

They had kept spirits up during her treatment by light-hearted banter like that. With the mental changes from Cisco's stroke, she feared that rapport would be lost. *Have to remember to work on that.*

The important thing was that he was alive, recovering, and would soon be home. Whatever needed to be done, she would do.

She went into their library and picked up *A Taste for Death* by P. D. James, which she had brought with her to Assisi Hill but never had time to read. She sat in her favorite reading chair with her legs on an ottoman, but she couldn't concentrate, her mind rehashing recent events.

Maryam had gone to the ravine at her regular time for three days, but Mother Josepha had not appeared. Maryam was unfazed. "She'll come when she's ready," she'd said. "She's made herself scarce before." But would she, now that her needs on earth had been resolved? Well, the religious matters were someone else's domain now, at least for a while.

Maryam had the dogwood shillelagh and would keep it until the sisters decided on a permanent home. It remained unchanged. Only a few days had passed since the cane was transformed by the miracle, but there was no drooping, dryness, or foliage loss.

Cora suggested that Maryam pull a leaf from the branch that had broken off the cane and see if it grew back. Maryam refused to do so. "You don't put God to the test, nor His saints," she said. "At least I don't. When we release this story to the world, the Commission for the Cause will want to run tests, but I won't be a part of it."

Cora was not so reluctant; she felt compelled to make the miracle uniquely hers, fearing that with time she would lose the immediacy of the experience she so wanted to keep. Before she handed over the cane, she took a small cutting in secret, carefully protecting it with wet paper towels and plastic wrap. Tomorrow, after Cisco was settled, she would dip it in rooting compound and, come spring, the tiny new tree would be planted in a place of honor in her yard. A symbol not only of the miracle she had witnessed but also of the miracle of faith, the tree would bring her closer to God. Once it was thriving, she could make cuttings for her sons, and perhaps, with the flowering of the small trees, faith would be strengthened in them as well. Cora's miracle garden, devoted to Sister Gardener and a place to gather cherished mementos.

It was Cisco's garden, really. He did most of the work. Would he recover well enough to work in the garden again? Would she tell him the story of this baby tree so he'd take special care of it? She'd work those details out later. Maybe the tree would even change his mind about religion.

She wondered if the little dogwood trees would be considered relics and if they would be labeled second or third class.

Then she remembered Sister Elizabeth's words that God did not perform miracles as magic tricks, but to change lives. Had the miracle she witnessed resolved her struggle with her faith? Belief in Josie and the miracle at Assisi Hill should have put all her doubts to rest. But a cane turning into a living branch, dramatic as it seemed at the moment, could lose impact over time and long term might not be the key to the Kingdom of God.

Cora wanted to believe Mother Josepha was the major factor in Cisco's recovery. But perhaps it wasn't God's intervention that had helped Cisco. Maybe there was no divine intervention, just medical science. Her logical mind still searched for rational reasons to explain the experiences of the past weeks, but she was more and more convinced the answers she sought had to be found not in logic, but in faith. However, after so many years of laxity, she needed time to return to her normal life and dwell on her experiences—to put everything in perspective.

She had wanted a sense of the divine to come alive in her heart, and she had learned that saints served as examples of how to lead spiritual lives and reminders that our lives will end. She did believe there had been a miracle, and it was done through Josie. She had Josie in her life now—a connection to build her faith on, if she could work out the steps.

Her first step would be something very particular to Cora—she would start a new notebook and list steps to a stronger faith, starting with getting to know Mary better, and Jesus. She thought her ideas would be successful this time, since they were grounded in personal experience. But she had to *take* the steps.

In her last talk with Sister Maryam before leaving the convent, Maryam inadvertently put Cora's own thoughts into words. "You have not only experienced a miracle, but you've made new friends—the most profound friendship with Mother Josepha. If you have not already taken your final steps toward recovering your faith, she will be your help and guide, and will support you and Cisco in the days ahead. I hope you won't hesitate to call on her," Maryam said.

Cora was already calling on Mother Josepha, but her image of the saint-to-be was of Josie. The young woman with unequaled compassion and spunk produced a warm feeling in Cora's chest, like a close personal friend. Love—that was the right word. Katy Mrozek's story was moving, but it was Josie that would be a continuous presence in Cora's life and to whom she would turn throughout Cisco's recovery. Perhaps she could even find time to write books about their lives. It could help their candidacy for sainthood. *After the dust settles.*

Cora propped a pillow behind her head and closed her eyes. She felt in her pocket for her rosary and twined it through her fingers, leaving her hand inside the warm space.

Soon Joe would go back to Indiana and she and Cisco would be alone again. What would their lives be like? She'd left her home two weeks ago, trying to deal with a crisis of faith and fear of death brought on by her struggle with cancer. This was replaced by Cisco's health crisis and her meeting with Josie that resulted in a new paradigm in their lives. She felt determined, but also fearful. What if Cisco refused the therapy that would improve his chances for a faster and better recovery, as he had been doing? She could try to persuade him, or she might give in to keep the peace. If he didn't approach therapy with the right attitude was it worth doing at all? Would he be able to live with AFib or would he need cardiac intervention? Was his thinking clear enough for him to make informed decisions?

Their other son Patrick, their daughters-in-law and grandchildren, they might influence Cisco. But the real decisions would not be made until she and Cisco were alone together.

She might be over-thinking. On the other hand, she might be over-confident and in for some unpleasant surprises. Did she have enough patience? She couldn't expect Cisco to be patient, because the part of his brain that controlled such emotions had been injured. It would be up to her.

Anything less than full ability, life as he always knew it, would be a severe blow to Cisco, who liked to stay in control. How should she handle things when they disagreed, those times when his opinion was clearly harmful? He'd want to drive, for instance, but she had been told he needed clearance, and that evaluations could not be done sooner than two months after his stroke.

Joe had warned her that Cisco's anger might not be easily controlled and this normally considerate man could now have bouts of violence. The driving issue held that potential. Should she be afraid? No, there were some things she absolutely would not consider. Fear *for* Cisco was very real. Fear *of* Cisco was not to be entertained.

Just as there were things she would not consider, there were things that were absolutes. She absolutely loved this man and could not imagine her life without him. Whatever the difficulties ahead, somehow she would handle them. Nothing was more important.

She fingered her rosary again and started to pray, thinking of Cisco, thinking of Josie, as she moved her fingers along the beads. *Hail Mary.* Despite the lump in her throat and the tight feeling in her chest, despite her shaking legs, her exhausted body called for relief and Cora dropped into sleep.

Her cell phone awakened her. It was dark in the room. She fumbled for the phone.

"Mom? We're almost there. Just turned off I-355."

"Okay." Phone in one hand, she reached for the wall switch and turned on the light, a little frightened. "Is everything still okay?"

"It's fine, Mom. We're tired, so it will be good to be home. An early night, I think?"

"Food? Maybe just some sandwiches, or I can cook—"

"We stopped for McDonald's, so let's just get there and talk about it. Be home soon."

"Soon. Okay." *McDonald's. Is Cisco supposed to eat that? Joe of all people should know.*

She rubbed her face with both hands, went to the bathroom, and then walked through the house, turning on lights. She switched on the light outside the front door and stared out the window. No cars yet.

Should she run outside to greet him and help him out of the car? Should she just watch and wait for him to come in? She unlocked the door, continuing to watch through a glass side panel. Her heart was beating furiously, her stomach empty and jumpy.

A car turned onto her street, moving slowly. *Why didn't I ask Joe what kind of car he rented?* She never thought of it. As the car drew nearer, she saw it was a dark blue SUV. It pulled past the house and turned into the far end of their circular drive. She waited, her hand on the doorknob. But the car didn't pull up to the front of the house. She heard a car door slam and realized they were coming in through the garage.

Cisco must have entered the garage door code. Or maybe Joe remembered it.

She hurried into the kitchen and opened the door to the laundry room off the garage just as Cisco stepped into it. He looked no different than he had when she left him at the airport, which seemed a lifetime ago.

As Joe wrestled luggage from the SUV's trunk, Cora grabbed Cisco and pulled him into the kitchen, then threw her arms around him and buried her head in his chest. She closed her eyes. Holding him felt so good.

Cisco was home!

# Afterword

*The Miracle at Assisi Hill* was inspired by the life of a real woman, **Venerable Mother Mary Theresa Dudzik. Josephine Dudzik**, later **Mother Theresa of Chicago**, was born in Plocicz, Poland, on August 30, 1860, and immigrated with her family to Chicago in 1881. She founded the Franciscan Sisters of Chicago on December 8, 1894.

In 1898 the Sisters opened the **St. Joseph Home for the Aged and Crippled** on Chicago's Northwest side, one of the first such institutions in Chicago. The order's mother house was built on the same site. The sisters began their move to Lemont, Illinois in 1926.

Mother Mary Theresa died on September 20, 1918, at the age of 58, after a long and painful battle with gastrointestinal cancer. On October 13, 1972, her body was exhumed from St. Adalbert Cemetery in Chicago under the guidelines of the Cause for Beatification.

The exhumation began at nine in the morning, on a cold, dark, misty day. Near noon, as the first bones were removed from the grave, the sun suddenly appeared and flooded the site with bright rays. **Father Henryk Malak**, who had started her Cause for Sainthood, was present throughout the entire exhumation process, which took thirteen hours. Mother Mary Theresa did not arrive at her new home, **Our Lady of Victory Convent** in Lemont, Illinois, until eleven that night.

The remains of Mother Mary Theresa now rest in a red marble sarcophagus in the Sacred Heart of Jesus Chapel at Our Lady of Victory Convent.

Mother Mary Theresa Dudzik was declared Venerable on March 26, 1994, and is currently awaiting the final steps needed for canonization.

The author urges readers to visit www.MotherTheresaDudzik.com for further details about her life and the status of her candidacy for sainthood. *The Chronicle by Venerable Mother Mary Theresa nee Josephine Dudzik 1860–1918* is available at Our Lady of Victory Convent in Lemont and can also be ordered from Amazon.

In *The Miracle at Assisi Hill*, the story of parts of Mother Theresa's life is told using the name Mother Josepha. The journal entries that appear in the novel are not meant to be from a real journal, but from a book written by the novel's main character, Cora Tozzi, sometime after the events of the story are concluded. However, Mother Theresa Dudzik's life, as well as the conditions in Poland and Chicago at the time, were well-researched and the journal is meant to convey the real life of this remarkable woman.

I have long been impressed by the unusually large number of religious institutions in and near the Village of Lemont. The more I explored them and their history, the more impressed I became. I was amazed to learn of a saint-in-the-making right here in my own town, and surprised that so few people knew about her. I thought it was important to introduce her to others, as well as the little-known good works done by the religious people who live among us. This book is my small contribution to this knowledge.

The religious communities referred to in the story are based on actual places but written as fiction, using made-up names. Lemont, known to some as the Village of Faith, has an unusual number of churches and religious institutions of many faiths—Lutheran, Methodist, Baptist, and Hindu to name just a few. Because I wanted to feature Mother Mary Theresa, I limited the communities in the story to some of the Catholic ones, to avoid overwhelming readers with what was a remarkable number of places. Even just the Catholic organizations is an impressive list.

For those with an interest in historical detail, the Catholic institutions in and adjacent to Lemont, in addition to the organizations included in the novel, include:

– Four Catholic parishes: **St. Patricks, St. Alphonsus, SS. Cyril & Methodius, and St. James at Sag Bridge.**
– **Everest Academy**, educating preschool through eighth grade children.

- **Viatorian Fathers Retirement Home**: Land adjacent to St. Marija's along 127th Street, purchased by the Archdiocese of Chicago in 1929 and leased to the Fathers in the 1940s.
- **Fournier Institute of Technology**: Philanthropist Arthur Schmitt purchased the Fathers' land and built a school to prepare young men for Christian leadership in business and industry. Closed in 1955.
- **St. Vincent De Paul Seminary**: Replaced Fournier Institute.
- **De Andreis Seminary**: School of Theology on same property as St. Vincent's.
- **Lithuanian World Center**: Largest organization of Lithuanian Catholics in the U.S., now located on portions of the former St. Vincent's property.
- **Holy Family Villas**: Nursing home and rehab center, operated by Catholic Charities of Chicago and the Lithuanian Catholic community.
- **St. Francis of Assisi Residence**: Independent-care senior residences on Holy Family property.
- **Bishop Lyne Residence**: Retirement home for priests on Holy Family property.
- **Poor Clares**: Cloistered, reflective order adjacent to Holy Family.
- **Carmelite Priory**: Provincial house and spiritual center of Carmelite priests and sisters.
- **St. Theresa National Shrine**: Shrine on Carmelite campus to honor St. Theresa of Lisieux, called The Little Flower, a Carmelite sister.

I tried to write the history and physical descriptions of Assisi Hill, St. Marija's Monastery, and St. Joseph Convent as accurately as possible, although residents of Lemont may recognize the real places and communities, **Mount Assisi, St. Mary's Monastery, and Our Lady of Victory Convent**, that inspired the story. The sisters, priests, and other characters and events of the novel are all my imagination, and not intended to depict actual people or events.

The buildings, grounds, gardens, and statuary described in the story are private property of the communities that own them and are similar to what can be found there today. The senior residence referred to as Assisi Manor was **Alvernia Manor**. Unfortunately, Alvernia Manor was closed during the writing of this book.

The sisters at Mount Assisi today are mostly engaged in professional activities including teaching. Some teach high school full time, others college courses, tutoring, and religious education programs.

The first Sister to occupy the **Mount Assisi** property was **Sister Salvatore Jama**. When the property was purchased by the Sisters in 1925 for their Provincial Center, it contained only one house. Sister Salvatore was sent to live there as housekeeper while additional housing was built. In 1931, after Lemont became the Provincial Center, Sister Salvatore was the person who designed and built the grotto, Way of the Cross, and Garden of Gethsemane. The shrines were constructed of stone found on the property, not the same stone used at St. Mary's Monastery. Sadly, erosion has made it impossible to visit the shrines today, and only the Garden of Gethsemane can be seen.

Today the **Franciscan Sisters of Chicago**, from their mother house at Our Lady of Victory Convent, continue to carry out the mission of Venerable Mother Mary Theresa Dudzik, living the gospel of charity by dedicated service, ministering to the poor and elderly through their numerous continuing care retirement communities.

The property of Our Lady of Victory also contains lovely fields, hills, and woodlands, and in 1936 stone grottos and stations of the Seven Sorrows of the Blessed Virgin Mary were constructed. In 1939, Stations of the Cross were added, and in 1947 the Grotto of Lourdes. The statuary is composed of cement with tufa rock, another type of limestone, used for the bases.

The unusual stone that so fascinates Cora Tozzi, found at St. Mary's Monastery, also fascinated me. It exists as I described it, but I was never able to exactly identify it. I was able to verify that it was ordered as a single shipment that arrived sometime in the late 1930s, and the builders completed all the work before the guest house was built in 1946. My research revealed that the stone is most likely some form of limestone, probably **karst limestone**, with crystals and geodes present in the composition, as I described in the story. The **stone tape theory** is real—theory being an important word here. I also found documentation of the theory that paranormal activity is increased near limestone. It is up to you whether or not to believe these theories.

The statuary gardens at St. Mary's Monastery and at Our Lady of

Victory Convent are in areas of the properties that can be visited by the public.

**St. Stanislaus Kostka** is a real church on the north side of Chicago and is still operating today. Josephine Dudzik belonged to that parish, and the events that take place there are based on research. **Father Vincent Barzynski**, the pastor during Josephine's day, was a real person.

The number of parishioners of St. Stanislaus at the end of the nineteenth century was astonishing. Today, the average size of a Catholic parish across the country is about 1150 families, or 3000 members. This is significantly larger in Chicago, with 3000 families and 9000 members. At over 30,000 members in the late 1800s, St. Stanislaus could have been the largest parish in the U.S. The numbers used in Josie's journal are real, amazing as that may seem.

**John Grabiec** is not a real person. His character was inspired by **John Gniot**, a widowed parishioner of St. Stanislaus, who had proposed to Josephine Dudzik and was rejected. John Gniot remarried another woman, but continued to be a good friend throughout Mother Theresa's life, supported her efforts to assist the poor and aged, and contributed significantly to the construction of the St. Joseph Home. **Sophie Wisneski** and the other founding sisters were also based on real people. Their names have been changed but the circumstances are historically accurate. Their remains can be found in the cemetery at Our Lady of Victory Convent. Similarly, **Tommy Tokarz**, the legless boy, was based on a real person.

Josephine Dudzik in real life essentially raised her younger sister, Katy. She loved Katy very much and considered her more of a daughter than a sibling. **Katy Dudzik** became a Sister of Charity of the Incarnate Word, took the name of **Sister Maria Barbara**, and trained as a nurse in San Antonio, Texas. Katy died at the age of eighteen after a visit to a sick farmer when the buggy she was driving overturned. Outside of those facts, the events in the novel surrounding Katy's death are entirely my imagination. There is no suspicion that she died in any other way or that she ever visited Coahuiltecans.

The parts of the story set in San Antonio use real places, but all of the characters with the exception of Katy are fictional. The resources Cora, Frannie, and Dan contacted are for the most part real, but their contacts and discoveries were made up. The existence of a **Coahuiltecan** village in San Antonio in the 1880s is possible, even likely, but not verified. The village in the story is my invention, as are all the Native American characters. The lifestyle and traditions of Coahuiltecans, both past and present, are as accurate as possible after considerable research. I am solely responsible for any errors in portraying these and other historical people, events, or places, and I apologize for any errors that may exist.

The character of Barney was inspired by my cousin, John Kirk. Rest in peace, John, knowing you are remembered by those that loved you.

Some years before writing this book, I was treated for tongue cancer, enabling me to share intimate details of the experience. The medical portions of the story are for the most part truthful, although the names of the doctors involved have been changed.

The research and the writing of this story, as well as meeting marvelous people along the way, all gave me many hours of joy. I hope you, my reader, enjoyed reading it.

# Acknowledgements

Writing is usually thought of as a solitary profession, but, in my opinion, it is the profession that best fosters friendship. It was not until I began writing that I learned to appreciate the opportunities to meet a host of wonderful people through writing groups, research, interviews, and author events. The list is endless, but I'd like to mention a few.

I could not have written about the religious organizations in Lemont were it not for the courtesy extended to me by representatives of the places that inspired this book. These kind people welcomed me, showed me around their buildings and properties, and answered what must have seemed to them my endless questions. Thank you to Deacon John Vidmar of St. Mary's Monastery, to Sister Jeanne Marie Toriski from Our Lady of Victory Convent, and to Sister Cindy Drozd and Sister Therese Ann Quigney at Mount Assisi. I hope you agree that my book represents you well, as that was of the utmost importance to me.

Twice a month I meet with other writers who belong to Room Seven Writers. They have patiently held my hand through rough first draft chapters, provided valuable comments, and helped me hone my work with astute suggestions, not to mention freely handing out the encouragement writers need so badly. Thank you to Rod Brandon, Luisa Buehler, Michael Cebula, Mim Eichmann, Jon Payne, and Lee Williams. Fred Meek, we miss you terribly. I have a tear in my eye as I write this.

Although other obligations have prevented me from participating fully in the Downers Grove Writers Workshop, I consider myself a part of this group as well and am grateful for their comments and support, especially Yvette Johnson.

A special thank you goes to my "beta readers," the people who were kind enough to take the time to read and comment on my entire completed manuscript. This final step before sending the manuscript to be edited made it a better book. I am grateful to Rod Brandon, Ken Kirk, Dan Melone, Sandra Miller, Barbara Monier, Jon Payne, Sister Jeanne Marie Toriskie, and Deacon John Vidmar. Some of you have so kindly corresponded via email with countless comments and suggestions that improved my novel.

My eternal gratitude goes to the doctors and professional staff of Rush Medical Center, too numerous to be mentioned individually, who guided me through the tough months of my treatment for tongue cancer and ongoing follow-up. Were it not for them, I may not have been able to write this story. I will remember you always.

I was fortunate to find two wonderful people to put the finishing touches on this story. Diane Piron-Gelman caught my errors and put the polish on my words, and Sarah Koz came through once again with her impeccable design concepts, error-free typesetting, and imaginative cover art. Thank you cannot be enough to say about your skills, patience, and respect.

Friends probably don't realize fully how important their support is. Among those friends I would like to mention Father Tom Koys from St. James at Sag Bridge, Sue Roy from Smokey Row Antiques, Augie and Traci Aleksy from Centuries and Sleuths Bookstore, my wonderful neighbors, and my many friends at the Lemont Public Library, the Lemont Area Historical Society, and the Forest Preserve District of Cook County. You guys rock!

I've left the most important for last: my family and my ever-supportive husband, Chris. I know my writing takes a lot of time away from all of you and I am grateful for your understanding. I hope you appreciate the value of reading throughout your lives and realize that the books I write are meant as a gift of myself to you.

# Book Discussion Questions

**The present-day story**

1 At the beginning, what does Cora Tozzi want? How does that change throughout the story? What was standing in the way of her goal(s)? What would be the consequences if she failed?

2 What did Sister Maryam want? How did her beliefs change during the story?

3 Why do you think Mother Josepha appeared to Sister Maryam instead of someone else?

4 How did Cora's struggle against cancer affect her life? How did it affect Cisco's life?

5 Have you ever had life and death doubts such as those that tortured Cora? How did you deal with them?

6 Why do you think the author included Frannie and Dan in the story? Did these characters add to your enjoyment of the novel?

7 What purpose does Sister Fatima play in the story? How did you feel about her initially? At the end of the story?

8 Cora, Sister Maryam, and Josie all had a particular devotion to the Blessed Virgin Mary, but in different ways and for different reasons. Discuss Mary's impact on their lives.

9 Do you think Cora did everything she could to help Cisco? Do you think her actions were admirable? Or were you critical of her decisions?

10 How did the miracle Cora witnessed affect you?

11 What do you think Cora's and Cisco's lives will be like in the future? How will they get on at home? Will Cora still over-involve herself in outside activities?

12 What is the status of Cora's faith at the end of the story?

13 Did the story seem like a love story to you? Discuss.

14 What scene(s) in the story do you remember the most vividly?

## Josie's story

1 Josie has doubts about her abilities but her faith in God enables her to achieve what others have been unable to do. Discuss the qualities that made her succeed.

2 Part of Josie's story is one of failure. She achieves her objective but is replaced. Was her replacement warranted?

3 What is your opinion of Mother Josepha's friend, Sophie Wisneski (Sister Anne)? Was she a help or a hindrance? Was she the true friend Josie thought? Or did Josie have a false picture due to her tendency to see only the good in people?

4 Were you moved by Josie's story? What did you find moving?

5 Do you think Mother Josepha should be canonized? Why or why not?

6 Do you think Katy deserves to be named a saint? Why or why not?

7 Cora and Josie both struggle with self-doubt. In what other ways are Cora and Josie alike? Different?

Pat Camalliere is the author of the popular, five-star-rated *Cora Tozzi Historical Mystery* series. She lives with her husband in Lemont, Illinois, a suburb of Chicago, where her stories are based. She serves on the board of the Lemont Public Library District and volunteers at the Lemont Historical Society, where she directs the society's archives. She is a member of the Chicago Writers Association, Sisters in Crime, and the Society of Midland Authors. She speaks locally on a variety of historical topics and to writers' groups, and writes a blog that features unique history stories. Visit her at patcamallierebooks.com, or email her at pat@pat camallierebooks.com.